THE *Oks* ARE NOT OK

Grace K. Shim

Kokila

KOKILA
An imprint of Penguin Random House LLC
1745 Broadway, New York, NY 10019
penguinrandomhouse.com

This book was edited by Zareen Jaffery, copyedited by Kaitlyn San Miguel, proofread by Ariela Rudy Zaltzman, and designed by Asiya Ahmed. The production was supervised by Rye White, Madison Penico, Natalie Melius, Misha Kydd, and Vanessa Robles.

Text set in STIX Two Text

Library of Congress Cataloging-in-Publication Data is available.

First published in the United States of America by Kokila, 2026

Manufactured in the United States of America
BVG

ISBN 9798217001842
1st Printing

The authorized representative in the EU for product safety and compliance is Penguin Random House Ireland, Morrison Chambers, 32 Nassau Street, Dublin D02 YH68, Ireland, https://eu-contact.penguin.ie.

For Jin and the family we grew together

Before the car comes to a full stop, my friends and I can hear the paparazzi. Everywhere I go, it's always the same:

"Elena! Over here!"

"Elena, are you wearing an original?"

"Elena, is it true about [insert latest gossip here]?"

I'm only seventeen, and yet, everywhere I go, my fame precedes me. It comes with the territory when your family owns It's Ok!, one of the fastest-growing clothing brands. It's a play on our last name, Ok, which is spelled like *okay* but sounds like *oak*. My haters say that as a soon-to-be senior in high school, I haven't done anything to merit this amount of attention, but take it from me: Being in my family *is* work.

Since my friends and I are early for our seven o'clock dinner reservation, we aren't prepared for the photographers in front of Koi when the car pulls up to the entrance. Not that it matters. With high-profile families like ours, we're always red-carpet ready. Faith's dad is a theater director, Melody's dad is a record producer, and Brynn's mom is a celebrity attorney. Willow's parents are prominent plastic surgeons, but she has aspirations for the silver screen. Aside from being classmates at Brenthaven Prep, we all have hopes to one day follow in the glittery footsteps of our successful parents. And yet as we step out of the car, it's obvious the paparazzi are here for one of us more than the others.

"Elena, who designed your outfit?"

"Elena, are you excited about the event tonight?"

"Elena, who was that guy you were with last week?"

Not only am I known for my family's successful business, I get paid to make appearances at parties—I'm the ultimate influencer. Tonight Steve Aoki is DJ-ing at an event to launch his collaboration with Billie Banks at the Hollywood Palladium. Something to do with sportswear or sporting goods? I don't know and frankly don't care, because the events aren't really about the products, are they? They're about drawing attention. And I'm good at that.

We barely get through the tunnel o' paparazzi unscathed. In the restaurant, as the maître d' swiftly ushers us to our usual table, we overhear the restaurant manager in a slight altercation. The five of us casually glance over.

"Who's that?" Brynn points to a disheveled guy with unkempt hair. He's talking to the waitstaff, gesturing wildly with his hands. "He's giving serial killer energy."

"He's looking straight at you, Elena. Do you know him?" Faith has her hands to her mouth like she's horrified. She takes after her father's dramatic flair.

"As if I'd know someone dressed in head-to-toe vinyl." I chuff. Pleather, maybe. But his jacket looks like a straight-up trash bag.

"Ew, I think he's trying to sit with us." Melody points as the guy takes two steps in our direction.

"If some rando thinks he can walk over to you like you're just some *regular* person, he'll have to get through the four of us first." Willow pretends to roll up her sleeves. Ever since I introduced her to the producer who offered her the lead role in *Parks and Trailers*, a new sitcom about teens living in a mobile home community, Willow has professed her undying loyalty to me.

Before the guy gets any closer, the manager swiftly steps in and ushers the unwanted guest out. When the door to the restaurant opens, it's like someone turns the volume up on the street noise. "Elena! Elena! Elena!" Then the door swings shut, and the sound becomes muted again.

Okay, so I know I'm not, like, supposed to admit this, but I love hearing the sound of my name being called out. Can't get enough of it. I'm *obsessed* with it.

"This is how it started with Kim K. My mom told me about it when she was representing her in the lawsuit against her stalker," Brynn says. "First they show up in public places. Then it's only a matter of time before they appear in your private home." She tsks, shaking her head.

Melody gasps. "God, I can't imagine what you have to endure. You poor thing," she says with an expression that's half sincere, half envious. She's doing voice-overs for animations in an attempt at becoming a pop star, and with her stardom not yet on the rise, who can blame her? Our friendships with one another boost our already high degree of social cachet, but it's no secret that I am by far the most established in my own right. Brynn, Willow, and Faith nod at me sympathetically with Melody.

"Aw, you guys. I don't know what I'd do without you," I say, touched by their concern even though I'm far from concerned. I have enough sense to know it's not particularly en vogue to admit my excitement over reaching stalker status. But, wow. Talk about milestones.

"Love you, ladies." I blow air-kisses at them.

"Love you more," they squawk back in unison.

I take it all in. My friends, the fans, the press—with all eyes on me, it's not an exaggeration, by any means, when I say I'm the envy of *everyone.*

My phone rings, and when I see who it is, my mood takes a complete nosedive. It's the one outlier who does not, in any way, want to be me.

"What?" I say in my usual greeting to my brother.

"Just because it's a club doesn't mean you have to drink," Gavin says, bypassing any form of a greeting. "Or at least be discreet about it. And because I know you don't know the meaning of the word, I'll tell you. It's to do something quietly without drawing attention to yourself. Oh, wait, you don't know what that means either."

The eye roll comes at once. "Okay, *Mom*." Which is kind of a funny thing to say, considering our mom doesn't get involved in my influencer business. In fact, she hasn't had an opinion about my life for as long as I can remember.

"Don't you take anything seriously?" Gavin sighs loudly into the phone. "You're going to have to grow up one day, and I'm not always going to clean up your messes."

"Um, no one asked you to, Gavin."

"If only that were true. I'm only calling because Dad told me to. So don't kid yourself."

Ah yes. The *real* reason for Gavin's call.

Ever since Gavin started attending the University of Southern California last year, Dad has taken him under his wing to be his protégé. Now that Gavin's been appointed the youngest executive in training at It's Ok!, it's been "Gavin, let me show you this" and "Gavin, let me show you that." Meanwhile, no one asked me if I got home safely from the wedding of a dictator's daughter in the world's most secretive and isolated country. Or that time when I came back from a weekend on the yacht of the wealthiest drug cartel in the Southern Hemisphere—both paid appearances, thank you very much. You've heard of the heir and the spare? Well, it's more like the heir and the . . . who cares? If I weren't a year shy of becoming an adult myself, I would seriously seek out emancipating from my parents. Except, at the rate at which they've been steadily ignoring me, I'm sure I'd be doing them a favor.

"It's the first week of summer break, Gavin. Don't you ever take a day off from being . . . you?" As the world's most unfun person, I imagine even Gavin gets bored of himself.

"Maybe you should try taking a day off from getting yourself in the tabloids by kissing someone else's boyfriend, or getting into a fight with a politician, or talking to a controversially racist person," he throws right back at me.

Admittedly, the aforementioned incidents were, on reflection, the results of poor decision-making under less-than-ideal circumstances. But aside from a few bruised egos, the media coverage did more good than harm, boosting my popularity even higher. I suspect that Gavin's concern over my well-being, Dad-mandated or not, is more out of personal interest.

"Are you afraid of being upstaged by your younger sister?" There was a time when Gavin was the only one in the limelight. I'm sure it bothers him now that I'm the one who appears on the front covers while he's buried deep in the back pages.

He lets out a humorless laugh. "Hardly. Being a public spectacle is a life no one aspires to."

I don't know why I bother. Gavin doesn't get it, and maybe he never will. To him, I'm just a brainless heiress. But however incompetent he thinks I am, it takes a lot to single-handedly wield more power in my little finger than the AI-engineered filters in Facetune can.

To prove a point (literally to no one but myself), I glance at the photographers practically pressed against the restaurant windows. The light bulbs go crazy, and I can hear the shutter-click frenzy through the double-paned windows. When I have their full attention, I look up cluelessly and mouth, *What's that?*, timing my finger to touch my lower lip at the same moment. The paparazzi predictably go nuts. The entire restaurant glances at the photographers outside, then back at me. Within seconds, everyone's eyes are on me. Now that's power.

So the story behind the catchphrase is from my first interview, when I was fourteen and It's Ok! was quickly becoming a household name. Gavin was sixteen and an intern at the company. Back then I wanted to be like Gavin. Call it naivete or willful ignorance. So when Gavin started doing interviews, I wanted to too. As soon as my acne cleared up and my overbite was corrected, my parents finally scheduled one for me. And it was a big one. *Vogue.* It still surprises me how much time my parents put into my makeup and wardrobe but how little they actually prepped me for the interview itself.

Anyway, I don't even remember saying it, but when I got an advanced copy of the issue, there it was: a full-page photo of me, doe-eyed, with my finger to my lip, and the caption read *What's that?* A whole hour of interview questions about myself that I answered with perfectly respectable responses, and the one question about the fashion industry—the *one* question I didn't know the answer to—happened to be the one they chose to focus the entire article on. Turns out the question wasn't even about a *what* but a *who*—my dad's number one competitor, Amancio Ortega, the founder of Zara. How in the fourteen-year-old hell was I supposed to know who that was?

With all eyes fresh on me, I knew if I wasn't careful, *Elena* would be the new *Karen*. So instead of seeing the press as my enemy, I made them my biggest asset. I figured, since my dad started his own business, so could I. Except instead of selling a product, I'd be selling my image. Three years later the joke's on them, because I've trademarked the catchphrase and made a substantial living off it. Now, not only do I get paid every time someone says "What's that?" in a movie, TV show, or song lyrics, but people pay me upwards of ten thousand dollars just to appear at clubs, parties, and in social media posts. For a seventeen-year-old, I'd say that's not bad.

"Whatever, El. You're on your own," Gavin says, like it should be some kind of a threat.

"I know," I say without a hint of irony before hanging up. It's been three years since the *Vogue* article, and I've been on my own since then.

At the rate I'm booking my appearances, I could make this a full-time career before I graduate from high school next year. I wouldn't even have to go to college. Who needs college or a job at It's Ok! when I can be my own CEO? I could move out on my own, and the best part is, I'd be making a lucrative career just by being me. Then my life could really start. Anyway, if Gavin thinks he's doing me any favors, he's the clueless one.

"Who was that on the phone? Not Liam, I hope." Brynn makes a face.

I shake my head. "Guys, that was, like, two weeks ago." They should know I don't do long-term. Relationships only hold me back from maximizing my lifestyle brand.

"El, no. You shouldn't use the term *guys* anymore. It's a symbol of exclusion." As an aspiring lawyer, Brynn often tries to emulate her mom. Like the time she tried to tell us she identified as a woman who didn't have cellulite, or the time she claimed her English teacher made a verbal agreement to give her an A on a paper she hadn't even written yet. I know it's harmless, born out of admiration for her mom, but Brynn should seriously do her research before she opens her mouth.

Maybe it's because my call with Gavin put me in a mood, but I can't help myself from correcting Brynn. "Actually, I read that *guys* is not considered gendered anymore and that it's widely accepted as a colloquial alternative referring to a group of people regardless of gender due to the fact that the English language doesn't have a designated gender-neutral form for the plural *you*."

When I finish, it's silent. Awkwardly so. The four of them stare at me as if I've spoken another language. As if I have three heads. As if they don't know who I am anymore. Their interest is waning, turning to their empty plates and bubble-infused waters.

"Good evening, ladies. Are we dining omakase tonight?" the waiter asks, cutting into the silence.

In a knee-jerk reaction, I peer up at the waiter, bat my lash extensions, and put a finger to my lip. "Omakase? *What's that?*" I say.

The entire table erupts in laughter, including the waiter. The paparazzi go nuts. And equilibrium is restored. I'm back to being the Elena everyone wants. The one everyone is familiar with. The one that says Elena Ok is okay.

Two hours later we pull up to the Palladium, and the vibe check is hot. I'm about to strut down the step-and-repeat with the logo of the brand we're here to celebrate printed all over the backdrop. Although, by the way the press is shouting my name, you'd think this were a party held in my honor.

"You look amazing, Elena!"

"The Pilates is paying off!"

"Elena, the camera loves you!"

Before I take my first step, my phone rings. I normally wouldn't pick it up, but it's my brand manager, Kiki Klineman. And I always pick up her calls.

"El, hon. I saw photos of you at dinner," she says in her usual no-nonsense monotone.

"Already?" I don't know why I'm surprised when she always seems to know the news before it goes to print. It's why I hired her.

"Don't worry. You look incredible," she says flatly. "Nothing urgent now, but call me in the morning. I've got a bunch of requests coming in for the summer. Some of them overlap, so we need to prioritize the ones that matter most."

"Fun! I can't wait to go through them with you."

"Me too," she deadpans. "But tonight enjoy yourself. You've earned it!" Kiki is a straight shooter with no emotions. But this is the most she's ever shown.

The second she hangs up, a champagne flute is handed to me. It's no surprise I don't listen to Gavin and I take the glass. Like Kiki said, I've earned a night of fun.

"Elena, over here."

"Turn to the left."

"Look to your right."

With literally everyone calling for me at all angles, I do a three-sixty while holding the glass up, giving them exactly what they want. The sound of the shutter click is music to my ears. As soon as I turn the corner and before I walk through the doors into the club, I swiftly pour out the champagne in a planter. When I get inside, an attendant takes the empty glass from me. Smug satisfaction rises in me, knowing I've proven Gavin wrong not once but twice. I *do* make responsible decisions, and I *can* be discreet . . . when I want to.

It isn't long before the party really gets going. The music is as intoxicating as the vibe, and my body can't help but move to the rhythm of it. Everywhere I go, I'm dancing. On the speakers, in the stairway . . . even in the bathroom while I wash my hands, I'm dancing like I don't have a care in the world. And why should I? Everyone loves me.

"Drink, drink, drink, drink!" a crowd chants at me the second they see me come out of the bathroom doors. So I do. Right after I take the shot, my phone vibrates in my hand. I answer without thinking.

"Ugh, what now?" I shout over the electronic music pulsing in the background.

"Someone's live streaming in the club." God, Gavin is so exhausting. Even on a Saturday night, he can't take a day off. "Drinking out of someone's belly button? Elena, have you *no* standards?" Of course Gavin notices the one time I slip up.

"I know who you are," I say, wiping my mouth from the belly-button shot in question. "You're Carlton."

"Jesus, Elena, just how drunk are you? I'm *Gavin*," he seethes. "Your older, much wiser, and *much more* responsible brother."

"No, I mean, you're Carlton from *Fresh Prince*," I say, completely sober. "You know, the really uptight one who doesn't know how to relax? You're Asian Carlton!" I cackle at the spot-on comparison. "Don't you have anything better to do than to stalk my socials? You need to get your own life, Gavin."

"I do have a life. Sonya and I were watching a movie when—"

"Ew, stop flexing your relationship status." Just because Dad is proud that Gavin's dating Sonya, he acts like he's cured cancer or something. According to Dad, Sonya Sinclair is perfect for Gavin. On paper that is. She's the heiress to Bucky's BBQ Sauce, which has been a staple in households across the US since her grandfather Bucky Sinclair trademarked and sold their family's secret recipe in 1960. Hailed as "The most American discovery since America itself," her family's business matches the caliber of success of our family's, and they're in the food industry, which ensures that our two families will never be in direct competition with each other. Dad thinks Gavin and Sonya's relationship elevates our status. You know, like a birds-of-a-feather type of thing. News flash: The only person who cares about Gavin's relationship with Sonya, aside from Dad, is Gavin.

"You can't make having a girlfriend your entire personality," I say.

"You can't make partying your entire personality," Gavin counters.

"Actually I can, Gavin." And because he won't take my word for it, I hold my phone up for Gavin to hear for himself.

"Elena, Elena, Elena!" the crowd chants when I cup my hand around my ear. Just because he—and my parents, for that matter—don't think I'm worth their time, it doesn't mean others feel that way too. And as long as people keep saying *"What's that?"* and are paying me to attend their parties, I don't see that changing anytime soon.

In the dark club, the strobe lights and mind-altering music make everything seem like a good idea. Like table dancing, kissing randos, and eating bacon-wrapped hot dogs from the questionable cart around the corner. And, okay, yes. The occasional drink is also a huge contributing factor. But who cares? I'm living my best life. In the day, however, the harsh lighting reveals the smeared makeup, the sweat stains, and the ugly truth that none of it was a good idea.

My head is pounding, and my mouth feels like sandpaper. I need water. And a maximum-strength ibuprofen. I try to peel my eyes open, but my lids are glued to my eyeballs. After several attempts, I finally pry them open, only to shield my face with a hand. *Ugh*, the light. Once my vision adjusts, however, I'm still squinting as I take inventory of my surroundings. That's not my bathrobe. I don't own a corded telephone. And this bedspread? I would never choose this print for myself.

I sit up to get a proper look around. Something about it seems familiar. It's a hotel room in The Beverly Hilton. I'd recognize these curtains anywhere. But whose room is this? When I attempt to get out of bed, my feet feel someone at the other end of it. I cover my mouth to muffle a gasp. *Oh* my God. This is bad. So bad.

Instinctively I pat myself down. I sigh as soon as I realize my jumpsuit is still on and still intact, with all its buttons firmly clasped. At least nothing happened between me and this mystery guy.

A quick scan of the room tells me we're the only ones here. Which means my friends must have abandoned me at some point last night. How could they do this to me? How could they stand by and watch me make the series of poor decisions that led me here? I could've been hurt, unconscious, abducted, or all of the above. For all they know, this guy could be a serial killer. I mean, a pretty young one with a Rolex and a diamond stud and . . . are those keys to a Ferrari?

Curiosity gets the better of me, and I move the sheet to reveal the mystery guy's face. When I get a good look at him, it all comes screaming back. Oh God. I used his belly button as a shot glass. Guess that explains the hangover.

Wait, that can't be right. I don't get hangovers. Despite what Gavin thinks, I don't drink. *Much.* Okay, fine. Sometimes I have an occasional drink or two. Maybe three if it's an all-day event. But it never gets out of control, and I *never* wake up in a place I don't want to be. At some point I must have stopped checking what was in the drinks I was being handed, because sober me would never have let myself end up in a hotel room with . . . seriously, who is this guy?

I didn't catch his name, but I'm less frantic knowing he's a vague acquaintance of an acquaintance and not a total random stranger. Now I feel a regular amount of panic, as one would waking up in the bed of a stranger in a hotel room. Holding my breath, I slide off the bed in an attempt to make my escape. But in my head, I imagined pulling it off way stealthier than I do in real life. My toe gets caught in the sheet, pulling it out from under the guy, jolting him properly awake. Awesome.

"Hmm, what? Oh," he says, taking note of me. "You're up." He smiles at me groggily. "How long have I been sleeping?"

"Since last night?" I legitimately don't know.

As he props himself up and leans back against the headboard, I get a better look at him. Although we shared an intimate moment last night when my lips touched his belly button, his face is barely recognizable to me. It's also kind of cute. He's rocking the nineties-boy-band look with his baby-blue eyes and disheveled blond hair. I'd definitely be interested in getting to know him if I were looking for a relationship, which I most certainly am not. When it comes to dating, it's always the same. As soon as I get close to anyone, it's only a matter of time before my public lifestyle gets in the way. I'm either going out too much, or I'm not around enough, or there's never any privacy. But I am so close to having my socialite status bankroll my lifestyle indefinitely, and I am not ready to give that up for anything—or anyone, for that matter.

"Did you sleep okay—"

"I have to be somewhere. So I'm going to take off," I say, pointing to the front door.

"Yeah, sure. I understand." He scratches the back of his messy bedhead. "Can I call you sometime?"

Call me? Speaking of . . . I'm looking for my phone, tossing pillows around with one hand and putting my shoe on with the other. "Yes!" I shout as soon as I spot my phone in the crevice of the couch cushions. "I mean, I'll call you." I go back to the bed to grab my wristlet on the nightstand.

"Cool. Do you want my numb—"

I put a finger to his lips to shush him. "Look. Don't take it personally, but . . . relationships aren't my thing." I wave and disappear out the door before Belly-Button Shot Guy has a chance to drag out this already-too-long conversation.

On my way to the elevator, I order a car service to pick me up at the back exit of the hotel. As an establishment frequented by many celebrities, The Beverly Hilton has a private entrance and exit for those wanting to avoid the paparazzi. It's a route I'm familiar with but hardly use, since being in the media spotlight is sort of the whole point of being a socialite. Today, though, I'm glad for the escape route.

I take the service elevator down, and before I exit the building, I use the single-stall employee restroom, which is thankfully empty. Because I have had to pee since I got up, and for some reason, using the restroom in the hotel room of a guy I hardly knew felt undignified. Apparently consuming alcohol from the belly button of a stranger is okay, but using his bathroom is where I draw the line.

While I wash my hands, I catch my reflection in the mirror hanging above the sink and gasp. Mascara smudged under my eyes, lipstick smeared across my cheek, and pillow creases on my forehead. This is the part of my life I don't want the public to know about—that I *can't let* the public know about.

The *Vogue* article was hurtful, but it taught me how the media game works. When it comes to the wealthy, the press is always looking for a story, which means I have two choices: I can let the media find their story, or I can supply them with it. It's no secret I choose the latter. It's why I hired brand manager extraordinaire Kiki Klineman. Every article, every post, and every collaboration has been curated for me to appeal to the masses. And it doesn't mean I can't have a relationship with the press that isn't mutually beneficial. As long as I give the media what they want—a carefree party it girl—I'll get what I want: a lucrative career as a socialite turned influencer. But I have to be smart about it. In order to stay in the public's good graces, I have to be seen at parties with alcohol, but I can't be caught hungover the next day. Which is weird when

I think about it, since it's only natural for one to lead to the other. But that's what it's like for women. You can't slip up, not in the public eye.

When I finish using the restroom, a driver in a black SUV with tinted windows is waiting for me in the alley behind the hotel. I hop in, and he takes me to the address I sent earlier. It's about a thirty-minute drive home, so I lean back and close my eyes. I'm so tired, I could sleep for days. It's a good thing it's summer. With all the events Kiki has lined up for me, I have a feeling there'll be many more days like this ahead of me.

I ignore my phone buzzing incessantly in my lap. I'm sure it's Gavin calling to lecture me on my poor life choices. As much as I hate to admit it, on some level, Gavin's not wrong. Belly-Button Shot Guy turned out to be this cute, harmless golden-retriever type. But I might not be so lucky next time. Going forward, I promise to make better decisions. For now I'll ignore Gavin's calls, since there's no sense in getting worked up over the PR nightmare, as Gavin will refer to it, when it can be fixed with just one, make that two, words: *What's that?*

Thirty minutes later, when the car pulls up to my home, there's a mass of press surrounding the gated entrance.

"Elena! How was last night?"

"Elena, who is that guy you were with?"

"Elena, Elena, Elena!"

Although I never tire of hearing my name being called over and over, this is getting out of control. "Drive past them," I instruct the driver, opening up the gate with the remote access on my phone. I usually don't let drivers beyond the front gate, especially when the press is here. But the paparazzi haven't been this aggressive before, and today they aren't shouting the usual words of affirmation.

"Elena, is it true about George Bronstein?"

"What's going to happen to you now?"

"Are you going to move?"

Move? Why would that even come up? And who the hell is George Bronstein? *Great.* Is he the guy from the hotel room? As soon as the car comes to a stop, I bolt out of it and pray that someone other than the paid staff is home. It's usually empty, or maybe it just feels that way when we're on our separate sides of the house. Although Mom has been more present than usual these past few days. The other day she even asked me if I wanted to do a mother-daughter trip to Korea this summer, which is highly uncharacteristic of her. We don't do things like that. But right now I'm banking on her uncharacteristic behavior to be home so she can explain to me what the hell is going on. I'll even settle for Gavin at this point.

As the gate starts to close, the press gets louder and more specific.

"Elena, what do you have to say about the IRS repossessing your family's assets? Does it have anything to do with the accusations of embezzlement and money laundering?"

The last reporter gets me to stop in my tracks. My head whips up, and I drop my hand from covering my face.

"Is it true that It's Ok! is guilty of money mismanagement? Is it going to file for Chapter 11?" another photographer asks.

Chapter 11? In my complete and utter shock, I respond without thinking. "What's that?" I say, right before the gate shuts, giving the photographers exactly what they want. The roar of camera clicks that follows startles even me. Not since the *Vogue* article first came out when I was fourteen was I this clueless uttering those two words.

When the gate closes and the press is out of sight, I finally check my phone.

BREAKING NEWS 

Updated 1 minute ago

> **Leading retailer It's Ok! is under investigation, sparked by complaints from multiple retail management companies of months of unpaid rent. This has caused the immediate closure of several of its international branches and a few here in the US. Thousands of It's Ok! employees are waking up to find themselves out of a job, and amongst them is founder and CEO Dale Ok. The IRS has seized all of Ok's assets while it conducts a thorough review of the management of the company's funds. For now, it is unclear whether money mismanagement can be linked to financier George Bronstein's recent criminal indictment for defrauding investors in a Ponzi scheme, also known as the Madoff 2.0 scandal, or if it points to ethical lapses at the highest levels of leadership. We reached out to a company representative for comment, but we did not get a response.**

What (and I can't stress this enough) *the fuck?*

EXCERPT

I wish I could say there is some magic formula to guarantee success, but there isn't. Everything I have was built by my own two hands.

The American Dream Achieved: The Story of Dale Ok, Founder of It's Ok!

TRANSCRIPT

60 MINUTES INTERVIEW WITH GLORIA OK

INTERVIEWER: You and your husband have created one of the fastest-growing US-based clothing brands. Your son's appointment at the company as an executive in training was just announced, and your daughter is well-known for her status as a socialite turned influencer. Clearly this is a family full of success stories. What would you say is the secret?

GLORIA: There is no secret, just hard work. As Dale would say, he accomplished everything with his own two hands.

INTERVIEWER: And how hands-on is he about the day-to-day running of the business?

GLORIA: *Very* hands-on. Nothing at the company happens without Dale's approval.

INTERVIEWER: Really? For such a large-scale business, that's quite impressive.

INTERVIEWER: It's Ok! has experienced significant expansion over the past year, including abroad.

GLORIA: Yes, it's true. Seventy-five new stores have opened in the US and twenty-five overseas.

INTERVIEWER: But recent data indicates a steady increase in online shopping. Given the shift in consumer behavior, is there any concern regarding the potential impact on the business?

GLORIA: As part of our growth strategy, Dale plans to reduce retail stores and shift our focus to expanding our e-commerce presence. We're also entertaining investment proposals to expand the company into fragrance and skincare.

INTERVIEWER: Speaking of investment proposals, we've heard rumors about It's Ok! being involved with financier George Bronstein. Is it true the company has invested in his business scheme?

<TRANSCRIPT PAUSED>

An hour later we've been summoned to a nondescript warehouse in LA's Fashion District. It's been unused for a while now, and some of the local vendors have been known to do shady business down here. How fitting that this is where Dad has chosen to meet with our lawyer. I didn't think he could be capable of anything this sleazy, but his secrecy about the company's day-to-day business, even with his own family, does make me raise a brow.

"Please. Sit." Mr. Ahn, my dad's personal lawyer since forever, pulls up some old crates and gestures for us to sit.

My dad declines, opting to stand with his hands folded across his chest in what I'm sure he thinks is a power move. My mom unties the silk scarf around her neck and sits on the scarf after laying it on a crate. I'm too frazzled to sit, so instead I pace aimlessly. Of course Gavin makes a show of sitting down, eyeing me specifically as he lowers himself to the crate, pretending not to take notice of the splinters burrowing their way through his Ermenegildo Zegna slacks. Like he's some kind of goddamn hero for not having standards. I would call him out on it, except now is not the time for snobbery, especially if any part of the article implicating It's Ok! is true.

Once we're settled, Mr. Ahn clears his throat. "Now, it looks bad, but—"

Oh, thank God, there's a *but*.

"—it's actually much worse than it seems," he unfortunately continues. Apparently, not only did the company fail to pay the rent for multiple retail locations for the past few months, but production had to come to a complete halt due to the nature of the investigation, causing the loss of ungodly amounts of money.

This can't be happening. I keep waiting for a camera crew to appear from a hidden room, because this has to be a joke, right? In the silence that follows Mr. Ahn's explanation, however, it becomes clear that no one is filming us and this isn't a joke. I make the mistake of glancing down at the phone in my hand. The notifications come in rapid-fire succession. I reflexively click on them.

"Oh my God, oh my God, oh my God," I mutter endlessly as I scroll through my social media feeds. I've been dropped from all the events I had booked for the summer. "I'm . . ." I gasp. *"Canceled?"* The tears come out at once. There go my summer plans to party my way to independence. Just like that. I've already called Kiki a billion times but got sent straight to voicemail, which is bad enough. But to find out via social media what she should have told me herself is a swift punch to the gut.

After staring at me open-mouthed for a long and drawn-out moment, Mom, Dad, and Gavin turn their attention back to Mr. Ahn.

"How could we be so severely in debt? How did it happen so quickly?" Mom asks Mr. Ahn. "Is it because of that no-good George? Please tell me we didn't invest in his scheme."

Mr. Ahn clears his throat. "It's unclear if George Bronstein's investment fraud charges are linked to you. What we do know is that you signed a significant number of lease agreements at a low, post-pandemic rate. But each clause indicated the subsequent, not to mention substantial, increase in rent per year, and the company just hasn't been able to keep up with the costs to uphold your end of the lease agreements."

Mom spins around to face Dad. "I warned you about this." She tuts. "I told you that we needed to close the international storefronts, focus on the US market only, and shift our goals to e-commerce."

Dad looks as utterly taken aback by Mom's directness as Gavin and I are. As the epitome of a trophy wife, Mom is often seen—in head-to-toe couture—but not heard. Gavin and I glance at each other, then back at Mom.

"What?" she says in response to our blank expressions.

"I didn't know you knew so much about the business," I say.

Mom sighs loudly, as if to say *duh*. "Why wouldn't I? I've been at the company since the beginning. Where did you think I was all those years when you were at school?"

"Charity events and fundraisers?" Gavin says, guessing at the same time that I say, "Ladies' lunches and pickleball?"

Disappointment washes over her face, but I can't tell if it's at us or herself. It's a stark contrast to the unflappable smile she normally sports. Now the smile is gone and, I take it, so is the fakeness.

"What can we do?" Mom asks, trudging ahead.

Mr. Ahn blinks a couple times before he says, "Well, nothing."

"What?" Gavin asks what we're all thinking. Surely we've heard him wrong.

"At this point we have to let the investigation run its course. With the IRS it could take anywhere between several weeks and months, depending on how far back the investigation needs to go."

"Months?" I flail. "Did you see what it's like out there? I can't live like this for another day!"

"For once, Elena is right," Gavin concedes. "The camera crews are camped outside of our gate. I rode in Sonya's trunk to get here. I can't live like this for the next day, let alone months."

"Then maybe it's a good thing the house is being repossessed," Mr. Ahn says, somehow cavalierly.

"Excuse me?" Mom shoots up. "Our home?"

This gets Dad to finally say something. "Surely they won't do that. Couldn't we appeal for some type of leniency—"

"This *is* lenient. They're giving you a few days to get your affairs in order," Mr. Ahn says matter-of-factly, as if he's explaining a math equation or reciting the definition of a vocab word. Instead of resenting him for his nonchalance, I find myself envying him. I'd give anything to trade places with Mr. Ahn, who has the luxury of being on the other end of this conversation.

"The only money they aren't freezing right now is the separate account Mrs. Ok made in Elena's name," Mr. Ahn says.

The three of us crane our necks to look at Mom, surprised.

"She can't have her own bank account. She's only seventeen,"Gavin blurts. He's not wrong. I distinctly remember opening the joint account with Mom.

"Gloria?" Even Dad must not know about my account since he's asking her for an explanation.

"What?" Mom holds out her hands in annoyance. "Because of who we are—" She winces. "Or were, I should say. The bank allowed Elena to have an independent bank account at sixteen. So I took myself off as co-owner when she started making money from her catchphrase and paid appearances." She sighs. "I only thought it was fair, since she earned it."

My jaw hangs open. Had I known I had full access to my money all along, I would have moved out sooner.

"Yes, the IRS felt that this money earned was unrelated to the corporate sales of It's Ok!, and as such, it falls outside of the scope of their investigation," Mr. Ahn goes on to explain. "More importantly, it should be enough to keep you afloat for now."

"Um, Gavin? Did you hear that? My party money saves the day." I tap him on the shoulder, and he glares up at me. "You're welcome," I say with an obnoxiously large smile.

"So we can stay at our house?" Dad asks.

Mr. Ahn clears his throat. "The money is not enough to keep your mortgage, and with no assets, you have no collateral. I'm afraid your house is no longer . . . your house." A deep and disturbing silence descends on us as we're stripped of our last shred of dignity. "But the good news is," Mr. Ahn says with forced enthusiasm, "Elena's money is enough to tide you over until everything gets sorted out."

"Okay, I guess that is something." Dad rubs his forehead, trying to convince himself this is good news when we all know it's not. "We have the condo in Westwood. I suppose we could stay there."

"Excuse me?" Gavin's head jerks back. "I share the condo with Sonya. Have you forgotten? Don't you know how that would make us look if we just kicked her out of there when it suited us?"

"I'm with Gavin on this," I say, surprising him. "Have you seen his place? It's *tiiiiiny*. There are only two bathrooms, and it's got a kitchenette. Like a house for squirrels or something."

"Wow" is all Gavin can say.

"I'm sorry, but the Westwood condo isn't in your budget either," Mr. Ahn interrupts.

Our jaws collectively drop.

"My condo isn't anywhere near the dwelling space for woodland creatures that Elena overexaggerated, but it's far from luxurious. It's modest at best. With a doorman. And a gym. And a spa— Okay, it's nice." Gavin recoils, reconsidering his aforementioned argument.

"But it's a microscopic fraction of the size, not to mention the cost, of our Calabasas mansion. Couldn't we afford at least that?"

Mr. Ahn, however, remains unmoved.

"So, like, going back to your earlier statement. How is this good news?" I ask. "I thought lawyers were supposed to tell the truth." I fold my arms across my chest.

"Mr. Ahn, just tell us. What *are* our options?" Mom asks, exasperated.

Mr. Ahn begins shuffling through his papers. "There is one piece of property the IRS is allowing you to retain." He hands my dad a piece of paper.

Gavin reads it from behind Dad. "Bl-aire?" he says slowly.

"Bel Air?" I squawk loudly, sighing in relief. "Oh, thank God. Finally some good news." I glance over at Mr. Ahn as I say this.

"No, not Bel Air. *Blaire*," Mr. Ahn, the beacon of joy that he is, clarifies.

"Blaire?" I say the unfamiliar word as if it's toxic. "Where's that?"

"It was a piece of property we purchased ten years ago," Dad says, suddenly remembering.

"Ten years ago? I was nine. Elena was seven," Gavin says. "How come you never told us?"

"We bought it when It's Ok! began expanding and our prospects were looking good," Mom explains in a kind of nostalgic but sad way.

"It was supposed to be our retirement plan," Dad says. "I had completely forgotten about it."

"Wait, you two purchased a piece of land for retirement and forgot about it?" All of a sudden, alarm bells start ringing, and red flags begin to shoot up. You don't somehow forget about the property you buy for retirement if it's an over-the-water bungalow in Bora Bora or a cabin in the Swiss Alps. I narrow my eyes at my parents. "Just where is Blaire?"

"It's in central California, between LA and San Francisco," Mr. Ahn explains.

I wrinkle my nose. "Nuh-uh. I'm not falling for this one. No one lives between LA and SF," I say.

Gavin makes a big show of rolling his eyes. "Is it near Bakersfield?"

"It's west of Bakersfield," Mom says.

"Is it close to Santa Barbara?" I ask, hopeful.

"It's north of Santa Barbara," Dad says.

"Well, where is it?" Gavin asks impatiently.

"Blaire is where Blaire is." Mr. Ahn has had enough of our ignorance and hands us his phone with a map pulled up.

Ridiculous as it sounds, it's exactly where Mom and Dad said it is—in central California, west of Bakersfield, north of Santa Barbara. It's a microscopic town called Blaire. I click on the town icon, and it reads *Population: 150.*

"Why are they allowing us to retain this one piece of property?" Dad asks out of curiosity.

"In the time since you purchased the land, Blaire has become a government-sanctioned National Radio Quiet Zone. That is, it is the location of a scientific telescope that has a lot of rules enforced on the town to keep it secluded," Mr. Ahn explains, "which, naturally, has made it a less desirable place of residence and subsequently driven down the price of real estate in the area. In essence, the property no longer holds value."

Well, there's a sobering sentiment. Our lives have been reduced to living in a place where no one wants to live.

"It could be good for you to stay out of public life during this time," Mr. Ahn says, probably noticing the utter defeat in our expressions. "There are a series of quotes from your autobiography that are starting to pick up momentum online." His eyes flick to Dad.

"Quotes from my book?" Unbelievably, Dad has the audacity to beam at the mention of his most prized possession—the story of his life. "That's a good thing, isn't it?"

"Not the way it's being circulated." Mr. Ahn shifts uncomfortably as he gears up to explain. "The quotes are probably being taken out of context, but people are accusing you of supporting a toxic work culture. Some are saying your status as a self-made man has not only made you successful but has also made you out of touch with reality."

I'd say he's out of touch, all right. Dad's expression sinks deeper, as if this was the worst of our problems.

"The good thing about Blaire is that the National Radio Quiet Zone makes it secluded in a way that no one will know who you are there. News travels slowly, and oftentimes only the big headlines reach the town. It's a good place to lie low and bide your time while we wait for the appeal."

Lie low? Of all the bombshells Mr. Ahn has dropped on us, this is the one that hits the hardest. Because I didn't build a career on my lifestyle by lying low. And without my very public—not to mention very lucrative—image to uphold, how am I supposed to move out and be on my own now?

Gavin sits back, rendered expressionless, probably from the shock. Mom is at a loss for words, and Dad seems more distraught over hearing his autobiography is portraying him as a corporate douchebag than being told we've lost everything. It wouldn't be the first time I didn't understand my own family. But how can they be willing to accept defeat so easily, especially when it's *this* extreme?

"There's got to be a way out of this," I say, desperately pleading with Mr. Ahn. Someone's got to come up with a reasonable solution. It may as well be me. "I was able to negotiate my way out of an arranged marriage to a prince in Bhutan—"

"What?" Dad startles.

Mom's head shoots up with eyes full of concern. "When did you—?"

"I didn't actually agree to the marriage. It was a misunderstanding over an innocent hand gesture. Anyway, my point is, I was able to get out of *that*. Surely we can do something about *this*. Can't we?"

"There is one way." Mr. Ahn hesitates before continuing. "Filing bankruptcy would allow you to reorganize and restructure your company and secure the future of It's Ok!"

"No," Dad says firmly. "Filing bankruptcy is admitting fault, and I didn't do anything wrong. I worked hard, and I stand by my decisions. I'm confident I can find my way through this."

I'll be the first to admit I don't have a close relationship with my dad, but even I can attest to his strong work ethic. His absence from home is evidence of his dedication to the company. Mom looks as if she's going to try to convince Dad to reconsider, then gives up. She knows better than any of us that when Dad's mind is set, there's nothing anyone can do to change it. Gavin has no opinion to offer at all, which is surprising, since he's the one who has just as much at stake in the company as Mom and Dad do.

Mr. Ahn shakes his head, shocked over what he's hearing. "Dale. As your lawyer, as your friend, I have to advise you to reconsider. It's in your best interest." Noticing Dad's hard stance, Mr. Ahn sighs. "Well, then, we just have to file a petition with the court and wait for an appeal date. In the meantime, the petition will prevent the creditors from taking collection actions against the company. At the very least it'll buy us time to strategize over how to proceed in the event that the case doesn't end up going the way we hope for."

"How much time?" Gavin asks, finally showing some concern. It seems like a delayed response. Maybe it's the shock, which is understandable. As an executive in training at It's Ok!, not to mention the publicly acknowledged heir to the fashion empire, Gavin currently has a future that is, arguably, in more jeopardy than mine.

"We have two weeks to appeal," Mr. Ahn says. "Then it's out of our hands."

There wasn't any part of the conversation that wasn't pure torture, but at least I know there's an end to this nightmare. Two weeks is recoverable. I'll still have most of the summer left. Maybe by then, Kiki can do some damage control and negotiate some events for me before school starts so I can get back to monetizing my appearances to earn a proper living. In a year my parents will expect me to go to college, and I can't tell them I have no intention of going until I have something better lined up for me.

It takes a series of steps only seen in international spy missions and heist movies to get our bags packed and sent to us in this abandoned warehouse. First we each arrange for our house cleaners to pack a specific list of essential items that can fit into only one suitcase a piece, a challenging feat in and of itself. Once they load the luggage into their car along with their cleaning supplies, they take them to their facilities. An hour later we arrange for a separate car service to pick up the bags from the facilities and meet an associate of Mr. Ahn's in an underground parking lot in his office building. There, he takes the bags and gives them to another car service, which is scheduled to pick us up in the dank and depressing warehouse where we've been since this morning.

While I wait, I check my phone to see if Kiki has called me back, but there's nothing. No messages, missed calls, or voicemails from her. My finger hovers over the keypad to call her again. A second later I think better of it. I've already left her a series of voicemails, increasing in batshit with each subsequent message. If I were her, I'd probably screen my calls too. But I'd be lying if I said I wasn't freaking out. Yesterday she couldn't wait to talk to me. Now I can't get her to return my calls. With my phone in my hand, a slurry of texts comes in. I fumble with my phone, too eager to read the messages, but I'm disappointed to find that none of them are from Kiki. They're from acquaintances and sponsors who are either pumping me for information or canceling my bookings. Both are depressing, so I delete those and read the texts from my friends.

MELODY

Just saw the news, El. Are you okay?

WILLOW

Is any of it true?

BRYNN

Of course not. I wouldn't be surprised if this was all part of a targeted prosecution that has more to do with the Madoff 2.0 scandal than It's Ok!

FAITH

Yeah, there's no way El's family are corporate scumbags.

Corporate scumbags? I didn't get a chance to read all the headlines, but it sounds worse than I thought. I'm not used to reading anything about me in the media that isn't affirming in some way, shape, or form.

Mr. Ahn didn't say we shouldn't tell people where we're going, but if I'm going to somehow recover from this major setback, I can't lose the respect of my friends, which means I definitely can't tell them we've been banished to a place with a population of one hundred and fifty—a town where no one wants to live.

Instead I decide to tell them that I'm going on a silent retreat for the next two weeks while the news of the investigation dies down.

Faith suggested going to one before as a joke. At least that's how the rest of us took it. We laughed about how absurd it seemed to spend a week or two in intentional silence, away from people, technology, and civilization in general. Except that's exactly what it sounds like it'll be like in Blaire.

Faith is overexcited for me, asking me to report back all the "deets of your journey." Brynn is skeptical, as per usual, telling me to take a tracking device with me for my safety. Melody must be confusing a silent retreat for a resort, because she keeps asking me if they have goat yoga and infrared saunas. As the discussion continues, Willow becomes notably quiet in the group chat.

Guess I can't say I'm surprised. With Willow's own future in jeopardy, she'll want to distance herself from any whiff of a scandal, even one with no merit. I've watched her work and hustle for every role as a side character, every job as an extra, to now starring in her own sitcom. She won't want to lose that by being associated with me, and I wouldn't want that for her, either, even though I was the one who got her the big break in the first place.

While I think of something to respond with, I overhear Gavin on his phone, probably talking to Sonya. *Barf.* Not that I have anything against her; she's been nothing but nice to me. But Gavin's relationship with Sonya is just so . . . fake. As in, not real. Knowing Dad, he's probably socially engineered their relationship, since that's what he tried to do with me.

After the *Vogue* article, Dad's idea of recovering my reputation was to negotiate a relationship between me and someone from a family of similar status. At first I was touched by his efforts to protect me from the harmful side of the media. He said that with the right partner, we could be a powerhouse couple, which would give us an added layer of protection. But then he went on to explain that because we'd be two people from major industry families, the press would be less inclined to make fun of me—get this—*the next time I said something dumb*. Can you believe that? After I learned the truth, I realized that his concern, like the proposed relationship, was a lie. Dad wasn't trying to protect me from the press; he was trying to protect the press from me. Because he believed, like the article implied, that I was too dim-witted to know anything about anything. I felt like saying yes to his negotiated relationship was as good as admitting that I believed it, too, which I didn't. I know I'm smart. So, out of principle, I rejected Dad's idea. That was the last time he considered me for any part in the family business.

"What's the situation like at the condo? Is the press still there? Are you okay?" Gavin pauses while he listens to Sonya's response. Even the way he asks is so formulaic. In fact, I wouldn't be surprised if he were reading off a script Dad wrote for him, which is reassuring to me in a way. If being in the family business means being a cog in Dad's machine, then I have no regrets.

"I'm so sorry about leaving you like that," Gavin says after Sonya finishes telling him everything. "I should be the one dealing with that mess, not you. If there was any other way—"

Presumably Sonya cuts him off. I think about what she's saying to him. How she's mad at him for running away and not manning up. How ironic it is that he's lost everything when he was the one lecturing others for not being responsible. How a person with his body type, long torso/short legs, shouldn't wear slim-fit joggers (as long as she's at it, she might as well say what we're all thinking).

"Wow, that's . . . incredibly understanding of you. You're seriously the best, Sonya." He pauses. "Yeah, I miss you too."

Apparently Sonya is more forgiving than most, which makes me dry heave a little. Even more surprising is finding out that their relationship, socially engineered or not, must have developed into something real. I've never envied Gavin. I mean, he runs at a stress level you know is going to lead to an early grave. And relationships never felt like a sacrifice at the time, but now seeing the way Gavin is with Sonya makes me think that maybe I have been missing out.

After Gavin gets off the phone, Dad calls him over to join him and Mom. They huddle together in a serious discussion, no doubt talking about the appeal, while I'm standing by myself in the middle of the empty warehouse. Even though I don't think I need a relationship to protect me from the media, I'll admit, at times like this, I wonder if it was worth turning down Dad's idea. Because sometimes not being part of the family business makes me feel like I'm not part of the family.

My phone pings incessantly in my hand. My friends have segued into chittering on about our graduation trip and if we should consider doing a silent retreat or something more typical, like the Maldives or the Amalfi Coast. When they can't come to a unanimous decision, they ask me which one I prefer. A reminder that despite my nonexistent status in my family, everyone else is curious to know my opinion on any given matter. Because I'm the one leading the life people want. My fingers hover over the keyboard as I think of how to respond. After a few attempts I delete the message and click off my phone. I can't come up with anything. Not now, when there's nothing about my life that's aspirational. We haven't even left LA yet, and I can already feel my social relevance fading. I sigh. This is what it must be like to be a *regular* person.

A car arrives, interrupting my thoughts. At first glance I dismiss it, seeing as it's a pickup truck. Can't be paparazzi, either, as the car is ancient and sputters as it makes its way through the empty warehouse. But then the car parks and a guy gets out, introducing himself as Rick, our driver. He says he's been hired to take us to Blaire (not to be confused with Bel Air). Once we reluctantly confirm our sad destination, Rick loads our bags into the back and opens the door for us to get in. But no one moves.

"Is there another car coming?" Gavin asks.

Rick scratches his head. "Not that I know of."

I know what Gavin's thinking. The truth is, we've never ridden together in a car of this size. Which is humbling, to say the least. But I'm not about to give Gavin the satisfaction of admitting it. Especially not in front of Rick, the first driver we've had who isn't wearing a suit.

"I've been told to be discreet and that this type of car would throw off anyone following you," Rick adds when he senses our hesitation.

Well, that's something we can all agree on. The Oks would definitely not be seen in a car like this. My, how the mighty have fallen.

"What's that smell?" I cover my nose and breathe through my mouth.

"It's a diesel fuel engine. You get used to it." Rick shrugs like it's no big deal we're breathing in a dense fume of carcinogens.

"Let's just get in," Dad says in a defeated tone. He opens the passenger door to the car and slides in.

Mom opens the back seat door behind the driver's side and climbs in. I wait for Gavin to get in first, but he just stands there, staring at me.

"After you," he has the audacity to say.

"I don't do middle seats." I purse my lips.

"This is not a time to have standards. You're the only one who can fit in the middle."

"Oh, so now you're going to admit I'm skinny?"

"Wow. Can you stop thinking about yourself for one goddamn second?"

"Can you stop being an arrogant ass for once? I have to sit next to the window, or else I'm going to yak all over you."

"I'll find you a bag." He motions for me to get in the car.

"Gavin, I'm serious! You sit in the middle."

Gavin peeks into the truck. "That space isn't big enough for one of my ass cheeks, let alone two. So you sit in the middle."

"No, *you* sit in the middle." I haven't eaten anything all day, and the acid is rising in my stomach, making me put a hand to my mouth and retch a little.

"Oh my God. You don't have to be so dramatic." He throws his arms up by his sides.

"What are you two arguing about? Elena, stop being a nuisance and get in," Mom calls out to us from inside the back seat of the truck.

Unsurprisingly I'm the one being called a nuisance, even though she has no idea what we're fighting over.

The commotion gets Dad to peek his head out of the passenger door window. "Everything under control, Gavin?"

"Yep," he says to Dad, then turns to me. "Fine, if it means that much to you." Of course Gavin gives in as soon as Dad gets involved. He reluctantly does the shame crawl into the middle seat of the car.

As soon as I get in and close the door, claustrophobia sets in. The last time I crammed into the back seat of a car this small was when I was backstage with Justin Bieber after his concert and we hopped into the back of his manager's Porsche to avoid the swarming paparazzi. Which is *so* not the same as this scenario. I haven't had to sit next to Gavin in the back of a car in years.

"Make sure to turn your phones on airplane mode. Else it'll drain your battery," Rick advises before we leave.

"Airplane mode?" Gavin pipes up.

"Mr. Ahn went over all this." Dad turns his head to face us. "Blaire is in a National Radio Quiet Zone."

"I thought that meant, like, quiet hours or something. Which is why I brought my AirPods." I wave the case in front of his face.

"I think you're thinking of noise ordinances. The Quiet Zone is in reference to radio frequency. As in, Wi-Fi and radio stations." The more Rick explains, the less I understand.

"Didn't you listen to anything Mr. Ahn said?" Mom says.

Not gonna lie, with all the bad news he gave us, I sort of tuned Mr. Ahn out. Kind of like how I'm tuning Mom and Dad out now. After I put my phone on airplane mode, I lean my head back and close my eyes, pretending this is all a bad dream.

Two hours later, when the car pulls over to the side, I wake up disappointed to find myself still in the back seat of Rick's truck and still sitting next to Gavin, the annoying mouth-breather that he is. Even more disturbing is what's happening outside of the truck. It's dusk, with just a sliver of light peeking from behind the horizon, revealing nothing but dirt and tall grass. No strip malls or gated communities. No tall buildings. In fact, no buildings at all. Civilization as we knew it, gone. Suddenly Rick startles us by getting out of the car and disappearing into the darkness. All we can do is sit and watch helplessly.

"Rude," I say. "He could have at least waited until we got to a gas station before pulling over to pee on the side of the road."

"I'm not sure that's what he's doing," Dad says, following Rick with narrowed eyes.

"I think there's something out there," Gavin says ominously.

A light turns on, and we collectively gasp. "Is this a torture chamber? Is he abducting us?" I shriek. Brynn told me about a case her mom worked on over some C-list celebrity who was embroiled in a human trafficking scheme on the side. Even though we've lost all our fortune, I'm aware that I'm a hot, young Asian girl with dewy skin and zero cellulite. I bet people would pay a lot of money for me. What am I saying? People *do* pay a lot for me. But this would be *so* different.

"The tenants moved out not too long ago. I knew it would be somewhat dilapidated. But this is . . ." Dad doesn't have to finish his sentence for us to know what he thinks.

"This . . . is a house?" Even Gavin's having a hard time covering up the dread he feels, which humanizes him in a way. At least beneath the facade he's not as down-to-earth as he pretends to be.

"This is where we'll live for the next two weeks," Mom confirms. "Our new home."

"*Temporary* home," I say, feeling compelled to make the subtle but very necessary distinction.

"At least we have a place to live," Dad says, though the defeat in his tone is unmistakable. He gets out, and we have no choice but to follow.

Our phones are on airplane mode, but we're still able to use the flashlight. The four of us walk with our luggage in one hand and our phones in the other, stepping only in the lit area in front of us. So far there's nothing surprising other than an overgrown lawn of grass and weeds that seems to go on forever. When we finally reach the screen door, it creaks as we open it and follow Rick in.

Rick gives us a tour, which is a gross exaggeration of the word, since he doesn't have to leave the main room to do it. The kitchen is attached to the living room we're standing in, with three bedrooms on one side of the hall, the bathroom on the other, and brown shag carpet as far as the eye can see, which I'm sure is hiding stains of dubious natures. Desperately, I try to find a silver lining somewhere, anywhere. But the more I look, the worse it gets. The vinyl countertops are peeling along the edges. The walls have mysterious burn marks in various places. And don't get me started on the smell. Every square inch of this place is covered in minor assaults on my dignity.

"There are a lot of quirks here. This will tell you everything there is to know," Rick says, handing Dad a thick binder. "It's basically a handbook of the town."

"Thanks," Dad says, relieved to receive it from Rick, though I don't know why. If a town needs a handbook to explain itself, I'd say our worries are far from over.

After Rick leaves, we inspect the place, opening the doors like each room is a crime scene, which is not far from the truth. The third bedroom is a closet with a consistent drip of brown water coming from the ceiling, leaving two bedrooms for the four of us to share. And I could have sworn I misheard Rick, since in the short time I've known him he's not been one to articulate his words, but when he said *bathroom*—singular, not plural—he indeed meant it.

"So, how is that supposed to work?" I point a finger to the dingy bathroom.

Dad walks in and looks around. "It's got two sinks. One for me and your mom, and the other for—"

"Dad, I beg you. Please don't finish that sentence." But it's too late. He's already said the dreaded words.

"—you and Gavin."

My head falls, along with my last shred of dignity. It's bad enough I have to share a room with Gavin in this hellhole, but the bathroom? Is nothing sacred?

EXCERPT

Always strive for first place. Because coming in second is nothing more than being a first-place loser.

The American Dream Achieved: The Story of Dale Ok, Founder of It's Ok!

TRANSCRIPT

60 MINUTES INTERVIEW WITH GLORIA OK

GLORIA: There's absolutely no truth to the rumor. I've advised Dale against going into pursuing any business ventures with George Bronstein. When someone's offer seems too good to be true, it usually is.

INTERVIEWER: Earlier you mentioned that Dale is the one who manages the company. But it sounds like you play a significant role in the business affairs as well.

GLORIA: Me? No. That is, of course we discuss business, but he's the one who attends the meetings and makes the decisions. Besides, Dale knows from experience that there is no get-rich-quick scheme. It takes years of long—and often hard—work.

INTERVIEWER: Is that because of his farming background?

GLORIA: [*hesitates*] His what?

INTERVIEWER: [*flips through her papers*] I don't have a note that says that his life before the business is off the record. Is it?

GLORIA: No, it's not. I'm sorry, I'm just having trouble seeing the connection. What does Dale's farming background have to do with the business?

<TRANSCRIPT PAUSED>

After the shock wears off, reality sets in. For the next two weeks, *this* is our new home.

I start to unpack, only to realize there's nowhere to put my clothes. Even the closet consists of a lone bar without any hangers. It seems like a delayed response, but I'm just now realizing there's no usable furniture here. Bedframes without mattresses, a kitchen table with no chairs, lamps without light bulbs. The list goes on . . .

"What exactly did you have in mind when you bought this place for retirement?" Gavin asks the question that's been on my mind since we arrived.

"We weren't going to live in *this* house, obviously," Dad says, taking inventory of the place. "We were going to tear it down and build a small but nice house, while the rest of the property would be farmed."

"We planned to grow produce like cabbage and radish that I could make kimchi with, and make herbal teas with ginger and ginseng," Mom adds. "It was meant to be a retreat from the city."

The more they talk, the less sense it makes. Farm? Cook? Make kimchi? I haven't seen them do any of those things, and by the look on Gavin's face, he's just as baffled as I am.

Dad opens his bag and begins riffling through it, looking for something in particular. And despite his grand plan of retiring quietly on a farm, the essential items among his things don't corroborate any of his story.

<u>Dad's essential items:</u>

- ***Suits, suits, and more suits***
- ***A laptop***
- ***Mysterious cables***
- ***Briefcase full of work documents***
- ***His autobiography***

If anything, the contents in his bag would suggest the opposite: that Dad has no plans of staying here for the long term. The only thing in his suitcase that seems out of place is the framed family photo we took last year. I'm sure he brought it to keep up pretenses that we are the perfect family for when this ordeal is over, since I have never known him to be the sentimental type. I'd be more offended by his dishonesty if it weren't a testament to his level of confidence that it'll be business as usual in no time—a kind of reassurance that we'll be out of here before we have a chance to settle in, which is a relief. Because I have a life to get back to. Speaking of . . .

I pull out my phone only to realize it's still in airplane mode. I'm about to switch it off when Mom stops me.

"You can't use that, remember?" she warns me. "There's no cellular reception or Wi-Fi here."

"We don't even have Wi-Fi here?" The gag reflex that comes after I say this out loud is involuntary but understandable. Just yesterday we were living in a ten-thousand-square-foot mansion, each of us with our own wing of the house. The dramatic fall from grace is going to take some getting used to.

“I need to get in touch with Kiki. I’m sure she’s flipping out right now over all my events being canceled.”

“You can’t,” Mom says matter-of-factly.

“You can go back to the limelight after we win the appeal,” Dad says confidently.

“If you’re sure we’re not in the wrong, then why does it matter if I talk to the press? I bet *Extra* or *Access Hollywood* is dying to get an interview,” I say, trying desperately to keep us in the good graces of the media. “Besides, it might help make our time here go by quicker. We might even get a show out of it. People love watching the rich slumming it. And just because it’s temporary doesn’t mean we couldn’t use the extra cash to make the living conditions here more . . . livable.”

The sound that comes out of Gavin is full of so much disdain, it startles me. “We can’t just *Simple Life* our way out of this mess. This isn’t a reality show. What we are going through is just reality. In fact, we’re trying not to get the attention of anyone, remember? So that means there can be no cameras and definitely no media involved.” Of course. Leave it to Gavin to be the *responsible* one.

“Gavin,” I say, spinning on my heel to face him. “To quote Sister George Michael from *Derry Girls*, ‘You will go far in life. But you will not be well-liked.’ ”

“That’s enough.” Mom preemptively stops us from going at it again. “Gavin is right,” she says, and I don’t know what’s more offensive: Mom’s declaration or the smug smile on Gavin’s face. “While the appeal is going on, our family’s reputation will be scrutinized more than ever. Frivolous articles about what you’re wearing, what you’re eating, what yoga pose you can contort your body into will not help our cause. This place is a blessing in disguise. The accusations are already painting us as greedy and out of touch with reality. With no high-speed internet or Wi-Fi, news about us hopefully won't reach these parts." Mom turns to me, pointing a finger. "So if you want to help the family, don't cause a scene here."

Before I can remind them that *causing a scene*, as they put it, is what's bankrolling our lives these next two weeks, I get distracted by Dad firing up his laptop at the kitchen counter after connecting it to a cable that fits in the uniquely shaped jack in the wall.

"I thought we didn't have Wi-Fi here," I say.

"We don't. But we have dial-up," Dad says as he waits for his computer to turn on. "Luckily I had enough sense to pack dial-up cables."

I glance at Gavin for clarification, but he looks just as lost as I am.

Gavin furrows his brows. "But I thought we couldn't use the internet."

"It's the old-fashioned way to access the internet. The connection goes through the landline, which doesn't disrupt the radio frequency," Mom explains while Dad types on his keyboard.

I only understood about half of that, but I don't care. All I heard was that we have internet access. Things are not as dire as they seemed. Gavin must be thinking the same thing, since we're both hovering over Dad's laptop.

On the speaker it sounds like a series of numbers is being pushed on a phone, and then there's a short ring before a god-awful static fills the air. I flinch at the sound, plugging my ears. A second later Dad beams. "Ta-da. Internet." He opens up a Google tab and types a web address on the keyboard, then we wait. And wait. And wait some more.

"Nothing's happening. Why is nothing happening?" I begin to panic.

"Is it frozen?" Gavin asks. "Should we restart it?"

"No, definitely don't restart it." Dad hovers protectively over the computer.

"Then what is it? What's the problem?" I ask.

"Just be patient. This is how dial-up works." Mom tries to calm us down. "It's not high-speed, but it's something."

It doesn't make sense at first, but it starts to sink in as we watch the page load line by line. About a decade later the website is up. I celebrate too soon, however. It takes another decade for the documents Dad needs for the appeal to download. After the last line loads, I finally make my move.

"What do you think you're doing?" Mom eyes me, wedging her way in front of the laptop.

I let out a squeak of annoyance. "You said I couldn't call Kiki, but you didn't say anything about email."

"Elena, in case you haven't noticed, it requires a lot of effort to use the internet here. We have to reserve it for business matters only," Mom chides me.

"But what about my business affairs?" My brows furrow.

Mom, Dad, and Gavin stare at me with a shared look that's all too familiar.

"My laptop is for essential business only," Dad says, typing in another web address in the tab.

Of course when they discuss their business matters, it's considered essential. However, my request to talk to my brand manager is dismissed as frivolous. Typical.

"What's Ih-khee-ah?" I say, sounding out the big block letters that pop up on the screen.

"*IKEA* is a furniture store. Don't you know anything?" Gavin rolls his eyes.

“Sorry for not knowing, like, all the furniture stores.” I glare at him. “Why can’t we just order the same stuff we had from Restoration Hardware? Don’t we have enough money—I’m sorry, I mean, don’t *I* have enough money—to pay for that, at least? I did make ten thousand dollars at my last event. And the cost of living can’t be that high here. Now, *that* would be criminal.”

Mom and Dad wince. I’ve noticed they do this anytime it’s mentioned that we’re living off of money I earned as an influencer. Like it’s drug money or something.

“No point,” Dad says, recovering quickly. “We’re not going to be here long, and we’re only going to get the necessities. Mattresses, tableware, and kitchen chairs.” He motions around the empty room.

“For all the meals we eat together?” I can’t help but snort at the notion of it.

“Now that we’re being stripped of everything, we’re going to be doing a lot of family dinners,” Mom says, as though it’s a punishment.

We haven’t had a family dinner since Gavin moved out almost two years ago. And even then it wasn’t like we couldn’t find the time to meet up. Gavin only moved downtown, less than an hour away from home. Maybe it was because of Dad’s late nights at the office or my paid appearances becoming more frequent. Or maybe it was because of Mom’s latest charity she’d be involved in or Gavin’s relationship with Sonya. But regardless of what the excuse was, there was always an excuse. Because when it comes down to it, having dinner as a family was never a priority for any of us.

After we select our furniture—though *select* is too generous a word; it’s more like *settle on* since the pages took so long to load that we just picked the first items that appeared—Dad signs off (whatever that means) and closes his computer. The cost of the furniture didn't amount to much, so we decided to splurge on next-day shipping. Small wins.

"Gavin," Dad barks. He motions for Gavin to follow him outside and get a lay of the land. Without hesitation, Gavin does as he's told and trails Dad like the loyal, trained dog that he is. His incessant need for Dad's approval never ceases to amaze me. Even more startling is the pang of envy that stabs me, seeing the way they are able to carry on with their lives in a semi-normal way, as if this scandal isn't affecting them in the same way it's affecting me. After the appeal is over, it'll be back to business as usual for It's Ok! and for Mom, Dad, and Gavin. Meanwhile, because I'm a socialite, my reputation is my livelihood. Their careers won't be defined by their offenses, and yet my name will henceforth be forever marred by the It's-Not-Okay-to-Be-Ok Scandal. To have everything I've strived for snatched from under me, through no fault of my own, is monumentally unfair.

My thoughts get interrupted when I notice Mom unrolling a sleeping bag *right onto the carpet.*

I gasp. "What are you doing?" Surely we're not sleeping on the ground. On *this* ground.

"In case you haven't noticed, we don't have any other options." She motions around the empty rooms.

"But the floor is so . . ." I shudder.

"Elena." She looks me dead in the eye. "My parents survived the Korean War. They were starving and had to start all over with next to nothing to save up enough money to give me a better life. Complaining was never an option for me. So unless you can make furniture appear with the flick of your wrist, I am going to roll out this sleeping bag and sleep on the floor and not complain. I suggest you do the same." She proceeds to calmly unroll the sleeping bag in her room and slip into it.

This new version of Mom catches me off guard. Usually over-involved in her charity du jour, Mom hasn't shown much interest in us. But now she's lecturing me on being grateful, taking away my phone privileges, and threatening us with family dinners. She's acted more like a mom in the past twenty-four hours than she has in the past four years. More than the reality check, though, it's the mention of her past that surprises me. She hardly ever brings up life before It's Ok!, and until now I had no idea her upbringing was much different from mine, considering how effortlessly she hosts dinner parties and manages the household staff.

I wonder if her strange behavior has anything to do with the interview she did with CBS last week. Ever since then she's been home more than usual. She suggested a mother-daughter trip, and now I find out that she created an independent bank account for me. I mean, what is that all about? I make a mental note to ask her about that later when things aren't so . . . strained. I may not know how to rough it, but I do know how to read the room.

I roll out a sleeping bag next to Mom's and slip into it, careful not to let any part of me touch the shag carpet. Just as I'm about to doze blissfully away from this place, Dad and Gavin come back to the house and report to Mom on the state of the property. They're talking animatedly, suggesting good news for once. My head pops up from the sleeping bag out of curiosity.

"You should see the place, Gloria. The previous tenants must have been farmers. There's an irrigation system in place, and the soil has already been fertilized." Dad's voice reaches a level of excitement I'm unfamiliar with. Partly because he spends so much time at the office that he's physically unavailable. And partly because when he is home, he's, well, emotionally unavailable. At least to me, that is.

"Jincha? That cuts down half the work if the land has already been cultivated." Mom matches his enthusiasm, which is a mystery to me how anyone can be that happy about anything he's said.

Dad nods. "Only a small portion, it seems, was farmed. The rest of the land has no crops to speak of, but at least it's been treated, so it's ready to be planted."

"There's even an herb garden full of chives and parsley," Gavin chimes in. He's not quite as animated as Mom and Dad are but seemingly happy nonetheless.

"I can make chive pancakes and cold noodles, just like we did on the farm," Mom says.

"When did you live on a farm?" I feel compelled to ask. "And how is this the first time I'm hearing about it?"

"Whatever made the tenants leave, it wasn't because they weren't good at what they did. The crops are flourishing," Dad carries on, completely ignoring me.

Somehow they're even able to find the timing of our arrival to this sad excuse of a house as good news. According to them, June is the beginning of the summer harvest, which gives them something to look forward to. I'd be more upset about the fact that they're all talking over me—as if I'm not even in the room with them—if there wasn't something more troubling on my mind. This conversation is starting to veer into long-term territory. And that can't be right.

Before panic ensues, Gavin asks, "Will we be here long enough to see the crops through? Two weeks doesn't seem like a long time."

"As long as we're here, we may as well make ourselves useful," Dad says. "It would be a shame to let all this progress go to waste."

"And temporary or not, this place belongs to us. It's been ignored long enough," Mom says.

It isn't the only thing that's been ignored. All I'm looking forward to is getting back to my paid appearances, the media frenzy, and saying *"What's that?"*—a life where I'm the opposite of ignored.

"Son, I'm going to need your help." Dad addresses Gavin as if they're in his office on the forty-second floor of the company headquarters on Wilshire Boulevard, not in a derelict shack in the forgotten land of Nowheresville. "With the appeal and the state of this property, there's going to be plenty to do."

"Whatever you need," Gavin predictably chirps.

"And Elena," Mom says.

My head pops up, startled by the sudden recognition. "Yes?" I respond, full of hope. Maybe they've come to their senses. Maybe they realize that now that we're on our own, four of us are better than three. Or maybe they just feel plain sorry for leaving me out, which I'm oddly okay with. They haven't acknowledged me throughout this entire conversation. At this point I'm not above pity.

"No one knows us here," Mom starts. "We wouldn't want anything to ruin the one good thing we have going for us, so make sure you don't use your phone." Both Dad and Gavin stare at me with the same look of warning.

I was wrong. So wrong.

As the three of them go on about their plans for harvesting the crops, I slip farther into my sleeping bag. I give up trying to relate to any of them. Even as our world is flipped upside down, one thing remains: Elena Ok is a nobody in her family. I can't wait until we get out of here in two weeks. Then I can go back to being a somebody.

In the morning I wake up to Mom and Dad talking with Gavin. Sounds like they are taking inventory of the house and making a list of what we need. When I don't hear words like *new carpet*, *new house*, *new life*—things I think should be on the top of the list—I stop listening.

"I think this is good for now," Dad says. "We'll add to it as we figure out what else we need."

"Yes, it's enough to get us started," Mom agrees.

Whatever is on the list, I hope it includes food, because yesterday, when we were told we lost everything, it included my appetite. Now that I've had time to sleep on it, my stomach feels like it's going to implode.

"Can you bring me back some egg-white frittata bites?" I call out from under my sleeping bag. "I have such a craving."

When the front door slams shut, I pop my head out of the sleeping bag. "Mom? Dad? What about my frittatas?" When I look around, my worst fear is confirmed: Not only did they leave, but they left me behind with demon spawn.

"What?" I hiss at Gavin, who is staring down at me from the kitchen.

"You're unbelievable." He shakes his head.

"Thank you," I say, only to annoy him. Which I'm successful in doing, since he disappears into the other room, closing the door behind him. I'm not sure how we're going to make it through the next two weeks if we can barely last a minute together before needing our own space.

As much as I'd like to sleep through the two weeks here, my body betrays me with the sudden urge to pee. My sleeping bag is the only safe surface I will allow my bare skin to touch. Thankfully I had enough sense to pack a pair of indoor slippers. I carefully get out of the sleeping bag and into my slippers by the time Gavin emerges from the room, dressed like he's going out.

"Where are you going?" I ask. As delightful as his company is, it's our first day here, and I'm not trying to get murdered. I'd rather not be left behind in this crime scene waiting to happen.

"To prune the herb garden," he says.

I wrinkle my nose. "Why?"

"Why do you care?" he says instead of answering my question.

I don't. But if I'm being honest, it does strike me as odd that without the business, the three of them are able to find something to work on together here. And it's farming, of all things. "Can I ask you something?"

Gavin's head pops up from tying his shoes, eyeing me from head to toe. "The answer is yes. Your satin two-piece pajama set and furry slippers make you seem completely out of touch with reality."

I groan angrily at him. Gavin makes it impossible to have a serious conversation with him. "You're the one who's out of touch with reality, going along with Mom and Dad's delusional plans of being farmers when I've never seen you grow anything, not even a sense of humor."

"Elena." He sighs, pinching the bridge of his nose. "Let's just get through this, okay? Then you can go back to doing whatever you want."

"Fine," I say. That's one thing I can agree with him on.

After he leaves to go "prune the herb garden," which I'm still not fully convinced about, I go to the bathroom. With my slippers on, I take great care to step only on the lighter parts of the shag carpet, since my slippers are 100-percent suede-lined with shearling. As soon as I close the door to the bathroom, however, I realize I can't pee. At least not in *here.* Brown stains around the faucet fixtures, a ragged shower curtain barely hanging up by three rings on a rusty rod, dust balls in the corners, and, not to mention, grime on every square inch of the place. My body shivers from a mix of disgust and claustrophobia.

Despite being in a bathroom with this level of grossness for the first time, I find myself in familiar territory. Turning something deemed undesirable into something of worth is, after all, my specialty. And this bathroom qualifies as just that.

Cracking my metaphorical knuckles, I unzip my toiletry bag sitting on the sink counter. My mom once hosted a charity event with Martha Stewart where I witnessed that woman use Chantilly lace trim and a glue gun to turn a plain wicker basket into a bassinet. It went from Hobby Lobby to haute couture in mere minutes. There must be something in my bag I can work with to improve the place.

Channeling my inner Martha, I rummage through my things. First I find a bottle of toner. On the bottle I read that the toner contains alcohol, which could be used as a disinfectant. But it's only half full, and even though it was gifted to me by the product's company when their new skincare line was launched, I'm not sure when I'll be able to replenish my stock. I tuck it back into the bag, deeming it too precious of a commodity to waste.

Next I find a packet of lavender-scented bath salts. I wouldn't mind a relaxing bath now, but not until the tub is up to my standards. Then my eye lands on something that can help. A bottle of hand sanitizer. I spray it around the tub first and then the sink. By the time I get to the floor, I'm spritzing the last remaining droplets. Thank God I can't say no to a deal and purchased the large scented bottle. After I finish cleaning, the room is not only bacteria-free but it smells like rain after a storm. Or at least that's what the description on the bottle suggests. And it's a marked improvement, if I do say so myself.

Now that the fear of catching tetanus or some kind of fungal infection is significantly reduced, I'm finally able to use the restroom. And just in time too. I was already doing a dance only kindergarteners and old people do. I was seconds away from having an accident that would make me have to disinfect the bathroom all over again.

When I'm done I wash my hands and face and start applying my seven-step skincare regimen. As I emerge from the bathroom feeling cleaner than I did when I entered it, a feat no one would have believed was possible before I took matters into my own hands, I can't help feeling a sense of major accomplishment. Now everyone can thank me for turning this bathroom from useless to usable. Except when I look around, I'm the only one here. A reminder that I'm alone in this family.

Who am I kidding? No one will thank me for a germ-free bathroom. They won't care about something they can't see. Like with the invisible germs, my parents can't seem to see the value in my work as an influencer. I used to think that if I could prove myself to them in terms they could understand—money, power, fame—then I'd finally be worthy of their praise. But I've become successful in my own right. I've become a bigger name than Gavin. And yet his future is still the only one they care about. I'm starting to think that no amount of success will make my parents proud of me, which is a bigger problem than I can handle. Because that means it's the person, not the achievement, they care about.

Of course I know my family loves me in that obligatory way. But liking me is a different story. As it was, our house manager, Carolina, used to do everything my parents didn't want to do, including spending time with me. And I'm good at finding solutions for all sorts of problems, but this isn't one of them. Even if Martha Stewart herself helped me, I couldn't fashion myself into someone I'm not.

Thinking about my family always gets my nerves riled up. Every part of my body is tense. While I look for a muscle relaxer, I find the lavender bath salts sitting on top of my toiletry bag. I decide to skip the muscle relaxer and draw a bath instead. Since no one else is here to enjoy it, I may as well take advantage of the now-clean bathtub.

Opening the packet, I pour a scant amount in the tub. The water is blessedly warm when I slip in, and the fragrant floral scent instantly boosts my mood. With my eyes closed, I'm able to forget where I am. Thirty minutes later, when my fingers and toes turn into shriveled raisins, I unclog the drain and dry myself off. Before putting the bath salts away, I read on the back of the packet that lavender is known for its calming effect. I'm surprised at how effective it is, considering how much my mood has changed even though my circumstances haven't. I tuck the rest of the packet into my toiletry bag like it's a precious commodity. With two weeks to go, I know I'll likely need it at least a handful more times.

EXCERPT

FORBES 20 UNDER 20 LIST

In keeping with the tradition of *Forbes*'s list of exceptional individuals making a global impact, this year the magazine is putting out a list of twenty under twenty. This is in response to the notable rise of entrepreneurs and executives disrupting industries at a younger age. We ask each person on the list to answer the same five questions.

#18—Gavin Ok. As the next in line to take over It's Ok!, a fast-fashion empire that is steadily supplying the fashion trends for anyone between the ages of fourteen and twenty-one one midriff at a time, Gavin Ok has a net worth that is already staggeringly high as an executive in training.

1. Q: As an individual not yet twenty years old, you have surpassed goals many people can only dream of achieving in their lifetimes. Do you worry you have peaked too soon?

A: Not at all. My father is a hardworking immigrant who built his life from nothing to become a leader in the fashion industry. Since I can remember, he has instilled in me to keep striving for achievement, no matter where I am in my life.

2. Q: Have you always known what you wanted to be when you grew up?

A: Yes, my father has included me in the business affairs of It's Ok! from a young age. In a way, it has made me feel part of the business my whole life.

3. Q: What do you think has been most influential in helping you be the success you are today?

A: As I mentioned before, my father has helped guide me in my path. Additionally, without a doubt, the education I'm receiving at the University of Southern California has been invaluable to my achievements. I could not have made it here without the top-notch education.

4. Q: The type of success you've achieved requires a rigorous work ethic that could potentially be overwhelming. How do you handle work-life balance? What sort of hobbies or activities do you do for fun?

A: I don't have time for hobbies. The way I see it, they're a waste of time. Achievement at this level doesn't happen without effort, and this sort of lifestyle isn't for everyone.

5. Q: Lastly, on a more personal note, with all the work you do to maintain this level of success, do you have time for a special someone in your life?

A: I do have a girlfriend at the moment. Sonya Sinclair and I are high school sweethearts. Her grandfather Bucky Sinclair is the founder of Bucky's BBQ Sauce. Like our family businesses, Sonya Sinclair and I make a great pair. Good taste and fashion go hand in hand.

With my hair in a towel, I wander into the kitchen, and my eye catches the clock on the counter. I'll be the first to admit I have no idea how long pruning an herb garden should take, but an hour seems like an unusually long time to be gone. Mostly fueled by curiosity and only a tiny bit out of worry for Gavin's safety, I go outside to check around the property.

Despite the gray cloud that's been following us since we got here, the sun's rays burst onto my face as soon as I open the door. I have to shield my eyes as I walk down the steps of our stoop to get a proper look around. In the daylight I'm disappointed to discover the place looks worse than it did last night. Every panel on the house is peeling in a color that can only be described as shit brown, and the concrete driveway is covered with veinlike cracks all the way down to the dirt road. On the side there's a shed that is horror-movie levels of decrepit, and behind it is a field that stretches farther and wider than I imagined it would. It isn't until I almost make a full circle of the property that I find Gavin.

"What are you doing?" I huff, annoyed he made me trek across this massive wasteland only to find him unharmed. Not only is he not near the herb garden, but he's sitting on the steps to the back door, reading something.

He folds the magazine in half and abruptly stands up. "I'm about to trim the chives."

"Sure you are." I eye him suspiciously.

"God, you're exhausting," he says in an exasperated way I don't understand.

"Gavin, you're being weird about reading a magazine." I raise a brow at him.

"I'm not being weird," he says unconvincingly. Now he's shoving the magazine deep into his back pocket, as if that'll make me forget I ever saw him reading it.

I couldn't care less about Gavin's habits, reading or otherwise, but his strange behavior does strike me as odd. I just can't understand what could possibly be making him this uncomfortable about reading a—I gasp, putting a hand to my mouth. So this is what he meant by *pruning the garden*.

"What now?" He sighs, irritated.

"You don't have to be embarrassed, Gavin," I say knowingly. "I won't say anything."

Gavin jerks his head back. "What are you talking about?"

"Looking at porn is nothing to be ashamed of. I mean, *I'll* definitely judge you for it, because you're my brother and no one should know *that* much about their family." I alternate between snort-laughing and gagging. I manage to keep it together long enough to finish my thought. "But you shouldn't let that stop you from being who you are. Exploring your sexuality is a natural thing."

"Ugh, Elena. It's not porn." He rolls his eyes so theatrically, all I see is white. "And if I seem embarrassed, it's because of my second-hand embarrassment over you thinking I need your approval to look at porn."

"Ha! So it is porn." I point a finger at him.

"You're missing the point." He shakes his head pitifully. "That may be how you operate in life, one pleasure-seeking opportunity after another, but some of us have responsibilities."

Ah yes. His *responsibilities.* I know what that really means. The way Gavin gets off on Mom and Dad's approval, I wasn't too far off the mark with the porn accusation.

"Where did Mom and Dad go?" I ask, suddenly reminded of them. I mean, how is Gavin supposed to win their approval if they're not here to witness him being responsible?

"They went to get supplies for the farm. Don't you listen to anything they say?"

"Honestly I try to block it all out."

"Typical," he mutters. Before I can challenge him by saying that it's typical that the family didn't include me in their conversation in the first place, he brushes past me to pick up the gardening shears on the ground. Of course, now that I'm here, he walks over to the boxed planters with tall grasslike strands and begins cutting them. Once he has a bunch in his hands, he places them in a reusable bag that's already filled with leafy greens.

"What's that?" I ask, pointing to the bag.

He cringes at my catchphrase. "These are herbs. This leafy one is parsley, and this one with the needlelike leaves is rosemary," he says, slow and high-pitched, like he's talking to a child. "Or are you unfamiliar with greens that aren't in the chopped salads you eat religiously? The ones with names as pretentious as you, like Green Goddess and Waldorf Astoria?" He reverts to his usual voice but maintains the same level of condescension.

"It's just *Waldorf,* Gavin. And that's not what I meant." I make a face at him. "Where did the herbs come from?"

"Where else would they come from?" he says, irritated by the question. "I had to trim the rosemary because it was blocking the sunlight from reaching the oregano. The parsley was getting overcrowded, so I had to cut the foliage off to relieve the stress. And the chives were also getting too tall, so I trimmed them."

"So you really were pruning the garden?"

He doesn't dignify my question with a response. Instead he stares at me, as if to say *duh*.

"When did you learn how to do all that?" It occurs to me, leveling my gaze with Gavin's, that we're staring at each other as if we're strangers. Is it possible that, while I've been trying to tell Gavin I'm not who he thinks I am, he's been trying to do the same about himself?

His eyes dart around self-consciously. "I mean, Mom and Dad said I should clean up the garden, so that's what I did." The arrogance in his voice is gone. In its place is an insecurity I'm not familiar with coming from Gavin. "I'm just doing what I was told to do."

Nope, I had it right all along. Gavin is exactly who I think he is. Not only that, but it now hits me that Gavin's act is not an act at all.

"Oh my God." I shake my head, laughing incredulously. "This is just like you to all of a sudden grow a green thumb."

"What are you talking about?" Gavin's eyes are half closed, like he doesn't have time for my nonsense.

"I always knew you thrived on Mom and Dad's attention, but to force an interest in farming?" I tsk. "That's desperate."

"Wow," he says, slow and drawn out. "Not only are your assumptions about my insecurity tendencies completely wrong, but you've now made it super obvious what your insecurities are."

I arch an eyebrow, unconvinced. "Then how do you explain your newfound hobby?"

He narrows his eyes. "How do you know it's a new hobby?" he challenges.

Gavin's right to call me out. I wouldn't know that about his habits, not firsthand. I learn about my family the way everyone else does: Google. Last week *Forbes* magazine put out its annual Who's Who list. This year they did a roundup of the top twenty under twenty, which included Gavin. And I'm pretty sure he specifically mentioned he doesn't have time for hobbies, calling them *a waste of time*.

"I would have read about it somewhere if you did." I pull out my phone to look up the article, then remember I'm not allowed to use it. I groan.

"Just because it isn't mentioned on Page Six doesn't mean it ceases to exist," he says. "Not everyone has to alert the press of every little thing they do."

"I don't alert the press of *everything* I do," I counter. "Sometimes they just show up without my knowledge." I sigh. The good ol' days. "And that's beside the point. Why is everyone in this family suddenly interested in farming?" Call it paranoia, but I'm starting to feel like they're all in on some secret mission that I'm on the outside of.

"Elena, I know this is a difficult concept for you to understand, but not everything is about you." He waves the bunch of limp chives at me, then continues walking. "I'm only now learning about Mom and Dad's interest in farming, same as you."

"If that's the case, then aren't you curious as to why Mom and Dad never mentioned they had property in Blaire or that they grew up on a farm?"

"In my opinion, it's better not to ask too many questions. Especially ones you don't want to know the answers to," he says, brushing me off. "Just follow their lead; it'll keep you out of trouble. You should try it sometime."

"That's the problem, Gavin. I am following Dad's lead. I'm being smart and steadily building my brand. But how can I get him to acknowledge me if he doesn't take anything I do seriously?"

His head jerks back, a little too dramatically if you ask me. "You want to be taken seriously?"

"I'm sorry, are you gaslighting me?" I spit back at him. "In case you haven't been paying attention, Gavin, I'm quite business-savvy."

A ridiculous sound escapes Gavin's lips. "What experience in business have you had?"

"Isn't it obvious?" I blanch. "I'm in the business of people. Why do you think people pay for me to attend their parties?"

He snickers.

I glare at him. "My point is, if you know as much about farming as I do, then why didn't Mom and Dad ask *me* to prune the herb garden? I mean, if you can do it, how hard can it be?" Leave it to my family to make me feel FOMO over something I can't even fake caring about.

"Since when have you been interested in what the family does?" Gavin glances at me sideways.

I wish I could take it as cavalierly as he meant it, but he struck a nerve. I want to tell him he has it wrong. It's the other way around. I've always been interested in the family. It's the three of them who haven't shown any interest in me. The resentment builds and builds until a defensive rage bubbles in me, preventing me from saying all those things.

"I'm not interested," I say instead. "I was just wondering when you had time for all these hobbies when you're the one who's been on the fast track to getting a business degree at USC so you can take over the family business."

Now *I* must have struck a nerve, because Gavin stops on the front stoop of our house. Instead of pushing the door open, he spins on his heels to face me. "Elena," he says, "when are you going to get it through your plastic head that you aren't as perceptive when it comes to people as you think you are?"

His caustic tone catches me off guard, so I respond with the first thing that comes to mind. "I don't know, Gavin. Maybe when you finally accept that you shouldn't wear clothes that accentuate your worst features?" I gesture to his stature of disproportion.

"Face it, Elena," he says, ignoring my comment. "There's a lot about me you don't know." But despite his bold claim, he predictably takes the corded phone with him into Mom and Dad's room to call Sonya, who I'm willing to bet is not just his girlfriend but his only friend. I don't feel the least bit sorry for him. With a personality like his, I'd say he deserves it.

While he's in the room, I take the towel off my head and brush my damp hair. I'm about to style it when I discover something disturbing. The walls, just like the rest of the house, are shoddy, and no matter which room I'm in, I can hear Gavin talking to Sonya. *Blech.* Their conversation is so polite and lacks spark, it's nauseating. Thinking quickly, I grab my phone. Mom said I'm not allowed to turn on cellular or Wi-Fi, but she didn't say anything about music. I tap on my phone to find my playlist and put my AirPods in so I don't disturb the Quiet Zone. Seconds later the electronic beat of my playlist drowns out the background noise. Sweet relief.

With the threat of overhearing Gavin's conversation with Sonya out of the way, I decide to unpack. Or at least I try to. Without drawers or hangers in the closet, there's no place to put my things, and I end up leaving everything in the bag. Next to my bag I discover Gavin's essential items by accident. And by accident, I mean I maybe, sort of riffled through his belongings. (How else am I supposed to pass the time without my friends or a phone?)

Gavin's essential items:

- ***A handful of business attire***
- ***A picture of Sonya***
- ***Business 101 textbook***
- ***A surprising amount of athletic wear (?)***
- ***Not one but two pairs of running shoes (??)***

Like he is in real life, his personal items are a snoozefest. Except for the athletic attire. Didn't think someone as wound up as Gavin did anything remotely leisurely.

Suddenly a noise startles me. Thinking I've been caught snooping, I reflexively throw Gavin's things back into his bag. I peek my head in the hallway expecting to see Gavin, but the door to the room he's in is still closed. When I realize it's not Gavin making the noise, I pop my AirPod out just as a loud knock at the door comes. I'm pretty sure Mom and Dad would not be knocking on the door to our new, but very temporary, home. But if this isn't Mom or Dad, who could it be? Gavin's head pops out of the room with the same puzzled expression on his face. We flinch when the knock comes again, this time with even more force, like someone's pounding on the door.

"Blaire law enforcement," a deep male voice announces through the door. "There's been suspicious activity happening in this location. Please open up."

Gavin and I stare at each other with the same helpless expression. Even though my head is swirling with a mix of fear and uncertainty, it's not lost on me that this is the most Gavin and I have had in common since we got here.

Despite announcing himself as law enforcement, the man standing on our stoop is dressed in overalls and has a beard covering half his face. Unless it's agricultural law he's involved in, I'm unlikely to believe him. I find myself leaning for protection into Gavin, who, at the moment, is the lesser of two evils.

"Sorry to trouble you today. I'm Officer Hartford. Are you the proprietor of the house?" he asks.

Proprietor? I swallow a laugh. I hardly want to be a tenant. "Are you kidding? I'd rather die than call this my house." Then I add a second later, "No offense."

He angles his face at me. "So you don't live here?"

"What she means is, we're living here. Temporarily," Gavin clarifies.

"So you do live here?" Officer Hartford scratches the back of his head.

Has he not been listening to anything we've said? *"We. Are. Staying. Here. Only. For. A. Short. Time.* Not"—I shake my head for added emphasis—*"forever."* I speak loudly and slowly in case he has trouble with comprehension.

Gavin jabs me.

"What the hell, Gavin? You don't have to break a rib."

“What’re you doing?” Gavin hisses at me.

“What does it look like I’m doing? I’m talking louder in case he doesn’t understand what we’re saying.”

Gavin blinks at me, open-mouthed. I’ve never wanted to gouge an eye out as much as I do now. And I’ve had to fight a dude trying to cut me in line for the bathroom at Coachella.

“Right,” Gavin drawls out. “And talking louder is going to get him to understand your words better.”

I know he’s trying to make a point with that all-knowing, holier-than-thou tone in his voice. So I ignore him. And apparently so does the man—I mean, *police officer*?

“Ma’am, I’m just trying to find the source of some suspicious activity going on at this location.”

If I weren’t so worried by the *suspicious* part of the sentence, I’d be more troubled by the *ma’am* part. (Excuse me, but I could pass for a mature twenty-year-old—twenty-one, tops!)

“Officer, I think you’re mistaken,” Gavin says, putting on his nice-guy act. “We’ve been doing nothing untoward.”

I snort. *Untoward?* It’s like he’s swallowed a Jane Austen novel.

Gavin shoots me a side-eye that could cut glass.

“I was talking to my girlfriend about our apartment. She wanted to know what to do with our bills since I had them linked to my account. But because those don’t work anymore, I had to—”

“Oh my God, Gavin. No one wants to hear about your boring-ass domesticated lifestyle, *okay*? Like, we get it. You’re in a committed relationship. Literally no one cares.” I internally sweat. Is Gavin that clueless? Was he really going to divulge why our accounts are under criminal investigation to a law enforcement officer (though the verdict on his official title is still TBD)?

“Jesus, Elena! Are you trying to help or not?”

Believe it or not, I was trying to help. But I can't seem to ESP my thoughts to my brother, someone I'm supposed to share DNA with. Honestly, the more time we spend together, the more I'm convinced we don't share anything, not even a single thought.

"Officer"—I put my sugary sweet voice on—"I was listening to music with my AirPods on. I have no idea what he was doing."

"You said you were wearing AirPods?" The officer's brow quirks.

I nod, though I'm less confident now that it feels like I'm being interrogated.

"I think I've found the issue here." Officer Hartford flips a page on his clipboard and starts scribbling something down.

"I think there must be a misunderstanding. I was wearing AirPods. I know this is a Quiet Zone or something, so there isn't a way I caused any noise disturbance."

"That's just it, though. This here is a National Radio Quiet Zone, which means we have to monitor the radio frequency waves being emitted so they don't interfere with the radio telescope. But considering this is your first offense, I'll only issue you a warning." He asks us for our names, which we reluctantly give him. Then he rips off a piece of paper and hands it to us.

"Just make sure to turn off your Bluetooth option on your devices and put them on airplane mode. It'll save me another trip here."

"You betcha." Gavin actually salutes the guy, like some character from an old-timey black-and-white movie.

It's a good thing Officer Hartford didn't seem to recognize us. I let my hair air dry, and the frizz is starting to take hold. I'm sure the tabloids would have had a field day if they knew what we've been reduced to.

"That was close," I say, patting down my unusually coarse hair.

Still holding the warning in the air, Gavin remains frozen. He doesn't even blink. I'm about to wave a hand between his face and the paper when I hear noises outside the door again. The sputtering of an old vehicle grows louder before shutting off completely, followed by the unmistakable thumps of footsteps up the front porch. I freeze.

Is Officer Hartford coming back? Did he just google our names and discover who we are? And now he's hoping to snap a caught-off-guard photo of us that'll appear in the tabloids? I can see it now in bold block letters: CAUGHT IN THE WILD, THE OKS ARE NOT OKAY.

The door opens before I have a chance to hide or run a flat iron through my hair.

"Omo." Mom puts a hand to her chest. "What are you two doing right in front of the door like that? You nearly gave me a heart attack," Mom says, even though she's the one who nearly gave us a heart attack.

Dad follows Mom into the house. "I saw a guy leaving in a truck. Did he leave from here?" he asks.

Gavin nods. "He's from law enforcement. Apparently Elena was using her phone," he divulges much too eagerly.

I cut Gavin a severe look. *That Brutus.*

"I wasn't using my phone," I clarify. "And honestly it wasn't a big deal. Only a slight misunderstanding over AirPods." *Nothing remotely close to leading a multinational company into possible financial ruin,* I think but don't say.

"He gave us this." Gavin's fingers tremble, holding the ticket up. For all his arrogance, he seems rattled. It surprises me because, one, Officer Hartford wasn't even the real police. And, two, who cares? We're not staying here long enough for some stupid ticket to matter.

Dad takes his time reading through the fine print. "It's just a warning, and there's no penalty. Nothing to worry about."

Mom reads over his shoulder. "Still, we shouldn't be so cavalier about our stay here. It may be temporary for now, but we don't want to do anything to jeopardize our appeal. What if someone finds out about it? The papers have a way of spinning things. They might make us look like we have a history with the law. So we must be careful not to break any more of the rules here. Don't use your AirPods again. In fact"—she holds out her hands—"I'll take your phones and wireless devices now."

I gasp. "You can't be serious."

"I am." She pushes her hands out farther, as if to say *gimme*. "You can't use them here anyway, so they're as good as useless."

Gavin parts with his devices much easier than I do. His level of nonchalance is as enviable as it is irritating. I guess not having a life has its perks. All I can do is watch Mom as she stows away our phones into a kitchen drawer.

"So, what else have you been up to?" Dad asks. "Other than getting in trouble the second we leave."

"I was talking to Sonya. So far Bucky's BBQ's stock hasn't been affected. I explained to her that it would be better for their family if we distanced ourselves from each other during the appeal, so we decided to take a break from our relationship. For precautionary measures." He raises his eyebrows at Dad, waiting for his approval like the trained monkey that he is.

"Good. Smart." Dad nods definitively with his arms folded across his chest like he's in some kind of board meeting. It's so weird when I think about it. How can he say *good* about anything Gavin just said? And don't even get me started on the *smart* comment.

"You didn't use your phone, did you?" Dad asks.

"No, of course not. I used the landline. I wouldn't be so careless as to use anything that could potentially interfere with the airwaves."

Gavin glares at me. As if he wasn't shitting his pants a second ago when the tech officer was making his inquiry. "Except there's something wrong with the phone," he recalls. "It kept clicking during my call."

"Clicking? How?" Mom's interest is suddenly piqued.

Gavin looks up thoughtfully. "Well, at first it made a short beeping sound, then it clicked. It did that a few times, then stopped. Then it would start again a minute later, then stop. You should get someone to look at it."

Mom slaps a hand on her forehead and sighs. "How can someone so smart be so . . . not smart?"

As much as I'd like to jump on this bandwagon disproving Dad's *smart* comment to Gavin earlier, I don't know what Mom is referring to. And according to the look on Dad's face, he doesn't understand either. So we wait for Mom to explain.

"The clicking sound is a call waiting." When my dad doesn't reanimate, Mom leans in, wide-eyed. "Which means another call was trying to get through."

Comprehension immediately floods Dad's face. "Mr. Ahn! The appeal!"

"Yes, Dale. The appeal," Mom says, like *duh*.

Dad scrambles to look up Mr. Ahn's number in the notebook he scribbled all the important phone numbers into. Before he finds it, the phone rings. He drops the notebook and lunges for it.

"Hello? Mr. Ahn?" Dad says frantically, followed by a long pause. "Uh-huh. I see. Yes, of course," he says, giving us no indication of whether it's good news or bad. The rest of the call is a series of yeses and noes while Dad paces the room. After about a million minutes go by, Dad finally hangs up and immediately rushes over to rummage through his briefcase.

"What did Mr. Ahn say?" Gavin asks, hovering over him.

"It's in here, I know it is," Dad mutters to himself.

"What's in there?" I ask, full of hope that it's something that can magically get us out of here, like a wand or perhaps a crystal ball with a bright outlook.

"I found it." Dad holds up a mysterious folder.

The less responsive he is, the more inquisitive we get.

"Let him speak." Mom shushes me and Gavin, then stares at Dad expectantly.

"Mr. Ahn said he was able to get an appeal date for Monday."

"That's in one week!" Mom's face lights up.

"If they find no wrongdoing, we can be back in our homes by the end of next week, just like he said," Dad says. "And these are the documents that are going to prove our innocence." He waves the folder in front of us.

"Finally good news!" I jump up and down, clapping.

"That's a relief," Mom says, sighing. "I'd hate to think we lost everything because of that no-good George Bronstein."

Gavin, however, remains stoic, which is surprising, even for him. Although he's usually devoid of emotions, you'd think he'd at least show some signs of relief knowing his future is close to being secured again. It goes without saying that I'd never be in his size tens, but that's how I would feel if I were in his shoes. Speaking of shoes, Dad is putting his back on, which makes me panic.

"Where are you going?" I ask. "You just got back."

"We'll need to prepare for the appeal with Mr. Ahn," Dad says, then turns to Gavin. "Make sure to wear your blue suit."

"Excuse me?" Mom places her hands on her hips, facing Dad. "What about me?"

"Gavin needs to learn how to run the business," Dad says cluelessly. "It would be a good experience for him to watch and learn."

"I've put as much time into the company as you have. I should be there if we're being accused of money mismanagement. Don't you think?" Mom asks with some serious side-eye.

"And leave Gavin and Elena home alone?" Dad doesn't say it directly, but he makes a serious assumption that Mom is supposed to stay home and babysit us. "After their run-in with the police—"

"Tech police," I clarify. What I don't say is that Gavin and I don't need a babysitter. We need a referee.

"They'll be fine," Mom says, not taking *no* for an answer. She joins Dad at the door, slipping on her shoes.

I'm about to ask them how they're going to LA when I notice something unfamiliar in our driveway. "What's that?" I can't seem to peel my eyes away from it.

"Elena, for the last time, that catchphrase isn't going to fix our—" Gavin stops when he gets closer and sees for himself. He shuts himself up, saving me the trouble. "I think it's a tractor," he says a second later.

"I know it's a tractor." I roll my eyes at him. Just how much of an airhead does he think I am? "What's it doing here?"

"The mayor lent it to us," Dad says.

"The mayor?" I didn't even know this town was big enough to have one.

"We went to the auto repair shop to ask if they had any cars they could loan us. The owner said they didn't, but he had a tractor we could borrow," Mom says.

"Wait. So was it the auto mechanic or the mayor who lent the tractor to us?" Gavin's brows furrow.

"Both," Mom says. "The man who owns the auto repair shop also happens to be the mayor."

"Is this one of those towns where the preacher is the doctor and the vet is the schoolteacher?" I ask only half jokingly.

"He was nice," Dad says pointedly to me. "In fact, he lent us the tractor at no charge. We haven't seen that kind of generosity in a while, right, Gloria? The Harringtons, the Sheffields, the Wentworths . . . they won't even return my calls," Dad admits.

"Yeah, that's true," Mom says, agreeing with Dad for the first time since we got here. "The only people who are taking our calls now are lawyers and the IRS."

"That's bleak," I say. I don't know what's sadder, the fact that this tractor is the nicest thing anyone's done for them lately or that they admitted to having crap friends.

"Anyway," Dad continues, unamused, "the point is, thanks to the kind people here, we were able to get a diesel-run piece of machinery that can get us around town without disturbing the radio frequency waves." He climbs into the driver's seat.

"You can't drive to LA in that thing," Gavin says, reading my mind.

"No, but it can take us to Bakersfield," Dad explains, "which is the nearest town with Wi-Fi access. There's a small remote workspace where we plan to meet with Mr. Ahn virtually. It's about thirty miles away, and since the tractor only goes up to thirty miles an hour, we'll have to take local roads."

Gavin must be doing the same mental calculations I am, because his face turns sheet-white at the same time that I feel the blood drain from mine.

"That's a two-hour commute!" He flails. "On top of your meeting, that could take—"

"All day," Mom confirms.

Sheer panic takes over me. On second thought, maybe we do need a babysitter. "What about us?" I plead. "I haven't eaten all day, and I don't see any frittatas. We'll starve to death." As I'm saying this, Gavin is mocking me from behind Mom and Dad so they can't see him. "Oh my God, Gavin. I'm going to kill you!"

"Elena!" Mom chides. "That's no way to talk to your older brother."

"Especially since he's the one who will be watching over you while we're gone," Dad says, wiping the smile right off Gavin's face.

"There's a store just down the street. You can get food there," Mom says, settling into the passenger seat. "And the furniture will be delivered later today."

"Food and furniture. That should keep you busy and out of trouble," Dad says, then turns on his engine with a loud roar.

Another f-word comes to mind as I watch them drive away. If they think leaving us behind in this place is going to keep us out of trouble, it shows how little they know us. Being stuck here with Gavin would drive anyone to the brink of insanity. Who knows what kind of trouble we'll be in by the time they get back?

I'm as unfamiliar with grocery shopping as I am with picking up dry cleaning or getting stamps at the post office. You know, Regular People Stuff. But I haven't eaten a proper meal since we got here, and my stomach feels like it's starting to eat itself. So I guess I have no choice but to go to the store. Besides, I'm *so* bored. I'll do anything to get out of the house, even if it means spending time with Gavin.

As sure as Mr. Ahn is that we won't be recognized here, I'm not so sure. My popularity in the media puts me at the top of all the algorithms, which means photos of me are mass-circulated in curated news feeds amplified by repeated exposure, making me hypervisible to the curious and incurious alike. And as the visual representation of my business as an influencer, my face has become an instant symbol of brand recognition.

Translation: I am as recognizable as the Starbucks mermaid or the Quaker Oats guy, only much leggier and *way* younger.

If I have any hope of maintaining my status after this temporary setback, I can't be caught looking like anything but a ten. So, on the not-so-slim chance I'll be recognized, I decide to wear a sheer top with a nude bodysuit underneath and a pair of cut-off denim shorts. By the time I straighten my hair with a flat iron, Gavin is halfway down our street. Typical. Before he has a chance to act like a hero, I chase after him.

Gavin hears me stumbling to catch up and glances behind his shoulder. "What do you think you're doing?" He slows to a stop.

"What does it look like I'm doing? I'm coming with you to the store."

"Dressed like that?" He arches an eyebrow. "Don't bother. I can manage."

"And let you get all the glory again? No thanks."

"What's that supposed to mean?"

"Everyone knows you thrive on Mom and Dad's approval, and being the responsible one is your way of getting it. But in order for that to happen, you have to make me look like the irresponsible one. And staying home while you go out to get groceries would be doing just that."

He has the nerve to be offended. "I don't have to try to make you look irresponsible. You're doing just fine on your own." He motions to my ensemble. "I mean, how you think those clothes count as essential items is beyond irresponsible," he counters.

"I am being responsible. With our reputation hanging by a thread, it's *essential* to look our best now more than ever. And as a one-of-a-kind, custom-tailored top designed especially for me to wear at the launch of Axe body spray's new product line for women, I know I look good in this."

"Okay, fine, whatever." He waves a hand between us to shush me. "Let's just go to the store."

Of course Gavin doesn't understand. No one will care if he gets spotted in those ill-fitting pants or last season's shoes. They'll throw a parade in his honor, hailing him as down-to-earth for buying his own groceries, while I, on the other hand, will be shamed for hitting rock bottom. It's the real reason why this top and these shoes are essential and why Gavin and I can never see eye to eye. How can we when he's the one benefiting from the double standard? So I do what I always do. Try to stay one step ahead of him. Except at the moment it's harder than usual. So I steel my ankles and power through the rocky terrain.

"Do you know where you're going?" I ask, hoping there's an end to this dirt road that seems to go on forever.

"Mom and Dad said it's on this street and that we can't miss it," he says, but he doesn't seem as sure as his words suggest.

In both directions of the road, there are long stretches of unmanicured fields with the occasional home here and there in the same deteriorating condition as ours. We slow our pace when we spot a group of people across the street. Their makeup-free faces make them appear young, but their off-brand clothes and severely outdated hairstyles are throwing me off. They could be anywhere between twenty and forty.

"Maybe they're going to the store. We should follow them," Gavin recklessly suggests.

A squeak of disapproval escapes my lips. "Gavin, no. In this town and those clothes, they could be headed to a windowless compound. Next thing you know, we'll be making soap out of animal fat for a charismatic guy named Harvey, who we'll be forced to worship with excessive devotion in a religion he made up." I smack my lips. "Trust me, we don't want to go anywhere they're headed."

"El, just because their fashion choices fall short of your standards doesn't mean they're in a cult."

"Doesn't mean they're *not* in a cult," I counter only half seriously. "And it's not just their fashion; it's . . . everything." I make a big sweeping motion of the space around us. "You know it's weird here.

Like we stepped into the twilight zone or a time machine."

A car passes by. It's one of those old cars from the Elvis movies Dad used to watch. The ones with big bubbles around the wheels that come in colors like baby blue and Chantilly yellow. By Gavin's silence I can tell he knows I'm right. Everyone's sort of in this weird time loop here, stuck in the 1950s rural Midwest.

Up ahead is a gas station and what appears to be a convenience store. The sidings are weatherworn, the windows are so scratched up that they're permanently foggy, and the roof is missing patches of shingles.

"I think this is the store." Gavin scratches his head, looking down both ends of the main road.

"Can't be. It barely has a roof." As I say this, a middle-aged woman walks through the door with a shopping bag hanging from her arm. She has the same outdated hair and clothes as the other people we spotted earlier. Funnily enough, just as she passes us, she pauses to look me up and down as curiously as I'm looking at her. As if *I'm* the weird one.

"Did you see that?" I chuff incredulously. She had no idea who I am.

"Yeah," Gavin says. "This is the store, and it's definitely open."

It's not what I meant, but that's the least of my concerns now. As Gavin pointed out, this condemned-adjacent building is indeed the store we're supposed to buy our groceries from. And just how is anyone supposed to shop from a place as unappealing as this? Even the bell attached to the door jangles pathetically as we push it open, as if it, too, would rather be anywhere but here. As soon as we step in, however, Gavin's eyes widen.

"It's actually . . . not bad," he says.

Looking around, I'm surprised to find myself agreeing with him.

The conditions on the inside are better than the outside, though it's not hard to be. Rows of tall shelves, filled with items reminiscent of our former lives, take up the bulk of the space. Lavender honey, seasonal fruit preserves, crème fraîche. There's even a whole section of housewares. Woven place mats, ceramic mugs, and a rack of semiwearable clothes. It's not Gelson's or anything. It's still just a convenience store, but it's clean and organized, like the ones I'm familiar with. Except for the scowling guy behind the counter, staring us down with narrowed eyes. Gavin grabs a basket, and I stick closely by him. The sooner we get out of here, the safer I'll feel.

Not long after, the door opens, and a young woman walks in, grabbing my attention. She's dressed in vintage overalls rolled up around her ankles, with hair a color that's somewhere between dark blond and light brown. She sparks my interest because, one, unlike the others we've encountered so far, she seems to have a sense of style. And, two, with another patron in this establishment, I now have the assurance of a witness to a potential hate crime. Halfway down the aisle, though, I frown.

As surprising as it is that this store has so many artisanal items, there are no ready-to-eat meals or canned craft lattes. Only rows and rows of ingredients that require a multistep process to result in something remotely edible. Eventually I manage to find essentials that don't require much, if any, prep—water, cereal, milk, and microwavable meals that are chock-full of preservatives and sodium that I normally wouldn't consume, but desperate times . . .

When I unload my haul into the basket Gavin's holding, I notice it's still empty. Instead of shopping, he's been studying each item on the shelf. Apparently there isn't a task he doesn't take seriously.

"Are you ready?" I ask. My eye catches the girl in overalls down the aisle. I smile at her, and she smiles back.

"Yeah, just a sec." He puts the vial back, muttering, "Saffron usually costs five times as much as this anywhere else."

My brow quirks. Since when does he know about the prices of obscure spices?

"That's because they're grown locally," the girl says, startling us.

Gavin and I crane our necks to face her. That's when I notice she's emptying contents from her basket onto the shelf and not the other way around.

"These were grown here?" Gavin says with forced interest. Or at least, that's what I'm assuming, since no one gets that excited over a spice.

She nods proudly.

"Is this your product?" I say curiously. She looks too young to be a . . . I'm not even sure what to call it. A saffron grower?

"The saffron? No." She picks up a different bottle off the shelf and shows us. "But the honey is from my family's bee farm."

"Cool," Gavin says, taking it from her and adding it to our basket. We thank her and move to the next aisle, where Gavin loads his basket with wild mushrooms and Parmigiano-Reggiano and . . . is that truffle oil? And he calls *me* delusional. Who does he expect is going to cook for us, Mom? I'm about to call him out for his unrealistic expectations when I get distracted by a revolving stand of cheap flip-flops that I get overexcited about. I don't wait to purchase them before tearing the tag off a pair and slipping them on. The state of the ground from the house to the convenience store, crumbling or cracked on every square inch, must be the worst I've stepped on. And as someone who's gone to several fashion shoots in third-world countries, I have stepped on some of the most uncultivated ground. By now my blisters have blisters. As soon as my arches melt into the synthetic rubber soles, I sigh. Sweet relief.

On the counter I place the price tag of the flip-flops along with the items Gavin unloads from our basket. We nod politely at the cashier. He grunts, presumably a hello, before he starts adding the items into an old-timey cash register that's a type of old that's historical. I wonder if it's in workable condition. Sure enough, the keys on the machine manually move a tiny plate that stamps the corresponding symbol of each key onto the paper receipt. Between the cashier's mannerisms, which are as ill-fashioned as his attire, and the clickety-clack of a machine that belongs in a museum, I'm not sure where I am or when I am. What's next? Ma has dysentery?

"That'll be thirty-nine even." His gruff voice startles us. Then he cranks a wheel that pushes the paper out, and he tears a piece off and hands it to us. Gavin is just as mesmerized as I am, staring at the receipt in his hand.

"What are you waiting for?" I say to Gavin when he doesn't move. "Pay the guy."

Gavin puts a hand in his pocket. A split second later, he tenses up. After patting down his other pockets, he deflates. "Yeah, I left my wallet at home," he confirms. "Elena." He stares at me expectantly.

My head jerks back, leveling my gaze with his. "*Elena* what?" I balk. "Don't tell me you expect me to pay? Weren't you the one who said you could manage buying the groceries without me?"

His nostrils flare. "Weren't you the one bragging about having *all this money*?" he counters while doing an imaginary hair flip.

I don't know what's more insulting—the accusation that this is somehow my fault, or that he honestly thinks that I'm so thirsty for attention that I'd stoop to something as basic as hair-flipping. What's next, twirling chewing gum around my finger?

"All of my money's in a bank account, remember? And I haven't carried a wallet in years. Don't you have a debit card or something? Since you're so responsible?" I seethe.

"Elena," he says through gritted teeth, "all of that is on Apple Pay, and we can't use our phones anymore, remember?" He points a finger to his head, as if to remind me I have a brain and should consider using it sometimes.

It's about now that I notice the cashier of dubious intentions watching us with intense curiosity. He's got that type of lethal combination of mullet and haphazard denim on denim that says he was born with a suspended driver's license. With his series of reckless decisions so bold, I can only guess what he's capable of. And if I'm not mistaken, has his glare become more menacing?

Gavin waits expectantly, as if the problem is going to solve itself, which, considering how he's gotten through life so far, tracks. So, once again, it's up to me to get us out of this mess. As a natural problem-solver, I've been able to get out of a lot of things. Speeding tickets, late fees, indecent proposals from wealthy shipping magnates . . . but *insufficient funds*? I'm in uncharted territory here. In my panic, images of us washing pots and pans to pay off our debt flash before my eyes.

"I can spot you if you don't have any cash with you." The girl from earlier appears from behind us, and just in time. I was beginning to think indentured servitude was our only option.

"Thank you," I say, at the same time that Gavin says, "No, we can't impose."

She pauses, unsure of how to proceed. When we don't move, she makes an executive decision and hands the cashier two twenty-dollar bills.

"Thanks, Hal," she says when she receives her change. Despite her cheerful disposition, he gives her the same grunt in response, making me realize the guy's attitude toward us is not personal but one of general disgruntlement. And it's no wonder. If I lived here—permanently, that is—I'd be perpetually angry too.

"Thanks for spotting us," Gavin says before we leave the store.

"No problem." She hesitates. "I don't think I've met you before. I'm Callie," she says.

"Gavin." He sticks his hand out awkwardly, then retracts it to wave at her.

I recoil from secondhand embarrassment. I've always known Gavin was socially awkward. At birthday parties, he was the kid who sat off to the side, removed from the rest of the group when they sang "Happy Birthday." And he was the birthday kid. But I thought he'd grown out of that. At least that's what it seemed like in all the articles I googled about him.

"You seem about my age. Are you in high school? Or college?"

"High school or college?" Then, inexplicably, he begins coughing. His brain seems to be malfunctioning. Right. Time to do damage control.

"Hi, Callie. It's nice to meet you. I'm Gavin's sister, Elena." I swoop in and flash my disarming smile.

Callie's expression changes. "Elena?" Her eyes light up in a way I'm more than familiar with by now. "You must be—"

"Yes, I am." I nod, smiling modestly. I knew Mr. Ahn was wrong. It was only a matter of time before someone would recognize me here. And if I had to put my money on anyone, it would be someone like Callie. She's cute in that no-makeup makeup type of way.

"That's what I thought." Callie seems delighted.

Now that I'm getting a proper look, I notice she's about our age too. I could even see us becoming friends. That is, if we were staying long enough to make friends. I give a subtle I-told-you-so look to

Gavin, who seems even more uncomfortable than before, which I didn't think was possible.

"I usually know everyone here, so I know when new people move into the town."

I blink at her. New people? As in, people she's never met before? I deflate. So, Callie doesn't recognize me.

"Or maybe I'm wrong. Have you been here long?" she asks, noticing the shift in my expression.

Without thinking, I say, "Yes," at the same time that Gavin says, "No." It feels like we've been here an eternity.

"What we mean to say is, we arrived here yesterday," Gavin says after a subtle but intense glance at me.

"But we're not staying very long," I add, recovering from the unexpected anonymity.

"Oh, I see," Callie says, seeming to buy our clumsy explanation. "That's a shame. It would've been nice to have more people my age around here."

I'm struck by her sincerity, since she obviously doesn't know who we are. Why should Callie care if nobodies like us stick around?

Gavin clears his throat. "How can we pay you back?"

"And I promise, we're not poor or anything. We left our wallets at home, I swear." Without the recognition, I feel the need to make the distinction.

Gavin side-eyes me.

"No, I believe you." Callie takes notice of my ensemble. "You wouldn't be able to find something as nice as this in any store around here."

"Thanks." I manage a weak smile. At least this outfit wasn't a total waste.

"You can find me here." Callie motions to the convenience store.

"I come to the store to restock the shelves every morning around this time."

"We'll make sure to run into you here to pay you back before we leave," Gavin says.

"No problem." Callie smiles. "Hope to see you around."

After we say our goodbyes, we head back down the dirt road with our groceries in tow. As we walk I stare at my pedicured toes in the cheap shoes. The burgundy polish clashing against the neon-pink flamingo-print flip-flops is like me in this town. I don't belong here. Because Callie wasn't the only person who didn't recognize me. No one did.

"What's wrong?" Gavin says when we pass by another couple on the other side of the road.

"Who says anything's wrong?" I say defensively.

"You haven't talked about that person's hairstyle or this person's clothes in a minute," he says.

"I'm just surprised that no one recognized us." The incident with Hal reminded me of how much I have to lose if I can't recover from this setback. Without my reputation, I have zero credibility. "I mean, considering how much It's Ok! has been in the news lately," I add so he can't accuse me of being a narcissist.

"No one wants to be associated with the George Bronstein scandal," he says, buying my explanation. "It should be a relief to know people here don't recognize us."

That's easy for Gavin to say. He receives validation in many forms, whereas I only get it in one.

"In fact, we should count ourselves lucky. If it weren't for Callie, the cashier could have called the authorities on us when we didn't have money to pay for our things. Then our cover would've surely been blown. We're not supposed to be drawing attention to ourselves, remember?"

"Not like you handled yourself any better. Your inability to answer her very basic question about yourself was so sus, I'd be surprised if she doesn't rush off to google our names on a wired computer somewhere."

"I panicked. I didn't know if I should tell her I was in college, because then she'd ask me where, and I wouldn't know what to tell her without giving up specific information about us."

I guess his explanation makes sense. Sort of. Telling anyone here that he attends USC, a school with almost fifty thousand students, would not have outed us in any way. But as much as Gavin can't understand my thought process, I can't begin to understand his.

EXCERPT

I work seven days a week. Anyone who works five days a week is missing out on two days of progress.

The American Dream Achieved: The Story of Dale Ok, Founder of It's Ok!

TRANSCRIPT

60 MINUTES INTERVIEW WITH GLORIA OK

INTERVIEWER: I would think his farming background would be very relevant to his business work ethic. Is that not true?

GLORIA: Well, yes. Working on a farm is incredibly hard work.

INTERVIEWER: Then why isn't it mentioned in his autobiography?

GLORIA: Dale doesn't like to talk about his humble beginnings.

INTERVIEWER: Really? Why not?

GLORIA: Korea has a hierarchical society, and status matters. For many of us, what kind of family you were born into determines your future. Doctors become doctors. Scholars become scholars. And farmers become farmers.

INTERVIEWER: But how does that affect him as a businessman in the US?

GLORIA: It shouldn't. But it matters to Dale.

<TRANSCRIPT PAUSED>

Not long after Gavin and I get back to our temporary place of residence, I hear a thud by the door and get overexcited, thinking my parents are back, not that I want to spend more *quality* time with them. But they act as a buffer between Gavin and me. And right now I'll take what I can get.

I peek through the window, and instead of Mom and Dad, I see a large IKEA truck on the road, which is still something to get excited about. It feels like Christmas morning watching the two men unload the truck, starting with four mattresses. No more sleeping on our crime-scene carpet. I glance over at Gavin, who is now standing beside me. Unsurprisingly he does not seem to share the same level of enthusiasm as I do.

"I wouldn't do that if I were you." I gesture to Gavin's forehead. "If we can't afford real furniture, then I'm pretty sure Botox is out of the question."

He barely glances at me. "El, aren't you at all concerned about the fact that the 'dresser' that you ordered came in a box that's six inches thick?"

"Who's a snob now?" I stare down my nose at him.

"Are you telling me you know what to do with that?" He gestures wildly at the boxes on our doorstep.

"What, like it's hard to assemble furniture? Just follow the instructions."

"Famous last words," he mutters.

There is nothing more motivating than a person's skepticism about your abilities, especially if that someone is Gavin. So as soon as the delivery men leave and Gavin and I bring in the boxes, I rip open the first box, preparing to make him eat his words.

An hour later wooden slats are splayed on the floor along with the tiniest baggie of screws and pegs and one questionable tool. I refer to the instructions, thinking they'll explain just how the hell this is supposed to somehow become a dresser, but they don't. How is this stick-figure comic strip that's not even remotely funny supposed to help us assemble the furniture?

"So, what's the first step?" Gavin says with artificial interest.

Assuming he's trying to prove some sort of point, I ignore him completely and gesture to the wooden slats. "Take that piece and put it together with the other piece with this peg-looking thingy."

Instead of doing what I tell him to do, he just stares at me, mouth agape.

"What?" I say, enunciating every letter of the word. "God, you're more annoying than cystic acne, the kind that has its own heart-beat."

"Like, what am I supposed to do with that? You're not making sense." He throws his hands out to his sides. "It's like you're not even trying."

"Put those two pieces of wood together with this thing." I repeat myself louder and slower, pointing more intently to the items.

Despite my very clear and very concise explanation, Gavin remains dumbfounded, which, honestly, says more about his intelligence than mine. "How about this?" he says, exasperated. "Don't try to interpret the instructions. You're just making yourself sound incompetent. Instead, why don't you read them out loud, verbatim?"

"Gavin." I stare directly into his pupils. "There are no words, just these badly drawn cartoon people. See?" I shove the instructions page in his face.

He pulls his head back, then takes the instructions sheet from me. After staring at it for a long time, he's at a loss for words.

"Bet my interpretations don't sound so bad now, do they?" I say with my arms folded across my chest.

"Aren't you the one who said it's not hard to assemble furniture and that all you need to do is . . . What's the phrase you used?" He taps a finger to his lip. "Oh, that's right. 'Just follow the instructions.' "

"Ugh, you're so annoying!" I crumple the instructions sheet and throw it at him. "If you're so smart, then you figure out what this means."

He catches the balled-up instructions and glares back at me. "You said it was easy, so you figure it out." Toss.

"No, *you* figure it out." Toss.

If I'm being real, I'm not sure I can figure it out. And I'd rather sleep on the probably bloodstained floor another night before admitting that to Gavin.

With neither of us willing to budge, we leave the pile of plywood on the floor. I storm into our room and slam the door behind me. Now I understand why this furniture is so cheap—there's only a fifty-fifty chance you'll actually manage to assemble it into something usable.

"How was your meeting?" Gavin asks when Mom and Dad get home later that evening.

"Long," Dad says.

"And dusty," Mom says, shaking the fabric of her blouse.

"Did Mr. Ahn give you any indication of how long it would take for the judge to decide after the appeal?" I ask.

"It could be anywhere from a couple hours to a couple days," Dad says. "Mr. Ahn thinks it may come down to our reputation."

"That means, while we're meeting with Mr. Ahn to prepare for the appeal the rest of this week, you'll have to keep a low profile," Mom says.

A low profile? That phrase does not exist in my vocabulary. "What if I come up with a pseudonym? With my full lips and my high cheekbones, I could easily be a Claudia or Shosh—"

"No." Dad is quick to cut me off.

Gavin snorts, and I scowl at him.

"Mr. Ahn thinks we shouldn't give false identities," Dad continues. "They would only make us seem guilty."

"Besides, it's too late. Officer Hartford already knows your name after you gave it to him when he issued you the warning," Mom adds, suddenly shifting the focus to me.

My shoulders sheepishly sag. "Again, it was an honest mistake."

"Even so, Mr. Ahn says that we're being painted negatively in the press. I believe he used the term *unlikable*." Mom's eyes ping-pong between me and Dad.

Dad shrugs, seemingly unbothered. "The point is, no one knows who we are here, and until our position is more secure, we shouldn't do anything to shine a spotlight on us," he says. "Like breaking the rules."

"I get it," I say, feeling their judgy eyes on me. "No loud parties."

"Not only that," Mom says. "But you also can't do anything that will interfere with the radio waves."

"Which means no cell phones, satellite TV, Bluetooth, or Wi-Fi." Dad stares directly at me.

"So what do you expect us to do?" I flail, exasperated. "I can't live this way for two weeks. Like some kind of caged animal."

"Emphasis on *animal*," Gavin mutters.

"If we want to find tenants before we leave, there's plenty for you to do," Mom's quick to suggest.

"Speaking of . . ." Dad points to the wooden pieces next to the stack of IKEA boxes. "What happened here?"

"The furniture arrived," Gavin says. Although I would've thought it was obvious. Then again, maybe they're not used to seeing furniture in small boxes either.

Dad shakes his head. "Why aren't they assembled?"

"Cheap furniture means cheap instructions," I say.

"I'm sure you could figure it out if you tried," Mom mutters.

"No, really. It's impossible," Gavin says, surprisingly backing me up. "The instructions don't make sense. And there's no Google Translate for Stupid."

"The mattresses are all we really need for the time being," I say. "We've taken the liberty of moving them onto the bedframes in the rooms, m'lady." I curtsy with my head bowed, doing a servant-from-*Downton-Abbey* bit. My parents aren't amused.

Dad frowns. "How are we supposed to settle into this place without proper furniture?" Since there are no chairs, he sits on an IKEA box next to the kitchen table.

"This is our home. We should make it feel like one too," Mom says, leaning against the kitchen counter.

"Can you please stop calling this *our home*? You're freaking me out." I shriek.

“Even if we don’t intend to live here, we need to make improvements to attract tenants,” Dad explains.

“Or maybe, once everything is settled, we can make this our vacation home,” Mom adds.

I laugh, then place a hand on my mouth when I realize no one else is laughing. Apparently I’m the only one who didn’t take Mom’s absurd suggestion seriously.

“If the house doesn’t look good by the time we leave, we’ll have to stay until it does. Maybe until the end of summer,” Mom says, like a threat.

“Don’t worry,” Gavin says, almost as if on command. “I’m on it.”

“I knew I could count on you,” Dad says to him. “Make sure Elena helps you.”

I don’t even whine about how Gavin is no better at assembling furniture than I am. What’s the point, when talking to my parents is no clearer than the IKEA furniture instructions? I can see what they’re doing, but the crucial explanation is missing.

“Maybe if you got to know the place, you’d like it better,” Mom says, mistaking my frown for thinking it’s the home I’m disappointed with.

“The observatory gives tours every morning at ten. Maybe you two could go to one.” Dad slides a brochure across the kitchen counter to show us.

“Yeah, sure,” Gavin agrees, much too easily.

I glance at it. There’s a satellite on the cover, which is a big nope for me. “I’m busy.”

Mom’s frown deepens. “Elena,” she says, like a sigh. She hesitates, wondering what to say next. Knowing Mom and how little she knows me, she’ll try to appeal to me to have a better attitude or be more open-minded. "Nothing," she says instead.

I'm surprised by the disappointment I feel that she didn't even try to lecture me. Then again, I wouldn't have listened anyway. So maybe she does know me.

We say good night and go to our rooms. Now that we have real beds, it makes our living conditions less bad. The downside? I have to share a room with Gavin.

"Since when are you busy tomorrow?" Gavin asks, not even a minute after we settle into our beds.

"Why do you care?" I sneer at him.

He hesitates. "You're not going to, you know, *pull an Elena*, are you?"

The offense is palpable. I want to challenge him to see if he even knows what *pull an Elena* means. Does he mean to take charge of my life? To turn something people consider worthless into something worthy? To capitalize on my popularity in the media by building a business off my image?

But he won't get it. So I say, "I just don't want to go. Is that a crime?"

He sighs. "I get that living here is beneath you, but couldn't you at least try? You're not the only one who's lost everything."

"*You* haven't lost everything; *I* have," I correct him. "I've lost the social clout I need to get booked for paid events."

Gavin snorts.

"I don't expect you to understand. Someone who's had their future handed to them on a silver platter." I must have struck a chord with him, because the smug smirk is gone from his face.

"Says the pot calling the kettle black," he retorts.

"Just saying, while Dad took you under his wing, I was left to fend for myself," I counter. "Unlike you, I've had to work for everything I have."

"Was it hard jet-setting to luxury international resorts on private planes? The one-star Michelin restaurants weren't good enough for you? You needed two or more to be satisfied?" He mock-cries, then abruptly stops. "News flash: No one feels sorry for you," he deadpans.

My cheeks flare, and I taste bile. If he thinks I'm taking our privilege for granted, he's *so* wrong.

I know what it seemed like on the outside. My life was a series of *Carolina, take Elena shopping. Carolina, take Elena to Cabo.* It's some people's dream to be waited on hand and foot, but it wasn't like that for me. I could tell what my parents were doing. In the aftermath of the *Vogue* article, my parents treated me like the idiot child they were burdened with. They were keeping me busy so that I wouldn't be in the way while they poured all their attention over Gavin. The one who would take over the business after Dad. The one who mattered.

If anyone is taking anything for granted, it's Gavin. Because once this ordeal is over and It's Ok! is up and running again, he will go back to being Dad's protégé while I'll have to find a way to rebuild everything I've created. After this I'll have to pay to attend parties instead of the other way around.

I'm sure a therapist will have a field day unpacking what kind of lifelong impact it had on me to be the only one not included in the family business, but that's for future me to worry about. Right now I have to figure out a way of getting in the public eye again so I can become financially independent in my own right.

When I wake up the next morning, Mom and Dad have already left to meet with Mr. Ahn, and Gavin is at the observatory for a tour. Taking advantage of the empty home, I don't waste a second. I grab the corded phone and dial the number I know by heart with renewed determination. Once the appeal is over, the first thing I'm going to do is ensure that I don't have to live under the same roof as my family again. That means I have to make sure I'll have enough paid public appearances to support my independent lifestyle. If anyone can get me back in the public eye, it's Kiki Klineman, manager to the biggest names splashed across the society pages and tabloids. I'm sure she'll know how to keep me relevant during my media hiatus. If only I could get through to her.

As the phone rings, my heartbeat races. I begin to worry Kiki won't pick up because I'm calling from an unknown number. Just as I'm thinking this, however, she surprises me by picking up the call.

"Kiki Klineman," she answers in her signature no-nonsense way. As a lifelong Manhattanite, she's direct, cuts to the chase, and has one goal in mind: to maximize her clients' earning potential.

"Thank God you picked up," I say breathlessly. I was beginning to lose hope.

"Elena?" The disappointment in her tone is notable. "I was going to call you."

"You were? Because I left you a bunch of messages. If I didn't know any better, I'd think you were avoiding me." I let out a nervous laugh. Kiki doesn't laugh.

"Elena, sweetie," she says icily. "I'm not avoiding you. I no longer represent you."

"You're dropping me?" The words come out like a shriek.

"Hon, I'm not dropping you, but the payment for your last invoice was declined."

"Invoice?" I don't recall paying her for her services directly. "Aren't you paid on commission?"

"That's correct. I get fifteen percent of all earnings from events booked through me. But with all your bookings canceled this month, fifteen percent of nothing is nothing. And as the contract states, if the commission fails to cover my fee, I need a minimum of twenty-five hundred dollars a month to retain my services. Bottom line: If I don't get paid, then I can no longer work for you."

A sound like a dying animal escapes my lips. I know she doesn't mince her words, but her tough love feels extra hurtful today. Then again, I've never failed to make a payment on anything before. So maybe this is warranted.

"Look, I'm sympathetic. You're not the first client to fall on hard times. But I'm not a charity. You get it, right? It's not personal; it's business."

No, she did not just give me the business equivalent of the breakup line *It's not you, it's me*, did she? "Kiki," I say with renewed vigor, "don't believe everything you read. It's all one big misunderstanding."

"Really?" Her voice falters slightly. Kiki never falters.

“Really,” I say confidently. Even though I don’t know exactly how we’re going to be cleared, I am relying on the assurance of my dad, who is, if nothing else, confident to the core. “We have an appeal in a few days, and our lawyer says if all goes well, everything will go back to normal in as early as two weeks.”

“Two weeks?” she repeats skeptically. “Then why don’t you call me when the appeal is finalized, and we can resume where we left off?”

“But you know as well as I do, a day out of the media is like years. If I wait it out, I’ll be vilified to the point of no return. Or worse, I’ll be forgotten about entirely.” I shiver as I say this; a film of cold sweat lines my forehead. “Isn’t there anything I can do now?”

“As much as I’d like to help, I don’t run on credit. Maybe you could start a GoFundMe?”

Virtual panhandling? As bad as things are at the moment, I am not at the point where I need to start begging for support, financial or otherwise.

“The funds are there,” I reassure her. “Or at least they will be there after we win the appeal.”

“Then as soon as your payment clears, I can start booking you for events. There are a couple gigs I could line up for you. One is for unwanted animals. I’m sure they’re desperate enough to have anyone come. Will you be in LA anytime soon?”

As appealing as that sounds (honestly she may as well have described it as a charity event for me, not the sad, unwanted animals), I realize I don’t have many options.

“Look, Elena,” she says, probably sensing my defeat. “This isn’t my first time strategizing a comeback. Many of my clients have successfully revived themselves from financial ruin. And two weeks isn’t going to do irreparable damage.”

I don't love her phrasing. *Financial ruin* has such a negative connotation. But I'll admit she's got me curious. "How?"

"Look at Martha after her incarceration. Kim K. after her sex tape. And Woody Allen after, well, all the times he got canceled. Every one of them was able to come back and rebrand themselves to become bigger than they were pre-fall. Netflix documentaries. Celebrity collaborations. Hosting gigs. If it worked for them, it can certainly work for you."

"I'm listening," I say. This new plan to rejuvenate my brand into a better one is an idea I can get behind.

"Use this time to think of content you can use to rebrand yourself. A charity, a noble cause—anything that gets you back in the good graces of the public."

"What do you mean? I don't create my own content; you know that. The press does that for me. They're everywhere I go."

"That was before It's Ok! became the bad guy. Any connection to the Madoff 2.0 Scandal is considered social leprosy. No one wants to be associated with the scandal, and that includes It's Ok! From now on, the media is not your friend."

"No, you have that wrong. People like me for me," I say adamantly. "Sure, I initially got media attention because of It's Ok!, but people stuck around for me. I'm endearing, and charming, and—*have you seen me?* My lifestyle is aspirational, and I work hard to uphold that image." Although it may seem contrary to vignettes you see online or in the media, turning ridicule into a monetizable catchphrase, paid partnerships with products that sell themselves, cross-promoting product placement at paid events—that takes work!

"Still, your name is synonymous with your family's business. You need to distance yourself from the company," Kiki says. "My advice? Don't do anything desperate to try to make yourself relevant. No one likes a clingy ex-girlfriend, and there's real power in making yourself obscure. Eat, pray, love your way through this time. People love that stuff. And when this all blows over and you're ready to come back in a couple weeks, we'll find some way to drum up the anticipation for your reappearance."

"Okay, I can do that," I say, thinking out loud.

"Great," she deadpans. "That one's on the house."

"Thanks, Kiki." I feel instant relief from hearing her plan, which reminds me of why I hired her in the first place. "I don't know what I'd do without you."

"I don't either," she says without a hint of irony. She hangs up without saying bye. I would have read into the way she abruptly ended the call if I wasn't so sure Kiki said what she meant and meant what she said. Besides, she's given me a lot to think about. As long as people think I'm spending my time eat-pray-loving and not living in squalor, maybe I can ride this out and still end up on top. And, bonus, this town might be the thing I need to come up with an angle to separate me from our family's name, which is synonymous with the fashion industry, since I can't imagine there being anything remotely fashionable here. Best of all, if it works the way Kiki said it would, I'll be back to making the steady income I need to move out on my own as soon as this nightmare is over.

Kiki must really be a miracle worker, because everything around me is starting to look better, not just my outlook. The mattresses in the room make it cozier, the bathroom is much improved, and the musty odor is gone. It actually smells pleasant.

No, wait. That's not my imagination. Next to the brochure of the observatory is a plate of food left for me on the kitchen counter. At least my mom didn't completely forget about me. It reminds me of Carolina's meals, which were presented to me on a marble tray under a glass dome. But, like, the poor man's version. I pare my expectations for whatever is left for me on the plate. Stale bread, a piece of cheese, maybe even an apple. Underneath a film of plastic wrap, however, I'm surprised to find something more palatable. Eggs Benedict?

It isn't until I peel the plastic wrap off that I notice the eggs Benedict look different from the ones I'm used to. Instead of an English muffin, the poached eggs slathered in hollandaise sauce are sitting on top of rice that has been shaped into a mound with a chopped-up layer of something in the middle. When I take my first bite, the flavors burst in my mouth. The mystery layer is sautéed chives, and the rice has been fried so that it's crunchy on the outside and chewy on the inside. At least we don't have to eat like we're prisoners, even though our accommodations may suggest otherwise. When did Mom learn to cook like this? What am I saying? When did she learn to cook, *period*?

Mom is not someone who works with her hands. Every year, Brenthaven organizes a community service day where we go to the inner city and paint over graffitied walls or plant flowers in under-funded communities. Parents are always encouraged to come and do the work with us, but Mom always declines. Instead she writes a check, which is the extent of hands-on that she gets. I guess if Mom is making an effort, I should take her suggestion to get to know the place better more seriously. And who knows? Maybe I will like it here.

I get ready to go to the convenience store, where I intend to pay Callie back with cash our parents left us, but there's something else I have to do first. Yesterday's outing was unsettling. I'm not used to being in a place where I'm not the life of the party. So, fueled mostly by curiosity and a little bit of denial, I've come up with a plan to remedy that.

The bell on the door jangles when I push it open, and Hal looks up. I nod at him. He grunts back, charming as ever. I waste no time and make a beeline to the refrigerated section in the back. If my time in the media spotlight has taught me anything, it's that *fun* and *alcohol* are synonymous. So I grab a subpar—but probably good enough for the locals—bottle of vodka and a jug of orange juice. In a town with a population of a hundred and fifty, I'm bound to run into someone as desperate as I am for fun. When I do, I'll invite them over. They'll bring their friends, we'll play drinking games, and, *bam*, I'll be back to being the life of the party. So maybe Gavin's right after all. Maybe I am going to *pull an Elena*.

I confidently place my items at the cash register and wait for Hal to ring me up. With money to pay him this time, I won't encounter the same embarrassment from yesterday.

He starts ringing up the items and stops when he gets to the bottle of vodka. "Do you have ID?" he asks.

On reflex I swat a hand at him, as if it's ridiculous he's even asking. "ID?" I giggle. When he remains unmoved, I falter. "I didn't bring one with me. Is that going to be a problem?" As much as I don't want to encourage him, I realize that without my reputation to carry me, I'll have to resort to something a little more foolproof. Leaning my body against the counter, I bat my lashes and then wait a beat before gazing directly into his eyes and pursing my lips ever so slightly.

"I can't sell this to you without seeing proper ID," he says in a voice resembling a low growl.

I blanch. How did that not work? "Are you sure you can't look the other way, just this once?"

He doesn't respond, but his expression—brows clenched and a glare that's just shy of menacing—says it all.

Then, in a moment of weakness, I hear the words come out of me before it's too late. "Do you know who I am?" Immediately I recoil. Am I that desperate that I've lost all sense of decorum? I mean, I may as well have asked to speak to the manager while I was at it.

"No, I don't. Should I?" he says, revealing what I feared the most. No one cares who I am here.

"No, guess not," I mutter pitifully.

"Great," he deadpans. "That'll be five even." For once I'm grateful that this place is the land of the forgotten. If this were LA, my Big Karen Energy would have gone viral by now, canceling me indefinitely.

I leave the store with a bruised ego and a jug of orange juice I have no intention of drinking. I'm in a daze, and I nearly walk right in front of a white Jeep Wrangler pulling into the parking lot. A second later, after the Jeep parks, the door opens.

"Hey," Callie says, walking toward me. "Sorry I startled you. It seemed like you were lost in thought."

"Yeah, I must have been."

"I just realized I know who you are. You're Elena Ok," she says, catching me completely by surprise.

"Oh my God, yes." *Finally* she gets it.

"You live at the property on Blaire Road, don't you?" Callie continues.

I falter. It's not exactly what I'm known for. And if she didn't know who I was before yesterday, I'm pretty sure that whatever she's learned about me in the past twenty-four hours can't be good.

Her lips curl up, as if she knows our secret. I brace myself for it. "My dad's Officer Hartford," she says. "He said he stopped by your place earlier for suspicious activity. He mentioned new tenants."

"Oh, right," I say, trying not to sound disappointed. So Callie doesn't know who I am, not really. "We learned our lesson the hard way. No more Bluetooth." I point to my ear and laugh, probably a little too loudly. Luckily, Callie doesn't seem to notice my strange behavior. Come to think of it, why would she, when she has no idea how I am normally?

After I regain clarity over the situation, I remember something. "I have your money," I say, handing her two twenty-dollar bills from my pocket.

"I almost forgot about that. Thanks." She pockets the twenties, then opens her trunk and pulls out a box of jars.

"So, do you work here?" I ask, taking a peek at the contents of the box. There are some jars of honey, which I remember Callie saying her family makes. But there's also a variety of other jars and oils along with them.

She stares at me curiously. "Oh," she says, then laughs. "I'm sure that's what it looked like. But, no, I don't work here. I collect the locally sourced products and deliver them to the store."

"But I thought the farmers all moved out of town because of some radioactive observatory," I say, thinking out loud.

She laughs again, then stops when she realizes I'm not joking. "Oh, you're being serious? Sorry, I didn't mean to laugh. It's just that most people move here because of the radio telescope at the observatory. I assumed it's what brought you here too."

I shake my head. "Our tenants left, so we're fixing up the house while it's empty."

"That makes sense," she says, easily buying my story. "Most of the families left when the observatory was built. Some of us, including my family, maintain a small portion of the property that was farmed long ago as a kind of homage to the past."

Farming as a hobby? Maybe that's why my family seems so at home here. They're among their people.

"Is it just you and your brother here?" she asks.

"No, I live with my parents as well. I'm only seventeen; they'd never let me move out on my own." *Yet.*

"We're the same age." Her face lights up, and I find myself smiling with her. "I'm an intern at the observatory this summer, but I'll be a senior at Blaire High School in the fall."

"Same," I say. "I mean, not that I'm going to Blaire High, but I'll be a senior in the fall too." A second later I realize she may ask more questions about where I go to school or where we came from—questions I don't want to answer. So I change the subject. "You're an intern at the observatory?"

She nods. "I'm headed there now and can show you around if you have time."

I wrinkle my nose. "Maybe next time," I say. Knowing Gavin is there at this very moment, I would rather be anywhere but the observatory. "What do people do for fun around here?"

"Fun?" She considers the word. "There's not much . . . ," she starts saying, and my frown deepens. "But Blaire does have one place where most of the locals hang out."

"Hang out?" I perk up.

"Yeah, it's a cafe. Would you like to go? I can take you there now," she offers.

"I don't want to make you late for work."

"Oh, you won't," she says with a curious smile I don't know what to make of. "Let me just drop off these things, and we can go." She lifts the box in her hand.

I tell Callie I'll wait for her by her car, since I'd rather not see Hal again. Somehow he is impervious to my charm. I'm a person who usually likes to confront my haters head-on, but in this case, in the absence of my cloak of invisibility, a.k.a. my reputation, I think avoidance is best.

Callie is back in a flash, and we both hop into her Jeep. She revs her engine on and starts driving down the path, and in the far distance I see a crossroads.

"Is it far from here?"

"Not too far. Just left at the fork in the road." She points. When we turn at the intersection, there's a satellite-dish-looking structure peeking out of the treetop landscape that looks like it came right out of a science fiction movie.

"That's the radio telescope," she explains. "Isn't it cool?"

"Yeah," I say, trying to conjure up enthusiasm.

"And this is the main building of the Blaire Observatory." She pulls into the parking lot of a stand-alone brick building that is bigger and notably nicer than anything else in this town, similar to the ones on Wilshire.

"Wait. I thought we were going to a cafe."

"We are," she says with the same coy smile.

Even though I don't comprehend, I follow her into the building, where she takes me through the large open space of the lobby, which is lined with linoleum-tiled floors and tall ceilings with exposed pipes, making it seem slightly industrial. There are a handful of people coming in and out of the elevators, but it's otherwise empty.

"The cafe's this way," she says, heading toward an archway at the end of the lobby. We're technically in the same building when we walk through the archway, but the look and feel of the place become strikingly different. Where the lobby is sterile, like a hospital, the cafe is cozy, with colorful red booths and natural-wood-paneled walls. "I'm sure you noticed, but Blaire is a small town, so the cafeteria isn't only for the observatory's employees; it's for everyone in the town," she says.

"Oh, that makes sense," I say.

"Why don't you find a table for us to sit at, and I'll grab us some water?"

"Great. I could use a Perrier." While Callie leaves, I look for a place to sit. Most of the tables and booths are occupied, and the room is filled with a white noise of pleasant conversation. It feels welcoming to be among other people. As though this were a civilized society. Maybe there's hope for this place after all.

That is, until I spot an eyesore.

"Ew, what're you doing here?" I find myself staring at Gavin sitting comfortably in one of the booths. "I thought you were on a tour.

Or did you just tell Mom and Dad that you were going so you could uphold your reputation as the responsible one?"

Gavin folds the menu and sets it down with an eye roll. "As it turns out, I did go on the tour. It just ended, and I happen to be here with a friend. He's getting me a drink."

"Ha," I say dryly. "Your first mistake was not coming up with a more believable lie."

Gavin somehow finds my comment offensive. "I am capable of making friends."

"Since when? And don't say Sonya, because she doesn't count." I tsk.

"He works at the observatory," he says, unamused.

"Sure he does, Gavin," I say, playing along. "And I bet he's really smart, good-looking, athletic, and all the things you imagined him to be." Just then, a guy who eerily fits the description I uttered approaches us. I'm stunned by his sudden appearance. I wonder if it would work if I wished for a different life.

Nope. Still here.

"Sorry about the wait," he says, handing Gavin a coffee. Then he sits down in the booth across from him.

This is Gavin's new friend?

After moving to an alternate universe where up is down and left is right, it shouldn't be a surprise to me to finally see the perks of having an older brother. Gavin actually made a friend who not only seems normal but is cute.

After thanking his new friend for the coffee, Gavin brings the cup to his lips, eyeing me in that annoying I-told-you-so way. As soon as he takes his first sip, however, his expression changes.

"I should mention that Blaire Labs might have state-of-the-art technology when it comes to radio frequency telecommunications, but it is quite lacking when it comes to craft coffee," the guy says to Gavin.

"No, it tastes great," Gavin says unconvincingly.

I've been standing here, listening to their exchange, and *no one* has acknowledged me for an alarmingly long time. I clear my throat in case Gavin's new friend has some rare condition that affects his peripheral vision. They both turn to me.

"Oh, hello," I say, shifting my stance to face the guy. "Gavin was just telling me about his new friend. And any friend of Gavin's is a friend of mine."

"Is that so?" he says, his eyes flicking between me and Gavin. "Then it's nice to meet you. I'm Brennan." His smile reveals a set of beautifully aligned teeth that nicely complement his strong jawline.

Yes, Chef.

"Is this your sister?" Brennan guesses when Gavin doesn't offer an introduction.

"I don't like labels," I say, wrinkling my nose.

Gavin rolls his eyes. Unable to ignore me any longer, he finally introduces us. "Elena is my annoying little sister," he says with an air of superiority.

"His younger, more sophisticated sister." I wrinkle my nose and smile at him.

Brennan turns to Gavin. "I didn't know you had a sister. She should join us. There's plenty of room in the booth."

"She's not staying—" Gavin says at the same time that I say, "I'd love to."

Brennan scratches the back of his head, confused. With great reluctance Gavin scoots over. I mean, I somehow manage to slide into the booth and sit shoulder to shoulder with him without retching. Would it kill him to try? Although it does help to be sitting across someone as genetically blessed as Brennan. And I'm even willing to overlook his worst flaw: befriending Gavin.

"Can I get you anything?" Brennan asks.

"Thank you, but my drink is coming." I detect a slight drawl in his accent. Not quite Southern, but like someone from the mid-Atlantic region. "You must not be from around here. You're too charming." I point a finger at him with a wink.

"I think I'm going to be sick," Gavin mutters loudly.

"Oh no. Are you okay? I hope it's not the coffee." All of a sudden I lose Brennan's interest to Gavin's sarcastic remark.

"What? No, I'm kidding. I was just . . ." Gavin hesitates and looks as if he's going to explain himself while debasing me, but he somehow doesn't. "It's just a little gas. I feel better already."

"Ew," I let out by accident. I know people aren't Gavin's strong suit, but honestly could he not have thought up a more socially acceptable cover-up story?

Just then Callie approaches us.

"Oh, hi. I didn't know you'd be here," Callie says to Gavin. "What's up, Supernova?" she says to Brennan.

"Calamity." He nods back at Callie.

Callie sits across from me, handing me a paper Dixie Cup with something bubbly in it. "They didn't have a Perrier, but they do have club soda, which is pretty much the same thing."

"Thanks," I say, even though she couldn't be more wrong. Not all sparkling waters are created equal. But I don't want to be rude, so I put the cup to my lips and take a small sip.

"You two know each other?" As soon as the words come out of my mouth, I roll my eyes at myself. Of course they know each other.

"We're both interns at the observatory," Callie says.

"I came here on an exchange program through my high school in April. Loved it so much, I decided to stay as an intern this summer."

"It's all part of our master plan. Next we're going to convince you to finish your senior year at Blaire High. Isn't that right, Supernova?" Callie pokes his side teasingly with her finger. He squirms, laughing.

"Supernova?" Gavin quirks a brow up at Brennan. "Because . . . astronomy?"

"That and because he's from NOVA—Northern Virginia, that is," Callie clarifies.

"But also because I'm super," Brennan adds, flexing his arm for emphasis. And, boy, does it emphasize the appeal of his physique.

“I knew I detected a mid-Atlantic accent.” I delicately tap his hand.

Brennan tips a confirming head at me. “Fairfield, Virginia. Born and raised.”

“And . . . Calamity?” Gavin asks.

“Don’t you know?” Brennan chuckles. “She’s a walking disaster.”

“I’m not that bad.” Callie laughs along with him. “My full name is actually Calamity Jane Hartford. My parents have a mutual shared love of the Wild West.”

I stifle a snort. That’s the most hillbilly thing I’ve ever heard. But so far what I’ve seen of Callie is nothing but kindness, so I keep the thought to myself. The two of them seem to have some kind of close rapport, like they’re family. Well, not like *my* family. But what I imagine other families to be like.

“How did y’all meet?” Brennan points to the three of us.

“Callie was nice enough to lend us money at the convenience store when we didn’t have any,” Gavin says.

“Not because we’re, like, poor or anything,” I quickly add. Jesus, is Gavin on a mission to make us look like pathetic losers? Because that’s about the only thing he’s succeeding at right now. “We’re only here for a short while, so we’re not used to not using our phones to pay for things.”

“That’s right. Gavin told me you’re making some improvements on your place to rent it out,” Brennan recalls. “And I totally get it. It took me a minute to get used to not using my phone here.”

“What about you two? How’d you two meet?” Callie asks Brennan and Gavin.

“Gavin was the only one who showed up for the tour today, so he was stuck with me.”

“Honestly I feel like I lucked out. I basically got a private tour of the place,” Gavin says.

"We ended early, so I offered to buy Gavin a drink at Blaire's finest dining option."

This janky cafe is Blaire's finest?

"Just kidding," Brennan adds, as if he can read my mind. "Blaire's only dining option."

I'm about to laugh until I realize Brennan is being serious. "One restaurant for the entire town?" I gape.

"I couldn't believe it when I got here either," Brennan says. "But working here has shown me how challenging it is to run a fully functioning business that's compliant with the National Radio Quiet Zone. With all the regulations, small businesses aren't able to make a profit in a town like this."

"Doesn't the town get assistance from the government?" Gavin asks.

"The observatory gets funding, but it's not enough," Callie explains. "That's why a lot of our stores, like this cafeteria and the convenience store, quadruple to cover all our needs. And because food is expensive to transport into town since we're so far out of the way, a lot of it is locally sourced. I may be biased, but I think it tastes better than any gourmet restaurant out there."

"It's true." Brennan nods. "They have an extensive menu, and they try to change it frequently."

I raise a skeptical brow, but at this point I notice Gavin's interest is piqued.

"Really?" He leans in. "What kinds of food come from here?"

"Mayor Beecham and his wife have a dairy farm that provides milk and cream, and then Jean has the most amazing garden and chickens that lay not only the best-tasting eggs you'll ever eat but the most beautiful ones you'll ever see. And my family has a bee farm. Our honey is used in everything from yogurt parfaits to honey-baked hams." Callie smiles proudly. "We're in a co-op that sells our products to the local store and this cafe, but we also take them to a farmer's market in the nearest town every Saturday to raise extra funds."

My face falls sympathetically. "Is it because you're poor?" I extend a hand and place it on hers.

"Elena! Don't be so insensitive!" Gavin chides me.

"I *am* being sensitive." I was trying to let Callie know that if she's fallen on hard times, she's in good company. I mean, who are we to judge? But leave it to Gavin to assume the worst of me.

"No, it's okay," Callie responds, more amused than offended. "I wasn't very clear. What I mean is that since most of the people in Blaire work for the observatory, many of our town's resources are allocated to maintaining it. But I'm sure you've noticed that the town needs maintenance, too—unpaved roads, overgrown fields, and buildings that have seen better days. A few months ago the town council agreed to let us sell any leftover resources to use the proceeds for beautifying our town."

"Thank God you said that. I was beginning to think everyone had lost their will to care. But now that makes sense. It's not that you've given up; it's that the town is po—" I rethink my word choice, lest I get another scolding from Gavin. "I mean, because this town is underfunded."

"From what I saw yesterday, the locally sourced items are severely underpriced," Gavin says, surprising me. "You could charge three times what you are now, and it would significantly increase your profit margins."

I crane my neck to face Gavin. Since when does he know so much about food prices?

"I'm sure you've noticed that Blaire is a small community. We know our consumers personally. And we're not looking to profit off one another. But we do sell our products at a slightly higher price point when we go to the farmer's market every month. Everyone, not just the co-op, pitches in." She nudges Brennan. "Including this guy."

"Just doing my civic duty." He blushes in that aw-shucks kind of way.

"He's being modest. When we first went to the market, we didn't know we had to bring our own booth, so we had nowhere to store our supplies. Poor Brennan here had to go back and forth to the truck so many times. If it wasn't for him, we wouldn't have been able to sell much."

"Happy to help," he says. "I know I'm only here for a short time, but I love that I've found a way to give back to the town that's given me so much."

Good looks and a good heart? I'm finally starting to see a silver lining in this town, and it's in the form of a six-foot, brown-eyed, ruggedly handsome do-gooder. Brennan might be the one redeeming quality about this godforsaken town. And since we won't be here long enough, it can't develop into anything serious. Besides, what's wrong with a little harmless flirtation?

"I can relate." I lean in, fluttering my lashes. "Charity is something that's near and dear to my heart." I place my hands on my chest.

Gavin's eyes narrow. "Since when?"

"Since forever. I'm quite charitable," I say through gritted teeth. After events I always donate my gowns to auctions for nonprofit organizations, and that time I did a GRWM collab with *Seventeen*'s prom issue, I negotiated the terms to have the magazine cover the cost of the venue for our junior prom in lieu of payment. If that's not charitable, I don't know what is. But I can't tell him that without revealing too much of ourselves in front of Brennan and Callie, so I'm forced to grin and bear it.

"That's something you and I have in common, then," Brennan says with a smile that reaches his eyes.

"Maybe there's something we can work on together while I'm here," I suggest. And who knows? Maybe we'll discover we have more in common than charity.

"I'm sure there will be plenty of volunteer opportunities while you're here, even if it's only for a short time," Brennan says. He leans toward me with a smolder-y look I'm more than familiar with. As the object of many people's affections, I know flirty when I see it.

"Yes, I'm sure Elena would love to volunteer. What about the next farmer's market?" Gavin suggests.

I know he's trying to pull one over me, but little does Gavin know that he's helping me with my master plan to spend more time with Brennan. "I'd love to come." I lean closer to Brennan, showing off all my teeth.

"That's perfect." Brennan flashes a wide smile that confirms he's as happy about this idea as I am. "You can take my place next Saturday, since I won't be able to make it."

As soon as my face drops, Gavin's lights up. "Sounds just perfect for you. Since you're such a charitable person," he says with sarcasm that only I can detect for some reason.

There's actually a word for this exact behavior Gavin is demonstrating: *Schadenfreude.* It's when a person experiences joy in response to other people's misfortunes. And, boy, is he Schadenfreude-ing hard now.

"You won't be able to make it?" In a last-ditch effort, I make sad-puppy eyes at him.

"Yeah, I'll be in LA."

"LA?" I almost gasp. This would have been useful information to know *before* I offered to volunteer at the farmer's market. I'd give anything to go to LA with Brennan.

"My parents are coming out here, and we're going to meet in LA since I've never been there before."

"You've never been there?" I gasp.

Brennan's lips tug up to one side. "I take it you have."

"Yeah, we used to live there," I say. Then I catch Gavin giving me a subtle but very distinct look of warning.

"I didn't realize you were from LA," Callie says, taking turns looking at me and Gavin.

"That was a while ago," Gavin says, shifting in his seat. He's not wrong. We've only been away a couple days, but already it seems like a distant memory.

"I've been to LA a few times," Callie says. "When I'm there, I realize how much I'm not cut out for city life. Everything is so spread out, people are constantly in a hurry to get somewhere, and there's always traffic on the 405 freeway, no matter what time of day it is."

"Yeah, that sounds about right," I say wistfully. God, I miss the chaos.

"What are you and your family going to do together?" Callie asks, turning her attention to Brennan. Even though I was hoping for Callie not to ask more about our lives in LA, it's weirding me out that she's able to move on from it so quickly. In my mind LA is the only city worth living in. It's the center of my universe, and it's throwing me off to know it's not everyone's center of the universe.

"My sister is ten, and she's dying to go to Disneyland. We're going to surprise her by going there."

It's one of my biggest pet peeves when people assume Disneyland is in LA. Anaheim is in Orange County, which, I cannot stress enough, is not the same as Los Angeles. But when Brennan says it, I don't feel the urge to correct him. His expression is so genuine, so sincere, like spring mountain water that's naturally pure and doesn't need to go through a filtration process to be drinkable. Maybe it's because I never had one, but knowing Brennan is a thoughtful older brother makes him even more appealing.

"I'm so relieved you're able to fill in for Brennan," Callie says, putting a hand on my arm. "I was about to skip next week, but honestly we need the funds. I'm so glad I won't have to now that you can come."

"Me too," I say, not quite matching Callie's level of enthusiasm.

After we finish our drinks, we throw our cups away in the trash receptacle and make our way out of the cafeteria and into the lobby of the observatory.

"This was fun," Brennan says.

"Next time you should try the food. The chefs are quite innovative. It's impressive what they do with what we have," Callie explains.

"She's right. My understanding of space discovery isn't the only thing that's grown since I started my internship." For added emphasis Brennan pats his gut, which, as far as I can tell, is nonexistent. "That's why I started running."

"Me too." Gavin perks up.

"*You too* what?" I'm compelled to ask.

"I like to run," Gavin confirms.

"Since when?" I wrinkle my nose at him. Doesn't exercise release endorphins or make people, you know, less uptight?

Gavin ignores me and looks at Brennan. "We should go running together sometime."

"I'd love that," Brennan says.

While they make plans to meet up, I press my lips together to prevent them from forming a pout. It should be me Brennan is making plans to meet up with. Not Gavin.

Since Callie and Brennan have to stay for their shifts at the observatory, Gavin and I walk back home. On our way down the dirt road, I'm still thinking about how my plan went so wrong.

Gavin glances my way. "Cheer up," he says, more sarcastic than sincere. "You've never been to a farmer's market. You might actually like it."

"Yeah, I won't be going to that."

"What?" His head jerks back. "Why not?"

"We won't be here next Saturday, remember?"

"Oh." His face falls at the reminder. Though why he's sad about it is beyond me. "Why didn't you tell Callie you couldn't make it, then?"

"I didn't want to let her down, not after she seemed so happy. Anyway, don't worry. I'll make up a good excuse by the time we leave."

"That's not the point, Elena." For some reason he's upset. "If you had no plans of going, why did you even offer to go in the first place?"

"Because," I groan, frustrated that my plan did not go as intended. "I thought Brennan was going to be there," I admit.

Suddenly Gavin stops in his tracks. I glance over, expecting him to be mad, but he's not. Somehow Gavin finds this funny.

"So that's what this is about." He makes a show of leaning his head back and laughing theatrically.

"What?" I say, irritated.

"El, and I mean this in the nicest way possible—"

"Doubt that."

"—in what world do you think Brennan would be interested in you?"

My cheeks flare. Just because Gavin can't appreciate my charm doesn't mean others can't. "I'll have you know, Gavin, people love me. There wasn't an event in LA that I attended that wasn't sold out. And *Entertainment Weekly* hailed me as 'a tabloid's gift that keeps on giving.' *I'm* the life of the party."

"I'm not talking about superficial stuff. I'm talking about what's in here." He taps his chest. "I spent the day with Brennan, and I know enough about him to know he's too . . . wholesome for you. He's the type of guy who's looking for his soulmate, not a good time. He's monogamous, long-term material, while you . . ." He eyes me from head to toe. "You don't even have girlfriend energy. It's actually kinda scary." He shudders.

Suddenly my insides twist along with every muscle in my face. Not only is Gavin insinuating I'm not good enough for Brennan, but is he making the serious accusation that I'm not good enough for anyone? Red-hot anger pulses through my veins.

This is why Gavin and I stopped being close. Not because Mom and Dad prefer him over me. Or because his future is secure and mine isn't. It's not even because he disapproves of my influencer business. It's because Gavin is, and always was, my biggest hater.

When the *Vogue* article insulted my intelligence, Gavin didn't reassure me that the article had it wrong. He made me feel like they had it right. But despite what he—or anyone for that matter—might think, turning what he considers a brainless catchphrase into a brand doesn't happen on its own. It takes intelligence to make it happen. And if Gavin can't see it now, then he never will.

"I think we got along better in LA." I fold my arms across my chest. "You know, when we didn't have to see each other."

"Then it's a good thing we'll be back there in a week," he says, matching my tone, which is confusing. What he has to be mad at me about is a mystery.

"Why wait, then? We should start now."

He chuffs incredulously. "Fine."

"Fine," I say. But when I notice he's still right by my side, I glare at him. "Stop following me."

"I'm not." He scowls. "This town isn't big enough for both of us."

Frustrated he's right on both accounts, I cross the street, and we walk the rest of the way on separate sides of the dirt road.

EXCERPT

Lead with authority. If you are confident, people are confident in you.

The American Dream Achieved: The Story of Dale Ok, Founder of It's Ok!

TRANSCRIPT

60 MINUTES INTERVIEW WITH GLORIA OK

INTERVIEWER: Shouldn't Dale be proud of achieving success despite his humble beginnings?

GLORIA: Dale doesn't see it that way. You see, by the time we immigrated to the United States, we were married and had to start working right away. No time for a college education. Dale started the business without a formal education, and there's a stigma attached to that. Many executives questioned his intellect. Often he's had to overcompensate by presenting himself as overly confident. And it worked in the beginning. We were able to get the business deals we needed to open our first store based on his assurance. Can you believe that?

INTERVIEWER: He must have been very convincing.

GLORIA: He was. But the bigger the company got, the bigger the stakes. And I warned him about letting his insecurities get bigger than him. The truth is, if he's not careful, his feelings of inadequacy will be the ruin of him.

<TRANSCRIPT PAUSED>

For the rest of the week, Gavin respects my wishes and leaves me alone, and in return, I take Gavin's advice to just do what Mom and Dad tell me to do. So when they tell us to "stay out of trouble" while they have to attend meetings over the weekend, I don't argue with them, I don't bicker with Gavin, and I definitely steer clear of the liquor section at the convenience store.

Instead I prepare for my reentry into public life. I pluck my eyebrows. I whiten my teeth. I do all the masks, not just for my face, but also for my hair, feet, and hands. Aside from my efforts, the one thing that's been sustaining me through the week is the breakfasts Mom has been leaving out for me. Who knew she could be so creative with such limited resources? Chive pancakes with crème fraîche whipped topping, a breakfast hash substituting wild mushrooms for corned beef, and "toast" made with a rice patty that was pan-fried until it was crispy, accompanied with a variety of jams. They remind me of the meals I'm used to eating and, with any luck, meals I'll be back to eating in no time. My friends already think I've been on a silent retreat, and having spent a lot of time in unintentional silence, it'll be closer to the truth than not.

We're even making notable progress on the house, too, which means we can hopefully find new tenants soon. Over the weekend

Mom and Dad bought dishes and silverware from a place called the Bargain Bin in Bakersfield, along with bedding, bathroom mats, and a shower curtain. With the furniture Gavin and I assemble, the house is actually looking livable. I mean, not for me. But, like, for someone else.

On Monday, after Mom and Dad leave for the appeal, I start packing. Even though Dad said it could take up to two days before the judge reaches a decision, I might as well get ready so we can leave the second the appeal is over. I'm neatly wrapping the cords around my hair-drying system when the front door opens and slams shut. I assume it's Gavin, so I ignore it. That is, until I hear someone who's not Gavin speak.

"It's time for a family meeting." Mom's voice startles me.

Family meeting? Two words I dread. But that's not the only troubling thing. I check my watch. It's not even noon. Mom and Dad weren't expected to be home for hours.

When I meet them in the living room, they're standing around the kitchen counter. Gavin follows in shortly after them.

"I saw the tractor pull in. What's going on?" he asks, catching his breath. A film of sweat lines his brow from . . . *running*? Guess he wasn't lying about that. But with Mom and Dad's sullen expressions staring back at us, that's the least of my concerns.

"There's something we need to tell you," Dad starts.

"And we'd rather you hear it from us than some journalist who is looking for a scandal," Mom says.

My stomach twists into knots. The energy in the room is eerily similar to when Mr. Ahn told us in the warehouse that we had lost everything.

"The good news is, the appeal is over," Dad says, barely smiling.

"And the bad news?" I don't celebrate. Clearly there's more.

Mom shifts uncomfortably. "It turns out, we don't have a strong enough case to appeal to the IRS. We simply don't have enough to cover all the losses from the decline in sales."

"What does that mean?" I say. It doesn't make sense. Every business ebbs and flows. Even I know that. "Isn't there a savings or relief fund you can draw from?"

"Well, there were some losses we didn't account for, and they're more than we have," Mom says gravely.

"So does that mean what I think it means?" Gavin carefully asks.

Dad reluctantly nods. "We have to file for bankruptcy."

As Mom and Dad explain what happens next, it only gets worse. Our house and furniture were repossessed, along with everything else that held value. Vases, fine china, paintings, etc. They're going to be sold in an auction where all the proceeds will go to paying off our debt. *A public garage sale*, for Christ's sake. I'll never be able to recover from the shame.

"The rest of our possessions were put into a storage unit until we know where we'll end up." Mom wrings her hands.

"What are we supposed to do now?" Gavin asks.

"All we can do is wait for a board to be appointed and for them to reorganize the company," Dad explains. "I'm sure I'll be offered an executive position, and my income will be enough to live on, but it won't be the same as what it used to be. So we have to prepare ourselves for a different life than what we had before."

The only thing that made it bearable to live here was knowing that we'd be going back to our old lives. And now we're being told that's not possible anymore? The air sucks out of the room. This is bad. So, *so* bad.

I'm not sad. I'm not even distraught. I'm mad, and I can only think of one person to blame.

"How did this happen?" I turn my attention to Dad, who has always maintained his innocence. "You said everything would be okay."

"I was . . . mistaken," he admits with difficulty.

"Mistaken?" That kind of response is an acceptable excuse when confusing salt for sugar or being caught out in the rain without an umbrella. But for driving a multinational, not to mention *multibillion-dollar*, business into bankruptcy? It's not even close to comparable.

"Turning on each other is not helpful, Elena," Mom says, coming to Dad's defense. "The thing we need to focus on is how to move forward. Now, I've already talked to Brenthaven. In the event that things won't be settled by the fall, your headmaster is making an exception so you can finish your senior year online and graduate on time. College applications are due next year, and we don't want to do anything to jeopardize that."

There are so many things wrong with that statement that I don't know where to start. As someone who has no interest in going to college, social interaction is the only part of school I care about. Now they're going to take that away from me? And how can she be so calm when she's telling me we might have to live here until the fall or beyond?

Before I have a chance to protest, Dad zeroes in on Gavin. "To ensure your studies aren't interrupted, I've already reached out to USC to find alternative ways to continue your education. The uncertainty of your position in the company may put a negative spotlight on you. Maybe you can take a year off or do online courses like Elena. Then, after your position at the restructured company has been secured, you can go back. Dean Rutherford hasn't returned my calls, but when he does I'll let you know." He smiles at Gavin, who, if I'm not mistaken, tenses up. "By the way, are you sure you haven't received your grades?"

"I haven't been able to check my email, but I'm sure they're in my inbox," he mumbles.

"If you want, I can call them and—"

"No, I can do it," Gavin answers much too quickly. "I'll call the registrar's office tomorrow," he adds, trying to cover up his suspicious behavior.

I narrow my eyes at Gavin. Grades were available weeks ago. But apparently I'm the only one who sees through his lie, since Dad seemingly accepts his answer.

"It's a good thing we have this home," Mom says, somehow finding the silver lining. "It could take months to settle on an agreement. Now that we don't have to meet with Mr. Ahn, we can focus on the farm."

"I've noticed the weeds are starting to take over the field." Dad stares out the window.

"I can help," Gavin chimes in.

What is happening? Living here was supposed to be a short-term solution, not a long-term plan. Why aren't Mom, Dad, and Gavin freaking out?

"That's it?" I flail, unwilling to accept the reality. "Are you saying that we should go on as if everything is okay? *In this house?*"

The three of them crane their necks to face me with the same familiar expression. The one that tells me they can't understand my outfit choices, my partying, my lifestyle.

"Elena," Mom eventually says, "what other choice do we have?"

"There's got to be somewhere else we can go. Somewhere more suited to the lifestyle we're used to."

Gavin lets out an incredulous laugh.

I turn to him. "You said so yourself, your apartment building has the type of amenities luxury hotels have."

"We don't have to live here forever, just until my new position and salary are negotiated," Dad says, as if that's a solution that suits everyone's needs.

"Maybe time away will give you some perspective," Mom says. It's surprising how unwavering her support for Dad is, considering how this will affect her lady-of-leisure lifestyle. "In time you'll learn that money isn't everything."

But it's not just money, not for me. In the short time I've been here, I've been reminded of what's at stake if I lose my reputation forever. Without my socialite status, my financial independence will all be gone. Then what?

In my silence, Mom frowns at me. "Elena, we understand that transitions are hard—"

"Transitions?" I huff incredulously. "You make it sound like what we're going through is natural or pleasant, when that couldn't be further from the truth! We're not going through puberty or metamorphosing into a butterfly. We're falling out of a burning plane, and unlike the rest of you, I don't have a parachute. Dad will end up with a new role at the same company, and Gavin is going to go back to school with job security." I turn to Mom. "And you can go back to pickling cabbage or pickleballing—whatever. But I can't sit here and wait it out. I don't have the luxury to do that," I protest.

"There's endless work on a farm," Dad says, attempting to reason with me. But as usual, he's way off the mark. "When we were growing up—"

"Please, spare me. This is not like the olden times," I say, putting up a dire hand. "We live in the modern day, and you can't expect us to know how the hell we're supposed to farm this place, let alone live here, when we're used to drivers, cooks, and landscapers—people you hired so that we didn't have to do any of those things. Maybe Gavin is used to this level of obscurity, but I'm not. My livelihood—the one that is supporting us through this time—relies on keeping up my very public image. So, please, don't tell me that there's nothing we can do."

Mom, Dad, and Gavin stare at me, stone-faced. Of course they find offense in my plea, ignoring the fact that my parents are the ones with unrealistic expectations and that Gavin has the emotional quotient of a brick wall.

After a long silence Mom eventually stirs. "You're right, Elena." Her face lacks so much expression that I can't tell if she's being serious or sarcastic. "You are good at having fun. It's admirable, really. I'm sure you'll figure something out."

The irony is that I'm finally getting the recognition I've wanted from my mom, but it's in the form of a backhanded compliment that I can't enjoy.

Dad slowly goes over to his suitcase and pulls out the framed photo of us. He leans it against the wall on the kitchen counter. "We need to start behaving like a happy family," he says. "Even if it's all an act."

I don't know what's worse—Dad's belief that pretending to be a happy family is going to make us one, or the fact that Mom agrees with him.

Later that night I hear Mom and Dad arguing through our poorly insulated walls. Gavin has earplugs in, and I'm not even sure he'd care if he heard. I tiptoe out of the room and lean close to their door.

"How could you do this, Dale?" Even through the door, I can clearly hear the hurt in Mom's voice. A stark difference from the brave face she was putting on earlier.

"He seemed trustworthy." Dad remains resolute, despite the outcome of the appeal.

"But I warned you many times that it wasn't a good idea."

"I'm not the only one who's affected by his scheme. Big companies like Saks, Neiman—they all bought into it."

"Yes, but you're the only one who lost everything."

"I was told it was a foolproof deal. If you had that kind of assurance, wouldn't you put everything into it?"

"It was your pride. I know it was. I've always warned you about it. You were trying to cover up your insecurity by getting yourself involved in bigger, riskier deals."

"Insecurity?" He scoffs. "I don't have—"

"Dale, just because you didn't go to college doesn't mean you're not smart. You just have to stop trying to prove it to others. Isn't it enough that you and I know that you're smart?"

"I don't know what you're talking about," he says. "In any case, it doesn't matter. George is gone, and so is our money."

"It does matter," Mom says in a softer voice. "You realize it seems like you chose him over me, someone who's been by your side the entire time?" She sniffs.

"Gloria, you can't see it like that. You know what it's like in the meetings."

For once Mom doesn't disagree with him. "Sometimes you have to listen to your instincts even if they go against the trend. Isn't that what you said in your book?"

"That's different. These men run the industry. How could we benefit from being on the outside of the fashion world?"

"How are we better off now?" This time Dad falls silent. "It was a gamble either way, and it would have been better if we lost everything knowing that you took a chance on us."

I go back to my room. I don't want to hear more. Now I know there's nothing we can do but wait to see how the board decides to reorganize the company and what type of role Dad has in it. Which means Mom was right after all. What other choice do we have but to wait it out?

I know it's possible to work my way back to what I was, but that takes time. In a year I'll graduate from high school, and my parents will expect me to go to college. How can I tell them I have no intention of going to college if I don't have anything better lined up for me? My future that used to be Swarovski clear is now fogged-up glass.

EXCERPT

Being a leader is not about being in charge.
It's about taking care of those in your charge.

The American Dream Achieved: The Story of Dale Ok, Founder of It's Ok!

TRANSCRIPT

60 MINUTES INTERVIEW WITH GLORIA OK

INTERVIEWER: But whatever Dale's motivations are, it seems like they've pushed him to a level of success people can only imagine. And now you live in a ten-thousand-square-foot mansion in the wealthy neighborhood of Calabasas. Tell me, how does that compare to living on a farm?

GLORIA: To be honest, everything happened so quickly, I hardly had time to notice the difference. In the early stages of It's Ok!, we were inundated with getting it set up and running. Once we made a steady income, everything happened all at once. The house, the press, the success. It was such a blur.

INTERVIEWER: Sounds like a lot of work.

GLORIA: We were used to the work. It was the rise in status that was a bigger adjustment.

GLORIA: The majority of the people in Korea are working class, with the poor at the bottom and the chaebol—high society—at the top. Dale said that now that we were chaebol, we had to act accordingly, like in Korea. When we had Gavin and Elena, we hired the best nannies. When they started school, we sent them to the best private school. We were determined to give them the life we didn't have.

INTERVIEWER: But the hard work made you who you are.

GLORIA: That's true. I never thought of it that way.

<TRANSCRIPT PAUSED>

The next morning, despite waking up in Blaire, the sun still shines and time marches on. Apparently I was wrong. Living in Blaire for the unforeseeable future is not the end of the world.

I eventually muster up enough energy to get out of bed. A quick glance around tells me Gavin is in the bathroom and my parents are outside. In the kitchen I find a film-covered plate of breakfast on the table. Today it's an egg omelet with a tangy sauce drizzled on top. Knowing it's going to be the best and only good part of the day, I savor every single bite. That is, until I'm rudely interrupted.

"What?" I hiss at Gavin, who is now lurking in the kitchen with his lips curled up at the corners.

"Nothing. It just seems like you're enjoying breakfast." And there it is again—a creepy smile.

"What's with the smirk?" I stare at my plate skeptically. "Did you lace it with something?"

"El, I need to tell you about something," he says somewhat seriously, which gets my attention.

"I think I know what you're going to tell me."

"You do?" He seems nervous and slightly embarrassed, which is understandable if this is what I think it's about.

"Yeah," I say. "I saw the Rogaine in your bag of toiletries."

“What?” His head jerks back. “That’s not what I was going to tell you! And that’s preventative—” He stops himself, drawing in a calming breath.

“Then what is it about?” I ask, more confused than before. The Rogaine was a pretty big deal to me when I discovered it.

“Honestly I was just trying to make conversation. But forget it.”

Make conversation? What’s his deal?

After he leaves the room, I eat the rest of my breakfast in the privacy of a Gavin-free space. No sense in wasting good food. As soon as I clear my plate, I’m summoned outside.

While Mr. Ahn is working on filing for bankruptcy, Mom and Dad are home for the next few days, and they waste no time getting to work on the house. Which, due to recent events, makes sense, since this is *their* retirement plan. What doesn’t make sense is why Gavin and I are involved in their plans.

“Now that our future is less certain, we have to find a way to monetize this farm. And we all have to pitch in.”

“You want us to be farmers permanently?” I flail. Haven’t we suffered enough?

“I thought this was for your retirement. Not *the* retirement plan.” Gavin is as shocked as I am. “Don’t you have a 401(k) or a Roth IRA?”

“Aside from your college funds, I’m not sure what the IRS will determine we can keep,” Dad says. “But don’t worry. I’m sure whatever we’re left with, we’ll be fine,” he quickly adds. “And it’s a good thing no one’s responded to our listing to rent out this property. Because now we can start planting metaphorical seeds as well. By using my business sense and my farming background, we can start a lucrative side business before going back to It’s Ok! Then we’ll be back in business and better than before.” Dad puffs out his chest, unusually confident for someone in his position.

“I thought farming the land was for when you retire,” Gavin says.

“I’m with Gavin. This sounds like a you problem.” I point to Mom and Dad.

“Well, none of us is working now, so we may as well get a head start on it,” Mom not-so-delicately points out.

“Help me unload the equipment,” Dad says, handing Gavin a shovel.

Not only is Dad going to build a farm, but he’s going to make Gavin—a guy whose idea of manual labor is switching out his closet from his winter wardrobe to his spring one—help him. Now, this is a plan I can get behind. I lean against the tractor, settling myself into a comfortable position. This is going to be good.

“What are you doing?” Mom hovers next to me. “You don’t think we’re going to sit by and do nothing, do you?” She motions for me to follow her. And just like that, the joy drains from me.

Mom drags me into the house to get some supplies. I take notice of a few unrecognizable items among her things.

Mom’s essential items:

- ***A bulky kitchen appliance unfamiliar to me***
- ***A bag of unidentifiable red powder (Is Mom an underground drug dealer???)***
- ***A heinously large sun hat***
- ***Pink rubber gloves that go up to her elbows***
- ***A large bowl big enough to hold a toddler***

A few minutes later, against my will, I find myself walking with her to the herb garden on the side of the house. She’s wearing the sun hat, which has a visor that’s almost as big as the bowl she’s carrying.

“Nice hat,” I say in a sarcastic tone.

"It may not be fashionable, but it does a very important job protecting my skin. You should at least wear daily sunscreen if this type of hat is not to your standards. I saw some early signs of sunspots. Then it's only a matter of time before the wrinkles start to appear."

I'm too young to have sunspots. Aren't I? And *wrinkles*?

I have the sudden urge to run back into the house and stare at my skin in a magnifying mirror, but my mom stops me. "We need to turn the soil and prepare it for a new harvest. But first we have to clear the old one."

I give her a blank look. I mean, she may as well be speaking another language.

"It's easy," she says, taking my cue. "All you need are gloves and a good attitude." I'm about to point out that I don't have either of those when she tosses a pair of gardening gloves to me.

"These are green onions." She shows me a row of tall green stems growing out of the dirt. "They're fully matured and ready to be picked."

"Okay, how do I do that?"

She reads my face, trying to tell if I'm making a joke. When she sees that I'm not, she says, "You just pull them out." Then she shows me by doing literally just that. She dusts the dirt off the white roots and places them in the large bowl. "See?"

She's right. It's not that hard. But after a million of them (okay, probably dozens), my back hurts, the sun is scorching, and I'm covered in dirt. I glance over at my mom, whose face is completely covered by the shade from the brim of her hat and, more notably, sweat-free. I hate to admit it, but I kinda, sorta do envy my mom with her ugly visor.

After I clear the planter and trim the rosemary bush, the chives, and the other herbs, she finally calls it a day. I follow my mom into the kitchen to do . . . *"More work?"* I exclaim as my mom hands me a bag of groceries from the fridge. After being covered in a film of dirt on every exposed part of my body, I thought we'd earned ourselves a break or, at the very least, a hot shower.

"Who did you imagine was going to cook dinner for us? Carolina?" Mom cocks her head at me, exasperated.

I bite my tongue from responding. The truth is, the thought never entered my mind. Now that Mom and Dad are home, I sort of expected the food to just . . . be there. God, I miss Carolina. I have enough sense to know my mom would be disappointed in me—more than she already is—if I admitted that, so instead I say, "Can't we DoorDash something?"

My mom doesn't dignify my question with an answer. "Help me unload the groceries."

I do as I'm told and begin taking out the contents of the bag. Staring at the inventory, all produce and meat, I frown. "I don't remember buying any of this."

"I had to go to the store when I noticed there wasn't anything but snacks and instant food."

"That was because I thought we were going to be here temporarily," I counter.

"Exactly my point. Now that we're going to be here for quite some time, I need to teach you how to take care of yourself. Starting with the basics."

Of course it's my luck that, after years of ignoring me, Mom is choosing now to all of a sudden start paying attention to me. Before I can let out a squeak of disapproval, she disappears into her room. When she reappears, she's got some kind of kitchen appliance in her hand.

"What's that?" Out of habit, I say it in my signature high-pitched voice. The only people who aren't amused by it are my family, which is being made super apparent by the apathy in my mom's expression. So I correct myself. "I mean, what is that thing for?"

Mom studies my face. "You really don't know what a rice cooker is?"

"I know what a rice cooker is." *Now.* Honestly Mom has been acting weird since we got to Blaire. And it's not just the apparent undertone of disappointment that's odd. Her behavior is off, too, like bringing a rice cooker and a giant bowl when we were told to bring only the essentials. I've never seen Mom use either of those things in the entirety of my existence.

"You eat a wide variety of cuisine at various restaurants, Elena. How is it that you don't know anything about the things that you eat?"

"I think you answered your own question there. I eat at restaurants. I do not cook."

She shakes her head, tutting in disapproval. "Is that how little you pay attention? Food is one of the basic requirements of survival."

"I pay attention. I don't eat at places that don't have at least four and a half stars on Yelp."

Mom ignores my response and shoves a carrot in my face. "Peel this."

"Okay," I say, grabbing it from her. Only to realize belatedly that I agreed to do something without knowing what it meant. "How do I do that?"

She gives me another *seriously?* look, handing me a knife.

"Okay, but how do I peel it? And don't give me that look again, Mom. I've never had to peel anything before, and you know it."

"Isn't it obvious? Use the sharp edge of the knife to cut off the skin." Her tone, though measured, has bite to it. And I'm nothing if not good at picking up on subtle cues, so I don't ask any more questions and start peeling the carrots while Mom is prepping the other vegetables and rinsing the rice. When she is about to open up the meat package, I hand her the carrots.

"Done," I say, presenting the final product on the cutting board with a grand gesture.

"Oh my God." She stares at the three carrots, open-mouthed.

"I know." I nod in agreement. "Not bad for my first time, huh?"

"What did you do to them?"

When I notice her expression is not one of wonderment but quite the opposite, I deflate. "Well, now you're just being critical."

"There's nothing left. There's barely even enough for a crudités platter."

"Mom, don't be silly," I say. "No one eats the carrots. They're hardly the star of a crudités platter."

"They're supposed to be for the Japanese curry I'm making." Her eyes narrow at me.

"*Okay.* How the hell was I supposed to know that?"

"Again, by using your common sense. Can't you see the picture on the package of curry?" She holds up the box to me, and now that I see it, I get it. It's her attitude I still don't understand.

I'd always been aware of my parents' general disappointment in me. But it was always from afar. That's why my socialite status mattered so much to me. Whatever insufficiency I was feeling with Mom or Dad or Gavin, I could always count on other forms of validation. Parties held in my honor, the paparazzi yelling for my attention, paid appearances at sold-out events. It was the yin to my yang, the balance of my life. Now that we're stuck together for the unforeseeable future, I'm not sure how I can counteract the negativity.

"So I didn't know how to make a Japanese curry. Why is that such a big deal?" I flail my hand in frustration. It seems like nothing will be good enough for her. "Don't you think you're being a little hard on me?"

At first I think she's going to lecture me about my outburst. But she surprises me by tilting her head with a saddened expression. "This is my fault." She sets her knife down on the cutting board.

"What?" I raise a brow, half skeptical, half surprised.

"I hired the best nannies, the best cooks, the best tutors—because I didn't want you to struggle. I made life too easy for you. Now that we're on our own, I can see you're not taking it well."

"Oh my God, Mom. What happened to us is a pretty big deal. My reaction is reasonable."

"Maybe," she says. "But that's all the more reason why I feel the need to make up for lost time and teach you how to do things that were always done for you."

Maybe I should be grateful that she's trying to make up for the many times she wasn't there for me. But I can't help but think it's too little, too late. Why couldn't she care about me when I was exhausted from back-to-back events, or when I was humiliated by tabloids publishing unflattering photos of me, or when rising gossip bloggers would try to generate more likes by spreading rumors about me—times when I needed her the most?

A few minutes later, Gavin comes back from working in the field just in time for lunch. After my tirade yesterday, things haven't been great between us. Still, I look to him for camaraderie after being forced into child labor. Instead I'm surprised to find him excitedly talking about the farm and the plans they have for it.

"Gavin and I cleared half the field today," Dad brags to Mom.

Gavin nods proudly. "We can probably finish the rest tomorrow."

"Then we'll have to decide what to plant." Dad considers it.

"What do you think about cabbage?" Mom suggests. "Like the kind we grew in Anbandegi."

"That's a great idea," Dad says. "I bet they have seeds for that at the convenience store. They have everything there."

"I can come with you," Gavin suggests. His enthusiasm doesn't waver and seems genuine, which means he wasn't faking a new hobby for the sake of Mom and Dad's approval. He's actually excited about working on the farm.

How can everything be different and yet somehow remain exactly the same?

At night I take another bath using the last of my lavender bath salts. As much as I didn't want to deplete my supply, I needed it. It's surreal how easy it is for Mom, Dad, and even Gavin to go on as if this were normal life. Like they've been living here for years.

"Elena, come on. It's been over an hour." Gavin knocks on the door. "It's a bathroom, not a magician. No amount of time in there can change who you are."

I groan. Gavin is the worst. Like, honestly. It's impossible to pretend I'm okay with living here with my family. Tomorrow I'll see if the convenience store has more lavender bath salts, because if today was an indication of what it's going to be like living here, I'm going to need a silo-sized amount to get me through it.

After I dry my hair and get into bed, Gavin comes in from the bathroom and settles into his bed. I'm about to doze off when I hear Gavin . . . *humming*? I was already in a mood. Gavin's good spirits make me snap.

I jolt up from under my covers and glare at him. "How can you be happy at a time like this?"

"Whoa, relax." He puts his palms up. Gavin telling me to relax is the role reversal I least expected. Especially considering our surroundings.

"No, Gavin. You need to unrelax," I low-growl at him. "We live here now."

"It's not that bad," Gavin says dismissively.

"Yes, it is," I say through gritted teeth. "Why do you think we couldn't find new tenants? It's so bad, no one wants to live here. People are abandoning their homes to leave this place, and we're being forced to live here." I let out a sob that I've been trying to keep in.

Gavin remains unmoved by my emotional outburst. "You seriously need to calm down."

Calm down?! I glare at him. Not today, Satan.

"This is *so not* how I want to spend my summer."

"You think this is how I want to spend my summer?" Gavin's head jerks back. "Living with you is the worst part about it."

But that's just it. Even though he may not like sharing a room with me, he's definitely happier about everything else.

"Actually I do think this is how you want to spend your summer." I assess him from head to toe. Something's changed in him these last few days. And it's not his fashion choice, which is a shame. He's more upbeat and less moody than before, with a look of serenity on his face that can only come from a person who has found inner peace. And who could ever be at peace in this situation? "You've been giving off orange cat energy since we got here."

"Orange cat energy?"

"Yes. Strange. Weird. Inexplicable," I say, loud and clear, so there's no room for misunderstanding. When he still doesn't get it, I realize my oversight. This is Gavin I'm speaking to. I'm going to have to be more direct. "Why'd you lie to Dad about your grades?"

This gets his attention. "Who said I lied?"

"I know report cards were released three weeks ago."

When he falls silent, I know I'm right.

"Did you fail every class or something?" I snort. Not because I'm callous, but because we both know that with a guaranteed career ahead of him, his grades won't matter in the end.

When I notice his hands are clenched into tight fists, I recoil. I may have taken it too far this time. "Hey, sorry. I'm sure it's not as bad as you think it is."

"No, trust me. It's pretty bad." He slumps down into his bed, blows out all the air in his lungs, and rakes a hand through his hair.

I'm taken aback by Gavin's vulnerability. I always knew he'd go to any school Dad wanted him to go to. I never thought he actually cared about his grades. "I'm sure Dad will understand." In fact, I know he will. As long as Gavin graduates, Dad won't care what his transcripts look like.

"No, he won't. Not this time."

"Dad didn't even go to college."

"I know. That's why it matters to him so much that I do. He won't understand why I threw away a chance to go to college when I had the opportunity he didn't."

That's when I realize Gavin isn't talking about failed grades.

University of Southern California

3551 Trousdale Parkway

Los Angeles, CA

March 20, 2026

Gavin Ok

1000 Wilshire Boulevard

Los Angeles, CA

Subject: Notification of Expulsion from USC

Dear Mr. Ok,

After a thorough investigation, it has been determined that you have violated the University of Southern California's academic integrity policy by using artificial intelligence (AI) to complete assignments and coursework that were expected to be your own work. Specifically it was found that the work you submitted for a midterm paper on business ethics was generated using AI tools, which not only constitutes a serious breach of the school's code of conduct regarding academic honesty but also begs the question of your understanding of ethics in general.

As a result of this violation, the school administration has made the decision to expel you from the University of Southern California effective immediately. This decision is final and in accordance with the school's disciplinary procedures, which were outlined in the student handbook you received at the beginning of the school year.

We hope that this experience serves as a learning opportunity, and we wish you the best in your future academic and personal pursuits.

Sincerely,

Barron Rutherford

Dean of the School of Business, University of Southern California

When I finish reading the letter, I stare at it for a minute longer, not knowing how to respond. I knew something was up, but expulsion?

"So, no more USC?"

"No more USC," Gavin says, unable to meet my eye.

"What are you going to do?"

"I'll think of something. I might take classes at the community college and transfer to another school," he says. "Since Dad suggested taking online classes, it'll be harder for him to track where I'm taking them from."

My head whips up. "Wait, what? You're not going to tell him?"

"By the time I graduate, I think he'll be happy enough with the diploma. He won't care where it's from."

"So is that why you're not in a rush to go back to LA?"

He shrugs. "I figure the longer we're here, the more time it buys me."

"What are you going to tell him about your grades? He'll know something's up when you don't have them by the time school starts in the fall."

"I don't know. Maybe I'll tell him before then." He sighs, rubbing his face. "Or maybe I'll have ChatGPT write a report card for me." He chuckles weakly.

"That's not funny," I say.

"It is, kind of."

"Okay, you're right." My lips tug up into a weak smile.

"I'll be fine," he says, probably sensing my concern. "Dad will make sure of that."

He's right. Gavin will be fine. Because once he settles into his new role in It's Ok!, Dad will ensure Gavin has a place there.

As I lay in bed that night, I'm still thinking about Gavin's expulsion. As big of a deal as it is, his enthusiasm for our extended stay makes sense now. Blaire is offering him a way out of a bad situation. And after observing the way Mom and Dad are in their element on the farm, I can see glimpses of why they like it here too. But that doesn't change the fact that while this lifestyle may suit them, it doesn't suit me. Which is why I have to take matters into my own hands.

Maybe there is a way to get back to LA before the bankruptcy case is resolved. If I can pay Kiki for a month, she'll be able to book me enough events where I could retain her services on commission going forward. I just need the seed money to get me started.

I'll be the first to admit that peddling honey and God knows what else this town produces in a booth isn't how I prefer to spend my Saturdays. But now that we're here for longer than the expected two weeks, I have no excuse to get out of helping Callie at the farmer's market. Besides, I've come up with a way to use this to my advantage, which makes me much more motivated to go.

After getting ready, I leave the bathroom with my blow-dryer case in my hand. Mom and Dad have already left to go to a secondhand store outside of town, and since the tractor can only take the two of them, Gavin is the only other person at home. When I pass him in the kitchen, he scrambles to hide the magazine he's reading. Ever since he confessed his expulsion from USC, we've been more civil toward each other. I don't give him a hard time about his eagerness to please Mom and Dad anymore, and in return, he hasn't given me a hard time for shirking my responsibilities. So instead of making fun of him, I make a beeline for the door to leave him to read his porn in peace. *Blech.* Words no sister ever wants to say about her brother.

Gavin surprises me by stopping me before I reach the door. "What are you doing with that?" He arches an eyebrow.

I look down at the blow-dryer case in my hand. "I'm going to try to sell it at the farmer's market," I say.

"At the farmer's market?" He stifles a laugh. "Who's going to want your secondhand department-store blow-dryer there?"

"It's not just a blow-dryer, Gavin." I roll my eyes. "The Dyson Airwrap is an *Allure* Best of Beauty award winner and one of Oprah's Favorite Things from last year."

He looks more confused than before. "Do you even know what a farmer's market is?"

Realizing I won't be able to get through to Gavin with logic and reason, I resort to something more convincing. I whine. "*Gaaaaviiiin.* If no one's going to buy this, what else can I sell? It's the most expensive thing I have that I'm willing to part with."

Gavin rubs the back of his head. "Why do *you* need to sell anything at all? Aren't you supposed to be helping Callie sell *her* stuff?"

I'd forgotten that Gavin doesn't know about my plan, so I fill him in on it.

"You're going to pay for Kiki Klineman's services, and then what? Move back to LA?" His mouth hangs open.

"That's the hope." I sigh wistfully.

"Why? Not one of your friends has called you since you've been here."

"Our phones don't work, remember? Besides, it's the summer. They're obviously busy. I would have been, too, if things hadn't turned out this way."

"Sounds like solid friendships."

"I'm not as naive as I seem." I cock my head to the side. "I know what kind of friendships I have. The kind that rely on one another for our collective reputations to build our brands. And with our family situation, I understand why they're distancing themselves from me. I bring them down rather than up. If I were them, I'd do the same."

"Brutal. And you want to go back to that?" He grimaces.

"Look," I say, setting the blow-dryer case down and taking a seat to face Gavin. "You may not want to go back to LA, but I do. Without USC and It's Ok!, your life is starting over, but mine is still there. I just have to hire back my brand manager, who has a plan to get me back into the scene."

"That's what you call a life? Partying, boozing, saying *What's that?*"

"Gavin, haven't you been paying attention?" I make a dramatic sweep of the place. "This whole time we've been able to live off the money I made off my paid appearances—*my money*! And that's just from the past year. Imagine what could happen if I didn't have school to get in the way. I'd be able to live on my own and do the things that make me happy for once. And who knows? Maybe I could even support you while you figure out what it is you want to do, so you won't have to tell Mom and Dad about USC." When I finish explaining my plan to Gavin, he still doesn't seem to get it.

"But for how long? Till you're thirty? Forty?" His pitch grows more incredulous as the numbers get higher. "You can't party when you're fifty."

"Gavin, I think you relied on ChatGPT to do your thinking for so long that you can't think outside the box." I shake my head pitifully. "Of course I'm not going to party forever. My career would evolve into something more multipurpose. I could host events or provide commentary at fashion shows. Maybe I could sponsor multivitamins or be the spokesperson for AARP one day," I say, half joking, half serious. "My point is, I have a whole life waiting for me that is full of exciting unknowns. I just have to take the first step. So will you help me find something of worth to sell at this hippie farmer's market?" I look at him pleadingly. *"Please?"*

"I guess if that's what you want," he says, even though I can tell he's not entirely convinced of my plan. Slowly he gets up to go to our room. I follow him. After rummaging through his bag, he holds out his hands.

"A Ferragamo leather belt and a Burberry tie?" I raise a skeptical brow. "If you don't think people would want to buy the Dyson Airwrap at this farmer's market, why would anyone want those luxury items?"

"It's all I have." He sighs. "Do you want it or not?"

I guess if the odds of selling any of our items are similarly low, I may as well take the ones that are easily stowable. I haven't told Callie of this plan, and I don't have any intention to, either, so I stuff the belt and tie in my bag as I head out to meet her at the convenience store.

"Glad you made it." Callie beams when she sees me approaching her Jeep.

That makes one of us. Even though I managed to pivot and turn this situation to my advantage, I can still think of at least fourteen things I'd rather be doing instead of going to a farmer's market. But I don't want to seem rude, so I smile back at Callie.

"I hope you don't mind, but we have a few pit stops along the way. We have to collect the inventory from the others."

"Of course. No problem," I say. I'm about to hop in the car when Callie motions for me to follow her.

"The first stop is in here," she says, heading in to the convenience store.

The door closes behind her before I have a chance to refuse, so I have no choice but to follow her in. I didn't leave the best impression the last time I was in here (or the time before that).

"Hey, Hal." She waves at him sweetly.

He grunts at us with narrowed eyes before disappearing into the back room. Happy as ever, I see. Guess I shouldn't take it personally, seeing as even Callie's imitable charm doesn't work on him.

"This store is interesting," I muse, glancing around. "Wallpaper, live bait, canned ham, and . . . what are these?" I hold up an item that looks like half a mitten. "Looks like someone ran out of yarn before getting to the finger portion of this mitten." Too bad, because it's super cute in an ombre pink.

Callie stifles a laugh. "Those aren't mittens. They're mug cozies."

"What the hell are mug cozies?"

"You wrap them around a mug, and they keep the contents warm and your fingers from getting scalded." She demonstrates for me by putting the cozy on a mug that is conveniently for sale next to it. She raises it to show me. "Cute, huh?"

"Yeah," I admit.

"Hal's going to give us a box to sell at the farmer's market today."

I blanch. "*Hal* made these?" Just as I say it, he reappears in front of us, sporting a glare more menacing than before.

"Crocheting brings me joy," he says in the most joyless tone. Guess I'll have to take his word for it. Hal hands the shoebox of crocheted cozies over to Callie.

"Wow, you've been busy." Callie's eyes widen at the inventory.

"What can I say? There's been a lot of motivation."

It's then that I see the ceramic bowl with his yarn sitting behind the register. On the outside of the bowl, it reads *I crochet so I don't unravel*.

"Hang in there, Hal. We're here for you if you need anything."

"Eh," he grunts, waving us away.

We say bye and get in the car. I climb into the passenger seat with the box of cozies and riffle through them. There's a rainbow one, an American flag one. There's even one covered in hearts.

"What's Hal's deal?" I ask when Callie starts the engine. "'Cause these cozies and that man do not seem to add up."

"Yeah, he's had a pretty rough year. His wife left him last year. Then his ma, who raised him as a single parent and ran this convenience store since he was born, passed away. And then a few months later, his dog died."

"Oh my God." I sigh. "His life sounds more tragic than a Darren Aronofsky movie."

She falters, probably not fully understanding my comparison, but continues, seeming to get the gist. "We keep telling him that maybe a change of scenery could help him move on, but he's adamant that he wants to stay and keep the store going, just like his ma would've wanted him to. But ever since he started crocheting, he's been much happier."

"If that's his happy face, I shudder to think of what it was before."

She laughs. "It was pretty much the same." Then, in a more serious tone, she adds, "That's why the people in town check in with him often. Because Hal's emotions don't present themselves in obvious ways."

"That's nice of people to do that," I say. Now that I know the source of Hal's pained expression, I feel awful for assuming the worst about him. And I'm glad he at least has the support of the people around him.

Not too far down the road, we turn into a long driveway, passing a small barn with the most stunning garden around it. An older woman with shoulder-length white hair tied back in a bandana approaches us as we pull up to the house. She's got a storage container in her hands. Callie and I hop out of the car after she parks it.

"Hi, Jean. This is Elena," Callie says. "She's new in town and going to help me today."

"Oh, hello. It's always nice to meet someone new. I'm Jean." She lifts the container up to me. "Mind taking this from me while I go get the rest of the stuff?"

"Sure," I say, taking it from her. I peek inside and find cartons of fresh blue eggs. They look like the fake ones I saw on display at the Four Seasons in Singapore, only these are real.

Callie follows Jean behind the house, and when they return, they each have a bucket spilling with bouquets of flowers.

"Those are gorgeous. What's the occasion?" I ask.

Jean lights up at the compliment. "These are from my garden. They're for the farmer's market."

"You grew these? *Here?*" My eyes widen. Even though I logically know that flowers come from nature, I usually only see them in crystal vases at high-end venues.

She places a hand to her heart. "Oh, my Gerry would be so happy to hear you say that. And it warms my heart to know I've been keeping up with his garden long after he left us."

"Your dedication to him even after all these years is relationship goals, Jean." Callie squeezes her arm.

"Aw, thank you, darling."

"Sorry we can't stay long, Jean. We have to make one more stop on our way."

"No worries. We'll catch up later. It was nice meeting you, Elena." Jean smiles at me.

"Nice meeting you too." I wave at her and get back into Callie's Jeep.

"Now, go get top dollar for those ranunculi. For Gerry!" Jean waves at us.

"We will." Callie waves back, then turns the engine on.

"She's nice," I say as we head back to the main road.

"Yeah, she is so sweet. And her husband, Gerry, was too. He passed ten years ago, but the way she carries his memory with her makes it feel like he's still part of this community. That kind of loyalty is hard to come by these days."

"Yeah, it is." As I say this, I'm struck with a hint of envy. Even though I defended my friendships to Gavin, I admit that the only loyalty we truly have is to our own reputations. My train of thought is interrupted when we pass by a field of cows. "Let me guess, we're picking up milk next?" I ask Callie.

"Close." She smiles. "This is a dairy farm, but Dr. Blaire isn't only known for her milk; it's what she does with it that's impressive."

"Dr. Blaire?" I raise a brow at the name.

"Yep." Callie nods, understanding my skepticism. "Mayor Beecham's wife happens to be named Blaire, which made for all sorts of good fodder for his campaign." She clears her throat. "A man so dedicated to the town of Blaire, he married someone of the same name," she says in a TV announcer voice.

I laugh. "That does make a conveniently convincing argument."

"And it worked. Now he's our mayor. Anyway, Dr. Blaire has a doctorate in animal sciences with a concentration in dairy sciences. Which is a fancy name for a really, *really* smart dairy farmer," Callie says. "It also means she knows how to make all kinds of things with cow's milk. Her homemade yogurt is, not to sound dramatic, life-changing."

When we drive up, Dr. Blaire is waiting for us with an ice chest. She seems slightly older than my parents, wearing a plaid button-down shirt and jeans that are half covered by a pair of galoshes that go up to her knees. She certainly doesn't look like any politician's wife I've seen before. But when Callie introduces us, Dr. Blaire instantly knows who I am.

"Hey, how's that tractor working out for your parents?" Dr. Blaire asks.

"Oh, er, great," I say, caught off guard. I completely forgot who my parents said lent us the vehicle.

"We've been meaning to stop by, but we wanted to give you some time to settle in first," she says.

What I want to say is that I'm not sure we'll ever be settled. "It's not quite there yet," I say instead.

"We'll wait before stopping by, then. Or we could invite your family over for dinner sometime." Dr. Blaire's warm smile is inviting, and I find myself agreeable to the suggestion.

"Is that your homemade yogurt I've heard so much about?" I ask, noticing the ice chest next to her.

"Guilty," she says, holding a hand up. "Now, don't forget to keep the ice chest closed, only opening it when you need to. There's a thermometer here on the outside. Once it dips below forty degrees, the yogurt will no longer be good to sell. But there's plenty of ice and this cooler is insulated, so you should be good for a few hours."

"Got it," Callie says. "Hopefully we'll be able to sell out before the temperature dips."

"Here's hoping." Dr. Blaire crosses her fingers and holds them up.

Callie takes one side of the cooler and I take the other, and together we hoist it into the trunk of her Jeep. After we say goodbye to Dr. Blaire, we drive down the main road again.

"Okay, now we're off to the farmer's market," Callie says as we pass a sign that tells us we're leaving the town of Blaire. "Sorry for the delayed start."

When I met with Callie over an hour ago, I didn't want to spend more time than I needed to helping her at the farmer's market. With all the stops we had to make, the real work hasn't even begun. And yet the most unexpected thing about it is that I don't mind.

"It's no problem. I enjoyed meeting everyone today," I say, surprised that I actually mean it.

After spending most of the morning driving around Blaire, we're finally on our way to Bakersfield, which is still thirty miles away. Thankfully Callie is as sociable as I am, and we find plenty to talk about on the way. As she drives, Callie tells me about how Dr. Blaire worked with the town council to create the beautification fund that is supported by the proceeds from their booth at the farmer's market. This season, Callie hopes her family's honey will be a substantial contribution.

"Eggs and dairy are year-round, but the honey and flowers are more plentiful in the spring and summer. So we're hoping to make more progress this summer than we did earlier in the year."

"How much have you collected so far?"

"Since we started this initiative in April, we've raised about a thousand dollars. We think we'll be able to double that by the end of the summer."

Although Callie seems full of hope, I'm less convinced. "That's not enough to make substantial changes."

"No, but it could buy the supplies we need, and we can all pitch in to do the work since the labor is what's expensive."

I admire Callie's grit. She doesn't hesitate to get her hands dirty if it means achieving the goal she has in mind. And in a way it reminds me of me. We're both willing to do what it takes to get what we want, and we're not above doing the work ourselves. I knew I would like Callie the minute I met her, but now I like her even more.

Thirty minutes later, we exit the freeway, and I see a large lot with tables and tents set up. The parking area is off to the side, and we have to lug everything to our spot, which is inconveniently located at the far corner from our car. We start with the cooler full of yogurt since it's the heaviest. She takes one side, and I take the other.

"I can see why you need help," I say, struggling to walk and talk at the same time. "There's no way one person could do this job alone."

"Yeah, I wouldn't have been able to do this without Brennan. Thanks again for covering for him."

"No problem. I'm glad it all worked out." Though I originally offered my help in the hopes of spending more time getting to know Brennan, I'll admit spending time with Callie is a close second.

Once we get all our items to our stall, we lay them out on a table with signs and descriptions of the products. Before the farmer's market officially opens, Callie says she's going to check in with the organizer. While she's gone, I stand back to check the display, and something doesn't look right. So I take liberties with the table and reorganize it.

"Where's all our products?" Callie asks when she comes back to a sparse table.

"It was too clutter-y. If people can't see what it is we're selling, then they won't stop to find out more. The scene will be like white noise for their eyes."

"Oh, I didn't think about that. I just put everything out so everyone knows what we have to offer." Callie scratches her head.

"We need to pick the best item out of the bunch." I determine right away that Jean's baby blue eggs are the most unique and eye-catching of the bunch, so I grab a carton and place it on the table. "Next you want to dress it up with accessories that enhance but don't overwhelm the product." Using one of Jean's bouquets, I rearrange it to create a nest-like structure made of flowers and place the eggs gently on top. "Now all we have to do is sit back and let the product draw in the crowd. Once they stop to gawk, we tell them about the honey that came from the nectar of these flowers. It'll naturally lead us to suggest Dr. Blaire's yogurt, which it pairs nicely with. Maybe we can even get them to buy one of Hal's cozies to use on the yogurt jars."

"You came up with all of that just now?" Callie is flabbergasted.

"What can I say? I'm a natural." I play it off like the idea just came to me, even though I'm literally describing my role as an influencer. As the one with the most influence in my circle, I always drew the biggest crowd, and my friends were noticed for it. That's how Willow got her first role starring in a new sitcom. Anyway, it worked for me then, and I know it'll work today.

At nine o'clock on the dot, the farmer's market starts, and the customers begin flooding in. The people here are exactly how Gavin described them, all Birkenstocks and reusable bags. I notice the bags are filled with lush green produce and packages of homemade granola. The closest thing to apparel is a hemp-woven scarf. Gavin was right. I'm never going to sell his luxury silk tie and Italian leather belt here.

It isn't long before I discover that this crowd also likes honey, artisanal yogurt, and fresh eggs. We even manage to sell almost all of Hal's handmade mug cozies. The items are selling faster than Callie and I can handle the payments. I've never worked retail, but I get a crash course in the rush. It's so busy that we don't even have a chance to eat. Finally, when it dies down, Callie gets us two bánh mìs at the Vietnamese food truck.

“I don’t know what it was like last time, but I’d call today a success,” I say with my mouth full.

“Today was definitely busier than last time. Thanks to your display.” Callie smiles. “It also helped that the granola people were placed right next to us. I had so many comments from customers who couldn’t wait to put the granola on top of the yogurt with the honey.”

“Same! That product placement was clutch.”

Callie raises a brow at me. “Charitable and knowledgeable. Can I count on you to come to the next one? Will you still be here?”

Dad said it could take up to two months before we know what his new role at It’s Ok! will be, and I haven’t had the opportunity to sell any of the items Gavin gave me yet. So the likelihood I’ll still be here the next time she comes to the farmer’s market is pretty high. So I say, “Yeah, I’ll be here for the next one.”

“Great,” Callie says with admirable enthusiasm. Callie’s optimism for my company is always at a hundred.

I see her eyeing the other products with a look I’m familiar with. “I’ve got this covered. Why don’t you look around?”

“Really?” Callie bites her lower lip, hesitating.

“Go on. There are only a few products left, and the crowd is dying down. I can handle this.” With my reassurance, she relents.

“Okay, but I’ll be quick.”

“Take your time!” I call to her as she leaves. When she’s gone I make my move and pull out the items I brought with me to sell. Carefully removing the display eggs, I put Gavin’s belt and tie on top of the flower nest. A few people stop by, more interested in the floral arrangement than the luxury goods. I manage to sell the last bouquet along with the display nest, but the belt and tie are still left untouched.

Suddenly I spot something in my periphery that sparks hope. An Hermès Birkin in a sea of canvas bags sticks out like an expensive thumb. The lady carrying it saunters down the aisles with it hanging on her arm, and even though she's wearing ill-fitting jeans with holes, the cut and color of the distressed fabric tell me they are the Balenciaga Super Destroyed Baggy Pants, which cost thousands (yes, thousands!) of dollars. Believe me, I know my denim. *Finally.* Someone who has style and, more importantly, the funds to purchase one of my items.

"Hello," I say as she eyes the items on our table. "Can I interest you in anything?"

She inspects the tie and seems curious. So I swoop in for the kill.

"This tie was purchased at the flagship store in London. It's only been worn once, and the classic Burberry print never goes out of style." Despite my best sales pitch, she puts it down, uninterested.

"What about that?" She points to my wrist. "Is that for sale?"

"This?" I clutch my wrist, caught off guard by her question. "It's an original, made by Damiani himself."

Her eyes widen at the designer's name. I was right when I guessed she had a taste for the high-end.

My friends and I got these at Melody's sweet sixteen. Her parents had them especially made for us. And we always wore them when we went out together. As hard as it is to part with something that gave me so many fond memories, I know that holding on to it isn't going to bring me back to that place. Only selling it will. So I agree.

"A thousand dollars," I say.

She hesitates, staring at the piece.

"It's very rare. Only five of these designs exist," I say, trying very hard not to sound too desperate.

She reaches into her bag and my lips spread to a smile. "Do you take American Express?" she asks.

My smile instantly disappears. Although Callie brought a credit card machine, it's only meant for the beautification fund. There's no way I can process this personal transaction on it.

"Sorry, cash only," I reluctantly say, no doubt effectively killing the sale. Even I never carried around that kind of cash before.

She begins riffling through her wallet. "I've got five hundred."

Callie will be back at any moment, and soon it'll be time to pack up and leave. Seeing as I don't have a choice, I agree to the deal and the lady pulls out the cash, placing the crisp bills on the table.

Even though it's more money than I've seen lately, it's practically highway robbery. This piece could have easily sold on eBay for ten times that amount. But I have to count my blessings. I have five hundred dollars more than I had before I got here. Which gets me that much closer to getting back to LA.

I wrap my bracelet in a piece of parchment paper that was used to wrap the jars of honey and hand it to her.

"Nice doing business with you," she says before walking away.

I wave goodbye to her since I can't get myself to say the words back. My only regret in selling the bracelet is that I was only able to get a fraction of what it's worth. Before I can dwell on it any longer, Callie walks toward me. I quickly shove Gavin's tie and belt in my bag.

"Wow, we did good." She eyes the empty table.

"We sure did," I say. "Did you get anything for yourself?"

"Just this." Callie shows me a different kind of jewelry than the one I parted with. A handwoven bracelet she bought from a girl who was raising money for her school. She must really be charitable, because that is a bracelet you couldn't pay me to wear.

We pack up our things and load the Jeep, which is much easier than unloading it was, since we sold everything we had. Before we get on the freeway, Callie notices something on her dashboard.

"Oh, shoot. My tank is empty. We should fill it before we get on the freeway." She spots a gas station ahead and turns into it. After she pulls up to the pump, Callie gets out and opens the tank of her car.

"This Jeep is diesel-run?" I ask while the fuel is pumping into the car.

"Yeah. Diesel-run cars don't have spark plugs, which disrupt the electromagnetic waves," she explains. "It's more expensive to operate, but luckily we don't drive too much in town. So a tank usually lasts me weeks." Easily believable, since even Gavin and I can manage to get from one end of the town to the other on foot. After the pump is done, Callie gets out to close her tank and pay for the diesel.

"How much did you say we made at the farmer's market today?" I ask when she returns.

"Three hundred dollars." Callie's smile stretches extra wide. "It's more than we made in the last couple of times I came here. Your display made all the difference."

"I'm so glad I could help." Staring out my window, I read the pump. Diesel is $4.31 a gallon, and Callie must have a twenty-one-gallon tank, because the total came out to $86.00.

"Just curious, but does the town reimburse you for the diesel?" I ask as we're driving off again.

"Nah, we decided to take it out of what we make since we know the town doesn't have much to spare."

I do the mental math. That leaves her with just a little over two hundred, which seems hardly worth the effort. We spent all morning working for her to make less than what I made selling my bracelet in two minutes. Not to mention the time and effort put into making the products when mine was gifted to me. On the drive back, when Callie isn't looking, I decide to slip two hundred-dollar bills into her bag and keep the rest for myself. As much as I need the money, it seems like a fairer valuation of the day's efforts.

When we pull into our driveway, Gavin comes around from the side of the house. I assume Mom and Dad are still at the secondhand furniture store since I don't see the tractor.

Gavin approaches the car as I'm getting out. "So, how was it?" he asks Callie apologetically, anticipating the regret in her response. Happily, she doesn't give it to him.

"It was great." Callie beams.

"Really?" Gavin looks at me skeptically.

"Really," I say without a hint of irony. It felt good to flex my influencer skills after not being able to use them for a while.

"You should come with us next time," Callie says. "We could use another pair of strong hands."

"Sure," he says. "I'd love to come next time if you want me to. Er, if you want *my help*, that is." His neck turns all blotchy.

Callie giggles in a pitch that registers slightly higher than what I'm used to hearing from her. "Elena has such an eye for detail. Her display brought in more customers than we could handle. Which was a good problem."

"Not sure what I can offer in that department. She knows what people want, and drawing a crowd is Elena's specialty."

"Somehow I doubt that," Callie says. "I'm sure it's in the genes."

That's weird. Not only is Callie complimenting Gavin but Gavin is complimenting *me* over something he has never appreciated. In fact, my ability to draw a crowd was the source of our many, *many* arguments in the past.

“Well, I better get back.” Callie climbs back into her Jeep. “Thanks again for your help today.”

“No problem.” I wave.

After she drives off I turn to Gavin.

“So now I’m *good* at drawing a crowd?”

“I was being polite,” he says. But the drunken smile on his face tells me otherwise. “By the way, did you make any money with the items I gave you?” he asks, changing the subject.

“Nah, I didn’t sell the things you gave me.”

“I told you that’s not the right market for luxury goods.”

“Yeah, you were right,” I say, even though he wasn’t. I also don’t point out another thing Gavin was wrong about. I don’t need to always make a show of every little thing I do. I don’t need to tell Gavin, or anyone else, about the money I got for my bracelet or that I donated part of it to the beautification fund to feel good about myself. It’s enough that I know I did.

EXCERPT

You can never go wrong when you surround yourself with people who uplift you.

The American Dream Achieved: The Story of Dale Ok, Founder of It's Ok!

TRANSCRIPT

60 MINUTES INTERVIEW WITH GLORIA OK

INTERVIEWER: You headed a charity for the homeless and a walk for breast cancer, and have raised funds for under-resourced schools. Seems like you're quite busy.

INTERVIEWER: Says here your title is a strategic advisor at the company. Can you explain what that means?

GLORIA: Since its inception, I came up with the strategy for It's Ok! on how to sell, where to sell, and what to sell. Dale said I was great at strategy, so that's what we decided my official role would be.

INTERVIEWER: Sounds like you did quite a lot. In fact, some would argue that that's what a founder and CEO does.

GLORIA: No, no, no. That's Dale's role. He's always made the business deals. I only advise him on how to do it.

INTERVIEWER: If it's okay, I'd like to know a little bit about you.

GLORIA: Me?

INTERVIEWER: Is that allowed?

GLORIA: Of course it is. It's just . . . these interviews aren't usually about me.

INTERVIEWER: I don't understand. Don't you work at It's Ok!?

GLORIA: Yes, I do. But these interviews are mostly about Dale, since he's the head of the company.

<TRANSCRIPT PAUSED>

It isn't until I get into the house that I notice it's way past noon, and Mom and Dad have been gone half of the day. Maybe they scored a barely used chaise lounge from a designer brand and are arranging for its delivery. Or maybe they're having to haggle with the vendor, since Dad only packed suits and and gives rich-people energy. Honestly I'm not sure what to make of it, considering we've never had to shop retail, let alone consignment. But Mom and Dad must have anticipated being out all day, since I find cut rolls of kimbap wrapped tightly with plastic wrap on a plate left for me and Gavin.

Since Callie and I barely had time to eat, I'm famished. I tear off the wrapper and put a piece into my mouth. The sautéed vegetables wrapped in rice and roasted seaweed burst with a mix of sesame oil and garlic. It's so good, I don't wait to finish the food in my mouth before I shove another piece in.

"You're going to choke eating like that," Gavin says, watching me stuff my face with unusual interest.

I try to tell him that he's wrong, but the words don't make it out of my mouth filled with sticky rice. Okay, so maybe I did overdo it.

Gavin picks up a sleeve of kimbap and pops a cut piece into his mouth. "Remember when Mom used to make these for us and we'd eat them on the way to school?"

"She did?"

"Yeah, when we lived in Koreatown."

"Vaguely," I say. I might've blocked that time out of my memory. Koreatown is a place to go for good eats or a good time. Not a place anyone aspires to live in.

"Korean sushi, that's what we called this." Gavin pops another piece into his mouth.

After finishing an entire sleeve, I reach over to grab another one. "I may not remember much from that time, but I'm glad Mom remembers how to cook. Except this one is a little different. It has a smoky flavor, like the SmokeShack burger from Shake Shack." Somehow this amuses Gavin.

"What?" I scrunch my nose.

"Nothing. I'm just glad you're enjoying it."

"I know what you're doing. You're food-shaming me." I narrow my eyes at him.

"I'm not food-shaming."

"Fine." I accept his answer and proceed to eat the second sleeve of kimbap. "So, what have you been up to while I was gone?"

"Just stuff," he says vaguely.

"Okay," I say, getting the hint. Clearly his magazine kept him busy all day long. "Honestly, Gavin. No explanation is needed. What you do in your spare time is personal. You do you—" I instantly recoil at the unintentional double entendre. "I mean, you know what I mean."

"Jesus, El. Stop. I'm trying to tell you something." This time I notice there isn't an ounce of embarrassment in his expression.

"Okay," I say. "I'm listening."

After he takes in a deep breath, he says, "I made that."

"You made what?" I look around, noticing nothing new.

"This." He points to the kimbap in my hand.

"Stop lying." I slap a hand in the air.

"No, really." Gavin disappears into his room and comes back with something in his hand. I recognize it as the magazine he's always reading.

"For the last time, Gavin, I don't care that you look at porn!" I put my hands up to shield my eyes, but it's too late. I see . . . "Wait, is that a dude? A fully dressed one?" I drop my hands once I confirm that this is not porn I'm looking at. "Who is that?"

"It's Roy Choi." Gavin pushes the magazine closer to me so I can see it properly. It's an interview in *The New Yorker*, which is, like, the exact opposite of porn.

"Oh, that's why he looked familiar." I suck my teeth. "If you wanted to meet him, I could have introduced you. I've been to several events with him. Just wish you had said something sooner. Who knows when I'll be at an event with him again?" Or *if*. I don't say that out loud, since I still have every hope that I can earn enough to pay for Kiki's services again soon.

"No, I don't want to meet him. I want to be him." He sets the magazine down.

"Okay, that's not creepy," I say, registering his intensity level as a hair below stalker status. "Gavin, do me a favor. Please never say that again."

He ignores me and continues without skipping a beat. "I've been reading about his life and how he dropped out of law school and went to culinary school. He trained at Michelin-star restaurants and then left to start a food truck that makes what he calls 'food that isn't fancy.' And not only that, but he became an international success because of it. But more than anything, I love that he blends his personal story with his professional training. That's what I want to do. Make fancy food with notes of my heritage. Like bacon-and-mushroom kimbap and eggs Benedict with sautéed kimchi."

"Wait," I say, processing what my brain is telling me. "If Mom didn't make this, then she didn't make all the other stuff wrapped in plastic. . . . That was you?" I say, finally getting up to speed.

Gavin nods, his face lighting up at my reaction.

"How?" I'm unable to mentally process how something so innovative came from a square like Gavin.

"I didn't use ChatGPT at school because I was lazy. I used it because I was busy learning how to cook. I took night classes, which made it hard to focus during the day. And, El"—he sighs dreamily—"I loved every minute of it. The challenge of making something new with the same ingredients is what gives me life. It makes me feel useful and accomplished when I create something people like. And I've never felt that way. Not at school or with Dad. When I cook, everything makes sense. It's what I'm meant to do, who I'm supposed to be."

"Gavin, I'm so happy for you," I say genuinely. But somehow I get the feeling that this isn't something everyone would be happy about. "Does Dad know?"

"No, he can't know. He'll be devastated. Even more than if he knew about me getting kicked out of USC."

"You really think so?" I know Dad has his heart set on Gavin working with him. But is being a chef that bad?

"Come on, this is Dad we're talking about. That man is so stuck in the past, he hasn't evolved since Adam and Eve. You cannot tell him anything he doesn't want to hear. If it doesn't line up with his set of values, it goes in one ear and out the other. And what's worse is how he doubles down on his stance anytime anyone challenges him. He'd never understand why I would give up a corporate job to work in a kitchen." Gavin shakes his head with a look of defeat. "It's why I started running. The mental load from trying to please Dad and stay true to myself was becoming too much. I had to find a way to relieve some of the stress."

I guess that explains why he started an exercise regimen, but it isn't a solution, at least not a long-term one. "Yeah, but how much longer can you keep something like this from Dad? You have to tell him at some point."

"The best way to handle Dad is to keep up the pretense that I'm doing things his way in order to do the things I want to do." Gavin's stance is firm.

I'm speechless. As the responsible one, Gavin doesn't disagree with Mom and Dad. He doesn't argue; he listens. He doesn't say no; he says yes. And when he's told to follow in Dad's footsteps, he follows. But when I hear Gavin tell me about his sheer determination to underhandedly pursue his passions despite Dad's unwillingness to support him, it's as if he's describing someone else. He's describing me. Suddenly it dawns on me that I might not be the only one who's been struggling to fit in in this family.

"Just promise you won't say anything to Mom or Dad about cooking. Not until I have a solid plan."

I nod, giving him my word. Even though I want him to be honest with our parents about who he is, I have to respect the way he's going about it.

"You know what's weird?" I say. "I've always had an entrepreneurial spirit but suppressed the urge to ask to be part of the family business because Mom and Dad always made me feel like it wasn't my place. This whole time you've been doing the same with cooking."

After my words sink in, he releases a heavy sigh. "El, I'm sorry. I never knew that's how you felt."

"How could you? We've never talked about this stuff before."

"True," he admits.

I always thought our differences kept us from being close. But maybe I had it wrong this whole time. Maybe it was our similarities that made it impossible to see each other for who we really are.

The phone rings, startling us. I want to say that it's because it's an unfamiliar sound to us, but the truth is, it's probably because we were lost in our thoughts. For a second it got deep between us.

Gavin picks up the phone. "Oh, hey," he says as soon as he hears who's on the other end, and he takes the phone to our room. I'm about to head into the bathroom to take a shower so he can have privacy talking to Sonya. But when I overhear part of his conversation, my ears inadvertently perk up. He sounds—*bro-y*? I usually don't have any interest in eavesdropping on any of Gavin's phone conversations, which, as far as I can tell, are a snoozefest. But if he's not talking to Sonya, then who is he . . . ?

I press my ear against the door and catch the last part of his conversation.

"Sounds good, man. I'll meet you at the cafe tomorrow." Gavin hangs up the phone, and before I can get my feet to move, he's at the door.

"Um, can I help you?" he says, clearly catching me eavesdropping.

"I forgot something—bra—tampons—cramps," I blurt out a series of words that usually repel him, but of course this time they don't work.

"Sure" is all he says, opening the door for me to come in. The smirk on his face lets me know that he's not buying my excuse.

I go into my suitcase and rummage through it until I find a bra I have no intention of wearing and a tampon I have no need of, then ball them up in my hand. "Who was that?" I ask casually before I head back to the bathroom.

"Brennan. He's on his way back from LA and asked if I wanted to meet him tomorrow for lunch. Then he offered to show me the lab where he works."

"Can I come?"

He raises a brow. "El, I really don't think Brennan is—"

"Look, Gavin," I start, realizing I need to break down our current situation to him in easily digestible, Gavin-sized bites. "You and I aren't much different. You have ambitions; I have ambitions. You feel stifled by other people's expectations; I feel stifled by other people's expectations. And can we agree that this is so not the summer we envisioned for ourselves?" When Gavin agrees, I continue. "For the first time I've started to see the flip side of being here. Not only are we cut off from the good parts of our lives—the private jets, the exclusive restaurants, being waited on hand and foot—" My voice trails, along with my train of thought, and I quickly pull myself back from digressing. "My point is, while we're in Blaire, we've been given a blank slate. You have the freedom to experiment with this new version of yourself. Without It's Ok! you get to explore who you want to be. And maybe I do too. I want to finally know what it feels like to be in relationships without my reputation overshadowing me."

"You do?" Gavin softens.

I nod. "Isn't it time we start having the summer we want?"

"Fine," he agrees. "You can come with me tomorrow to meet Brennan."

I squeal. "Thank you, thank you, thank you!" Then I do something really out of character. I hug Gavin.

Of course Gavin is awkward after the hug and fidgets with his sleeve.

Mom and Dad come home a few hours later with some items that aren't too exciting but do help improve the place. Like curtains that functionally work but fashionably miss the mark and area rugs that are in not-great condition but a step up from the shag carpet that needs replacing.

Dad makes Gavin go with him to clear the rest of the weeds from the field while there's still daylight, and Mom makes me help her with dinner in the kitchen. Today I cut the tip of my middle finger with a knife, nearly burn myself with the wire rack in the oven while pulling out a baking sheet, and singe my hair on the stove while stirring a pot too closely. I know I told Gavin I'd keep his secret for him, but it would do both of us a huge favor if he would just come clean about his culinary skills. The only success I have in the kitchen today is not getting criticized by Mom. Since they returned, she's seemed distracted, preoccupied with her thoughts. Even at dinner she's quiet.

"I had a great time at the farmer's market with Callie today," I say in an attempt at small talk with my parents.

"That's nice," Mom says, more interested in the contents of her bowl than in continuing the conversation.

Gavin shifts uncomfortably in his seat at the awkward silence. "Elena and I are going to get a tour of the lab tomorrow," he adds. I can tell he's as desperate as I am to make this less weird.

"Tomorrow?" Dad startles, looking up from his plate. "We'll be busy preparing the field so we can start planting as soon as we figure out what the people here like to eat."

Mom's head jerks back. "What happened to growing ingredients to make kimchi and side dishes for other meals?" Mom raises her voice. "What happened to that plan?"

"Gloria, I know what I'm doing. Just leave it to me to take care of it."

"I'm not sure that's a good idea. Remember the last time you said you'd take care of everything?" Mom levels her gaze, matching Dad's intensity.

"What's gotten into you? This is the way it always was in Anbandegi."

"Well, this isn't Anbandegi. And that was almost thirty years ago, Dale. Things have changed. For such an ambitious man, how can you think so small?"

Mom and Dad have been doing this a lot lately. Bickering. I can hear them through the paper-thin walls at night after Gavin falls asleep. I can tell he's not used to hearing them argue by the way he's staring deep into his plate, trying to tune it out. It goes without saying that I'm not as good at pretending as Gavin is, so I can't help but speak up when the opportunity strikes.

"Why does it matter what other people like?" I ask. "We're not hosting dinner parties here, so who cares what we grow?"

"The farm can provide for us, sure. But I've been thinking about how it can help us on a larger scale. The profit from selling produce can pay for the expenses it takes to run a farm, like water, fertilizer, and equipment."

"Ew, can we please not say *fertilizer* at the dinner table?" I wrinkle my nose and set my fork down.

"The point is, the farm could provide for us in a bigger way, with enough left over to buy the ingredients for kimchi and whatever else you want to make," he says to Mom.

"It's not what we had planned for," Mom says, disappointed.

"I'm sorry," Dad says earnestly. "I made the mistakes that got us here. And now I am accepting responsibility for it. By monetizing the farm, we'll have a side income to supplement my salary when I go back to working at It's Ok! so you don't have to work again." Dad announces this like it's a good thing. Mom's face suggests otherwise.

"Are you at least going to let us know what the plan is?" Mom asks, irritated.

"I've been paying attention, and the people here are American to the core. They like potatoes and corn, not kimchi and kalbi. A bit late in the season, so we have some catching up to do. So don't make too many plans with your new friends," he warns Gavin.

It's just like Dad to think he knows about this town without actually getting to know the people who live in it.

"Sounds like you thought of everything. Guess there's nothing left for me to do. Again." Mom drops her spoon in her empty bowl with a loud clank.

"Yep, I've got it all under control," Dad says, completely oblivious to Mom's passive-aggressive behavior. "With Gavin's help, we can meet the people and build the relationships we need to grow a successful farm and business."

"It's settled, then," she says. "You and Gavin figure out the farm, and Elena and I will do the housework. I'm tired of doing both jobs anyway." She sighs.

Dread floods me. More time in the kitchen with Mom? That won't end well.

"How about this?" I say, suddenly coming up with a plan. "Before you start planting, why don't we find out what the people here want instead of guessing? Callie's family is in a farming co-op with two other families here. Farming is a side job, and they sell what they make to the cafe. I can introduce you to them to get their input on what needs they have."

Dad takes his time considering my suggestion, which is honestly insulting. Is he that resistant to seriously entertaining an idea from me? Because let's be real. If this were coming from Gavin, he not only would have jumped on the opportunity to partner with him on this venture, but would have praised him for his ingenuity.

"Elena already has a working relationship with the co-op," Gavin chimes in. "Because of her, they sold out all of their inventory at the farmer's market. Their profit margins went through the roof." That's not exactly what happened, and the profit margins were definitely not as high as he's indicating, through no fault of my own. But I know he's exaggerating the truth in a way that only Dad will recognize, using buzzwords like *profit margins* and *inventory*. So I nod, grateful to him.

About a million seconds later, Dad eventually agrees. "Okay," he says. "As long as you can manage helping your mom with her work."

I grimace. It's not exactly the outcome I was hoping for. Luckily Gavin swoops in at the opportune time.

"I can help with that," he says. "I'll cover for Elena at home so she can go with you."

Dad is again hesitant, but Mom answers before he has a chance to protest. "Great," she says. "At least one man in this family isn't afraid to try new things."

Dad is probably the only one who doesn't register the underhanded jab directed at him. But Gavin and I are too relieved to worry about that. Somehow we've both gotten ourselves out of our old patterns and into new ones.

While Gavin and I are getting ready to meet Brennan the next day, Dad wastes no time gathering data for his business proposal for the farming co-op. He mutters incoherent words that I'm assuming are swear words in Korean while the web pages take forever to load. I don't blame him, since I've seen sloths move at a faster rate. True to her word, Mom is not getting involved in any more of Dad's business affairs. Instead she spends most of her day tending the herb garden.

When I go to the room to change, Gavin passes me on the way to the bathroom. He does a double take at my face. I know yesterday-Gavin would have said something snarky, like how I've overdone it with the makeup or how my lashes and lips make me look like a llama. But to his credit, he says nothing. Wow. Look at us. We *can* get along.

"I can see if Callie can join us," I suggest. In the likelihood Brennan and I do hit it off, that would make Gavin the third wheel. A group thing could ensure everyone has a good time.

"No," he says much too quickly, which strikes me as odd.

My brow quirks. Does he not like Callie? The sweet-as-pie, girl-next-door Callie? Who couldn't like her?

"What's going on? Why don't you want to hang out with Callie?" I ask.

"What? That's not it at all," he says unconvincingly.

"Just tell me," I say. "I thought we were trying to, you know, get along better. Especially since Mom and Dad are fighting all the time."

My guilt trip seems to work, and Gavin softens. "If you have to know." He hesitates, as if he's gathering the courage to tell me his deepest, darkest secret. "I kind of, sort of have . . ." He mumbles the last part inaudibly.

"What was that? You have a rash? *Down there?*" I say loudly to get him to see how ridiculous he's being. Also because it's fun to mess with him.

"God, Elena. Grow up." He pinches the bridge of his nose.

"You grow up!" I say back to him. "You're being weird, okay? So just tell me what's going on."

"All right," he relents. "Every time I'm around Callie, there's something between us that makes my throat close up. Like I can't breathe or something."

"What are you saying? You're allergic to Callie?"

"No." He gives me a look. "I think I . . . sorta, kinda, *maybe* have feelings for Callie."

I wait for more, but there isn't. "Gavin, do me a favor," I say. "If you ever get close enough to Callie to confess your feelings, never *ever* repeat those words to her."

"Elena, be serious."

"I am serious. I've met people who work at the DMV with more passion than you."

"Okay, fine. I like Callie. Happy?"

I press my lips together, but it's no use. The smile cracks through.

"Oh my God." Gavin puts a hand to his face. "You're going to be so extra about it, and I just can't handle that right now."

I let out the squeal I've been holding in. I just love playing matchmaker, and Gavin knows that about me. "I can't help it. I think Callie's great. She's naturally pretty, fun, and doesn't have a superficial bone in her body. And, bonus, she's got great taste in friends." I point to myself.

"No, that's not good news."

I groan. Why does Gavin always have to see every glass as half empty?

"Is it because you think she's out of your league?"

He jerks his head back. "What? No."

"Then, is it because you're insecure about your style? Because I've been dying to do a makeover on you since you bought that pair of leggings two years ago."

"Elena, just stop." He puts up a hand to shush me. "I have a girlfriend. Remember Sonya?"

I pause. "Aren't you guys, like, on a break or something?"

"Yeah, but what if we, I don't know, decide to start dating again?"

"Oh my God, even your breakups are boring." I snore.

"It's more complicated than that. You know how status and all that matters to Dad."

"I do," I admit. Dad is a series of contradictions, and this is one of them. Despite his humble beginnings, Dad can be a pretty big snob.

"Anyway, we dated for over a year. And even though Dad wanted us to be together more than I did at times, I admit that we complement each other well. Sonya is bold and caring, and I'm sensitive and hardworking."

"Are you actually describing your relationship? Or the pairing of a Zinfandel with a panko-crusted halibut?" I shake my head at him.

He stares at me, unamused. "Not every relationship is the kind that sweeps you off your feet. Look at Mom and Dad."

"You're not twenty years deep in a marriage. We're talking about dating. And those relationships should sweep you off your feet."

"Oh yeah? How many relationships have you been in?" He narrows his eyes at me with pursed lips.

"That's different. I had too much of a life to settle down."

"While I didn't?" he says, seemingly offended.

"No, you didn't," I say plainly. "You were too busy playing the role you were expected to. No one expects anything from me, so I do what I want." As soon as I say the words, I realize this is the root of our differences. That ever since It's Ok! took over our lives, our paths had been set for us to go in completely opposite directions.

"Is that how you really feel? That no one expects anything from you?"

I shrug, unable to meet his eye. Although I've always felt this way, the directness of his question is a first.

"I'm sorry," he says. And by the softness of his tone, I can tell he genuinely means it. "I would have suggested to Dad to include you in the business earlier if I had known."

"It's okay," I say. "I don't blame you. I know how important first-born sons are to Dad."

It surprises me how sad I feel when Gavin doesn't disagree with me. It's not like he can change who Dad is any more than I can.

I clear my throat, getting back to the task at hand. "Now that we've been given a blank slate here, I can help you make the most of it."

"What about Dad? He'll find out about USC after things settle at It's Ok! If I don't have Sonya to go back to, he might not survive the whole ordeal."

"We'll worry about that when the time comes. And besides, who knows if Callie's even interested in you?" I joke with him to put him at ease, even though I'm pretty sure the feelings are mutual. When he still doesn't budge, I place a hand on his shoulder, tipping my head toward him. "Isn't it about time we start living our lives and not Mom and Dad's?"

Reluctantly he nods. "Fine," he agrees. "But no makeover." He puts a finger up to warn me.

I make no promises.

After making a quick call to Callie, Gavin and I head to the cafe, where we made plans to eat lunch with her and Brennan before their shifts begin. We arrive fashionably late and spot Brennan and Callie waiting for us at the front of the observatory.

"Hey, the band's back together," Brennan says in a familiar way that I find oddly comforting—surprising because, one, I've only known them for a short time, and, two, Gavin is part of *the band*.

"How was LA?" I ask.

Brennan gushes about how magical Disneyland was and how exciting it was to see the familiar backdrops of the LA landscape he'd only seen in movies.

"It's good to be back, though," he says, surprising me. I would've thought he'd be dying to stay there now that he's had a taste of LA, not to mention real civilization with cell service and Wi-Fi. But if it means Brennan is happy to be here with us, then I'm not going to argue with him.

We head into the cafe and spot an open booth. Instead of sitting next to Callie, Gavin sits next to Brennan, so I take the seat next to Callie. We share two menus since they are trifold and open up to the size of a small poster. While Callie and I hover over a menu, huddled close together, all I can think of is what a missed opportunity this is for Gavin. If he wants to get to know Callie, he better step up his game.

The menu is, as they said, extensive. In addition to the usual diner foods, such as hamburgers, sandwiches, and salads, the cafe also has a variety of not-usual diner offerings, such as chicken Milanese, döner kebab, and steak au poivre—dishes I'd order even if I weren't in Blaire. If I had known how appetizing the food was, I wouldn't have helped myself to a second serving of Gavin's egg soufflé this morning. Who am I kidding? I'd have eaten seconds even if I'd known about the menu at the cafe. The eggs were so light and fluffy, it was as if I were eating a cloud. I'm too full now to order a meal, but I can go for something sweet.

Brennan and Callie both order sandwiches from the deli, and Gavin gets the steak while I get an ice cream sundae.

"Why does your shift start so late today?" I ask after the waitress leaves with our orders.

"Every once in a while, we have to work the night shift," Brennan says.

"The night shift?" I wrinkle my nose. "How do you keep yourselves from sleeping on the job?" Working at a lab during the day already sounds like a snoozefest. I wonder how they manage it at night.

"Sleep is the last thing I'm thinking of when I'm at the lab," Callie says dreamily. "So much activity happens at all hours of the day and night, and it's exciting to think that we might be the ones to first notice it happening."

"Right?" Brennan nudges Callie. "Every night I come to work wondering, *Is today the day we discover a new star? Or find signs of water in a place we didn't know existed?*" The nerd-off happening between them is something I can't seem to understand. Science has never been my thing.

Soon, the food arrives, and the presentation is even more impressive than the extensive menu options. Gavin's plate has chopped parsley sprinkled along the edge, with pearl onions in a red-wine reduction.

"This is a perfect medium rare." Gavin marvels at the pop of pink when he slices into his steak. "Oh my God," he mutters with his mouth full. "So tender. You should try it."

Brennan and Callie take a bite, but I decline. "Maybe next time. I'm not hungry." Instead I grab a fry off Gavin's plate.

Gavin eyes me skeptically. "Not hungry, huh?" he teases.

"Everyone knows there's a separate stomach for dessert." I dip the fry in my ice cream before eating it. At first the three of them stare at me with unreadable expressions. Ordinarily I wouldn't be self-conscious about my quirks and habits. But their reactions remind me that I'm not the trendsetter here that I was known to be in LA. Fries with ice cream isn't that weird, is it? Maybe it's not a universally enjoyed combination like peanut butter and jelly, but I'm pretty sure it's a thing.

"You do that too?" Callie says.

"It's the only way to eat ice cream," Brennan says.

"Right?" I say, relieved that this is something we can agree on. "The sweet and salty combination always hits."

"Actually, I eat it that way too," Gavin says with an expression as surprised as I feel. Considering our different tastes in fashion, hair, and almost everything else, I wouldn't have thought we'd have the same taste in food combinations.

"Great. You can help me eat the rest, since there's no way I can finish it." I shove my bowl toward the middle of the table.

“Same.” Gavin pushes his plate next to my sundae.

We take turns dipping fries into the ice cream for dessert. This simple yet distinct common ground releases a tightness in my muscles, like letting out a breath I didn't know I was holding in. Somewhere in the transition from LA to Blaire, I lost track of who I was. I guess it's been a while since I've been able to just be me without worrying about anything else.

“I wonder who even came up with this combo in the first place,” Callie says, thinking aloud.

“It had to have been an accident, right? Like some fries fell into a bowl of ice cream or something?” Brennan grabs another fry and sweeps it across the melting ice cream.

“Seems plausible. More so than if someone just came up with the idea out of the blue. I mean, fries with ketchup make sense, but fries with ice cream?” Gavin shakes his head. “I don't see it.”

“Sometimes accidents make the best inventions. Like, did you know the radio telescope was discovered by accident?” When Gavin and I stare at Callie with blank expressions, she continues. “It's true. When an engineer working at a phone company noticed static interference on the phone calls, he discovered it was radio waves coming from movement in the solar system. That's how we got the radio telescope.”

Gavin and I share a look that says *nerd alert*.

“Callie knows everything about this place,” Brennan says, noticing our expressions.

“I do not,” Callie protests. “You know how the radio telescope was invented.”

“Yeah, because you told me!” He points a finger at her, laughing.

“I guess when your dad works at the observatory and your mom teaches at the local school, it's bound to rub off on you," Callie sheepishly admits.

I keep waiting for Gavin to chime in, but he doesn't. There have been plenty of opportunities, and their relaxed banter should put him at ease. What's his deal?

After we finish off the fries and ice cream, we pay the bill and head out of the cafe. As we're walking, I lean into Gavin when Brennan and Callie are slightly ahead of us.

"Why aren't you talking to Callie?" I hiss at Gavin.

"I knew we shouldn't have asked Callie to come today. Every time I try to speak, it's like the words keep getting caught in my throat."

"Well, figure out how to get them un-caught soon, before you find yourself permanently in the friend zone."

He rolls his eyes but doesn't argue with me.

"Since I already gave Gavin a tour of the facilities last time, do you want to show Elena around while I take Gavin to the lab?" Brennan asks Callie in the lobby of the observatory.

Let's be real, there isn't any part of this observatory I'm interested in learning more about. I'm only here to make sure Gavin doesn't botch things up with Callie. So splitting up is not an option.

"Why don't you give me the CliffsNotes version of what I missed so we can stick together?" I suggest.

Gavin gives me a subtle glance, indicating that he knows what I'm doing, which is a good reminder for him. Because with the way he's avoiding Callie—both in distance and in peripheral vision—he needs more than a reminder. He needs an intervention.

"The lab isn't the most exciting place in the observatory, but it's where the real action happens," Brennan says while we wait for the elevator.

"The lab?" I raise a skeptical brow. "I'd have thought the telescope was the main attraction."

"The radio telescope does have an important job of collecting the signals from space, but it sends the data directly to the lab," Callie explains. "And the analysis is where the actual discoveries are made."

"So you don't need to get close to the telescope to use it?" Gavin asks.

"No, but we can give you a tour of it if you want," Callie offers.

"How close can we get to the telescope?" I ask.

Brennan and Callie exchange a knowing look. "I think we can get pretty close, right, Callie?" Brennan asks.

"Yeah, I think I can arrange that," Callie says, pulling out her phone.

"I thought those were banned or something," I blurt. I haven't seen my phone in weeks. I'm starting to forget what it looks like.

"We don't normally get to use them, but today is a maintenance day," Callie explains. "It's when the telescope is temporarily shut down and not collecting data, so radio waves won't interfere with it."

"More importantly it means today is the perfect day to ask for a tour of the telescope," Brennan adds as Callie steps away to make a call.

"Who's she calling?" I ask.

"Her dad. He runs security here," Brennan says. "It's a good thing Callie joined us today, since he's the only one who can give us the proper clearance."

"It *is* a good thing Callie joined us," I enunciate ever so slightly.

Gavin doesn't acknowledge me, but the blush that blooms on his cheeks tells me he heard every word.

Callie's dad is going to meet us at the base of the telescope to give us the clearance we need to see it up close, so we follow her to the back exit of the lobby. As soon as the door opens, we see the satellite dish towering above us.

"Oh my God," I say, immediately overwhelmed by the sight. It's not like any kind of satellite I've seen before, and it's more massive up close than I could ever have imagined. Rather than a solid piece of equipment, the structure is built with LEGO-like pieces assembled to create a modern structure.

"I know," Callie says. "My whole life I've lived in this town, and it never gets old."

I glance over at her, and it's true. She's as struck by the sight as I am.

"It seems to go on for miles," Gavin observes, just as taken with the sight.

"Two acres of surface area on that bad boy," Brennan says with his eyes fixed on the satellite dish.

Something behind us catches Callie's attention, and she turns around to wave. "Hey, Dad," she says. When I turn to see a man in denim overalls and a trucker hat approaching us, I suddenly remember that I've met Callie's dad before. And under less-than-desirable circumstances, to say the least.

“Calamity.” Officer Hartford walks over to us, giving Callie a side hug and a kiss on the top of her head.

“You remember Gavin and Elena, right?” Callie motions to us, and I instantly turn bright red.

“How could I forget?” Officer Hartford nods at both of us.

Gavin stiffens. He sticks out a hand and gives him a firm handshake. “Uh, hello, Officer Hartford,” he says, reverting to the stuffy persona he usually puts on in front of Dad—and all dads, it would seem. Though I can’t say I blame him. Meeting the father of the girl you like would be intimidating for anyone.

I manage to mutter a hello with a wave.

“And you know Supernova, of course.” Callie motions to Brennan.

“Good to see you, my boy,” Officer Hart says affectionately. No wave, no handshake. They give each other a hug. “You both making the new residents feel right at home here?”

“Oh, no.” I shake my head forcefully. “We’re not residents here, not permanent, at least.” Though we’ve been informed our stay here is going to be longer than initially expected, I’m not ready to admit this is my permanent residence. Not now or ever.

“Brennan and Callie have graciously offered to show us around,” Gavin says, nudging me.

“Oh, right. They’re the best,” I say, fumbling with my words to make up for my honest mistake. Even though I can’t understand why anyone would choose to live here, I should be more conscientious about how others feel about living here.

“There’s no one better than these two to give you the tour. They live and breathe this stuff,” Officer Hartford says, thankfully not following up on my comment about being temporary residents. Since Officer Hartford is still on duty, he leaves us to resume his job. Now that we have the clearance we need, Brennan leads us up the metal stairway to the satellite dish. When we reach the surface of the telescope, we stand in silence, taking it all in.

"I know it's a radio telescope, but I still don't understand how it works," I say, shielding my eyes from the sunlight bouncing off the bright white surface.

"I'll let Callie take the lead, since she's a bigger nerd than I am." Brennan smirks at her and takes a step back beside me. Callie gives him a playful eye roll but seems to take the jab as a compliment.

"Think of it as a bionic eardrum." Callie puts a hand up to her ear and cups it. "It can hear things far beyond what we can see through the strongest ocular telescope," she whispers, leaning into us.

Gavin is the closest to her, so she's practically whispering in his ear. It would be the perfect opportunity for the two of them to have a moment, except I notice Gavin shying away from her. Guess that's my cue. If it were up to Gavin, he'd never have a moment with her, so instead of stepping back to give him clearance, I lean against him, preventing him from doing so.

Gavin notices. But more importantly, so does Callie. Her eyes are clapped on Gavin's, even though Brennan and I are standing right behind him.

Gavin clears his throat. "What's it listening for?"

"We send a signal out, and when the radio wave hits something, the waves sends the signal back to the satellite, where a machine in the lab prints out the findings. The higher the frequency of returning waves, the closer the object. Conversely, the smaller frequency waves suggest the object is farther away. With that information scientists can create a map of an area in space without even seeing it."

"Oh, that's cool," Gavin says, effectively letting the conversation die out between him and Callie. *Amateur.*

"What else can the telescope tell us?" I ask.

"The telescope is also like a time machine," Callie says. "When we look into space, we're seeing what happened light-years ago, so in essence we're looking into the past. How our universe assembled itself, how the solar system was formed. Even the big bang."

"That's fascinating, right, Gavin?"

His head pops up like a Whac-A-Mole. "Uh, yeah. That's really fascinating." Smooth, Gavin. Real smooth.

Callie, thankfully, doesn't seem to notice. She seems to be in her element. "What's even more fascinating is how the same molecules from then are not only still with us now, but they're the same molecules we're made of. So essentially we're made of star stuff," she says with a passion I haven't seen in anyone our age before.

Instead of asking another follow-up question, I give Gavin a subtle nudge. It's time he takes the lead.

After an awkward second, Gavin clears his throat. "So when people use the saying *the universe is telling me* . . . you can use it literally."

"I guess." Callie giggles, and I give Gavin a nod of approval. "I never thought of it like that. Except the universe never gives me the answers I'm looking for."

"Yeah? Like what?" Gavin relaxes and inches closer to her.

"Like if I should apply for out-of-state colleges or follow in my parents' footsteps and work in Blaire. Or if I should go to Florida to visit my grandparents instead of interning at the observatory over the summer."

"Or maybe the universe did give you an answer, and you're right where you should be."

My eyes widen at the marked improvement. Didn't think Gavin was a fast learner, but he's proving me wrong.

"Maybe." She blushes. Then, probably realizing they're not alone,

Callie quickly composes herself. "Then again, space exploration is one of the great unknowns. Even new discoveries often lead to more questions rather than answers."

The smile on my face is less about the discoveries out there and more about the ones happening here. Gavin's nerves are completely subdued by Callie's passion for her work, and Callie seems responsive to Gavin's advances, subtle as they are. Their conversation has relaxed into a natural back-and-forth cadence. Now that my work is done, I take a step back.

"So, have you discovered anything cool lately? Like UFOs or aliens?" I ask Brennan, trying to give Gavin and Callie some space.

"No," Brennan says. "Not yet at least."

I blink. Even though I was the one who asked about the possibility of extraterrestrials, I never expected to be taken seriously. And not by Brennan, of all people. "So, wait. You really think aliens are out there?"

He shrugs. "I mean, isn't that what space exploration is? Discovering new and often unimaginable things in our universe?"

To me, people who believe in aliens come off as out of touch, eccentric, or even delusional. But Brennan is none of those things. The unlikely response from someone I least expect pulls me out of my head. Maybe I've been so focused on what this town doesn't have that I can't see what it does have.

"The only thing I know for sure is not to rule out the possibility of anything," Brennan says.

"Yeah, I can agree with that." I sigh, taking it all in. And I'm not just talking about the cloudless blue sky above the expansive satellite dish hovering over the lush treetop landscape. Listening to Callie and Brennan talk about their day-to-day, collecting data coming in from millions of miles away, puts into perspective how small and narrow my world is. There's a whole universe out there full of unknowns, and it's making me wonder . . . Maybe I'm limiting myself by wanting to go back to my old life. Maybe the universe has something bigger in store for me than even I can imagine.

"Looks like it's time for our shift to start," Brennan announces.

"Already?" Callie seems disappointed.

"Guess time flies . . . ," Gavin says to Callie, then forcefully moves his eyes to Brennan so it isn't obvious he's just talking to Callie. Although he doesn't fool me. I know smitten when I see it.

"Guess so." Callie hides a smile behind her fist.

I'm so happy with Gavin's progress with Callie today that I'm willing to overlook that cheesy line that came out of his mouth.

As we climb down to the ground level, Gavin and Callie are in the middle of a conversation. So I thank Brennan for the tour.

"That was fun today," I say.

"Why do you sound surprised?" Brennan's brows furrow.

"Nothing against you or Callie," I backtrack, realizing my faux pas, "but I've never been interested in anything science-y. It's actually kinda my worst subject in school."

"I can't say I relate. I've always been good at science. Maybe you had the wrong teacher," he says with a boyish grin.

"Maybe," I say, matching his playful tone. Then, almost immediately, an unusual sensation creeps up my neck, making the temperature rise in my cheeks. What is happening? Am I . . . *blushing*?

I'm not the one who gets flustered. It's usually the other way around. Then again, Brennan, I'm quickly discovering, isn't like the "nice guys" I'm used to. The ones whose true intentions reveal they're more interested in the things I can do for them (money/fame/status) rather than in me as a person. But with Brennan, I can tell his good looks and good nature go more than skin-deep. Every part about him is as advertised. He likes science. He likes helping others. And I still can't figure out if he likes me, per se, but it's clear he likes spending time with us. Hopefully I'll have more chances with him to find out. Between encouraging Gavin to initiate conversation and making sure he and Callie had space, I barely had time to banter with Brennan today. But somehow, as Gavin and Callie rejoin us, all smiles, it doesn't feel like I missed out on anything.

"What were you two talking about quietly?" I ask Gavin as soon as we leave the building to walk back home. I've been dying to know.

His face reddens at the question. "You saw that?"

"What can I say? I'm observant."

"Callie offered to show me how to harvest honey on her farm next week."

"Like a date?" I jab him in the side with a finger.

"Ow." He jerks away, avoiding my jab along with the question.

"It's a date," I squeal, determining for myself.

"She's just showing me how to make honey."

"I'm sure she is." I waggle my brows at him.

"Grow up, El," he says, but he's unable to hide a smile. And more importantly he's unable to tell me definitively that this is not *not* a date. Which makes it all worth the many missed opportunities with Brennan today. I guess that's the upside of being here longer. I can work on my relationship status later. But first I need to help Gavin with his.

As soon as we get home, I sit him down on his bed and tell him to listen up.

"Here's what you need to wear," I say, holding up an appropriately suitable—and, more importantly, suited to his body type—outfit for a first date.

"I told you, no makeovers." Gavin has his hands up, warding me off.

"I know you did," I say. "I just didn't agree to it."

"Elena," he says.

"Gavin," I say in his naggy voice. "Why do you always have to say no before yes? Just save us some time and do what I say." I put my hands on his shoulders, gently forcing him into a sitting position on his bed so he can listen to the short but imperative presentation I have planned. "From what I've learned about you these past few weeks, you are nothing like the uptight rule follower that your style would suggest. I'm just trying to make your outside accurately match who you are on the inside."

"These aren't uptight. They're smart," he says defensively, motioning to his slacks and button-down dress shirt. "Dad says to dress for the job you want, not the one you have."

"My point exactly. Are you going to a board meeting or a date?"

"A date, but—"

A wry smile appears on my lips when I finally get him to admit this is a date. "But nothing," I say, cutting him off. "These slacks are boring; you need something more relaxed. That way she'll be relaxed, and you both can be yourselves when you get to know each other better."

He agrees with me, albeit begrudgingly, and takes the T-shirt and shorts I laid out for him.

"Now that you look more like you, let's have you sound like you." And because he has a confused look on his face, I explain, "You need help in the conversation department."

He opens his mouth to argue with me, but soon after closes it when he realizes he has no argument. "Fine. How do I start the conversation?"

"*You* don't. She does. Let her do the talking, and you do the listening."

"That's not what Dad said when I first started dating Sonya. He said I need to lead with authority. To take charge of the situation so she knows I'm a strong man who can take care of her."

I purse my lips with a hand on my hip. "Did he also tell you to pee all around her so that the other territorial males would stay away?"

After letting my words sink in, he gestures for me to continue. "Point taken," he says.

"Okay, so, first start by asking her questions about herself. Listen intently to her responses. Then—and this is an important step—when she finishes telling you something interesting about herself, follow it up with another question related to what she said, and whatever you do, do not, I repeat, *do not* follow up by relating it to something about you."

He blinks. "That's it?" he says after a beat. "That's the secret?"

"You'd be surprised by how little it takes to be a decent human being. Taking a vital piece of information about the other person and making it about yourself doesn't make you a good listener. It makes you a narcissist," I say. "Trust me, Gavin. It's the same reason why you shouldn't wear a strapless dress with tan lines, why you shouldn't wear tube socks with shorts, and why single men with no children shouldn't drive panel vans—because that kind of behavior isn't a good look."

"Okay," he says, convinced. "So basically don't do anything Dad told me to do."

I wouldn't have put it that way, but it happens to be true. So I agree with his assessment.

The tufts of his hair have finally grown out, but Gavin has not adjusted to the appropriate style the new length requires. "I don't have time today, but next time I'll do your hair."

"No." He puts his hands up firmly. "I have limits too."

My eyes bulge just slightly at his sharp tone. "Got it. No hair."

His brows furrow skeptically. "Why are you smiling, then?"

"Because," I say, taking inventory of him, "my work is starting to take effect. You're finally finding your voice."

He rolls his eyes familiarly. What's not familiar is the smile that accompanies it.

It's been a week since I've officially run out of lavender bath salts, the only remedy that keeps me calm during this transition period. And yet a noticeable peace washes over me that I haven't felt in a while. Hanging out with Callie, Brennan, and Gavin was not only unexpectedly pleasant, but it felt similar to the type of fun I used to have after going out to an event or a party. Which I know doesn't make sense, like comparing apples to apple martinis. What's even weirder is that today wasn't even about me. It was about Gavin. Helping Gavin become the person he wants to be has reignited my sense of purpose that's been missing since we got here. My life is starting to make sense again. In Blaire, that is. Not sure what it means for my life back in LA. By now more than two weeks have passed, and I'm no longer at the silent retreat I told my friends I was at. I wonder where they think I am.

Then I remember I don't have to wonder. Today is maintenance day, something I just learned about. It's the one day a month when the use of radio waves is allowed. I check the clock. The town will have cellular reception for one more hour. So while Gavin is in the bathroom showering, I don't waste any time. I find my phone where Mom left it in the kitchen drawer and turn it on. I wait impatiently for the screen to illuminate, silently praying the battery isn't drained.

With my eyes clenched closed, I jump when a rapid succession of pinging comes from my phone with the messages and voicemails coming through. Success!

I start reading the messages right away. The latest ones from my friends are time-stamped from the day we moved to Blaire. Noticing that their texts were no longer being delivered since my phone was on airplane mode, I bet they stopped sending messages. The rest of the texts are junk, so I ignore them and begin the daunting task of sifting through the barrage of voicemails.

I delete the ones that don't matter, beginning with the least important ones. First are messages from superfans with blocked numbers professing their undying love for me. *Gross.* As much as I value each and every one of my fans, the weirdos don't count. Delete. Next is the bulk of messages from reporters and media producers wanting a statement or an interview. *Leeches.* Delete. Then there are a handful of messages from people I haven't spoken to in forever who are coming out of the woodwork out of gossipy interest. *Ew.* Delete. One by one I swipe left on the messages of no importance. When my inbox is cleared, I'm startled to realize that it's not the only thing that's empty. Where are the calls offering to lend me a hand or a shoulder to cry on? Or the ones calling me to go on an In-N-Out run or shopping spree? Where are the calls asking me if I'm doing okay?

My mind starts to rationalize the radio silence from my friends. I bet they're busy vacationing, or their careers are pulling them in different locations around the world. But when it comes down to it, every version of the truth I come up with leads me to the same conclusion. No matter how busy people are, no matter how far they go, people make an effort if it's important to them. Right?

When the water shuts off in the bathroom, I return my phone to the drawer in the kitchen. By the time Gavin comes out of the bathroom, I'm in bed, pretending to sleep. With my eyes closed, my mind is racing.

As all of my friends have aspirations to be public figures, I understand why they would want to keep their distance from me publicly. But that shouldn't stop them from sending me private messages. Looking back I can see that my friends and I only hung out when there was an event to go to, a premiere to attend, or a party to make an appearance at. I was the gateway to fun and exciting things. Now that the paid events are gone, does that mean my friendships are too? Was Gavin right? Were our friendships so shallow that I could easily be dropped as soon as I wasn't needed?

EXCERPT

Confidence is the key to making any outfit shine, but when you wear it with a suit, no one will doubt your abilities.

The American Dream Achieved: The Story of Dale Ok, Founder of It's Ok!

TRANSCRIPT

60 MINUTES INTERVIEW WITH GLORIA OK

INTERVIEWER: Why don't we start at the beginning? Where did you grow up?

GLORIA: I grew up in postwar Korea. It was an economically poor time. My parents were recruited, along with Dale's parents, to cultivate the land in Anbandegi, in the eastern coastal city of Gangneung. It's about a three-hour drive east of Seoul. I have to say that because everyone thinks all of Korea is Seoul. Kind of like people in Korea think California is LA. [*laughs*] Anyway, when my parents first started farming, the government gave us a bag of rice every day we worked the uncultivated, mountainous land. The inclined terrain made it impossible to use agricultural machinery. We had to use handheld tools like shovels and pickaxes.

INTERVIEWER: Sounds like it was tough.

GLORIA: It was hard, but even harder was finding something to harvest. The landscape seemed impossible to grow anything. We nearly starved. Then we discovered the moisture in the high altitude was the perfect climate to cultivate cabbage. Today Anbandegi is famous for its cabbage, which is known for its sweet and rich flavor.

INTERVIEWER: That's quite a story.

GLORIA: It is. You see, in failing, we learned how to succeed.

<TRANSCRIPT PAUSED>

The following week, Dad and I get ready for our meeting with the farming co-op. I had hoped Gavin would be back from his date with Callie, but three hours later he's still out, which I consider a success, even without knowing the specifics of what went on. I'm still not letting him off the hook, though. The second he comes home, he owes me an update.

The meeting with the co-op is taking place in Jean's backyard, since her garden provides the perfect backdrop for the occasion. So I put on a Dolce & Gabbana chambray shirt and pair it with slimming black leggings. On the way out, I slip on sensible flats. It's classy yet relatable. But also practical. As nice as Jean's farm is, it's still a farm, and it's completely covered in dirt. There are no concrete pavers, no elevated deck, and no slabs of stone leading into the garden. When I'm satisfied with my look, I head out of my room to get Dad.

For the past few days, he's been busy writing his proposal. I offered my help, considering I'm more familiar with this group of people than he is, albeit marginally. Still, he declined. For a foolish second, I thought meeting the co-op together would make us business partners or that he'd make me his protégé. Or, at the very least, that he'd warm up to hearing more of my ideas. But I guess if Dad is going to Dad, even in Blaire, I should be happy he even took me up on my offer to organize this meeting in the first place. Bright side? Since our meeting is at four o'clock, I'm relieved of my sous-chef duties tonight.

"Ready?" Dad says by the doorway, carrying his briefcase. I'm a little surprised to see him dressed in a suit considering the meeting is taking place in a field next to a barn and not in a glass-walled conference room on the thirtysomething-th floor of a high-rise.

"Yep, ready." I smile at him. Guess you can take the man out of the corporate world, but you can't take the corporate world out of the man.

I follow him out to the tractor and climb into the passenger seat. Although he's not dressed the part, Dad seems to be in his element, comfortably wielding the heavy-duty farming machinery. I, on the other hand, am not so comfortable with it and hold on for dear life, closing my eyes and mouth to keep dust, debris, and bugs from entering any of my orifices. Thankfully everything in town is about a five-minute drive, and we're not in the tractor long before it's parked in Jean Bakewell's driveway.

The pathway leading up to the front porch is lined with rows of lavender bushes. "I've never seen so much lavender in one garden." Dad stops to inhale the scent. "And it's more fragrant than a bottle of perfume."

I draw in a deep breath and agree with him. "Just wait until you see the arrangements she makes with it." I motion for Dad to follow me to the front door. When I knock I'm caught off guard to see a woman who's not Jean answer.

"Hi, you must be Elena. Jean is in the back setting up. I'm Callie's mother, Annabel. I've heard so much about you." Annabel holds out her hands expectantly for a hug. Remembering how Mr. Hartford gave Brennan a bear hug, I'm guessing Callie's parents are both huggers. So I have no choice but to lean in. Even though this is supremely awkward for me, she gives me a squeeze that is comforting and sets me instantly at ease.

"Nice to finally meet you," I say when she releases me. "Callie speaks so highly of you."

"Aw, that's sweet."

"This is my dad, Dale Ok." I introduce Dad, who, compared to Annabel's warmth, is frigid. He holds out his hand and shakes hers stiffly.

"I would have put in a little more effort if I had known this was going to be a formal affair," Annabel says, taking notice of Dad's attire.

"Don't be silly," I say, swatting a hand at her. Her jeans and galoshes aren't quite designer, but they're practical and tell us that she takes her job seriously. We're here to sample her farm-to-table products, after all. "You're perfect the way you are." I look expectantly at Dad to chime in, but he doesn't. I can tell by the judgmental expression on his face that he agrees with Annabel.

Even though he should feel overdressed, he thinks she's underdressed. As a leader in the fashion industry, Dad always said that you are what you wear, and what you wear says a lot about you. I'm pretty sure he's thinking that these people are not serious.

"Dad, what was it that you said about your tea the other day?" I ask before an awkward silence lingers.

He seems truly puzzled. "Elena, this is a business meeting. Now is not the time for—"

"You said the honey elevated the flavor. Made it taste ten times the value of the cost." If I'm being technical, I believe he said that the honey made the otherwise unbearable tea drinkable, but I'm paraphrasing. For obvious reasons. Dad may know what sells, but

I know people. And you can't sell a product without selling the idea first. "Isn't that right, Dad?"

Annabel beams. "I'm glad you like it."

"Oh, *you're* the bee farmer." Dad finally catches on. I swear, for a man who built a company from nothing, he can be pretty dense.

Annabel nods proudly.

"I always enjoy honey in my tea, but yours had the most unique flavor I've tasted. What's your secret?" Dad asks.

"I'll tell you." She smiles, leaning in.

Dad waits with bated breath.

"It's Jean's flowers." Just then Jean pops up from behind her. "Oh, here she is. Jean has the most beautiful garden, and her arrangements always sell out at the farmer's markets."

"Flowers?" Dad blinks. "This is honey we're talking about, right?"

"It benefits us both, really," Jean explains. "We need the bees for pollination, and the nectar from the flowers makes the honey so rich in flavor." She stops herself from going on. "Well, don't just listen to us talk about it. Why don't you try it for yourself?" She motions for us to follow her through the side gate. "We've got it all ready for you."

The spread they have set up for us in the backyard is exquisitely charming. And not just for Blaire. For anywhere. Dr. Blaire is placing a chilled bowl of yogurt at the center of a rustic wooden table next to a variety of jars of honey. Along the sides are floral arrangements with bouquets of ranunculi and dahlias from Jean's garden that are elegant yet understated, like the bouquets we took to the farmer's market.

"Hi, Dr. Blaire. It's nice to see you again. I believe you've met my dad before." I point between Dr. Blaire and Dad.

"Yes, it's nice to see you both." Dr. Blaire smiles at me and Dad.

"You as well." Despite the fact that they've met each other before,

Dad shakes her hand. "Thank you again for lending us the tractor."

"Oh, it's no problem. We're always happy to lend a helping hand," Dr. Blaire says graciously. "And we can't wait to hear what you have for us today. Please, make yourselves comfortable."

"This is lovely," Dad says. His smile falters, taking inventory of the place setting. "Will your husbands be joining us?"

The women exchange glances. It's clear from their collective expressions they know what Dad is thinking.

"Not that I know of," Annabel says, placing her hands on her hips.

"I hope that's not a problem." Dr. Blaire folds her arms across her chest.

"Sorry, Charlie. It's just us," Jean says.

Instead of reading the room, Dad thinks it's a good idea to correct Jean. "My name is Dale," he says, putting a hand to his chest.

Dad is one more comment away from offending everyone in the room, including me, so I take it upon myself to spell it out for him. "It's just an expression, Dad," I explain in a kind but serious tone. "Jean and her husband tended the chicken farm together. When he died ten years ago, Jean took over everything, even his beloved garden. She discovered she had a knack for it, and now, instead of one business, she runs two."

"It makes me feel closer to Gerry. He loved his ranunculi," Jean says with a wistful look in her eye.

I smile at Jean kindly before glancing over to Annabel. "The Hartfords harvest honey, but only in the summer, after the flowers bloom and the bees are done pollinating. Which is perfect for Annabel, because she works at the school. During the school year, the beehive is used as an educational resource in the insect unit of the science curriculum. Callie said you're a first-grade teacher?" I look to Annabel for confirmation.

Annabel nods, smiling proudly. "The kids call me Mrs. Hart for short." She points to a heart-shaped enamel pin below the collar of her shirt.

"How sweet," I say, then turn to Dr. Blaire. "Not only do Dr. Blaire's cows provide the dairy for the town, but she is the one who is working with the city council to raise funds for the town beautification initiative," I say.

"It helps to be married to the mayor." Dr. Blaire cocks her head with a cheeky smile.

"You see, Dad? *Their* products are the ones we're sampling today. And if we want to partner with them on some potential collaborations, then we're talking to the right people," I assure him.

"Oh, of course." Dad bows apologetically. "I'm sorry if I've offended you, but in my experience with business, it's usually men who attend the meetings."

"What kind of business did you do?" Jean asks.

"I'm a retail enterpriser," he says proudly. Then, a second later, his lips curve downward. "Or I was. I guess you could say I'm retired now."

"Semiretired," I say. "He's venturing into a different market now. Produce." I gesture to the spread on the table.

Dad's smile returns. Not all the way to what it was before. But close.

"On that note, let's dig in." Annabel motions for us to sit while Jean grabs us a bowl each.

Before I have a chance to pick up a spoon, I feel something reach for me under the table. It's Dad. He squeezes my hand. For a split second, I wonder if he's confused. Because Dad isn't like that, not with me. Then he smiles, letting me know that he's grateful I'm here. I have to blink back the tears that come almost at once. It's the first time my dad has included me in his business affairs, let alone acknowledged me for my accomplishments. The taste of what I've been craving from Dad all these years is overwhelming. But if I want Dad to be proud of me by the end of this meeting, I have to be able to get through it. So I pull myself together.

We start filling our plates, drizzling honey over the yogurt and enjoying it with a side of Jean's hard-boiled eggs. Although it's a simple meal, Dad and I agree that it's surprisingly satisfying.

"When the ingredients are as fresh as these, you don't need to add this or change that to enhance it. It tastes best in its natural form," I say when the table is being cleared.

"You know what the secret is?" Jean asks, and leans in. "It's us." She turns to each side of her and smiles at Dr. Blaire and Annabel.

"It's true," Dr. Blaire says. "These cows are like family. They live a great life, the way I care for them. And research shows that cows that are less stressed produce milk with higher fatty acids and vitamins, which makes it tastier and healthier."

Jean and Annabel nod, agreeing with Dr. Blaire. And I'm surprised to find that Dad does too.

"I think I understand what you mean," he says. "It was like that when I grew up on a farm. Our family was known to produce the sweetest cabbage, and we credited it all to the care we put into cultivating it."

"You worked on a farm?" Dr. Blaire's eyes widen with interest.

"So you know what it's like to live like us," Annabel says.

"It's not quite the same. The conditions are much more agreeable here. You can grow pretty much anything. But back where our farm was, the land was so rocky, and the climate was harsh. We struggled to grow anything. So when we discovered cabbage thrived in those conditions, we treated it like a precious, rare jewel."

"I can see why it tasted so sweet, then." Jean smiles at Dad kindly.

What these women are hearing for the first time is what I'm hearing for the first time too. I want to know more about Dad's past, since he never talks about his life before It's Ok! But I realize now is not the time, so I suppress the urge to ask more questions.

Annabel brings a kettle of water with chamomile tea and honey. She hands us mugs with crocheted cozies on them and explains to Dad that they're handmade by Hal and sold at the farmer's market as well. Dad's cozy has a heart on his, and mine is yellow with a smiley face, like an emoji. I can't believe the guy I assumed was a convict is the same guy who crocheted this. I laugh at myself for having made such an error in judgment. Guess even I'm susceptible to making mistakes when it comes to reading people.

"What's so funny?" Dad asks.

"I'll tell you later," I say when I realize the table is quieting down. One by one the women turn their attention to my dad.

"Although we're happy to just be in your company, we're also excited to hear about an idea of yours." Annabel smiles.

"Especially one that could benefit the town," Dr. Blaire adds.

"Yes, we're all ears," Jean says.

Dad clears his throat. "Thank you for having me—for having *us* today," he corrects himself, looking at me. My smile stretches wide. "My family and I are starting a small farm that I think could contribute to the products of this group of talented entrepreneurs." He goes on to explain that we could grow enough to produce more than what our family needs. He could sell the surplus to the cafe and even contribute to the sales at the farmer's market. Using research on the town's demographics, he has the crop rotations planned out to suit the needs of the people. Before he can pass out the spreadsheet, they stop him.

“This all sounds great, and as our main priority is to provide the food for our town’s needs, adding you to our co-op aligns perfectly with our mission. But . . . potatoes and corn?” Dr. Blaire looks to the others, and they share the same skeptical expression.

“What’s wrong with potatoes and corn?” Dad’s head cocks to the side.

“Nothing. It’s just that we’re looking for something new. As you’ve probably noticed by now, we have all the basics. But people here are craving something different from what we’re used to. And we’re used to potatoes and corn.” Dr. Blaire shakes her head.

“Not sure how they’ll draw in more interest at the farmer’s market either. They’ll hardly stand out in the crowded market,” Annabel points out.

“Annabel’s right,” Jean says. “The farmer’s market only happens once a month. People have to wait for it. Some plan their meals around it. They’re not waiting for things they can easily get at their local grocery stores.”

“Then how about kale and little gem lettuce?” Dad tries again. “Those are very popular where we used to live.”

“Those have also been done to death here. We like healthy foods, but it doesn’t mean we want to eat the same supergreens all year round. We want variety,” Dr. Blaire says. “We have to start thinking beyond our basic needs. We have to think about what else we can provide to increase the quality of life for the people of this town.”

It’s clear by the way Dad is quietly taking in this information that he didn’t prepare a plan B. So I take this opportunity to speak up.

“This might be off topic,” I say, “but something you said reminded me of when I first got here. Not having Wi-Fi and the things I was used to having was a real shock to my system, and I wasn’t exactly happy to be here." The three women, along with my dad, stare at me intently.

"And at the time, all I had were my lavender bath salts. They were a gift from the Hotel George Cinq, which I went to in Pari— Never mind. It's not important. My point is that the bath salts gave me a break from my anxiety, helping me to see that things were not as bad as I perceived them to be. All because of a tiny moment of relaxation." I pause to gauge their reactions before I go on. When I see that I'm still holding their attention, I continue. "And while the convenience store has a lot to offer, as you said earlier, it doesn't have the items that meet people's needs beyond the basics. Care is essential, and that includes self-care. I couldn't find anything that offered the same effects as lavender bath salts, and there was no self-care section to speak of." The three women murmur in agreement.

"I couldn't agree with you more. There is a demand for products we don't carry, but the convenience store simply can't maintain that type of overhead." Dr. Blaire shakes her head solemnly.

"What ideas do you have?" Jean asks.

"I've been getting to know more about all of you, and there's a unique story behind each of your products. Honey has been a way for you to engage with young learners. The nutrient-rich dairy is a product of your love for animals. The garden is a tribute to Gerry. Even the cozies are a way for Hal to cope with the changes in his life. And the care that this town needs is something you have." I turn to Jean. "Everyone knows your lavender is not only the prettiest; it's the most fragrant. You could create a whole brand of products that promote relaxation. Lavender salts, teas, oils. In fact, this could be an opportunity for business synergy. You could partner with Dr. Blaire and make a milk bath."

"I like what I'm hearing," Jean says. Annabel and Dr. Blaire nod, agreeing with her. Their encouragement is fuel for my brain. The wheels begin cranking.

"When I was at the farmer's market, I noticed a parent who couldn't finish her shopping because her toddler was restless. If we had lavender honey ice cream or honeycomb ice cream, parents could shop while their kids got a handcrafted, artisanal treat. We could consider that proactive self-care." They laugh.

When I finish my impromptu presentation, Jean, Dr. Blaire, and Annabel clamor with excitement over my suggestions.

"This town has everything it needs, but it definitely could use a little TLC. And while we're working to improve the outside of it, we should think about how we can use our resources to help the people who make up this town," Dr. Blaire says.

By the time we leave, the three women are talking animatedly with one another. Jean and Dr. Blaire are discussing how to make the lavender milk bath, and Annabel is looking up recipes for honeycomb ice cream. All because of my suggestions.

I'm still in a daze when Dad and I walk down Jean's driveway. As soon as he gets into the tractor and shuts the door, Dad turns to me.

"How'd you do that? How did you know that this is what the town would need?" Dad asks me on our way back home.

"Because I got to know them, Dad," I say. "Sometimes doing isn't enough. You have to listen to people too."

"Today . . . you made me proud," he says with a fondness I've only seen in him when he addresses Gavin.

"Thanks, Dad." The lump in my throat is so big, my voice comes out like a whisper. Today's meeting was a success in more ways than one.

As soon as we get home, Dad opens the door, and we do a double take at the state of the place. It doesn't look—*doesn't smell*—like our house. Unlike the usual grab-and-go station set up for us on the kitchen counter, the table is neatly set with plates and silverware. And the aroma . . . it's interesting and strong in a good way that makes my mouth instantly salivate. Stepping back outside, I check to see if I'm at the right house. Yep, it's unfortunately the same house on the outside. Dad and I stare at each other, perplexed.

"You're back," Gavin says, greeting us from the kitchen with an apron tied around his waist.

"What are you doing standing out on the porch?" Mom says from behind him. "Come in." She motions for us to join them.

Slowly Dad and I reanimate. So this isn't a dream. This is our home. Er, temporary home.

"Sit," Mom urges us when we are inside.

"Did you buy new stuff?" I ask, noticing the plates and silverware have a shine the ones from before didn't.

"I used an old trick with baking soda and apple cider vinegar to buff out the scratches. It's simple, really." Mom waves it off as if it's something she does on a daily basis.

"Wow," I say, genuinely impressed. I didn't know my mom knew how to deep clean. Since we had a staff of maids, I didn't know she knew how to *regular* clean.

"And these lights. They work now." Dad points to the janky fixtures hanging above the dining table that are now fully functioning. I didn't realize how much of a difference lighting could make, but the soft glow on the table instantly brightens the place. "Gavin, I'm so proud of you," Dad starts, but Gavin's quick to cut him off.

"I can't take any of the credit. Mom did that too."

"Mom?" I crane my neck to stare at her.

"We had very poor electrical connections when living on the farm, so I know what to look for. Turns out the wire had gotten disconnected, so I reconnected it." Again Mom downplays her ability.

"Okay, that is seriously cool," I say.

She smiles appreciatively.

Dad seems puzzled. "What about dinner, then? When did you have time to—"

"That's all Gavin." She gestures to him by her side. He smiles nervously.

Despite Mom's very clear explanation, Dad still doesn't seem to understand. So she explains, "Dale, just wait until you try what your son cooked for dinner. I have never seen anything so different and yet taste so familiar at the same time."

"I call it spaghetti-bokki," Gavin says more confidently after Mom's strong endorsement. "It's like ttuk-bokki, but I replaced one starch with another, taking out the rice cakes and exchanging them for spaghetti noodles." He presents a platter with the same cheap lattice design around the edges that all our other plates have. Except it doesn't look like a cheap meal. Far from it. Tiny garnishes of thin slices of green onion sprinkled with parmesan make this meal reminiscent of our former life.

Dad jabs a finger into the saucepan on the stove and puts it to his lips. "This reminds me of the street vendor we used to go to."

"I know. I didn't even teach him how to do it; he just knew what to do," Mom says to Dad, and Gavin's smile is so wide, it's about to rip his face into two.

"Don't take her word for it. Try it," Gavin urges.

Dad and I just came from sampling an array of delectable bites from our meeting, and yet we both find ourselves sitting down, eager to eat.

Mom, Dad, and I begin twirling the pasta onto our forks while Gavin watches us with anticipatory interest. Dad is the first one to take a bite, slurping the longer noodles that aren't neatly wrapped around his fork. Mom and I do the same. Holding his breath, Gavin intensely studies our faces.

"I don't know whether I should be eating this with a fork or chopsticks," Dad says after swallowing. He wipes his lips on a napkin, leaving a dark crimson stain. He shakes his head in disbelief. "The flavor, the texture. Even the color of the sauce takes me back to Korea." He holds up the napkin to show us.

"Right?" Mom leans in excitedly at the shared emotion. "While he was making the sauce, I felt like I was fourteen again, hovering around the ttuk-bokki stand and eating the hot rice cakes slathered in the spicy sauce."

"It's definitely familiar but also has something else," I say, thinking aloud. I've had ttuk-bokki before, but I'm not as familiar with it as my parents are. I'm more familiar with the American aspects of it. Like the al dente noodles and garnishes that aren't normally paired together but make unique and surprisingly good flavor combinations. "It also kind of reminds me of the pasta at Wolfgang's."

"Exactly. It's classy comfort," Gavin says. "It's my version of Roy Choi's 'food that isn't fancy.'"

"That is seriously brilliant," I say, staring at him as if for the first time. This version of Gavin differs from the boring, predictable person I thought I knew. He's creative and innovative when he's passionate about something.

"Thanks. That means a lot," he says. His sincerity catches me off guard, making me supremely awkward.

"Oh, I— You're welcome," I say clumsily before twirling my fork aimlessly on my plate. I didn't realize my support meant so much to him.

Between bites, Mom and Dad take turns saying things like "Unbelievable" and "How remarkable" and other comments about how uncanny it is that Gavin was able to so accurately capture in a dish a memory that only existed in their minds.

Eating dinner together is unusual, but the conversations that accompany it are even more out of the ordinary for us. "This is nice," I say.

"I agree. We haven't had a family dinner like this in . . ." Dad drifts off.

"It's long overdue," Mom says, finishing his thought. A reflective lull takes over our table. I can tell by the thoughtful expressions on everyone's faces that we're enjoying this rare family dinner together.

"In Korea," Mom says, breaking the silence, "the word for *family* is *shik-gu*, which translates to *mouth to feed*, because we share our food with people who are the closest to us. It means food is essential, but so is family." She looks around the table before staring directly at Dad. His features soften, and for the first time in a while, Mom and Dad exchange a glance that conveys more hope than despair.

After we've finish eating, in a completely unprecedented turn of events, Dad offers to wash the dishes. And I help.

"I didn't know you knew how to wash dishes," I say semi-jokingly. Actually, come to think of it, I don't know how to wash dishes either. I'm just making it up as I go along. Soap, sponge, water. I mean, it's pretty self-explanatory, right?

"It's true," Dad says. "Men aren't supposed to wash dishes."

My skin prickles. "Excuse me?" I lean back to stare Dad in the eye.

"I mean, that's what I was taught growing up," he goes on to explain. "Kind of like how your mother and the other women in our village weren't supposed to deal with the merchants when selling our produce to the markets. Everyone had a job on the farm, which is how we managed the endless work."

As disappointed as I've been with Dad for his lack of interest in me, it occurs to me that I'm no better. I haven't asked him about himself since, well, ever.

"You never told me you grew up on a farm."

He nods, then goes back to washing the plate in his hand. I deflate, thinking he'll revert to engaging only in conversations that are limited to a need-to-know basis.

"Men were responsible for financially supporting their families, so we left the housework to the women," he continues, surprising me. "It's why I wasn't expecting to meet with those women today. Because I'm used to dealing with men when it comes to business and farming. But if I didn't change my perspective, I would have missed out on an opportunity with the co-op. And it's making me curious to try other things I'm not used to." He hands me a dish to dry after washing and rinsing it.

"Maybe you're better in boardrooms than in kitchens." I point at the food stains on the dish he just handed me.

He grimaces. "It's my first day on the job. Cut me some slack?"

"Okay." I laugh. "How about I wash the dishes and you rinse?"

"Deal." He smiles.

Mom hears us laughing and comes over to us. "I take it the meeting went well."

I glance over at Dad, who meets my eyes with a smile. "It did," he says. "It went really well. Elena was right to introduce me to this group of women."

My smile stretches wider. I'm still not used to hearing the unfamiliar words of praise from him. I hope we'll be able to join the co-op soon, since it'll give me many more opportunities to show Dad what I'm capable of. Most surprising of all is my excitement over my involvement in farming. I mean, who am I? Guess it really means I can turn any bad situation into a good one. And it feels good to finally be included in the family's business.

When we're done with the dishes, we dry our hands, and Dad joins Mom in their room while I go to mine, where Gavin is reading in bed. I'm about to tell him about my day when I suddenly remember his.

"So? How'd it go?" I singsong as soon as the door closes behind me.

"Must I?" He drops his head back dramatically.

"Yes, you must. It's my payment for playing matchmaker." I poke him in the chest. "Now spill."

"Argh." Gavin makes a face, pretending to be annoyed. "Fine," he says, putting his book away. He rolls over onto his side and glances at me casually. "It was . . . nice" is all he says.

"Are you serious?" I throw my pillow at him. "Try harder. Did my plan work?"

"Surprisingly it did," he says, sitting up and tossing my pillow back to me.

I catch the pillow and let out a squeal. "I knew it would! Tell me more." I sit on the edge of my bed, leaning toward him.

"After I got to the farm, she started showing me the process of extracting honey. I listened while she explained it, showing me the step-by-step. First she removed the honeycomb frames from the hive. After she scraped off the wax caps, she spun the honeycomb in a centrifuge to separate the honey. At the end I got to help her strain the wax bits out of the honey to get the final product. We had to squeeze it manually through a cheesecloth together. It was so cool."

"I bet it was," I say suggestively. "I'm envisioning the pottery scene in *Ghost* when Demi Moore and Patrick Swayze's hands lock while shaping clay on the potter's wheel together."

His brow quirks. "Never saw it."

"You don't have to watch the movie to know the iconic scene. It did the impossible by making pottery sexy."

"I think I get where you're going with this." He smiles bashfully. "There was a moment when we were straining the honey. My hands weren't securely fastened around the cheesecloth, so when I squeezed it, honey oozed out of the top. Callie had to help me by clamping her hands on mine. Then some of it accidentally got on my lip, and she tried to wipe it off, but by then our hands were too sticky, so she suggested another way to get the honey off my lips. By using her—"

"Ew, ew, ew." I plug my ears. "I get it; you don't have to tell me *everything*."

He laughs, rolling his eyes. "Anyway, we had a great time. I even got to show her how to make whipped honey to add to coffee, teas, and desserts. Having an extensive repertoire of recipes involving honey, she was surprised to learn a new one."

"Sounds like you had an amazing time."

"Yeah." He smiles drunkenly, thinking back on it. "I didn't have to remind myself to think of follow-up questions. Everything Callie says is so interesting. The questions came naturally. Did you know she lives in the house she was born in?"

"She's lived here her whole life?"

"I know. She told me about what it was like to grow up without Wi-Fi. Since it wasn't something she grew up with, she doesn't miss it. Which is interesting when you think about it. She's got such a different perspective on life than anyone I've ever met." The way his face lights up tells me this could develop into something more than *like*. He's never talked about any girl like this.

Suddenly I'm thinking of Sonya. "Did you tell her about your past?" I ask.

His expression changes. "Not entirely. I mean, I didn't lie about how I felt trapped going down the path Mom and Dad expected me to, and I told her I wanted to go to culinary school. . . ."

"I think you should tell her the truth," I say, startling Gavin. I can understand why he didn't tell Callie all the details. But in order for this relationship to make it—and I hope it does—I feel like it can't start with lies. "You didn't do anything you should be ashamed of. The company filing for bankruptcy is out of your hands, and getting expelled from USC speaks more to your abundance of ambition rather than a lack of it. If she's as cool as you say she is and as accepting as I know she is, I'm sure she won't think badly of you because of it," I say.

"I guess," he says with less certainty. "Didn't think you'd want anyone here to know the truth about our past." He glances at me sideways.

"I know. But it sounds like you like her, Gavin. Like, really, *really* like her. And I'm happy for you, which is why you can't mess this up." I see now that this is what Gavin needs. In order to change, he has to break the patterns of his past. "You said so yourself, your time in Blaire is your chance to be the person you've always wanted to be. But that can't happen if you're not honest with her. Because in the end you're still pretending to be someone you're not for the sake of their opinion."

What I say must resonate with him, because he nods, agreeing with me. "I hear you. And you're right," he says. "I'll tell her. When the time is right."

I suppress the urge to make him tell her now before it gets more serious. The more time that passes, the more personal it'll feel to Callie when she learns the details of Gavin's past.

"What about you?" he asks, startling me.

"What about me?"

"Would you be okay with Callie knowing who you are?"

It seems belated, but it didn't occur to me until now that Callie is *our* friend. And the advice I gave him is the advice I should have given myself.

"I wouldn't want her to know who I am," I say, surprising myself. Not because I'm ashamed about our family's scandal or because I don't trust Callie not to leak our whereabouts to the media. But the version of Elena that Callie knows is the best version of myself I've ever been. And part of me wants to hold on to that for a little while longer.

"So you get it, right?" Gavin asks. "How we reveal the truth about ourselves to Callie—and anyone here, for that matter—has to be delivered delicately."

"You're right," I admit.

"We'll tell her when the time is right. Together," Gavin says, and I nod, agreeing with him.

Even though the crops are still TBD, that doesn't stop Dad from prepping the field for harvest with Gavin the next day. Which leaves me home alone with Mom. As soon as I get out of bed, Mom is chiding me for the state of the room and the laundry and everything else. When I finish cleaning my side of the room and start a load of laundry, I reward myself by flopping onto my bed and staring up at the ceiling. Still, Mom is unrelenting. Despite my success in making progress with Dad, I'm not making much progress with Mom.

"Come, learn how to make kimchi." Mom motions for me to join her with a *butcher knife* in her hand.

Seeing as I don't have a choice in the matter, I drag my feet to the kitchen. Along with her coveted giant bowl and a bunch of large Napa cabbages, there are ingredients spread out on the counter. Most of them are label-less, and the others have Korean writing on them.

"The first thing you have to do is cut the cabbage into quarters, keeping the core intact so it doesn't fall apart." The level of confidence she has when spearing her knife into the heart of a cabbage is frightening. But also kind of badass. "Next we have to season the cabbage. The salt will not only flavor the leaves but also soften and preserve them." After she slips on rubber gloves that go up to her elbows, she begins rubbing coarse salt onto the cabbage, careful to get in between each leaf. As she finishes the quartered cabbage, she submerges it in a bucket of water. "Once we salt all the cabbages, we leave them in the water for six hours."

"Six hours?" I shriek incredulously.

"You have somewhere you need to be?" She stares down her nose at me, and I clamp my mouth shut. As if it couldn't get any worse, she adds, "Don't just stand there and watch. Put the extra pair of gloves on and do what I'm doing."

I sigh, glancing over at the ugly-as-sin pink rubber gloves.

"Unless you want your hands to prematurely age and be shriveled into prunes by the salt, then be my guest. Use your bare hands."

That gets me to slip the gloves on and begin slathering the salt onto the leaves like she's doing. We lapse into silence, and the monotony of the task makes my mind wander. The coarse salt against the cabbage reminds me of body scrubs I used to get that would leave my skin feeling like a baby seal. Suddenly I'm deeply pining for my old life. And I'm not talking about spa treatments, tranquil music, and plush bathrobes. Although I wouldn't turn those things down either. But before Blaire, our lives kept us busy in a way that didn't leave us any time for one another. At least then I could blame the emotional distance between us on the physical one.

In some ways Mom understands me. She knows how much my appeareance matters to me. Once I was photographed checking the mail in my pajamas, and a tabloid printed it with the headline IS ELENA OK O.K.? The article was as misguided as its impossible expectations of women. My way of dealing with an industry that scrutinizes women as harshly as the media does is by spending an ungodly amount of time on looking my best. Mom knows how to use what I care about (my appearance) to get me to do something she cares about (learning how to make kimchi). But beyond the superficial, she doesn't know me, and I don't know her. Now that we are here, we have the opportunity to get to know each other. Be closer. Have a relationship. And *this* is how she chooses to spend quality time?

"Remind me again why this is important?" I ask.

"Kimchi is a staple in Korea. We eat it with everything."

"I mean why do you think that I specifically need to learn how to make it?"

"Because," she says, wiping her brow with the back of her glove, "I've let other people do things for you for too long."

I let out a loud sigh. *This again?*

"It's time for you to learn how to take care of yourself."

That gets me to snap. Because I've been taking care of myself for a while now. Longer than she knows.

"You're right, Mom." My harsh tone makes her flinch. "By hiring people to do everything for me, you did me a disservice. But teaching me how to cook and make kimchi is not going to make up for that." My words seem to knock the wind out of her. But instead of slowing down, I keep going. I need to tell her how I feel before I lose momentum.

"After the *Vogue* article came out, I was humiliated. With the magazine's circulation of 1.2 million copies a year, when I say everyone was laughing at me, it's not an exaggeration by any means. And that includes Dad, Gavin . . . and you." I look her in the eye. "I was fourteen, Mom. A kid. All the hired help in the world couldn't give me what I needed most: my family."

"Elena, I had no idea," she says, genuinely shocked. "You seemed to enjoy the way the article portrayed you."

"What choice did I have?" My voice grows defensively louder. "I had to find my way through it somehow. So I turned *What's that?*

into my catchphrase. I figured I couldn't be the joke if I was in on it. Right?"

For the first time, she doesn't disengage at the mention of my catchphrase. Instead her face falls.

"But I realize now that I was only convincing myself that the catchphrase was what I needed. Because I didn't want Carolina to take me to this gala or Kiki to book me for that party. Or for someone to buy me a new dress or a bag to make me forget I was sad. I needed someone to tell me it was going to be okay and wipe my tears away. I needed the unconditional support from my family. I needed you, Mom." My voice cracks as the tears well up in my eyes.

Mom's eyes are watery too. "I'm sorry for not being there for you. I did what I thought was best. Even now I'm trying to do what I think is best before it's too late." She pauses. "Elena-yah," she says, trembling.

I give her a curious look. "You haven't called me that since I was little."

Even she's taken aback. She blinks, releasing the tears from her eyes. With the kimchi gloves on, she wipes her cheeks with her shoulder. I do the same when my tears trickle down my cheeks. Like how the salt works to break down the toughness in the leaves of the Napa cabbage, our tears seem to break down the barrier between us. It relieves the heaviness from before, making it possible for the gap to close between us.

"Being here is reminding me of when I grew up on the farm," Mom says with a lingering smile. "Every fall, the women of our village would get together for kimjang. It's when we would make enough kimchi to survive the winters."

"Survive?" I sniff. "Was it that bad on the farm?" For some reason I imagined my parents' farming experience to have been similar to what it's been like here. And I definitely didn't think hardship for them meant life-or-death.

"On the farm, losing a harvest to a harsh winter meant starving, and we relied on kimchi to survive, since it can last up to nine months. In a way kimjang symbolizes our resilience. It shows our determination to survive." She blinks back to the present and turns to me. "I didn't realize until now that losing everything and moving to Blaire sent me into survival mode. I'm sorry for putting my trauma on you."

"Oh, Mom," I say, overwhelmed with guilt. "I'm sorry too. I shouldn't have lashed out at you. I was frustrated because I thought you didn't see the value in me. That I was always falling short of your standards. But now I know I was wrong. It wasn't about me." My head dips sheepishly. I should know by now that not everything is about me.

"But this *is* about you." She motions to the cabbage. "Kimjang is more than just making kimchi. It's also a time for mothers to teach their daughters for the first time. Every region has its own unique way of making kimchi, and my mom taught me to make kimchi with fresh oysters since our village was close to the ocean. While we preserve the cabbage, we preserve our fond memories. Every time I make kimchi, I think of my mother, and I hope one day you'll think of me." She peers over at me, her eyes filled with insecurity. "You think that's possible?"

I nod, unable to speak. Mom wanting to share this time-honored tradition with me makes me overcome with emotion. All I ever wanted was to be included in the family.

While we wait for the salted cabbage to soak in the water, she shows me how to make the paste that flavors the kimchi. Some of the ingredients are obvious, like red pepper flakes, ginger, and garlic. And some are a surprise to me, like pears, rice flour, and the oysters she mentioned earlier. Making kimchi is actually kind of fun, and surprisingly it's the one thing I don't suck at making in the kitchen. It isn't long before I begin to think of someone else who would appreciate this moment more than me.

"Is it only the women who participate in kimjang?" I ask.

She gives me a knowing look. "Being on a farm was hard, especially for the women. Not only did we labor in the fields alongside the men, but we also had to take care of all the domestic duties. Cooking, cleaning, child-rearing. Men were the only ones who were given recognition, even though they had one job and women had many." Her face hardens as she describes it. Then she turns to me and softens. "Kimjang was intended for mothers and daughters to bond. Growing up I thought it was special. I can see now that kimjang should be for everyone."

I nod, agreeing with her.

Mom's childhood sounds so different from mine. I can't begin to imagine it. "What was it like in Anbandegi?"

She starts to explain, then stops herself. "Do you really want to know? Shouldn't we be focusing on you? I may not have been there for you before, but I want to be there for you now."

"I appreciate that, Mom. But this is important too." There's been a lot we missed out on in each other's lives. And that goes both ways. It's time we started getting to know each other. So I ask her more questions about what it was like on the farm. She tells me about how even though the farm was successful, it was always susceptible to failure due to weather, the economy, and other things outside of their control. The instability growing up made her and my dad want to move to the United States and make a different path for themselves.

At the mention of Dad, it occurs to me that they had the same upbringing. I understand better his obsessive devotion to work. Knowing he had to overcome so many hurdles, that he had to work harder to prove himself. It helps to let go of the resentment I built up, thinking he preferred work over me. Still, something about it confuses me.

"Why doesn't Dad ever talk about his time on the farm?" I ask. "You'd think he'd be proud of his accomplishments, coming from such humble roots." Even in his autobiography, the story of his life, he doesn't mention it.

She sighs as if she shares my confusion. "Your father has complicated feelings about his background. Farmers were among the lowest class in Korea. When he came to America to start his own business, he felt that coming from such a low-status family hindered his credibility."

"But this is America. There's no class system here. At least not one that prevents people from moving up in society."

"I know. And it's not like that anymore in Korea either. At least that's what I've heard. But it's not easy for him to forget about the past that made him who he is. Even I know that. It's why we bought this place." She sighs nostalgically. "It was hard, but after we got married and came to this country, we looked back on so many fond memories. Growing our own food was so rewarding, but we could never enjoy it since our livelihoods depended on it. Once we opened our first shop in the Fashion District and had enough money to live well, we planned on retiring here. We wanted to live a quiet life on a farm without the stress of being dependent on it." She smiles at the memory. Then it quickly turns into a frown. "At least that *was* the plan." She sighs. A flash of hurt appears for the briefest second.

"That was our mistake," she says, coming to. "We thought as long as we had enough money, we'd never experience loss like we did on the farm." She inches closer to me. "Sorry for being so hard on you. I was only trying to teach you to be self-reliant before it's too late. Because if you're not careful, you might find yourself dependent on a man."

It occurs to me that Mom's warning is a reflection of her feelings about the position she finds herself in now. Dad didn't consider Mom when he pivoted to joining the co-op, which has changed their future. Not because Dad was uncaring or because Mom didn't have a voice, but because it's what they were taught about marital expectations when they got married. And maybe it made sense then, but it doesn't make sense to me.

"You said it's not too late for me to learn how to be more self-reliant," I say, the earlier edge from my tone gone. "Maybe it's not too late for you too."

Her head jerks back, and for a second it looks like she's going to challenge me. Slowly she closes her mouth and doesn't say anything.

On Monday the following week, I'm woken up by a call from Mr. Ahn. Through the door I can hear Dad's side of the conversation. From what I gather, the items for the public auction have been sorted through, and the rest of our belongings have been placed in a storage unit, waiting to be claimed by us.

"We have to leave now if we want to get to LA and back before it gets late," Mom announces, standing at the door of our room.

"We have to go too?" I ask. Not that I don't want to go to LA, but to go collect our old things from a public storage unit like we've been evicted from the city dulls the appeal.

"Can't we just leave it there until we get back? It'll be, what? Like a month or two?" Gavin asks groggily. He was up late again last night, talking to Callie. He always tries to be discreet, taking the phone under the covers, which muffles his words but doesn't dampen the giggling. *So* much giggling.

Dad frowns. "Until I start working my new role at the company, we have to economize. Paying for the storage unit seems unnecessary since we have the time to take care of it now."

"And we only packed for two weeks. We should move the rest of our belongings—or what's left of them—here," Mom adds.

"How are you going to bring it all back on the tractor?" Gavin asks.

More importantly . . . "How are we going to all fit in the tractor?" I ask.

"I was thinking we could squeeze into the tractor until Bakersfield. From there, we could rent a car to go to LA and back," Dad says.

Surprisingly, sharing a seat with Gavin isn't the worst part of Dad's proposal. "You want the four of us to ride the two-person tractor to Bakersfield? Why don't we just wear a sign that says: We're poor," I deadpan. "Besides, that seems like a lot of effort to bring our things back. I'm sure someone can lend you a vehicle. One that has doors and windows." I sit up when I remember something. "Jean has an old truck she uses to deliver flower arrangements. I'm sure she'd lend it to you."

"That could work." Dad considers it. "I remember seeing it. It's a four-seater, so it can fit us comfortably."

"But I have plans to go to the town council meeting with Callie. They're going to discuss what they can do with the beautification funds they've earned so far. I can't miss it." I'm surprised to hear myself say those words and actually mean them.

"And what about the soil?" Gavin says. "If we're going to plant soon, it needs to be turned."

I crane my neck at him. He's starting to sound like a real farmer.

Mom and Dad exchange wary glances with each other, wondering if we can be trusted while they're gone for the day.

"Fine," Dad says.

"But make sure you get along," Mom warns.

"We will," Gavin and I promise at the same time.

After getting ready I leave by nine to meet Callie while Gavin stays behind to work on the field. At first when Callie told me to meet her at the town hall, I couldn't believe that there were parts of Blaire I still didn't know about. It's been weeks since we arrived here. I'm sure I've walked the entire length of Blaire and back at least a hundred times by now. Then, when she told me where the town hall was located, I realized I passed by it all the time. It's wedged between the convenience store and the observatory in a one-story stand-alone building. The unremarkable features and the building's bland color make it blend into the backdrop of the tall grass, which is why I've never noticed it before. I would have missed it today, too, if it weren't for the steady stream of people headed in that direction.

At the foot of the building, Callie spots me and makes her way over.

"Hey, you made it." She smiles brightly.

"And apparently so did everyone else," I say, looking around.

"If there's one good thing about living in Blaire, it's that we can count on one another . . . to not have plans." Callie and I laugh. "Let's go up front to get a good seat."

While we walk to the front row, we spot Jean, Dr. Blaire, and both of Callie's parents. We wave to them, and they wave back. Callie's mom mouths, *You got this*, while her dad pounds his chest with his hand and points at her confidently.

"Wow, your parents are super supportive," I say with a hint of envy.

"Yeah, they're the best." She smiles back at them, then finds a seat in the front row. "Make sure to save a seat for Supernova." She points to the empty seat on the other side of me. Brennan appears as she says this.

"Hey, this seat taken?"

"It is now," I say, peering up at Brennan through my lashes.

"Thanks," he says, and waves to Callie. She waves back.

"I didn't know you'd be here," I say in a not-unwelcoming way.

"Wouldn't miss it. You know me. If there's a way I can help, I'm there." Brennan's smile widens. "I'm glad to see you here, lending a hand," he says, genuinely pleased.

"Me too," I say, matching his sincerity. I may have faked it the first time we met, but I'm starting to realize that charity, the kind I have to roll up my sleeves for, is actually growing on me. When he's not looking, I wipe my mouth for drool, because *damn*. I'd forgotten how good-looking he is. His smile that lights up his whole face. The cute dimples on his cheeks. And were his eyes always this blue? The light reflects off them, creating literal twinkles in his eyes. Now that I've helped Gavin in the relationship department, maybe I can focus on myself.

Mayor Beecham calls the meeting to order and introduces the members of the council, who present today's agenda. When it's time to discuss how to allocate the beautification funds, the floor is open to suggestions on what should be prioritized. Callie gets up first and suggests making improvements on the outside of the convenience store, arguing that, since it's the sole provider of our most basic needs, repairing it will improve much more than the store. I couldn't agree more. I'd say a facelift on the town's most frequented place of business is long overdue. I steal quick glances over at Brennan, hoping to catch his eye, but his stare never wavers. He's mesmerized by Callie. And I can't tell if his expression is one of particular interest or general awe. Because Callie's managed to captivate everyone with her proposal.

Her suggestion isn't just the best one of the day; it's the only one. So the council votes unanimously to allocate half of the beautification funds to restore the facade of the convenience store. In support of her proposal, about twenty volunteers, including me and Brennan, offer to help with the labor. With that many volunteers, it won't only cut down the cost; it'll ensure the job will be completed in a timely manner.

After the motion is passed, the meeting comes to a close. On their way out, a bunch of people come up to congratulate Callie: Mayor Beecham and his wife, Callie's parents, and Jean, to name a few.

"That was amazing, Callie," I say once I have the chance.

"You should seriously consider a career in politics. You won by a landslide," Brennan says.

"It helps to not have any competition." Callie laughs, and Brennan and I laugh with her.

With the volunteers gathered around, we decide to head to the convenience store to assess the damage. That way we can get a head start on purchasing the materials we need to start working as early as next Monday. At the convenience store, we give Hal the news that our petition to fix up the outside of the store was approved, which he's happy about. At least I think he is. I may no longer be wary of Hal, but I still can't tell his happy face from his . . . not-happy face.

From the outside, Callie surveys the building and jots down which items need to be replaced. The roof is the most obvious concern. "Repair is not an option, so we'll need a new roof," Callie mutters, scribbling on her pad. Next are the wood panels on the sides. The ones that aren't as damaged can be patched up, but there are quite a few areas that are rotting or splintered. They'll need to be replaced before painting the entire exterior. After writing it all down, she does a quick calculation and frowns.

"What's wrong?" I ask.

"With the amount of materials and tools we'll need for the roof and siding, we're already at budget. That doesn't include the cost of paint."

"I've got some paint." Hal's gruff voice startles us. We crane our necks to face him.

"You do?" Callie lights up with hope.

He nods. Then, without further explanation, he disappears behind the store to an outside shed. After unlocking it, he goes in, then comes back a few minutes later with paint cans in hand. To my dismay, the paint we're presented with gives us little to work with.

"Brown again?" The words escape me before I have a chance to run them through my filter.

The group of volunteers turn their attention to me.

"It's the same color it's always been," Hal says by way of explanation.

"That's my point. I know the structural stuff is important. But how will anyone know the building's updated if it looks the same on the outside? If we're going to improve the place, we should, you know, *improve the place.*"

"But that's going to cost money. Should we ask the town council to use the rest of the funds for paint?" Callie suggests uncertainly.

I'm as conflicted as Callie is. Completely depleting the funds for one project when many other places are in just as dire need as the convenience store makes overall progress seem hopeless.

"I have all kinds of paint in the back," Hal offers.

"What colors?" I raise a skeptical brow.

Hal grunts. "What color are you thinking?"

I look up thoughtfully. "As a central fixture of the town, the convenience store is the heartbeat of Blaire," I start, thinking aloud. "The color, then, would set the tone for the town. It should be inviting, warm, and charming."

"What about lavender or honey, since they're some of the main products our town is known for?" someone suggests.

"I like the idea," I say, tapping a finger to my lip. "But while pastels like yellow and lavender have a cheerful vibe, they lack the sophistication of the products that are sold in the store."

"What about blue, like the eggs from Jean's chickens?" Brennan suggests. "They're unique and something the town is known for."

"That's perfect." My eyes meet Brennan's, and for the briefest second, I swear I feel the energy shift between us. Maybe not a spark, but a small electric crackle. "Not only does it have a deep undertone that gives the light blue a hint of sophistication," I continue, forcing myself to go on, "but it's cheerful and inviting, like this town." I glance over to Hal. "Do we have anything in a hue similar to chambray or Santorini?

Hal blinks at me. A second later he disappears back into the shed and then returns with two different buckets of paint. "We have blue and bluer," he says, placing the two buckets at my feet. His description leaves much to be desired, so I don't celebrate right away. When I pry the lids off, one reveals a light shade of robin's-egg blue, and the other is a deep navy.

Callie and Brennan exchange an approving glance.

"I can't decide between the two," Brennan says. "Would it be possible to use both?"

"The dark blue could be the main color, and the light one could be used for accents. What do you think, Elena?" Callie smiles at me hopefully.

They're right. The two colors complement each other nicely. More to the point, as the original brown is our other choice, it's our only viable option. "I could work with that," I say. It might not be Chip-and-Joanna-approved, but it's close enough.

Once that's settled, we set a start date for Monday the following week. Then Hal goes back into the store, and we leave to go home. Brennan, Callie, and I head down the dirt path.

"What's wrong?" I ask Callie when I notice her gnawing on her lip. After the progress we made today, I'd have thought she'd be on cloud nine.

"I'm just not sure it's enough." She sighs.

"Are you kidding?" I say. "Didn't you see the list of people who signed up to help?"

"We have enough people to do the work. It's the funds that are slower to come by. So far I'm the only one who can go to the farmer's market to raise money. I wonder what will happen with the beautification initiative if I go out of state for college." Concern lines appear across her forehead.

"Worry about that when the time comes. Like you said, you don't know where you'll end up," I say, trying to make her feel better. "Besides, once you graduate, I have no doubt you'll move on to bigger and better things." Callie is a natural altruist. I'm sure she'll find another project no matter where she is.

Callie gives me a funny look. "Once I graduate, Blaire will still be my home."

It's not the response I expected. My plan after graduation was always to leave and never look back. "So you really like living here?"

Again, she stares at me curiously. "Well, yeah. I grew up here."

There's a slight defensiveness in her tone that makes me realize I may have offended her, which is the last thing I want to do. "I didn't mean anything by it. I'm not gonna lie, when I first got to Blaire, not having my phone was the hardest adjustment for me. But it's more than that. Now that I've gotten to know what it's like here, I can see that it takes effort to live here. The farming co-op, fundraising, the manual labor." I motion to the convenience store behind us. "All this work to keep up the town is making me wonder if it's worth it."

Callie surveys the area around her with an expression that tells me she's not seeing what I see. Cracked pavement, decrepit buildings, and messy, overgrown fields of tall grass and weeds.

"Just because it's hard doesn't mean it's not worth the work. In fact, I would say it's all the more reason to keep at it," she says. "With fewer people in town, the need here is greater than anywhere else. And like I said, Blaire will always be my home, whether I end up staying or moving elsewhere."

I've never met anyone like Callie. With my friends, our conversations were always centered on ways to bolster ourselves, not others. For example, when Brynn offered to set up a meeting for me with Kiki, she knew it would benefit her if my popularity rose, just like I knew Willow's exposure would help boost my popularity, since I helped her get her starring role on a new sitcom. Until now, it never crossed my mind that I could find fulfillment in doing something for others without expecting anything in return.

Of course I know that charitable acts are an important part of being a well-rounded person and are inherently good. Back in LA, my family always donated to various causes and made it a point to volunteer when we could, because that was what was expected of prominent families like ours. But what Callie is describing goes beyond the occasional service act. She's not volunteering her time because she has to or because of the promise of something in return. She's not even doing it because she feels obligated to. She's doing it because she wants to.

It's clear that Callie and I have had a different upbringings. So I shouldn't be surprised that her response to the town's needs is different from mine.

"Is that why you're so invested in improving the town?" I ask, turning my attention to Brennan. "Because you know your time is limited here?"

"It was at first. But like Callie said, Blaire is such a small community. Even in the observatory, I didn't expect to be as involved. As an intern, I thought I'd be getting coffees or taking lunch orders. But because there aren't many who work here, everyone pitches in. So far, it's been an incredible experience. With any luck, I'll be able to get a job here one day."

"You want to end up working here?" I raise a brow up at him. "In Blaire?" I add for clarification. I understand Callie's reasons for wanting to stay. She's grown up with this lifestyle. And it's one thing to experience what it's like to live here. But Brennan is from a big city like me. Being in Blaire has got to be as much of an alternate universe for him.

"That's the hope," he says without a hint of irony. "Believe it or not, there aren't that many job opportunities for planetary scientists, and the field is highly competitive. I can only hope to one day work at the Blaire Observatory. It's why I'm so invested in the town's beautification initiative. In a way, I feel like this is my home, and seeing the impact of my work is something I can't put a price on."

"Right?" Callie says, matching his sentimental expression. "It's like that with farming too. There's nothing like seeing the actual fruits of your labor. I think it's a primal urge to provide for not only yourself but those around you."

"Exactly," Brennan says. And there it is again. The look of hopeless admiration plastered on his face, like he's completely and entirely enamored by her. Which, I guess, makes sense. A small town, similar interests, and a finite amount of time together? It's totally giving summer rom-com. Except I don't see this one ending in a happily-ever-after, not if Callie is giggling half as much as

Gavin is on the other end of his conversations with her. Still, it's surprising to feel the sting. Not because of the rejection. Okay, fine, maybe a little of it is. But now that I've gotten to know Brennan better, I see that Gavin is right. Brennan is the type looking for a long-term girlfriend. Which makes me wonder: If Brennan isn't interested in me, is Gavin right? That I'm not girlfriend material? And if he is, does it mean I'm not girlfriend material now or ever?

By the time I get home, it's almost five. Thank God that Gavin is in the kitchen making dinner. We worked through lunch, and now I'm starving.

"How was it?" he asks, whisking a bowl of something.

"It was great," I say, closing the front door behind me. "And long. Now I'm exhausted and hungry." I flop dramatically onto a kitchen chair and sigh. "What have you been up to?"

"I've been experimenting with a new recipe." His face lights up with an expression not much different from when he talks about Callie. "It didn't end up taking long, so dinner should be ready soon," he says.

Even though Mom's not here, I can hear her voice nagging me, so instead of standing by idly like I want to do, I decide to help Gavin in the kitchen. I scan the counter for something to do. There's a carton of eggs, soy sauce, sugar, and onions. I can't tell what he's making from the random assortment of ingredients on the counter, so I pick up a head of garlic and begin peeling it. A minute later he stops me.

"Please don't," he says. "No offense, but you're really not good at this stuff."

"I'm okay with that." I shrug. "I mean, no one's good at *everything*," I tease. "What're you making anyway?"

"It's a surprise," he says.

I consider forcing it out of him, but seeing how much he's enjoying being in his element, I decide against it. Instead I sit back down at the kitchen table and finish telling him about the meeting with the town council. Not too long after, Mom and Dad come home with a trunk and two suitcases in tow. I help them unload them from Jean's truck. Mom and I take a suitcase each, and Dad brings in the box.

"That's everything?" Gavin asks once we're inside the house.

Dad shakes his head. "We couldn't bring everything back, so we had to decide what to keep."

"It was easier to do than we thought. So many of our items are either out-of-date or not practical," Mom continues. "Ball gowns and tuxedos."

"Tennis rackets and golf clubs," Dad adds.

"We kept the items that still held either monetary or sentimental value, and we donated the rest. This is what was left." Although it makes sense, it's sad to see the remnants of our old lives amount to so little.

"What are you making?" Mom asks Gavin in the kitchen.

"Something I've been experimenting with." He tries to shield her from seeing it. Though I'm guessing she'll figure it out—if I could tell just from the smell, Mom definitely can. The aroma of Korean barbecue is something we're very familiar with. Still, Mom respects his wishes, and instead she helps Dad unpack the items in the living room. Seeing as I've been banished from the kitchen, too, I join them.

As I begin going through the suitcases, I'm reminded of items I had forgotten about. Rhinestone-studded bags, fur-lined wraps, crocodile leather belts—things that would make me stick out here in all the wrong ways.

It's then that I notice how much my style has changed in the short time I've been here. I still care about my looks, but in a more subdued, practical way. I've set aside my pigmented matte lipsticks and sleek ponytails for soft lip tints and beachy waves. I replaced my patent leather stilettos and lace bodysuits with sensible slides and fitted T-shirts. And I've completely abandoned my bracelets and belts since they get in the way when I'm doing chores around the house. What am I supposed to do with all these things? I glance over at Mom and Dad, who haven't made much more progress than I have. Their things have been sorted into piles like mine. When Gavin announces dinner is ready, we decide to leave our stuff scattered across the living room and finish organizing after we eat.

At the kitchen table, Gavin makes a show of presenting to us his latest creation. But instead of the expected bulgogi, he reveals a plate of something else.

"Hamburgers?" Dad looks up questioningly.

"Something wrong with hamburgers?" Concern crosses Gavin's face.

"From the smell, that's not what I thought it would be," Mom says.

"I used bulgogi marinade in the seasoning of the meat patties. That's why it smells familiar," Gavin explains. "They're bulgogi burgers."

"Yum," I say, hearing two different but quintessentially classic cultural dishes combined into one. What's not to like?

"I'm still playing with the recipe, so I made way too much." Gavin sits down to join us.

"It's better than not having enough," Dad says.

"I couldn't agree with you more," I say as my stomach growls hungrily.

"I used your kimchi to make an aioli," Gavin says to Mom. "Let me know what you think."

Our eyes widen with interest, staring at the red sauce oozing out of the sides. We eagerly grab a burger each and put them on our plates. But before we can take our first bites, we hear a car door close outside our house.

"Are we expecting anyone?" Dad asks, looking around.

When the three of us shake our heads, he gets up and peeks outside. "It's the mayor!" He startles, hiding behind the door.

"What?" Mom jolts up. "I wasn't expecting company." She frantically looks around the house. Items are strewn about in disarray.

Gavin and I stare at each other, confused. "Where are you going?" Gavin asks Dad, who disappears into the room.

"I'm getting my jacket on. I can't let him see me like this."

"Good idea. I'll hide these secondhand plates." Mom scrambles to stuff them into a kitchen cupboard.

"Why does any of this matter?" Gavin's brows furrow. "We've lost everything, but no one here knows that."

It doesn't surprise me that Gavin says this. Between the two of us, he's been the more sensible one. But in this instance I find myself agreeing with him.

"Everyone here lives like this. And besides that, what's there to be embarrassed about? Like you said, we have everything we need. Isn't that what's important?" I remind them of what they chided us over when we first got here.

"We may be okay with living like this, but I'm trying to conduct business in this town. We can't be seen living like everyone else," Dad says. "What kind of example would I be setting?"

"And if food is what we're trying to sell, then we can't be seen eating like beggars," Mom adds.

"Excuse me?" Gavin's head jerks back. "Were you lying to me earlier when you said it looked good?"

"No, of course not. But people eat with their eyes, and with mismatched plates and off-brand silverware, they won't give the food a fair valuation." Mom frets.

"The mayor has so much influence. This is so not how I wanted our business to be introduced to the town." Deep creases line Dad's forehead and eyes.

For all their talk about perspective, my parents don't seem to have a clear one now. But ready or not, a knock at the door comes, and with all our lights on and the obvious noise we're making, Dad has no choice but to open the door.

"Mayor Beecham." Dad immediately straightens his posture at the sight of him. "Dr. Blaire. What a nice surprise. Please come in."

"Don't mind if I do, Dale." The mayor's voice booms from behind the front door. Like his voice, he has a big presence.

"Sorry to barge in like this." Then Dr. Blaire says much quieter, "Daniel, honey, they're sitting down to dinner."

Mom joins Dad by his side. "No, please come in."

Gavin and I stand as well. "Hi, Dr. Blaire," I say.

"Elena, it's nice to see you again. And this must be your brother, Gavin. I've heard so much about you."

"Likewise," Gavin says, sticking his hand out to shake hers. "It's a pleasure to finally meet you."

"Sorry for the interruption. We were hoping to catch you before you sat down to dinner," Dr. Blaire says.

"We're eating earlier than usual since I skipped lunch to go to Hal's after the town council meeting," I explain. "You couldn't have known."

"Ah, I see." Dr. Blaire nods. "Well, we would have come sooner to welcome you to the town. But we wanted to let you settle in first."

“We heard you borrowed Jean’s truck to move some things in,” Mayor Beecham says. “Figured now was a good time to visit.”

“Still getting settled, as you can see,” Dad is quick to say.

“It’s a work in progress,” Mom says self-consciously.

“What house isn’t?” Dr. Blaire says, paying no attention to the mess. “You should see the state of our home. This one is good at starting projects around the house. Not so great at finishing them.” She points to her husband, shaking her head.

“I guess we’re all works in progress.” Mayor Beecham shrugs. Everyone laughs, effectively setting Mom and Dad at ease. “Speaking of works in progress”—Mayor Beecham gestures outside—“Blaire says you have plans to grow produce and join the co-op.”

“The former tenants left the field in such good condition that we’re almost ready to plant new crops,” Dad says. “Just need to figure out what it is the town could benefit most from.” He shares a knowing look with Dr. Blaire.

“We can’t begin to thank you for lending us the tractor. It’s been a huge help,” Mom says. “Really, you must charge us for it.”

“No, no, no.” Mayor Beecham puts his hands up and waves off Mom’s notion. “In Blaire we take care of one another. I can’t in good conscience profit off of any of our residents, no matter how new they are to the area.”

“If there’s anything we can do to repay the debt, please let us know.” Mom seems touched.

“Being in Blaire, we depend on one another. So I’m sure there’ll be a day I’ll call on you for a favor.” Dr. Blaire smiles kindly.

“What’s in the cooler?” I ask, noticing the insulated bag Dr. Blaire brought in with her.

“Oh, I almost forgot.” She hands the cooler to us. “It’s a test batch of the honeycomb ice cream you suggested. I think it turned out better than anyone expected, and I had to bring you some since it was your idea."

I squeal. "I can't wait to try it after dinner."

"Speaking of . . . Daniel, we should get going and let the Oks get back to their dinner."

He nods, agreeing with her. "Wouldn't want to keep you from it." He inhales deeply. "Whatever it is, it's making my mouth water."

"You should join us. We have more than enough food," Gavin offers. Mom and Dad seem mortified by the suggestion at first. Then Mom warms up to the idea.

"Yes, please join us." Mom gestures to Mayor Beecham and Dr. Blaire to sit.

Before they can refuse, I pull out two plates and place them in front of the extra chairs.

"It seems it's decided. You must stay," Dad says, changing his tune.

"If you're sure it won't be any trouble," Dr. Blaire says hesitantly.

"At this point it would be rude to refuse," Mayor Beecham says. He's already sitting down, making himself comfortable at the table.

Gavin goes into the kitchen to retrieve the burgers that were previously hidden. When he sets the plate down on the table, I can't help but notice how the now-cooled burgers are deflated and the buns are flattened. Maybe it was because Mom made the point that people eat with their eyes, but they seem unappealing, even to me. Mayor Beecham blanches. A nervous look washes over Mom and Dad, as if the thing they feared the most is coming true.

"They taste better than they look, I promise—" Gavin starts.

"What? No, I'm sure they taste delicious. It's just . . ." Dr. Blaire's glance cuts to her husband.

“From what we’re smelling, I’m surprised to see that they’re burgers.” Mayor Beecham inhales deeply. He shakes his head. “Yeah, no. I’m not getting burger smell at all.”

“It’s because I used a different recipe. I mixed a bulgogi marinade in the patties and then grilled them with onions topped with a kimchi aioli.”

Dr. Blaire and Mayor Beecham exchange an *aha* glance. “That sounds more like what we’re smelling,” Dr. Blaire says.

“And more to the point, what we’re about to eat.” Mayor Beecham takes a bite. “Oh my God, this is heaven,” he says with his mouth full.

“Daniel Beecham, manners,” Dr. Blaire chastises him playfully. But when she takes her first bite, she does the same. “Sorry, it can’t be helped,” she says.

The four of us collectively sigh and are able to eat now that our fears are put to rest.

“I’ll let you in on a little secret,” Mayor Beecham says, and we lean in. “Being the mayor of this town comes with its perks. Many residents of Blaire have us over, and I was hoping to be invited to a meal one day here.”

“Daniel!” Dr. Blaire says, equal parts horrified and amused.

“Oh, honey, it’s fine. The Oks don’t seem like the judgmental type.” Mayor Beecham gestures to us. Even though that’s exactly the type of people we thought they were, I’m relieved to discover that neither of us is being judgmental. I look at Mom and Dad, and they, like me, seem relieved to hear it. Like it’s a compliment.

“What a delight,” Mayor Beecham says after finishing his last bite. “One of the best meals I’ve had.”

“Me too. The cafe tries to keep things interesting by changing its menu options frequently. But nothing as interesting as these burgers." Suddenly Dr. Blaire's face lights up. "You should work with the chef there to put this item on the menu."

"What a great idea," Mayor Beecham says.

"What? Is that possible?" Gavin perks up at the suggestion.

"Of course it is. Don't you know who you're talking to? I'm the mayor of this town." Mayor Beecham puffs his chest out.

Dr. Blaire rolls her eyes. "Even so, you don't need his approval. Just submit your recipe to Justine, the manager at the cafe. She'll know what to do with it."

"And make sure to share this recipe with the chef too. This aioli is tangy and spicy." Mayor Beecham dabs his finger in the aioli drippings on his plate and puts it in his mouth. "I can't get enough of it."

"I can't take all the credit," Gavin says. "That's my mom's kimchi."

"You made this?" Dr. Blaire marvels. "I just love kimchi, but, as you can guess, we don't get much of it here. Every time Danny goes into town for business, it's one of the items I ask him to bring back."

"Really?" Dad asks, surprised.

"I just made a batch. I can give you a jar if you want," Mom offers.

"I'd love a jar," Dr. Blaire says.

I can't help but notice Mom's smile stretches wider than I've seen it in the past few weeks—in the past few years. And it's all because Dr. Blaire showed appreciation for something Mom values in herself. Making kimchi, as I've recently learned, is her way of providing for the people she cares about most. In fact, as I look around the table, I notice Gavin's more at ease than I've seen him before in a group setting, and Dad is laughing louder than I'm used to hearing. I can even feel myself engaging more in this dinner party than any other party I've attended.

When the evening winds down, Mayor Beecham and Dr. Blaire thank us before they leave, taking a jar of Mom's kimchi with them.

After we clear the table, I open the cooler of ice cream Dr. Blaire left behind. Inside is a small metal canister with enough ice cream for a petite scoop, which is all we can manage after the burgers. At the table, we each take a spoon and decide to eat right out of the container.

"Oh my God," I moan. The richness of the ice cream and the crunchy bits of sweet, candied honey are sinfully decadent.

"This . . . is ice cream?" Mom seems unconvinced. "The texture is smooth, more like Greek yogurt."

"That's because Dr. Blaire keeps her cows happy," Dad tries to explain, but it only confuses Mom more.

"It kind of tastes like the one Van Leeuwen makes," Gavin observes.

"Right? That's what I had in mind when I suggested the idea, but this is way better," I say.

"No, definitely better," Gavin agrees.

"I'm sure it'll be a hit at the next farmer's market." Mom smiles at me.

"You know what else I think would be a hit?" I say, thinking aloud. "Your kimchi."

"What?" Mom blanches, unsure that she heard me correctly.

Instead of explaining, I look to Dad to take over. When he meets my gaze, he seems to understand.

"After the meeting with the farming co-op, Elena got me to see what this town needs." Dad smiles at me. "What the town is looking for are things they don't have, and today Dr. Blaire pointed out that kimchi is one of those things."

"Are you saying what I think you're saying?" Mom's eyes light up.

"I'm saying I hope you're ready to work tomorrow. Because we'll be spending all day planting cabbage, radish, cucumber, and whatever spices you need to make kimchi."

Mom literally jumps for joy, clapping her hands with unbridled excitement. “Dale, I’m so glad you came around to the idea.”

“Thank Elena. She got me to see what the town really needs.”

“Elena.” Mom reaches out and pulls me in for a hug. It feels warm and comfy, like I imagine a mug would feel with one of Hal’s cozies wrapped around it.

“Knew you could do it.” Gavin gives me a nod of approval.

My time as a public figure has made me the object of envy and desire to many. But the look in Mom’s, Dad’s, and Gavin’s eyes makes that pale by comparison.

I thought we were fish out of water in Blaire, but maybe I was wrong. Gavin’s cooking, Dad’s farming, Mom’s kimchi-making, and my contribution to the town’s beautification are making me think we’re more in our element here than we were in LA. They’re also making me realize we do have something in common. We all want to be recognized for our talents. And more importantly, we want that recognition from one another.

The phone rings the next morning, waking me up. I peek over at Gavin's bed, expecting him to answer it. When he's not there—or anywhere else in the house—I remember he had planned to speak with the manager at the cafe, which isn't as Karen-y as it sounds. After Dr. Blaire's suggestion last night, I bet he isn't wasting any time getting his bulgogi burger and kimchi aioli added to their menu.

"Hello?" I answer, wiping the sleep away from my eyes.

"Elena? It's Jean. I made the new products you suggested—lavender salts, lavender sachets, and lavender tea."

"Wow, you must have been busy!" It's only been a week since our meeting with the co-op.

"I had to if we want to sell them at the next farmer's market."

"You're right. The next one is in two weeks, which doesn't give us much time to create a whole new product line."

Jean starts to ask me if I'd be willing to try the products for research, and I say yes before she has the chance to finish her question. I wish I could say that this was part of my plan all along, but sampling self-care products is an unexpected perk of the job.

I quickly get ready and walk over to grab the bag of sample products she has for me. As soon as I leave the house, I do a double take at Mom and Dad working in the field. *Together.* Between the bickering and the passive-aggressive silences, I was beginning to worry about them. But watching them side by side—him digging a hole and planting a seed in, her covering it up with dirt and watering it—is giving me life. I don't want to keep Jean waiting, so I have to force myself to keep walking, resisting the urge to continue creepily staring at my parents being cute.

After picking up the samples from Jean, I hurry back home, eager to try out her products. I reach the house at the same time Gavin does.

"So, how was it? Did the cafe accept your recipe?" I ask.

"They did. And not only that. The head chef there let me cook it for them to sample."

"Oh my God, Gavin, that's amazing!"

"I swear, cooking in a professional kitchen validated that it was where I should be. It felt like I was in my natural environment."

"You're giving me goose bumps!" I show him my arms. "You have to tell Mom and Dad. They'll be so proud of you and happily support you when you tell them you want to go to culinary school."

"You think?" He rubs the back of his head.

"How could they not? Gavin, this is a big deal. A restaurant is putting your food on their menu. I mean, *I'm* even proud of you!"

That convinces him. "Maybe you're right." He smiles dreamily. "Where are they?"

"They're planting cabbage. *Together*," I say with wide eyes.

"Seriously?"

"Seriously." I point at them in the field.

"They look so happy," he concurs. "I don't want to interrupt them."

I nod, agreeing with him, and we quietly go into the house together.

"Where'd you go this morning?" Gavin asks when we're in the kitchen.

"I got some samples from Jean." I present my loot to him, fanning out the products on the table.

"What are these?" He holds up a sachet.

"They're dried lavender sachets. You're supposed to hang them in your closet or drawers, and they make your clothes smell nice." I take one and go into our room. "Here, let me show you." I open my closet. But when I see the state of it, I frown. After I unpacked the items Mom and Dad brought back, my closet is now bursting at the seams. I can't imagine trying to fit my entire wardrobe in this space. I swear, this closet was made for people who must not have an appreciation for fashion, which, in Blaire, tracks.

"You should seriously consider downsizing," Gavin says.

"Problem is, I can't wear them, but I can't throw them away. They're too nice."

"You could always sell them at a consignment store."

I make a face. Then, a second later, I reconsider his suggestion. With the brand names and the pristine conditions I've kept them in, I'm sure I could earn enough to pay for the retainer fee I'd need to hire Kiki back.

"A high-end consignment store? Does such a thing exist?" I ask, thinking aloud.

"Let's go ask Callie. She may know of a place," Gavin suggests.

I grin teasingly. I know what he's doing. He's trying to find an excuse to hang out with her. Despite their obvious interest in each other, they're taking things slow, and in Blaire it means their progress is moving at a crawl. If slow burn was a sport, they'd be serious contenders for first place. What I'm most surprised by, though, is the natural ease with which he suggests meeting up with Callie. The opposite of the uptight, awkward version of him from the first time we met her. Between the two, I like this new version of Gavin much better, so I don't tease him about it, and I follow him out the door.

At the convenience store, we find Callie restocking the shelves, as we knew she would be. She glances over when the bell jangles on the door as we open it. Her face lights up noticing us. She quickly finishes putting the last few jars of honey on the shelf before setting her box down.

"Hey." She smiles. "Didn't know I'd be seeing you here today."

"We're unpacking some of our old things, and Elena had an idea to sell some of her gently used clothes," Gavin says.

"Sell? Like, here?" Callie looks around skeptically.

"No, not here," I say. If I have no use for them, no one here would either. "Is there a consignment store nearby?"

"A consignment store?" She taps her finger to her lip, looking up. "There's a thrift store in Bakersfield. We could stop by there on the way to the farmer's market in a couple of weeks."

"Okay," I say. "That could work. I'll bring them with me."

Callie picks up the empty boxes. Gavin and I each take a box to her car. Gavin opens the door for me and Callie, and we say bye to Hal, who grunts back a bye to us.

"Maybe you could come to the farmer's market with us," Callie suggests once we're by her car.

"I'd love to, but I can't," Gavin says.

Callie seems disappointed. Until Gavin explains he can't make it because he'll be working at the cafe.

"What?" she says, confused and surprised. "How did that happen?"

Gavin fills Callie in on how Mayor Beecham and Dr. Blaire suggested he talk to the manager at the cafe to have his food added to the menu. Not only did they accept his recipe, but they also invited him to work there part-time.

"I can't wait to try it," she trills excitedly.

"How about tonight?" Gavin suggests.

"I can't," Callie says. Now it's Gavin who seems disappointed. "Today is the first active day of the Perseid meteor shower. Are you two going?"

"Going?" To a meteor shower? How would that work? A second later I'm wondering if I even know what a meteor shower is.

"It's a tradition for people here to get together after the sun sets to watch the first sighting of the meteor shower. It's fun," she says. It shouldn't be a surprise that this is what the town does for fun, considering the majority of the people work at the observatory.

"Yeah, we're in," Gavin answers for us. He's back to being all smiles.

"Okay, bring a blanket, and we'll meet here before going to the abandoned field between the convenience store and the observatory."

"Come again?" I say. I'm not sure what watching a meteor shower entails, but what I'm hearing so far is not promising.

"The abandoned field is the most remote part of Blaire and the best place to watch the meteor shower." She points in the direction behind the convenience store. "And in order to get the best view, a chair isn't going to do it. So you'll have to bring a blanket to lie down on to get the full experience."

"On the ground. On *that* ground?" I point to the grassy field Callie mentioned, imagining ants and ticks and a variety of other creepy crawlers—my worst nightmares. I shudder. "Is there a place where we can see the meteors but don't have to be on the ground?" A glass cabin, perhaps?

Callie looks up thoughtfully. "There is another place we could go," she says. "Why don't we meet at my place?"

Gavin and I agree. "I'll meet you anywhere as long as it's not on the ground," I say.

Later that night Mom and Dad take their blankets and a picnic basket to meet Mayor Beecham, Dr. Blaire, and Callie's parents, as well as most of the others in the town, on the abandoned field, while Gavin and I walk the extra block and a half to Callie's house.

I'm about to knock on the door when Callie appears from the side gate. "You made it." Her smile stretches extra wide, like she's surprised we came. As if we had other plans or something. "Come on back. Brennan's already here." She motions for us to follow her. When we come around to her backyard, Gavin and I startle at the sight.

"You have a trampoline?" I gawk. Brennan is jumping up and down, getting some serious air.

"You've never been on a trampoline before?" Callie glances sideways at me.

"Of course I have," I somehow say with conviction, even though I can't recall when or where. "It's just been a long time."

"What about you, Gavin?" Brennan asks when he notices Gavin's hesitation. "You game?"

I'm pretty sure I know what Gavin's response is. Mr. Play-It-Safe doesn't like roller coasters, and he definitely doesn't do trampolines.

"Sure," he says before kicking off his shoes and joining Brennan on the trampoline.

Gavin's up for it? This will be interesting.

"What about you?" Callie eyes me.

"Why not?" I say.

Callie and I join the boys, and at first it's chaotic. There's no rhythm or pattern to our movements, just wild, frenetic energy that sends us crashing into one another. But after a while, we get into a groove. And with more confidence, my jumps get higher and higher.

"This is seriously so cool!" I say breathlessly. The exhilaration of my stomach dropping and my hair whipping around wildly reminds me of that time I was in a convertible zipping through the Hollywood Hills. I couldn't tell then if the unsettling feeling in my gut was from the adrenaline or the reckless driving, but now I know it was the lifestyle I was leading that made me nervous. Always living on the edge, pushing the envelope, trying to portray an image of a person leading an extraordinarily exciting life. Except it wasn't always exciting. It was exhausting and, at times, frightening. Here, jumping around on Callie's trampoline, I'm having all the fun without any of the fear. It's the most carefree I've felt in a while. I can tell Gavin feels the same way, too, seeing his smile reach his eyes, something I didn't know was even possible.

"Have you ever double-bounced before?" Brennan asks breathlessly.

"What's that?" I say. I can't help but notice that I don't say it in my usual signature way.

Brennan doesn't answer me. Instead his eyes dance around mischievously, and he gears himself to time his next jump with mine. The precise timing of his landing with mine catapults me higher than I expected, and I flail in midair. It causes me to miss my footing when I land, and my body flops onto the trampoline with a bounce. In an attempt to avoid landing on me, Gavin, Callie, and Brennan fall too. Now we're all lying on the trampoline in a fit of giggles.

"I haven't had this much fun in . . ." I try to think back to the last time I had this much fun, but I can't. My memory doesn't reach that far.

"Me too," Gavin says, probably feeling the same way.

"Why didn't you tell me you had a trampoline?" Brennan asks Callie. "I'd have come over sooner if I had known." I can't help but notice that his tone and his mannerisms are less flirty and more platonic than he was at the town hall meeting. So maybe I imagined it? Maybe Brennan doesn't have heart-eyes for Callie.

"It's been a while since I've been on it. I forgot how much fun it is." Callie sighs, smiling. "Most of my friends go away for the summer. But the beautification initiative just launched, so I had to stay behind for the farmer's market," Callie says. "It's the summer before my senior year, though, and I was kind of sad thinking I'd be spending it without any friends. That changed when you three showed up. This is the best summer I've ever had."

I feel slightly guilty thinking that this is the worst summer for me. But being with Callie is the best part about it, so I don't feel like I'm lying when I say, "Me too."

"Me three," Gavin says.

"Me four," Brennan says.

The four of us lie on the trampoline with our heads in the middle of it. The night sky is blanketed with stars.

"This may sound ignorant, but these are the same stars people see in other parts of the world, right?" I ask. "I'm only wondering because they're brighter than the ones I'm used to seeing, and there seem to be more of them."

“They’re the same ones,” Brennan confirms. “They just seem brighter here because there isn’t any light pollution to drown out their shine.”

“If you think these are bright, wait until the shower starts. You’ll be blown away,” Callie says.

“Wait, I think I see them.” I point to the lights flickering above us.

“I see them too.” Gavin squints.

Callie and Brennan glance at each other before bursting into laughter.

“What?” I ask, only slightly self-conscious. It’s clear they’re laughing at us, but not in a mean way.

“Those aren’t meteors,” Callie says.

“Or anything celestial for that matter,” Brennan adds. “They’re fireflies.”

“Ah,” I say, cringing. “That would explain it. I don’t do bugs.”

“You must be city folks,” Callie says in a fake Southern accent.

“Not from round these parts, eh?” Brennan adds, playing along. He doesn’t have to try as hard as Callie to get that Southern twang.

Gavin and I share a laugh.

“You’re from LA, right?” Callie asks, dropping her accent.

The question silences our laughter. I glance sideways at Gavin, who seems as conflicted as I am. It was easier to hide certain details of our lives when we thought it would help our chances in the appeal. Now that the appeal is over, there’s no reason why we can’t be honest about who we are. But I can’t seem to get the words out.

“Yeah,” Gavin says before the silence becomes awkward. “I lived in a condo on the twenty-sixth floor in Westwood, far from the natural habitat of an insect.” He gives me a subtle look that tells me it’s okay. I think he means that he wants to open up to them more, and I do too.

“What, bugs in LA don’t take elevators up to the twenty-sixth floor?” Brennan teases.

“The only type of bugs I’m used to are ones trapped under cups, waiting for someone to get rid of them. And that someone is not me.” I don’t tell them it’s Tony, our gardener, or Carolina, our house manager, or any of the other staff members we had on our payroll who got rid of the bugs. Still, it feels good to share a part of my life with them, even one as trivial as this.

“No, you? The person who didn’t want to lie on the field to watch the meteor shower tonight?” Callie says, pretending to be shocked.

“It was my secret plan to jump on the trampoline,” I say, even though I had no idea she had one.

“Honestly I’m glad it was. The trampoline was such a good idea. Even the view here seems better,” Brennan says.

“What part of the sky should we look at?” Gavin asks.

“All of it,” Callie says.

“Well, that narrows it down,” I tease her. She takes it lightly.

“Let’s just say you won’t miss it,” Callie says.

“She’s right; the meteors are everywhere,” Brennan says, leaning toward Gavin. “It’s impossible to see it all, but it’s a pretty amazing sight when you try to see as much of the shower as you can.”

It seems obvious, but my eyes can’t seem to take in the entire sky, and by the looks of it, Gavin seems to be thinking the same.

“You good?” Brennan asks Gavin when he notices him shifting his head around.

“The trampoline is fun and all, but lying down on it is a different story.” Gavin looks awkward trying to tilt his head back. “It dips in all the wrong places, giving zero support where you need it the most.”

“Let me get you something to make you more comfortable.” Brennan lifts himself to a seated position.

"Nah, I should be okay. Just need to find the right position."

"You sure? It's really no trouble." Brennan offers again.

My brow quirks. Brennan is being super attentive to Gavin. And his expression is similar to the way he gazed at Callie at the town hall meeting when he was completely enamored by her. Come to think of it, Brennan is like that with everyone. Me, Officer Hartford . . . even Hal. So maybe I was wrong. Maybe I'm not as good at reading people as I thought I was. Because I now realize Brennan isn't flirting with me, or Callie, or any of us. It's just his nature to be friendly with everyone.

"You stay. I'll grab some pillows for us." Callie pushes herself to a standing position.

"I'll help," Gavin offers, getting up to join her.

"Thanks, city boy," Callie jokes. Watching the two of them disappear into the house to get the pillows, all giggles, I surprisingly feel relief for Brennan. Knowing that he isn't interested in Callie, not in that way, means he won't be crushed when he finds out that her interests lie elsewhere.

"How's the search for tenants coming along?" Brennan asks when it's just the two of us.

"Still searching," I say. "Although my dad is hopeful the observatory will bring in a new resident soon."

"And then you'll go back to LA?"

"Yeah." I can't help but notice I say it with less certainty than usual. I was already skeptical about getting back my socialite status when I thought we'd win the appeal. Now I'm not sure what the future holds anymore. "What about you? Where do you see yourself next year?"

"I'm hoping to get into Caltech, since they have one of the best space science programs."

I perk up when I hear he might be in LA next year. Once we're able to go back to our old lives, it's always been my plan to leave this place and never look back. It's the people I've met here who will be harder to leave. But knowing Brennan and I might end up in the same place next year helps to think we could stay in each other's lives. Then, a second later, I remember Brennan's long-term plans.

"And Blaire is where you want to live?" I ask for confirmation. Surely this isn't the only place that studies space exploration.

Brennan lies back, resting his head on his arm folded behind him. "You know when they ask kids what they want to be when they grow up? They say things like firefighter, policeman . . . astronaut." He peers over at me with a boyish grin. "Well, I was *that* kid. When I learned that the radio telescope could reach the farthest parts of the universe, I was sold. But there's no guarantee I'll end up in Blaire. I still have a long road ahead of me. First I have to graduate college and then get my PhD. By the time I can apply for a job at the observatory, so much could happen. New discoveries could shift the demand within the field of astronomy, technological advancements could change the way we approach space discovery, or budget cuts could even shut down the observatory altogether."

"Doesn't that scare you?" Just thinking of what it might be like if I can't get back to my influencer business makes me break out into a cold sweat.

"Nah. I'm in the business of exploring the unknown." He gives me a toothy grin. "But one thing's for sure. Blaire's a place I want to call home. I'll find a way to get back here, one way or another."

I fall silent. I've never felt that way about any place. I've always looked to leave every home I've ever lived in. Even just last month, I couldn't wait to move out of my house and be financially independent from my family. To finally start living the life I wanted. Or thought I wanted. Now I'm not so sure.

Gavin and Callie come back with some pillows, and we get comfortable right as the meteor shower starts. The bursting lights are small but captivating, and the absence of light pollution competing for our attention makes the celestial objects shine brighter than anything I've ever seen in the night sky. As I watch the meteors, I can't help but think that being away from the city is giving me clarity on other parts of my life too.

Although I can see the downsides of it now, I don't regret my influencer lifestyle. It was the solution that got me out of a bad situation. Through it all, I discovered my real talent as an entrepreneur. And to be the envy of so many people is, I'm not going to lie, the biggest natural high. But as much as I try not to let it bother me, I can't stop wondering if Gavin was right about me. It's true: I've never been in a long-term relationship, but it's always been my choice. Now time away has made me realize that most, if not all, of my friendships were superficial. And it's making me wonder if being surrounded by shallow relationships for so long has made it so that I don't know what it takes to be long-term material.

Being here has shown me I don't need to be in the spotlight of many to feel valued. As long as they're the right kind of people, I only need a few. It's not rocket science, the whole idea of quality over quantity. But the point is, now that I've had a taste of what it feels like to make deeper connections, I want to keep going. And who knows? Maybe I can be long-term material too.

Gavin and I get home at the same time as Mom and Dad. It's late, almost midnight, but no one seems remotely tired. In fact, Mom and Dad must have had as much fun as we did, based on how they buzz excitedly as they recall their night watching the meteor shower.

"Dr. Blaire brought her homemade cheese, and we ate it with crackers and drizzled it with Annabel's honey," Dad says.

"It was divine," Mom says.

"Then the meteor shower started, and it was like being at the Hollywood Bowl. But better." Dad shakes his head in disbelief.

Mom nods. "What about you two? Did you have a good time?"

Gavin and I take turns telling them about our night while Mom folds the blankets they took with them. When I tell them about how I thought the fireflies were meteors at first, we share a laugh, knowing how any of us could have easily made the same mistake. Just as Dad is putting away the blankets in the hall closet, he startles us.

"Look what I found." Dad holds up a box in his hands to show us. "Life!" As he says this, his breath rouses a cloud of dust to appear in the space between us.

"Are you sure you don't mean *death*? Because surely something must have died in there." I fan the dust away from me.

"Oh, I've played this before. It's a board game." Gavin reads the box carefully. “Except the logo looks different.”

“It says it’s the original game from 1960,” Mom reads off the box. “Should we play it?”

“Sure, why not?” I say, since we’re all wide awake. Besides, I haven’t played a family game in . . . well, there’s a first time for everything.

A few minutes later, we’ve cleared the table, and Dad reads out the instructions to us. “It says to first choose the banker. I think we all know it’s me.”

“Why you?” Mom asks.

“Because it says so right here in the instructions: ‘Choose the banker. *He* will be responsible for all the money.’ ”

Not sure these directions based on outdated gender norms make a strong argument, but I let him have it. I don’t want to be the banker anyway. Gavin and Mom don’t push it either.

“Okay, now pick a car and put a little peg in it,” Dad instructs us.

I choose a blue peg because that’s my favorite color.

“Elena, come on.” Dad eyes me. “Just take the pink peg.”

“What’s the big deal? I like blue better,” I say, not for one second taking him seriously. But Dad doesn’t budge. “It’s just a peg, Dad. Calm down.”

“I think I’m going to want a blue peg too.” Mom swoops in to change hers from pink to blue.

“Gloria, no—”

“I do like a good pink,” Gavin says, cutting Dad off. We exchange a quick smile. Even in our disagreement, we’ve reached a new level of getting along. And I’m not saying I take pleasure in watching people squirm, but it’s fun to mess with Dad, especially ’cause we’re all in it together. Even Mom.

“Fine, let’s move on,” Dad grumbles. “We spin to see who goes first.”

The old spinny wheel miraculously still works, making a *tick, tick, tick* sound as it spins and lands on a number.

“Oh, yay! I get to go first,” I say when my number ends up being the highest. I rub my hands together and spin the wheel again, landing on the number four. Right off the bat, I have to choose between the business or college route. Business gets me working faster, but the salary is lower. If I go the college route, I take the longer path to getting a job, but the salary potential is higher. We’re playing a game, so I go the college route.

“Good. Wise choice,” Dad says approvingly.

“Honey, this isn’t real life. It’s just a game.” Mom nudges him.

“I’m only saying it was a good choice. This route may take longer, but look at the earning potential.”

Gavin gives me a subtle look and smirks. “I think I’ll start working right away.” As I knew he would, he moves his car to the business side of the game.

“Gavin, no—” Dad starts to say, but Mom shushes him by placing a hand on his shoulder.

“Not only is it a game from the 1960s, it’s cisnormative, supremely biased, and elitist,” I point out. “You can’t expect us to take the game seriously.”

“Besides, is it so bad to go to a trade school? Plenty of famous chefs went to culinary school instead of a four-year college,” Gavin says.

Dad cocks his head to the side. “Being good at cooking and making a career out of it are two different things. It’s a good skill. But there is no way a kitchen job can bring the same amount of success as an office job.”

Gavin's face falls. My whole body deflates at the sight, as if it were my dream Dad was puncturing with his words. A protective rage bubbles in me.

"Success isn't always defined by money, just like college doesn't guarantee success," I say encouragingly. Gavin has made so much progress following his dream that it kills me to think he might revert to following someone else's. Gavin meets my eye and gives me a tight smile of appreciation. And because I feel like Dad isn't completely convinced, I add, "Besides, there are plenty of successful people who didn't graduate college. Bill Gates, James Cameron, Ralph Lauren . . . you." Right after I say this, it's crickets. Literally, the chirping of the insects from outside our non-dual-paned windows is the only sound we hear.

"But—but . . . that's not how you win the game," Dad stammers, referring to the instructions on the box. "It says here that the player with the most money wins. And going to college gives you a higher salary." His face turns a shade darker, and we all know he's not talking about the game anymore.

"Like you said, it's just a game," Mom reminds us. "Let's try to have fun with it." Probably sensing the tension rising, she spins the spinner and chooses the college path, effectively ending the debate about college.

It's my turn next. And even though I'm over this game already, I spin and move my car to the GET MARRIED space.

"See, this is what I'm talking about. Which one do I give you now, blue or pink?" Dad scratches his head, staring at the pegs. "Pink, I guess?"

"How about no peg?" I suggest.

Mom, Dad, and Gavin crane their necks toward me, staring with the same look of confusion.

"No peg?" Dad's brows furrow. "But how would that work?" He stares off like he's trying to do mental math that doesn't add up.

"Are you coming out to us?" Gavin asks.

"What? No." I give him a look.

"Elena, it doesn't matter what peg it is. You can pick whatever color you want," Mom tries to reassure me.

"That's just it. I don't want another peg in the car seat next to me," I say. And to clear up any further confusion, I add, "I don't know if I ever want to get married."

Gavin seems to be the most confused by that. "But every time you go out, you're always with a different guy. . . ."

"Exactly," I point out. "I've never been in a long-term relationship. How do I know I want to commit myself to someone for life?" I shrug.

"Elena, don't be silly." Dad swats a dismissive hand at me. "Getting married and having kids is what women do. Just put a peg in the car. I don't care what color it is."

That's what women do?

"Are you saying I can't be a woman without a man?" I ask combatively.

"I'm not saying you can't be a woman without a man, but what would you do if you didn't get married?" He blinks at me with sincere curiosity.

This is a crushing blow. Worse than when he dismissed the culinary arts as a possible career option for Gavin. Did Dad learn nothing from our time here? Did he forget that it was my ingenuity that got him into the co-op? Is he not able to recognize the accomplishments of the women who run it? If this is how Dad truly feels, there's no way he'll recognize my potential.

Surprisingly Mom is the one who backs me up. "Elena has

a point," she says, spinning the wheel for her turn. "She's only seventeen. She doesn't need to make any declarations now. In fact . . ." As Mom moves her car to the GET MARRIED space, she puts a pink peg in her car. "It would be nice to have a wife for once."

Gavin and I exchange a glance. When it comes to taking sides, Mom is always on Dad's, even when he's being unreasonable. But her comment, subtle as it was, makes me feel like at least she'll support me and Gavin when the time comes. The tension softens on Gavin's face, and I can tell he's thinking the same thing. Dad still seems confused by all of us, so by the time it's Gavin's turn to "Get Married," he doesn't comment on his choice when he picks a blue peg to match his pink one.

After that's settled, we keep playing, taking turns moving through the path and snaking around the board. When it's Gavin's turn again, we watch in awkward silence as he moves his car, landing on SONS AND DAUGHTERS.

"I'm not sure Gavin is suited for kids," I joke to lighten the mood. Only one person doesn't find the humor in that.

"Of course he needs kids," Dad insists. "The more the better. Says here, you get twenty-four thousand dollars per kid at the end." He holds up the rules to show us.

I know it's a game, but the way he says it sounds calculated and insensitive. As if children only add value if they are profitable.

When it's my turn to land on SONS AND DAUGHTERS, Dad looks to Mom. "Gloria, your turn," he says, expecting me to pass my turn. But I surprise him by putting a pink peg in the back row of my car.

"You can't have kids. You don't have a spouse," Dad points out.

"Dale, what kind of statement is that?" Mom says, beating me to it. "Of course she can have kids."

“Yeah, there are plenty of single parents,” I say. “Sandra Bullock, Hoda Kotb, Charlize Theron . . .”

Dad still doesn’t seem convinced, so Mom adds, “Besides, let’s be honest. She’s the one who’s going to take care of the kids anyway. Not her husband.” That line we were toeing a few minutes earlier? Well, consider it effectively crossed. Because I might have thought I imagined it the first and even second time. But there was nothing subtle or passive about this comment.

Unsurprisingly Dad . . . does nothing. He’s great at pointing out flaws and shortcomings when it comes to others. Himself, on the other hand . . .

The rest of the game doesn’t get any better. For all his “sensible” talk, Dad buys all the stocks and tries his luck at each opportunity to play the market. But despite his best efforts, he never spins the right number, making him lose money each time. I can’t ignore the similarities, but it goes to show that in Life—and in real life—you can make all the right moves and still end up with nothing.

The last space on the game board is DAY OF RECKONING, an ominous—if not doomsday—ending to the game. It’s time we count up our money, and the one who has the most wins the game. As Dad pointed out, each player collects twenty-four thousand dollars per dependent. With no kids, Gavin is out of the running. I don’t have a spouse, but I collect the money for the carload of children I have, landing me in first place. Mom trails behind me as a close second. But it’s Dad who is in last place. When it’s clear he doesn’t have enough to move on, his expression turns somber.

“I reckon you don’t have enough to be a millionaire,” I say with a deep Southern accent in an attempt at levity. He remains unmoved.

“Wait a second. There’s a chance I can still win,” Dad says, suddenly coming back to life. He reads out loud the instructions off the box. "'If a player doesn't have enough money to be a millionaire, they can try their chance at becoming a Millionaire Tycoon. All they have to do is put everything they own on a number and spin the dial. If it lands on that number, they win the game.'"

"But you don't have enough to win, even if the dial lands on your number."

"I can use my car as collateral," Dad says, moving his car to the number.

Mom tilts her head at him. "Dale, isn't it enough that you have your car and family?"

"That's loser mentality. No one wants to end up with just a car and family," he says, not seeming to get the connection to our real life. Then a scary thought enters my mind. Maybe he does get the connection, and this is how he really feels about us.

"I refuse to end up on the Poor Farm. I need to be on Millionaire Acres," he says with more determination than when we first started the game. I'm not even sure who he's talking to at this point. To us or himself.

By now everyone's abandoned the game. Except for Dad, who's gearing up to spin the spinner. He's the only one paying attention as the spinner slows to a stop.

"I win!" Dad pumps his arms in celebration. Gavin and I can only stare at him incredulously. Mom seethes.

"And how does it feel?" Mom asks. "Is it worth it? To make it to the top but have no one to celebrate with?"

"Gloria, what are you talking about?"

"We may have lost the company, your title, the bulk of our wealth. But even though it seems like we've lost everything, there's still something we have that can't be taken away from us." She glances at me, then at Gavin, before turning her attention back to Dad. "And if you're not careful, you could lose that too."

She goes to her room and slams the door behind her. Gavin and I do the same.

More than anything, this game was a reality check. These past few weeks, I thought Dad was starting to see us more clearly. That I'm more business-minded than he gave me credit for and that Gavin has talents he was too closed-minded to appreciate. But now I can see that the changes in Dad's perspective only went skin deep. Like Mom told me before, it's not easy for him to forget about the past that made him who he is, and that includes societal values.

It's one thing to lose at the Game of Life, but in real life? I can't make the same mistakes. Last night was a reminder that living here with my family is not a winning strategy and definitely not a long-term solution. But if I want to be able to live on my own, I have to find a way to earn a proper living. And that can't happen until I hire Kiki back. I've accepted the fact that I have to lower my standards in order to achieve my goal. That means being open to any opportunity that comes my way, including the charity event for the sad and unwanted animals Kiki suggested in our last call. There's still time to be considered for it. That is, *if* I can hustle.

After thinking about it for the rest of the week, I come up with an idea that I plan to present to Callie when we meet at the cafe for tea. Instead of selling my clothes to a consignment store, I decide to propose the idea of sectioning off part of our farmer's market table for some gently used items. In exchange, I'll offer half of what I earn from selling my things to the town's beautification proceeds. I figure if I have to split the profits with anyone, I'd rather they go to Blaire than a consignment store.

"What are you doing?" I ask when I see Gavin and Mom in the kitchen, hovering over a giant bowl in the sink.

"I'm teaching Gavin kimjang." Mom smiles affectionately at me.

I smile back at her. At least Mom isn't reverting to the gender-normative thinking from her day. Gavin slips on the pink rubber gloves, eager to get started. It lifts my mood to see Gavin so motivated. After the botched game night, I would have thought Dad had discouraged his culinary pursuits. Speaking of . . . "Where's Dad?" I ask, realizing he's nowhere to be found.

"Where do you think?" Mom says, and Gavin nods toward the window, indicating Dad's whereabouts.

I sigh knowingly. Ever since Dad realized the profitability of kimchi in Blaire, he's been so extra about it. At least he finally came around to Mom's idea, which makes her happy. And busy. So busy. Is it possible the bowl has grown in size since we got here?

"Where are you off to?" Gavin eyes me.

"I'm going to meet Callie. Wanna come?" I ask in a mildly playful voice, which Mom doesn't pick up on but Gavin certainly does. His ears and neck are almost as red as the bag of dried red pepper flakes.

"Nah, I'm going to stay with Mom. Tell her I said hi."

"Tell her yourself." I stick out my tongue at him teasingly just before I leave. He smiles, rolling his eyes.

Not too long after, I'm at the cafe with Callie. Apparently, when she suggested meeting up for tea, she meant actual tea and not, like, the inside scoop on the local goss. Which is a huge letdown, not gonna lie. We get seated, and the waitress takes our order. I get chamomile, and Callie gets oolong.

"Is Gavin coming?" Callie asks.

I shake my head. "He's making kimchi with my mom."

"Oh, okay." Callie tries to pretend she's not disappointed, but the frown on her face tells me otherwise.

Neither of us has addressed the elephant in the room, so I decide to rip the Band-Aid off. "I know he's my brother and all," I start slowly, "but I'm also your friend, so I hope that whatever happens between you two doesn't make things weird between us."

She sighs, relieved. "I'm so glad you said something. I didn't know how you'd feel about me and, you know, your brother." She peers up at me shyly.

"Are you kidding? I wanted this to happen."

"What a relief. I was worried I'd have to choose between you two, which would be impossible because I like you both so much."

"But, like, in different ways, right?" I wiggle my brows suggestively.

Her face grows a darker shade right before my eyes. "Elena!" She slaps me playfully. We laugh.

"Of course I'd never make you choose between us. That would hurt me as much as it would the both of you," I explain. "Gavin and I have never had mutual friends before."

"Really?" The pitch in her tone is one of genuine surprise. "You two get along so well when we're together, like it's natural to be in the same social circle."

Thinking back, I realize she's right. "I guess we do get along." *Now.*

The teas arrive, and while we wait for them to cool down, we go over the new products we'll be bringing with us to the farmer's market next Saturday. After the rave review I gave Jean on her lavender bath salts and sachets, she's working on making a small batch to take with us. Dr. Blaire can make a big tub of honeycomb ice cream but is still working on the lavender-honey combination, since Jean was tied up concocting the other items.

"Maybe we can bring your mom's kimchi with us instead. Gavin told me she's made more than your family can eat."

"What a great idea. I'll tell her. She'll be so thrilled."

"It's so exciting to see our booth expanding."

I see this as a segue to suggest my other idea of selling my gently used, name-brand clothes.

"I love the idea of having a section for clothes."

"Really?" Callie's enthusiasm for my idea exceeds my expectations. "I'd rather have the profits go to the beautification fund rather than a consignment store. But if it's okay with you, would it be possible to split it fifty-fifty? It's just that I want to buy my parents an anniversary gift, and I want to surprise them with something nice," I add, feeling the need to come up with an explanation.

"Of course you can," Callie says. "And that's sweet that you want to surprise them."

"Er, yeah." I shift uncomfortably at the lie.

"How long have they been together?"

"Twenty-five years strong," I say. Although, after last night, I'm not so sure how strong they are.

"Speaking of relationships, that reminds me." Her expression changes. "Last week at the lab, Brennan mentioned there's someone he's interested in." She presses her lips together, arching her brows high.

I gasp. "Who, me?"

"No, Gavin," she deadpans, then slaps my shoulder playfully. "Of course you!"

"Do you really think Brennan has a crush on me?" I ask skeptically. "I mean, there was a time I thought he might have been flirting with me," I admit to Callie. "But when I noticed that Brennan acts that way with everyone, not just me, I realized it must be his personality to be overly friendly. If anything, I thought he was interested in you more than in me."

"There's no way," Callie says, not entertaining the thought for a second. "We're like family. Besides, Brennan said it was someone new to the town. I checked the county registrar's office. Your family is the only one that moved here in the past three months, so it can't be anyone else."

I'm still unconvinced. How can Callie be so sure when Brennan hasn't shown me any more attention than he's shown anyone else? Unless . . .

"I thought we might have had a moment when we were deciding what color to paint the convenience store," I recall. "Like we were reading each other's minds thinking about the same color. But that's ridiculous." I swat a dismissive hand at Callie. "I mean, it's just paint, right?"

"Maybe it's not just paint." Callie wiggles her brows.

"Maybe it's not." I brighten. It's a good thing Brennan signed up as a volunteer to fix the convenience store. Callie may be onto something.

"But you didn't hear it from me." She zips her lips.

"Of course." I zip my lips. So maybe I did get some tea after all.

On Monday morning Gavin and I get ready to work on fixing up the convenience store like we planned to. What I didn't plan on, though, is Mom and Dad joining us.

"You're coming?" I ask.

"Of course. The town has been generous to us," Mom says, tying a scarf around her hair. "I couldn't say no."

"And attending could be a good networking opportunity," Dad adds, slipping on his suit jacket.

"Dad we're going to remove and replace decaying wood," I remind him, inspecting his attire skeptically. "You might want to reconsider your suit."

He shrugs like it's no big deal. "Every encounter is a business opportunity."

"Suit yourself." Honestly, if Dad doesn't care, I shouldn't either.

"By the way, how is Sonya taking the news?" Dad asks Gavin out of the blue.

Gavin instantly tenses up. "She's taking it okay." He fidgets, unable to keep his eyes focused on anything. I can tell he feels like he's being disloyal to Callie.

"Good." Dad nods. "Once I'm assigned my new role at It's Ok! and you go back to USC in the fall, everything should revert to the way it was. Like you and Sonya."

The last time Gavin and I talked about Callie, we had planned on telling Mom and Dad about his budding relationship with her. But the strained look on Gavin's face is making me think he's changed his mind.

"Hey." Gavin pulls me aside when Mom and Dad walk ahead of us. "Um, so, yeah. Callie's going to be there today, so . . ."

"Let me guess. You don't want to tell Mom and Dad about her."

"After the way family game night went, I don't think Dad's position has changed enough. He wouldn't be able to handle learning about Callie and my expulsion at the same time. And he's bound to find out about USC sooner rather than later."

"Yeah," I say. I can't disagree with him there.

"But I'll tell Mom and Dad the truth soon. I promise."

"And Brennan and Callie too," I add. Even though I can understand why the deception is necessary, it doesn't sit easily with me.

"And Brennan and Callie too," he promises.

When we get to the convenience store, there's a large crowd already gathered in front. I find Callie right away and tell her that our parents don't know yet and that Gavin wants to tell them before they find out.

"I totally understand. I wouldn't want to start off on the wrong foot with your parents."

"Really?" I peer over at her. When she nods reassuringly, I feel actual pain in my chest. Ugh, even her willingness to go along with this plan is a testament to her good nature. Gavin owes me. He owes *us*!

Gavin sticks with Brennan and the rest of the carpentry team, who are busy cutting out and replacing the deteriorated parts of the wood siding, while Callie and I strip the paint off the intact ones. True to her word, she doesn't go out of the way to interact with Gavin aside from saying hi and goodbye.

I take a break from scraping off the paint and look around. "Where's Hal?" I ask, noticing I haven't had the pleasure of seeing his scowling face this morning.

She stops working and scans the area for him. "There he is," she says, pointing at the entrance of the store.

"I didn't recognize him under the shadow of the awning." He's quietly observing the volunteers from a distance.

"Yeah. He's probably having a down day," she says.

"What's a down day?"

"A day when he's down."

"Oh. I didn't think that's what it literally meant." Then, a second later, after I've had time to understand, I add, "Is he okay?"

Callie presses her lips together and shrugs. "I can't say I know how he feels at the moment, but it could be because the work we're doing today is changing the way the store looked when his ma was running it."

"Oh my God. I'm the one who suggested the paint." I put my palm to my forehead. "If it weren't for me—"

"No, don't be so hard on yourself. We've been telling him to repaint it for a while. He thinks keeping the store as it was when his ma was alive is keeping her memory close to him, but the store's falling apart. And how is that going to honor her memory? Anyway, everyone was surprised when he went along with the idea of a new color when you suggested it. Maybe he's ready to move on from his grief, and I think the new color will do him good."

"How do you know when he's up or down? He always seems so . . ." I look again to confirm before I say, "Grumpy."

"On the surface, he seems the same. But once you pay attention to him or know him as long as we have, you see the signs."

Sure enough, when Hal doesn't think anyone's looking, he lets down his guard. The creases around his eyes release, making him seem downcast, and he lets out a sigh. As soon as a person turns the corner, his scowl comes back into place.

"Some people wear their emotional armor so well, it fools us into believing they're doing okay. But even for them, it gets to be too much. And we've gotten to know how to support him." Then she says, "I'll be right back."

Callie goes to her car and grabs a box, then casually walks over to Hal and hands it to him. "Would you mind stocking the shelves? I forgot to do it earlier, and my hands are tainted with paint thinner."

Without hesitation, he takes the box from her and disappears into the store.

"Hal doesn't like attention," she says, rejoining me. "So I gave him something to do."

Callie never ceases to amaze me with her acts of kindness, making me feel worse about the deception by the minute.

Between the prepping and the painting, we spend the next few hours in concentrated silence. When the siding is all fixed, half of the team works on the roof, and the other half, including Brennan, joins me and Callie to paint.

“That side is all prepped. What should I do next?” Brennan asks me.

“The last thing we need to do before painting is cover the windows and fixtures.” I grab a large plastic sheet and hand Brennan a roll of painter’s tape. “The plastic sheet isn’t an exact fit, so we’ll have to fold it to fit the window.”

“Got it.” Brennan tips his head toward me. A second later, though, it looks like he doesn’t “got it.”

“Um, are you okay?” I stifle a laugh as I watch him wrestle the plastic sheet down.

“It’s fine. I’m fine,” he tries to reassure me, but it doesn’t look like he’s fine, so I tape down my corner first, then help him with his.

“Fold the bottom under, then the side. Like this.” I model my instructions for him.

“The wind, my fat fingers . . . ” He mutters a few excuses.

I suppress a laugh. “Plastic sheet, one; Brennan, zero.”

“I’m better with heavy lifting when it comes to this stuff.”

“How about this? Why don’t you hold up the ladder while I tape those windows?” I suggest.

“Deal.”

Brennan grabs the ladder and moves it under the window. When it’s steady, I climb up and tape the sheet to the glass. After I’m done, Brennan moves the ladder off to the side while I start covering up the hardware on the doors and light fixtures with painter’s tape. Before I can reach for another piece, Brennan has one ready for me, perfectly timed. When we’re finished prepping the exterior of the convenience store, he trails me to the storage shed. Without being asked, he brings out the buckets of paint while I carry the box of brushes and rollers. We fall into an efficient rhythm, almost like choreography, and I can’t help but notice how weirdly good at this we are. Because I’ve never done this kind of work before and yet, somehow, this works.

Once the supplies are laid out, I gather the volunteers. Aside from the handful of people working on the roof, the rest of us, including my parents, pick up brushes and begin painting.

Gavin and Callie join us to make it less obvious when they catch stolen moments between them. I glance over at my parents to see if they notice, but they don't. In fact, they're so focused on painting that they don't seem to notice anything around them. You'd think it's a race by the way they've taken over the whole front right side of the building.

News articles and interviews often heralded my parents for their work ethic, but I never understood it. To me work was the reason for their absence from my life, and for years I resented them for it. Having a front-row seat to Mom and Dad taking this job—and every other job they've done in Blaire—so seriously, I'm starting to see what others do. Still, the botched family game night is making it impossible to fully let go of the resentment. Can there be such a thing as too much of a quality as highly regarded as work ethic? It seems like Dad has been reliant on himself for too long to notice any other way of doing things.

A splatter of paint on my face jerks me out of my thoughts. "What was that for?" I say to Brennan when I realize he flicked his brush at me.

"We'll never get this done at this rate," he says playfully.

"*I'm* the one slowing us down?" I dab my finger into my tray and flick it at him.

He winces, wiping the paint off his eyelid. "Bold move." He grins mischievously before swiping his brush on my arm.

I gasp, then flick my brush back at him. We do this back and forth a few times, and the moment is like something out of a Hallmark movie, which, I'm not going to lie, is, like, a really cute look for me.

"Okay, now we're really not going to make any progress if we keep this up," I say. As fun as this is, there's a nagging sensation creeping over me to stop fooling around, which is odd. I can't remember the last time I preferred *manual labor* to anything else.

"Truce?" He peers up at me.

"Truce," I say. Then quietly, under my breath, I add, "For now."

With the brush in his hand, he smirks mid-stroke. I resist the urge to flick him again with the paintbrush, and we both somehow manage to get back to work.

It isn't until we finish for the day that I realize I haven't taken a break and I'm completely parched. Right as I'm about to look for my water bottle, Brennan hands it to me. Okay, now that's weird. Is he a psychic?

"How'd you . . ."

"Looked like you could use it," he says, again reading my mind. "We've worked up a sweat."

I self-consciously wipe my brow. It's true. I haven't worked this hard since my last F45 cardio session. The water feels cool and refreshing. And so does Brennan's attentiveness. Suddenly, I'm reminded of what Callie said. Could Brennan really be interested in me?

"We make a pretty good team," Brennan says, staring at the progress we made today.

I'm starting to think we do too.

In fact, if Brennan *is* interested in me and I *am* ready for a long-term relationship, there's no reason why we can't be more than just a good team.

Mom is busier than ever getting her kimchi ready for the farmer's market. When Callie's mom heard we had wiped the convenience store clean of their supply of mason jars and still needed more, she offered the ones that were left over from her honey. So while Gavin goes to get them, Mom gets started on yet another batch.

"Wanna come with me?" Gavin asks me on his way out.

He knows I'm always down to hang out with Callie. But between Gavin's job at the cafe and Callie's internship, I know they don't get to spend a lot of time together, so I make up an excuse. "I'll stay here to help Mom," I say.

After Gavin leaves I join Mom in the kitchen. She's hovering over the big bowl, filled to the brim with cabbages and a kimchi paste concoction. With her pink rubber gloves on, she slathers the mixture around, making sure each piece of cabbage is coated with the red peppery goodness.

"Can you get the jar of chopped garlic in the fridge?" She motions behind me. By now she knows my help in the kitchen is best limited to noncooking tasks.

I rummage through the fridge that somehow became packed overnight. "I can't find it."

"It's behind the kimchi," Mom says.

Which one? There are more jars than shelf space. After playing Tetris with the jars, I finally find the container of chopped garlic. She instructs me to put a healthy amount into the vat, and she continues mixing it together.

"I didn't realize there were so many different kinds of kimchi," I say, putting the jar back in the fridge.

"There are over a hundred types," she says, popping a piece of cabbage covered in kimchi paste in my mouth.

The crunchy texture of the not-yet-pickled cabbage mixed with spices is refreshing. "So good."

She nods, agreeing with me. I hold the jar out while she fills it with the fresh batch of kimchi. When it's full, I screw the lid on it tightly and set it aside.

"This batch is your best one yet. I have no doubt everyone in town is going to love it," I say, holding out another empty jar for her to fill.

"The only thing that would make it taste better would be cabbage from Anbandegi. We grew the sweetest cabbage I've ever tasted."

"Really? I'd like to try it someday."

"I hope you do. But you know what I think?" She pauses, glancing over at me. "I think it tasted sweeter because I worked hard for it."

"Is this one of those sneak-attack lectures about how I need to be more self-sufficient?" I raise my brow at her.

"Not this time," she says, laughing. "With all the hired help and your father running the business, I hadn't felt a sense of purpose in a while. And everything seemed . . . tasteless." She turns to face me. "Making kimchi for this town is giving me purpose. That's why this batch tastes so good."

"Now, that I believe." I smile at her. "I'm so glad you're doing this."

"Me too." She gives me a side hug, careful not to let her kimchi-stained gloves touch me.

Not too long after Mom and I clean the kitchen, Gavin comes home with jars from Callie's house. He also brings with him an unexpected, but not unwelcome, guest.

"Hey, Brennan." I angle my good side toward him.

"Hey, Elena. Hi, Mrs. Ok." He nods politely since his hands are full.

Mom smiles affectionately at Brennan, then at the box in his hands. Her eyes widen. "That's more than I was expecting."

"Guess that means you'll have to make more kimchi." I give Mom a knowing look.

Mom smiles at me. "I don't need all of them now, though. How about this? Elena, make space in the hall closet for Brennan. I'll show Gavin where to put these in the shed." Mom slips off her rubber gloves, lays them gently on the bowl, then leads Gavin outside to the shed.

"I didn't know you were coming over," I say to Brennan as I open the hall closet.

"I ran into Gavin on his way to Callie's. Figured as long as I was there, I could help."

"I'm sure you could," I say, staring him up and down. There's something else he can help me with. "Gavin's going to work at the cafe later, and my parents have plans to go into town. You could keep me company while they're gone," I say, fluttering my lashes.

Instead of reacting to my suggestive tone, he's completely unaffected. "Sorry, but I can't." He turns me down without an explanation.

So I try again. I compliment him, flip my hair, and laugh too loudly—all of my go-tos that usually do the trick, but none of them work. In fact, he does something I've never seen a guy do to my advances: nothing.

"Well, I better go," he says after setting the box down. "Tell Gavin I said bye."

"Okay." I wave.

By the time he's out of sight, Gavin and Mom come back from the shed.

"Did Brennan leave?" Gavin asks.

"Yeah. And he said to say bye to you," I say flatly.

Gavin picks up on my mood. "Did something happen?"

"It doesn't make sense. I thought we had a moment the other day," I say, thinking aloud.

"El, I'm sorry. Maybe Brennan isn't interested in dating anyone right now."

"But that's just it. A reliable source said he is interested in someone." I don't give Callie away since I gave her my word, although I'm pretty sure Gavin can figure it out. "And the same source strongly suggested it was me."

Still, Gavin remains unconvinced. He leans against the wall and hesitates before he speaks. "Look, El. I've seen how invested you are in expanding the town's booth at the farmer's market, and the people here are buzzing with excitement over your efforts to improve the convenience store. When it comes to something you believe in, you are all in. And the results?" He whistles. "They surpass everyone's expectations. Even your lifestyle brand. I can see that now." A sheepish expression crosses his face. "My point is, I know that you give a hundred percent of yourself to anything you set your mind to. And I'm sure dating is no different. So before you put yourself on the line, make sure you know all the facts. I don't want to see you get hurt," he says.

By now I'm used to Gavin's unsolicited advice. But this one hits differently. Unlike before, there's no judgmental undertone of disapproval at the heart of his message, and he doesn't sound like he's reading off a script Dad provided for him. This time he's not acting like a caring older brother. He is one. I smile appreciatively at him.

Gavin smiles back. "Just don't do anything unless you talk to Brennan."

My smile falters. As much as I want to take Gavin's advice, especially after his overprotective-big-brother spiel, I can't. It's not like I can ask Brennan directly if he's interested in me. Not without risking our friendship by making things supremely awkward in the event he says no, however slim the chances are. No, I definitely can't ask Brennan. But someone else can. . . .

"What? Why are you looking at me like that?" Gavin fidgets self-consciously.

Here's the plan: Gavin is going to meet with Brennan tomorrow morning before he starts his day at the observatory. Since Gavin will be starting his shift at the cafe at the same time, he suggested grabbing a coffee there. While they talk, Gavin has been instructed to bring up my name in a series of conversational starters we work on together. They include, but are not exclusive to, my incredible fashion sense, my charitable nature, my entrepreneurial spirit, my endearing personality. There's so much material to work with, I'm sure Gavin won't have a problem bringing up my name in conversation. It's his social acuity I'm worried about.

Gavin isn't the best at picking up on subtle nuances in a person's mannerisms that could, in certain situations, convey more than a thousand words. There's so much that is told through indirect communication that can only be deciphered through keen observation. A far-off look or a deep sense of longing. A flash of hope or a shadow that crosses an expression. Or even a modulation of the pitch in the inflection or intonation of Brennan's voice. For example, he could say, "Elena is amazing." Which would suggest he's already aware of my many attractive attributes and ready to profess his love. Or he could say, "Elena *is* amazing," which would suggest a new revelation that he's considering worth exploring. The distinction between the two, though subtle, makes all the difference. Needless to say, I can't leave it up to Gavin to relay every detail. How can I know for sure how Brennan feels about me if Gavin doesn't know how to read those social cues?

When I conclude that Gavin is an unreliable narrator, I come up with a backup plan. After Gavin leaves I'll wait ten minutes before following him to hear for myself what Brennan thinks of me. And to appear less conspicuous, I'll change into something less Elena. It's like that time I had plans to go to a Taylor Swift concert but the paparazzi had been camped outside of my house all day. Kiki told me to lie low so we could best optimize my earning potential, and I always listen to her. But after doing back-to-back-to-back publicity events, I was tired of saying yes to everyone and saying no to me. Long story short, I disregarded Kiki's advice and went to the concert anyway. I was in my boundaries era. The point is, since I was wearing unflattering clothes that were loose around the hips and midsection and I had greasy, unstyled hair, no one recognized me when I went to the concert, and I was able to hide in plain sight. It worked then, and I'm sure it'll work now.

Donning clothes I was able to procure at the convenience store (there's something I never thought I'd say), I head out the door without a dose of dry shampoo or running a flat iron through my hair.

I wear my hair down to hide my best features—angular jaw, high cheekbones, and pouty lips. . . . Well, I guess it's impossible to cover all my assets. Regardless, I've hidden enough of my distinguishable attributes to make me less recognizable.

When I get to the cafe, I spot Gavin and Brennan right away. They already seem to be deep in conversation. When they're not looking, I slip into the booth behind them. Luckily they don't notice. I only hope I haven't missed too much.

"Speaking of the farmer's markets," Gavin says, "Elena's contributions have been surprisingly successful."

A grin instantly forms on my lips. Being here has made me realize what I've taken for granted all these years, and Gavin is one of them. He is a good older brother. And maybe he always has been.

"Surprisingly? How?" Brennan says, taking the bait.

My smile grows even larger.

"I've never seen her this motivated about anything," Gavin says.

"Really?" Brennan says. "She seems very goal-oriented to me. In fact, I'm not sure how to say this without sounding vain, but I'm pretty certain she might be showing interest in me."

He knows? Of course he does; I was laying it on pretty thick.

"But you're not interested in her?" Gavin guesses.

"Nothing against her, but I'm interested in someone else."

My heart sinks. That confirms it. Brennan does have a crush. Just not on me. Suddenly my face burns with embarrassment. Is this what it feels like to be a B-list celebrity?

"You are?" Gavin asks.

"I wasn't really looking for a relationship or anything, so this one caught me by surprise. I came to Blaire hoping to learn a lot about science and maybe make some friends along the way. Luckily I've been able to do both. I already had more than I could hope for during my time here, which is why my feelings for this person caught me completely off guard. And it's funny, because you know me." He lets out an awkward chuckle. "Stumbling on discoveries is kinda my jam, so I should be in familiar territory. And yet . . ." He hesitates. "This new and unexpected discovery is making me nervous."

"Oh yeah?" Gavin asks. "Anyone I know?"

"Maybe?" Brennan says teasingly.

"Anyone you're willing to tell me about?"

"Maybe?" Brennan says again in a playful, almost coy way.

Not that I want to hear about the person who has captured the attention of Brennan so that he can't entertain the idea of liking anyone else, but I also kinda, sorta do. So I lean back deeper into the booth to hear his response.

"You," Brennan says.

I wait for Brennan to say more, because that can't be the end of his sentence, can it?

"Me, what?" Gavin asks, thinking the same thing.

"It's you," Brennan says. "I thought maybe we had a connection."

Oh. That.

I was expecting to be shocked by the name responsible for claiming Brennan's affections, whoever it was, but I never would have guessed *in a million years* that it would be my own brother, of all people. I can't be mad at Gavin. Clearly he didn't know how this was going to end. At least he tried to help me. And it does help to know that I truly didn't have a chance.

"I thought you were into women?" For some reason, Gavin thinks this is a reasonable response. I have to physically stop myself from reaching over and smacking him on the head.

Despite Gavin's poorly worded question, Brennan doesn't seem offended. "I am," he says. "But I am also attracted to men."

"Oh," Gavin says.

Wait. So I did have a chance with Brennan, and he still picked Gavin? I'm back to being wounded. Somehow it hurts more the second time.

"I should mention that Callie and I are kind of a thing. We haven't made it official yet, but we've been hanging out, and I'm ready to take our relationship to the next step."

"Guess I shouldn't be surprised. The chemistry between you two is pretty obvious," he says. "You make a good couple."

"Thanks. And I'm sorry things didn't work out. . . ."

"It's all good. I really am happy for you and Callie. She's like a sister to me, and you— Well, I think we both know that you're not like a brother to me." They both laugh. "But I'd like to think we're friends."

"Totally," Gavin agrees.

"I just hope Elena is going to be okay," Brennan says. "She seems to have a very intense personality. Wouldn't want to crush her spirit."

"Elena will be fine," Gavin says. "She has the attention span of a Chihuahua. She'll move on to the next thing in no time."

My senses jerk me back to the not so distant past. Is Gavin insulting me?

Brennan laughs. "You sure about that? She seems to wear her emotions on her sleeve. Especially when it comes to what she wants."

"Oh, you should have seen her before. You would've thought she had no ambition whatsoever."

"Really?"

"Trust me. At the rate she was partying, the only thing on her college application would have been a disco ball emoji and an Insta handle."

Brennan laughs. A little too loudly.

My skin prickles as soon as I hear the familiar guffaw, and my anger is solely directed at the one person who should have my back. Gavin is family. He should be on my side. Instead he's laughing about me. When he agreed to sus out Brennan's feelings about me, I finally thought we were through with the petty bickering. But I was wrong. *So* wrong. Gavin isn't on my side, like he wasn't all those years ago, and he never will be.

When the waiter comes to take their payment, Gavin has moved on to my appearance and how deep my superficiality went. If he didn't have to stop to pay the bill, who knows how long the Elena-bashing session could have gone on for. While Gavin and Brennan are preoccupied with splitting the bill, I take the opportunity to sneak out of the booth. On my way out of the cafe, I bump into someone.

Callie is as startled to see me as I am to see her. "I was going to surprise Gavin before my shift started, but I'm glad I ran into you. We finished making our first batch of lavender-honey ice cream. Do you want to come over later today?"

"Ice cream makes everyone feel better," I muse. Though I doubt it'll have any effect on me today.

"Right?" Callie says. "We're so grateful for your suggestion. We're even thinking about naming the flavor after you."

"Really?" My mood lifts. At least there are other people here who recognize my efforts.

"My shift ends at five. We can meet at my house to sample the ice cream. If you think it's good, we can make enough to sell it next Saturday. We just need to figure out how to arrange our table now that we have so many new products. Which is a good thing," Callie reassures me. "Thanks to you, we'll earn enough to replenish our beautification fund and more."

"I've been wondering about the farmer's market," I say, thinking out loud. Callie's recognition of my talents gives me an idea. "What if, instead of going out to a different town, we have the people come to us?" If I want to make money faster, I have to save where I can. And I can't spend half of my profits on diesel.

Callie blinks. "I'm not sure I follow."

"Sorry, I'm just spitballing here. But what if we held our own farmer's market?"

"How could we? The cars would all have to be compliant, and it would be a bigger drain on our resources if we had to monitor the vehicles that came into our town or did anything to disrupt the radio telescope."

"What about maintenance days? Since they happen once a month, we could use those designated days to organize the farmer's market. With the addition of the new products, we're quickly outgrowing the booth. This way we could set up multiple booths, each dedicated to a different product. We could call it the Blaire Fair."

"That's perfect!" She gasps. "We'll just have to think of a way to get the word out there. Blaire isn't really a town people talk about."

"True," I say. That is a snag I wasn't prepared for.

"Let's keep thinking of ways to market it. In the meantime, I'll go get the permit for it." Callie literally takes my idea and runs with it, rushing off before I have a chance to say bye, which is a good thing. Because I can't live with Gavin for much longer, not after today. And if I want to get out of here, I need to hire Kiki back ASAP. I make my way through the lobby, and just as I walk out the front entrance, I hear someone call my name. At first I think it's

Callie, so I stop. Before I turn around, she calls out to me again.

"El? Is that you?" It's a voice I recognize, but not from anyone I'd know here.

I slowly spin on my heels, and my jaw drops when I'm faced with the last person I'd expect to see here.

"*Willow?*"

"Oh my God, El. *It is* you." Willow prances over from the parking lot with her hands flopping around by her sides, a cross between a fairy and a T. rex. She jingles like a Christmas ornament from all the dangling jewelry she's wearing.

"What are you doing here?" I haven't heard from her all summer; she can't be here to see me. Can she?

Willow air-kisses me on each side of my face. "I know. Like, what is this place, and what am I doing here?" She gags.

I'm simultaneously offended and relieved. On the one hand, she is insulting the place I now have to call home. On the other, she's telling this to me with such brutal honesty that it occurs to me she has no idea I live here.

"Remember that show I'm doing? *Parks and Trailers*?"

"Oh, right. How's that going?" I feign ignorance. How could I forget when I was the one who got her the role in the first place?

"So great." Willow beams. "In fact, we're on location filming an episode here. We're on break, and this is the closest thing to an Urth Caffé within miles. I mean, can you believe it?" She snort-laughs.

I force myself to gloss over the dig on the cafe and zero in on the bigger news. "You're shooting an episode here?"

"I know!" she squeals. "Oh my God, El. There's so much I have to fill you in on. Is this near your retreat?"

So apparently my friends still think I'm on a silent retreat. And more importantly, they didn't abandon me.

"Yeah," I say vaguely. "Tell me more about this episode."

"Okay, so my character is in a post-breakup funk that gives desperate vibes. So the director looked up the most desolate, sad place in the US, and this tiny town called Blaire popped up. I never knew it even existed. Then again, if its claim to fame is being the country's most forgotten town, it tracks." She looks around in disgust. "I mean, what even is this place?"

"It's kind of cozy," I say, unable to help myself from feeling defensive, "in that ironically retro way."

"Elena, no. It's only retro if it was once cool. And there's no way that this red-vinyl-and-wood-paneled aesthetic was ever cool."

The sour taste in my mouth makes my lips pucker. I think back to my first time feeling like this place was warm and inviting. But one comment from Willow is all it takes to snatch that away. No matter how much I try to resist it, the power of her opinion is undeniable, and it reminds me of how impressionable the public is too.

"You're right." I hear myself agreeing with her. "I can't take it anymore. My parents are making me stay here until the bankruptcy is settled and my dad's new role at the company is finalized. But that could take months."

"Noooo," she says, deep and guttural. As if there could be nothing worse than living in Blaire.

"That was my reaction when we got the news. I'm dying to go back to LA, but somehow my parents seem content being here. They're even talking about me getting my GED so I don't have to go back to Brenthaven."

"Oh, El." Willow cups my cheeks and makes a sad, pouty face. "No matter what your family did, no one deserves to live here like this. Least of all you."

"Exactly! I shouldn't be blamed for their mistakes." *Finally.* Someone who understands me.

Willow gasps, suddenly lighting up. "How about you move in with me? You could stay in my guesthouse, and we could go to school together." She claps her hands, celebrating her idea.

"Really?" I clutch my chest, touched. And Gavin said I didn't have friends. Well, he's wrong about that, among so many other things. "You'd do that for me?"

"You poor, poor thing." This time her expression turns quickly from sympathy to pity. "I mean, isn't it enough that your parents squandered the business, leaving you destitute? You have to be subjected to living here too?"

I was willing to overlook her earlier comments. I had the same reaction when I first got here, and I understand more than anyone that living in Blaire takes some getting used to. But something about the way she's droning on about it is rubbing me the wrong way. I'm about to tell her that it's not that bad here once you get used to it. But at that moment, a young woman approaches us. By her cargo shorts and athletic shoewear—casual, functional attire suitable for behind-the-scenes work—I'm guessing she's a production assistant.

"Here's your order." She hands Willow a paper bag.

I smile awkwardly at the PA while Willow opens the bag and inspects it.

"Ew, what is this? I didn't order this." She shoves it back.

The PA peers up at Willow, confused. "It's your lunch. A burger—no patty, no bun, mayo on the side."

By the description of the order, I can understand why the contents seem unappealing.

"That's what I ordered, but that's not what this mess is. And why is the mayo red?"

"It's kimchi mayo." The PA reads off the receipt.

"Gross," Willow mutters. "No wonder no one wants to live here."

The PA takes back the bag even though she doesn't understand what's happening. I can't say I blame her. Willow is being utterly impossible when the order was made to her specifications.

Even though I'm mad at Gavin, a protective rage stews in my gut.

"Oh, before I forget, I have to get a photo of us." Willow whips out her phone.

"A photo?" I self-consciously run a hand through my hair. My fingers get caught in the oily texture.

"Proof that this place exists. No one will believe it otherwise." She plasters her cheek next to mine and purses her lips.

"No one? Who are you going to show this to?" I'm not ashamed of this town, not like I was before. But people can be mean. Without getting to know what it's like here, they can be ruthless. Before I can protest, she angles her phone at us and takes a burst of photos.

"You're not going to, like, share that with anyone, are you?" I hate the nervous lilt in my tone.

"Oh my God, are you, like, embarrassed people will think badly of you because you've been reduced to living here in this sad town?"

"No, that's not it. It's just that you caught me off guard. I don't have makeup on, and I'm dressed like a slob." It's not the real reason I don't want her to post these photos of me, but it's also kind of true. Because I tried to downplay my looks, I look worse than I normally would. Of course, it's just my luck that my disguise didn't work on Willow the way it did on Gavin and Brennan.

"You know I don't post anything without Facetuning it. So don't worry." She touches a finger to my chin and pouts, looking at me pitifully. "No one will know anything about your life has changed."

Before I can convince her to delete the photos, a sleek black electric car rolls up.

"Gotta run. But I'll be in touch about the guesthouse. Kisses!" She prances off the same way she approached me and follows the PA into the car. After she leaves, I stand there, frozen, trying to process what just happened.

"Elena!"

I blink myself back to the present to see Callie running toward me.

"I got it." She's waving a piece of paper in her hand.

"What did you get?" I ask, still wrapping my head around the fact that I was talking to Willow just a moment ago.

"The permit for the Blaire Fair!"

"Already?"

"I caught the mayor in between his meetings, and he thought it was a great idea. Said it could create more revenue for the entire town, not just the beautification fund. The observatory, the cafe, and the convenience store. He printed and signed the permit right then and there."

"That's amazing!"

"And just in time too. Maintenance day is coming up on Thursday."

"I can't believe we pulled this off." I am so torn by the news. Willow offered me a place to stay in her guesthouse in LA, where I can go to school, get back in the social scene, and maybe find a way to hire Kiki back without having to pay a retainer fee. Now that Willow is an up-and-coming star, if I'm in her orbit, I can resume my life as a socialite. I don't need the Blaire Fair anymore. Still, it doesn't diminish the pride I feel over seeing my idea come to life.

"It's all because of your idea." Callie's face lights up so much that her pale cheeks are almost glowing. She looks angelic. Combining that with her innocence, I start to feel guilty. Or, in any case, I feel like I owe it to her to tell her the truth.

"So, Callie, I just wanted to say something. About Gavin."

Her face lights up even brighter at the mention of his name. All the more reason she deserves to know. So I tell her about Sonya. How Gavin is technically still dating her. The apartment they share. I even show her a picture of them together.

As soon as Gavin gets home after his shift ends, he's in my face before the door closes behind him.

"What did you say to Callie?" His face is red and puffy, and his eyes are bloodshot too.

I thought news in this town moved slowly, but apparently not all news.

"She had a right to know," I say, surprised by his anger. It seems short-sighted, but I was so upset with Gavin when I told Callie about Sonya, I wasn't thinking about how he'd react.

"I should have been the one to tell her, not you. Now it looks like I was hiding something from her. That I was some kind of two-faced fraud who was too much of a coward to be up-front."

"Wouldn't have been the first time."

His head jerks back. "What's that supposed to mean?"

"What's this?" Mom opens the door to her room to join us.

"What's all the yelling about?" Dad follows behind her.

"It means that you've been secretive about a lot of things." I narrow my eyes at Gavin.

"You wouldn't dare," he warns me.

The thing about dares is that I've never been known to back down from one. Gavin would have known that about me if he'd actually taken the time to know me. If I were a more loyal sister, I might have felt inclined to continue covering for Gavin. Then again, why should I when he's never been loyal to me? So I tell Mom and Dad everything. About USC, about Callie. I even tell them about Gavin's culinary pursuits. By the time I'm finished, they appear to be more devastated than when Mr. Ahn told us we lost everything.

"What about college and Sonya?" As usual, Dad fixates on the things that matter to him. "How will you be successful without those things?"

Blood boils in my veins. "Are you serious right now?" Not only is Dad not focusing on the bigger issue of Gavin's deceit, but I take particular offense to his bold claim. "There isn't just one way to be successful, and if you could open your narrow mind just a tiny bit, you'd see that I'm proof of it. I mean, the only reason why we're able to afford these secondhand, weatherworn, off-the-rack things is because of *my* success."

Mom and Dad wince with the familiar repulsed expression. It sends me over the edge.

"Is my influencer lifestyle so beneath you that it's impossible to acknowledge what it's done for us? If it weren't for my party money, we'd be even worse off."

"Elena," Mom says, "we're not ashamed of you. We're ashamed of ourselves." She looks to Dad, who confirms it. "We're supposed to be taking care of you, not the other way around. You're still in high school, and Gavin is in college." When a pained expression crosses her face, I feel instant remorse over my misunderstanding. That is, until Mom continues. “And this is how you treat us? Gavin, how could you be so dishonest?” Then she turns to me. “How could you keep this from us?”

“That’s rich coming from you, Mom,” I say, the fire in my pit reigniting. If I’m going to be accused of having shortcomings, then everyone else is fair game. “When was the last time you were honest with Dad about what you wanted?” I turn to Gavin. “Or told Dad how you felt about his toxic masculinity?” As soon as the words leave my mouth, I regret them. But it’s too late. Like regular diarrhea, the verbal kind can’t go back in once it’s out.

Mom and Gavin are too concerned with Dad’s reaction to be mad at me for airing their grievances along with mine.

The color drains from Dad’s face. Too stunned to hold himself up, he slumps down onto a kitchen chair.

“Is that how you think of me?” He glances up at Mom. Then, a second later, he turns to Gavin. “Is that why you couldn’t tell me the truth?”

Gavin lets out a frustrated sigh and takes a seat facing Dad across the kitchen table. “Elena’s right,” Gavin says, but his hardened face tells me he’s merely stating a fact. “It’s like you have so many good qualities, Dad, and you’ve been able to accomplish so much. But because that strategy worked for you, you think success looks the same for everyone.”

Mom and I are frozen. Dad rubs his forehead in disbelief. “Gavin, if you felt that way, why didn’t you tell me?”

Gavin sighs, resting his arms on his knees and leaning on them. He looks up at Dad in an almost childlike manner, struggling to find the courage to say what’s on his mind. “I didn’t want to let you down.” His voice cracks, and he quickly clears his throat before continuing. “I could tell you wanted it so badly for me. So I tried. For you. Only I couldn't keep up with it. You have these unrealistic expectations of me. Of all of us."

"Is that true?" Dad looks at me and Mom.

I'm pretty sure I've said enough, so I shrug, but Mom doesn't meet his gaze, which is enough to answer his question.

He sighs almost devastatingly. "I raised you the way I was raised. On the farm, men were taught to be strong and provide for the family. Women maintained the children and the house. I didn't think anything was wrong with that. Our family seemed happy. Like a team." He turns to Mom. "It seemed to work when we first came to LA. Right, Gloria?" He desperately searches her face for an answer.

"It did," Mom agrees. "Until it didn't. When the business started taking off and you left me behind, we were no longer a team." He deflates at her words. "But it's not too late to learn from our mistakes," she says, reassuring him that what she's about to say next is coming from a place of love. "We learned on the farm which crops couldn't grow, but more importantly we learned which crops thrived. If you don't learn from the past, then you'll never reach the level of success you're looking for. Because that type of success doesn't exist."

Although I feel guilty about the way this conversation started, I'm not sorry it happened. We've felt this way about Dad for a while, and if we want to get through this, we can't keep trying to *act* like a family. It's time we start *being* one.

"I used to think that's what we wanted. A thriving business to buy nice things—a big house, the best schools, the finest foods money could buy. I wanted our kids to have a better life, an easier one than the one we lived." Dad stands up from the chair with great effort, as if the heaviness from the conversation is weighing him down. Slowly, he walks over to the family photo leaning against the kitchen wall. He stares at it for a long time. The intense expression on his face tells me that he's looking beyond the surface of the photo.

Dad always said he cared about us, but to me, actions spoke louder than words. Being a workaholic made it seem like he was more interested in money and success than in his own family. But now his actions are making me see that I was wrong. He wasn't just doing it for show; he really does care about us.

"It seems that this business has done more to tear us apart than keep us together." Dad shakes his head.

"We wanted so much for them that we tried to do it for them. Now they need to live their own lives, just like we did ours." Mom puts a hand on Dad's shoulder.

Dad reaches to put his hand on hers and looks at her. "You're right," he says. The smile on his face seems forced, but his words feel genuine.

"I shouldn't have spoken for you." My eyes flick between Mom and Gavin.

"No, Elena. You shouldn't have," Mom says flatly.

"I'm sorry, Mom."

She doesn't say anything. Instead she nods with her lips pressed in a line, acknowledging my apology. Which is more than I can say for Gavin, who's too upset to meet my eye, let alone answer me. And maybe I'm still mad at him too.

"Look, Gavin—" I start. But I'm cut off by a loud ruckus outside our front door.

Mom and Dad peer out the window facing the front of the house.

"It's the press." Dad abruptly moves back from the window.

Mom ducks behind the curtain. "How did they find us?"

"What are they doing here, Elena?" Gavin's head whips over to me.

The three of them stare at me in an all-too-familiar way.

"I don't know," I answer honestly. But it doesn't stop the uneasy feeling rising from the pit of my stomach.

So, Willow's a liar.

Not only did she not Facetune me, but she posted the photo on all her socials with the caption: *Me and my poor friend Elena Ok, who has lost everything, including her will to live.*

Now that her #Blaire post has gone viral, the media outlets have gotten wind of my location and are camped out in front of our house. The dial-up internet was so slow loading the comments, so I didn't read them all. But even if we did have high-speed internet, I don't know if I could read any more. Most of the comments fixate on the drastic change in my appearance, assuming that my unstyled hair; ill-fitting, off-brand clothes; and makeup-less face mean that I'm sad, alone, and weary living in Blaire. The truth is, I've always felt this way, even when we lived in LA. I was just better at hiding it.

The scathing comments aren't just about me either. They're about Blaire too. How poor the town is, how obvious it is that no one wants to live here, and how it's no wonder that no one knew of its existence before. It's only a matter of time before the town becomes a public spectacle. After today I will henceforth go down in Blaire's history for putting back on the map the town that's been forgotten about. An achievement I would have been proud of under different circumstances. Instead of highlighting its good qualities, Blaire has become a laughingstock—all because of me.

For the past hour, we've been cooped up inside our house since the reporters have been camped out outside. Mom and Dad think it's a good idea not to make any comments or public appearances, and for the first time, I agree with them. Gavin and I are in our room, and even though he isn't speaking to me, it doesn't mean it's been silent. There may not be as many reporters as I'm used to, but they are loud and unrelenting nonetheless.

"Elena, have you really lost everything?"

"Elena, what's going to happen to you now?"

"Elena, are you okay?"

"Ugh," I groan loudly. I can hear them even with my head buried under my pillow. "I can't believe Willow posted that photo of me."

"I can," Gavin says, breaking his silent treatment.

"How could she post that when I'm going to live with her?"

An incredulous noise escapes his lips. "Yeah, she had no intention of following through with that." The edge in his tone tells me he's still upset with me, which reminds me that I'm still mad at him too.

I sit up. "Of course she did. I got her the job on the show. She owes me."

"Do you even hear what you're saying? Friends don't owe each other anything except respect." Gavin scoffs. "She wasn't trying to help you. She saw an opportunity to boost her self-image, and she took it. I don't know why you're so surprised. You do it all the time."

I gape at him. "I'm not like that at all."

"Oh yeah? Why did you tell Callie about Sonya?" He stares at me with wide, accusing eyes.

"Because. She deserved to know the truth about you."

"And what about you? Didn't you think she needed to know the truth about you too?"

"That's different. I'm not in a relationship with her."

"Yes, you are!" He shoots up from his bed, startling me. "A friendship *is* a relationship. Don't you understand that not every person owes you something or needs to pay you for your company? Callie isn't like that. She's looking for friendship, no strings attached. She deserves to know the truth about you as much as she does about me. So don't kid yourself into thinking you were doing her a favor."

"You're right," I say, sitting up to match his cold, hard stare. "Maybe I don't know how deep and meaningful relationships work like you do. But can you blame me? If my own family abandoned me when I needed them the most, why should I expect anyone to be there for me?"

His face contorts in confusion. "That's what this is about? Public validation to make up for not getting attention at home?"

"Is it so hard to believe that I want to feel valued? I'm tired of being ignored in this family. While you were supported and praised your entire life, I was a joke."

He lets out a humorless laugh. "For the last time, the *Vogue* article was the joke! We didn't give it a second thought. But you certainly did. And now it's all you ever think of."

"What was I supposed to do? You abandoned me!" I point an accusing finger at him.

"Just because we didn't take it as seriously as you did, that doesn't mean we abandoned you. When you turned it into your catchphrase, that was when you decided to be on your own."

Is he really trying to make this about me? Because Gavin's wrong. *He's* the abandoner.

"As long as we're calling each other out, your responsible-big-brother act may have fooled Mom and Dad, but I can see through it. You lied to them, just like you lied to me about Brennan."

His head jerks back. "*Brennan?*"

"I heard you two talking at the cafe." I purse my lips at him.

"You what?" He arches his brows in disbelief.

"I didn't know if I could trust you to ask him how he felt about me without messing it up, so I followed you. And I was right not to trust you. Because I heard everything you said about me. I heard you making fun of me. It was *Vogue* all over again!"

Gavin stands up now, clenching his fists. "Did you hear the part where I said I misunderstood you all these years? That everything you do—from the money you've earned to support us, the way you got Dad to harvest what Mom wanted, and the impact you made on the town's beautification initiative—has shown me that you are a strong, capable, and determined person who will always end up more than fine?"

What? When? I must have left before I heard that part of the conversation. Still, it doesn't explain what I did hear. "Then why did you say all those insulting things about me?"

"I was trying to reassure Brennan that you weren't the fragile person he thought you were. He mentioned how you were flirting with him pretty hard, and he was worried you wouldn't take the rejection well. I wanted to let him know that you may seem like a vulnerable person, but you have an amazing ability to turn a bad situation around and make it good. And that quality has gotten you far in life. Once I got him to see that, he no longer saw you as weak but as strong. Don't you see? I was being a good brother!" Gavin is practically shouting at me.

His explanation is starting to make sense. But if he's been a good brother, then that means I've been a bad sister. And I don't want to believe that. I can't believe that. So I grasp for things that still don't add up.

"Brennan thought I was fragile? Because I flirted with him?" I scoff. "I only flirted with him because I thought that's what he wanted. He gave me the impression he was interested in me first, not the other way around."

"Of course he was interested in you. Brennan is a guy who values charity and giving back. So when he saw you dedicating your time to the town's beautification initiative and putting in hard work, he was drawn to you. Don't you get it?" Gavin says, still frustrated with me but no longer angry. "Because of your silly little catchphrase, you're so conditioned to think that dumbing yourself down will make you more popular. You can't see what respect looks like when it's staring you in the face. Brennan was being nice to you because he respects you."

"For the last time, the catchphrase isn't silly, and neither am I!" When is he going to get it through his head that it's not that deep? It's just a catchphrase, a couple of harmless words. And yeah, it pokes fun at me, but what Gavin doesn't seem to understand is that I was going to be laughed at no matter what. At least this way, I get something out of it—I'm making money and finding a way to support myself.

"You have no idea what it's like to be me. The intense scrutiny that women have is a thousand times more than what you and Dad and other men in the industry have to deal with. We have to be pretty, but we can't think we're pretty, or else we're self-obsessed. We have to be fashionable and wear clothes that accentuate our bodies, but we can't reveal too much, or else we're slut-shamed. And we have to be smart but not too smart, or else we're boring," I say. "The truth is, the media is more forgiving to men than to women. By using my catchphrase to my advantage, I'm just trying to be smart about it."

"Enough with the TED Talk, Elena." He sighs, exasperated. "Look, I get that society likes women who downplay their intelligence. And at first I knew it was an act. But at some point, you started to believe it. Because I can see the way you treat people. They're nothing but numbers or statistics. Some kind of metric that can measure your worth."

"That's not true! I have lots of friends—"

"Oh, really?" He points to the media outside our window. "Is that how a friend treats you?"

"That's one person."

"Oh yeah? Who else has stuck by your side during this time?"

"It's summer, Gavin. Everyone's busy."

"Too busy to pick up a phone and call?"

Gavin isn't saying anything I didn't already know. But putting voice to it is like forcing me to stare at my reflection in the mirror. And I don't like what I see. Not at all.

"But once we get back to LA and I get my brand manager to fix all of this for me—"

"Then what?" Gavin says. "You'll have friends who will call you? Fans who will follow your every move? All of them will be there until your next downfall. What kind of a life is that?" He lets out an incredulous sound. "Face it, El. There's nothing to go back to. Your day in the sun is done. You're like a one-hit wonder—all vibes, no substance."

The more Gavin talks, the less certain I am about the life I so desperately wanted to go back to. I feel the ground slipping from under me.

"As much as you think you were gaming the system with the

catchphrase, somewhere along the way, you bought into it. Because your self-worth is now tied to the public opinion of you. That's exactly why you told Callie. Because if you don't get all the attention, then no one can."

"No, that's not true," I protest. As much as I want to believe I'm not capable of being so deceitful, I can hear the insecurity in my tone.

"Name one thing you did for anyone here that wasn't selfishly motivated," he challenges me.

It isn't until Gavin points it out that I begin to question my own motives. At the farmer's market, I tried to make money to hire Kiki back, and at the convenience store, I tried to spend more time flirting with Brennan. Does that mean Gavin is right? Is everything I do selfishly motivated?

Gavin takes my silence as admission. "You made it so clear that this was temporary. That once we got out of here, you'd leave, and this was just a means to get you what you needed. You think being selfless means doing things for others. But true selflessness is doing things for others even if they come at the cost of something you want."

As much as I want to argue, I can't. Gavin's right. How could he know that I cared about him—about Mom, Dad, and everyone else in Blaire—if my goal was to leave as soon as I could?

By this point I've run out of excuses and am left with nothing but the truth. It wasn't all for my own selfish needs, but I admit it was a selfish way to fill that void. I hurt so many people along the way. Now I can see that the only thing I succeeded in when I turned the *Vogue* article into my catchphrase was reinforcing what everyone thought about me: That I don't know what I'm talking about. That I'm clueless. That I'm a joke.

EXCERPT

Keep your focus on the step ahead of you.

That's how you become a leader in the industry.

The American Dream Achieved: The Story of Dale Ok, Founder of It's Ok!

TRANSCRIPT

60 MINUTES INTERVIEW WITH GLORIA OK

GLORIA: We haven't been back to Anbandegi since we moved out of there. I heard it's famous now for stargazing, since the elevation and remote location give you one of the best views.

INTERVIEWER: I think I read that it's become better known after a K-drama was filmed there.

GLORIA: Yes, that's right. I was surprised to see my hometown in a K-drama.

INTERVIEWER: The views were incredibly scenic. It must have been surreal to grow up there.

GLORIA: At first, I didn't believe the stars on-screen were real. Because I never noticed them when I lived there. Guess that's what happens when you focus too much on the work. You miss the opportunity to see the beauty around you.

<TRANSCRIPT PAUSED>

The next morning I wake up to an unfamiliar sound. I jolt out of bed and kick off my blankets. "Do you hear that, Gavin?"

"What?" he mumbles, half asleep.

"Listen."

He props himself up. "I don't hear anything."

"Exactly." I leave Gavin in his bed and peek through the window around the house. No vans camped on our street, no cameras pointed at our house. They're gone. It isn't until I check the back window that I see someone out in the field. It's Dad. His unflappable work ethic never ceases to surprise me, especially given everything that's happened in the last twenty-four hours.

At first I'm disappointed. I had hoped that the one good outcome of our blowout yesterday would be forward movement. But it looks like Dad is reverting to his old habits again. Instead of spending time with his family, he's pouring all his attention into his work. Even his movements with the farming equipment seem more intentional, pounding the earth with his tool with more force than usual. That's when I notice he's not tending the soil; he's unearthing the crops that had just begun to sprout.

Without changing out of my pajamas, I rush outside.

"What are you doing, Dad?" I ask, running over to him. "Why are you destroying the crops? Are you really going to walk away from the farm, just like that? I'm sure the co-op won't kick you out for my mistake. I'll explain to them that—"

He raises a hand to stop me. "I'm not giving up on the farm. Don't you know me better than that? I'm no quitter." Dad tilts his head and looks at me with an expression I can't tell is serious or not.

"Then why are you digging it up?"

"I'm sectioning off a piece of the farm." He spears his tool into the ground and leans on it. "For Gavin."

"What?"

"Until yesterday I didn't realize he felt that way about me—that you both felt that way about me. On the farm we were constantly afraid of losing everything. We worked hard to make up for the loss. Now fear drives me to work compulsively. It's why I was a workaholic at It's Ok! and why I spend so much time with the co-op now. I'm afraid of losing everything." His expression softens. "But after I heard what you and Gavin think of me, it made me realize I could lose you. And no amount of success will matter if I lose my family."

I can't say I can't relate. Though the catchphrase did what I hoped it would do at the time—resurrect my reputation with the public—it came at the cost of my reputation with my family. And if I'm not careful, I'll lose others I care about.

"I'm not good with words—I'm more of a doer." A slight smile appears on his lips. "So this garden is for Gavin to grow what he wants. A symbol of my support for his dreams. He's a good cook, and I know he'll do well."

"I think so too." I choke up. I'm happy Gavin is finally getting the support that he needs. "Gavin's Garden," I say, looking at Dad's progress.

"Gavin's Garden," he repeats, smiling. "I like that." He wipes his brow.

"Can I help?" I ask, partly out of guilt. Not for the first time, I've misunderstood Dad's intentions.

He pauses, glancing around. "I noticed some new weeds sprouted. You feel like pulling them out?" he asks skeptically.

"Sure," I say. I grab a tool from the shed and rejoin Dad on the field. Except when I look around, I can't find any weeds.

"They're everywhere." Dad points around us.

"These?" I do a double take. "They look too pretty to be weeds." I point to the purple flowers blooming on top.

"Some weeds don't have deep roots, so they have to find other ways to protect themselves. They bloom to mimic flowers and they're prickly on the outside," Dad says, and again, I can't say I can't relate. "The thing about weeds is, they're not a problem that can be solved with a one-time solution. They require constant maintenance. And if you wait too long, they'll find a way to take over everything you've worked so hard to cultivate."

"Dad," I say, feeling like his weed analogy is hitting too close to home. "I'm really sorry. I didn't mean to dump on you like that yesterday, but I felt like it had to be said."

"I know," he says understandingly. "You are a doer, like me. The way you speak, with such authority and confidence, I see so much of myself in you." His smile reaches his eyes, which stare at me as if for the first time.

"Really?" Inexplicable pride blooms in me. I haven't been Dad's biggest supporter, criticizing him more than praising him, but this moment is making me realize it's because I never thought I had his support.

"I've always thought that too. It's how I came up with the catchphrase after the *Vogue* article. I took your approach to business and applied it to my circumstances," I say, standing taller than before.

"I was too closed-minded to see it before, but I can see that now. You're a natural entrepreneur, like me," he says. Then his smile falters. "Do you really not want to go to college?"

I shrug. I never planned on it, but I also didn't plan on my social status tanking. So I'm not sure of anything at the moment.

He does a slight headshake. "I can't say I understand it. I've accomplished so many things . . . except a college education. It's the only thing I regret about my past."

"You can still go. There's no time limit on that."

He swats the air with his hand. "I can see now that it wasn't the college experience I wanted. It was what the degree symbolized. I thought I needed it to give me the credibility necessary to succeed in the business world. When I started It's Ok!, I should have realized I was enough without it. But instead I passed my insecurity on to you and Gavin."

"You? Insecure?"

He lets out a light laugh. "My insecurity comes from wanting to give you and Gavin the best possible lives."

"I appreciate that, Dad. And I can see how much you sacrificed for us. But what I needed most was you. I needed to have a deep relationship with you to keep me grounded."

He frowns. "Using my insecurities to fuel me is my best quality . . . and my worst. I wanted you and Gavin not to suffer in the same way your mom and I did. But in trying to achieve that, I neglected so many other things. I can't change the past, but I can hope for a better future. And if you tell me that college is not the best path for you, I'll understand." He pauses. "Maybe not right away, but I will," he assures me.

"Thanks, Dad. I haven't quite made up my mind, but it helps to know I have your support either way," I say. "It's all I've ever wanted." It surprises me as much as it does Dad to hear my voice crack.

"Elena, I'm sorry." It's a simple statement, but coming from someone who isn't used to expressing his emotions or admitting fault, it means a lot.

"I'm sorry too," I say. We've both made mistakes.

We have a long road of healing ahead of us. But watching the care Dad puts into the land has shown me what he's capable of. The fields are in good condition, the new crops are sprouting, and soon they will be thriving. As long as we're willing to put the work into it, I know our relationship can flourish too.

When I get back into the house, it's almost noon. Gavin opens the pantry and announces we're out of food. Since it's my fault I've made our family social outcasts in Blaire, I take it upon myself to go to the convenience store. As I approach the store, I'm surprised to see the paint job and roof completed. When did that happen? A second later I roll my eyes at myself. Just because my life came to an abrupt halt doesn't mean everyone else's did.

The door jangles when I open it, and I brace myself for whatever reaction people might have when they see me. Public stoning comes to mind. Thankfully the store is empty except for Hal. I zip through the aisles, placing eggs, milk, yogurt, and other items in my basket. I'm sure Gavin will be able to make something with these—that is, if he's even in the mood to cook. Although he said some harsh things last night, I can't say I didn't deserve it. It was all true. And I'm still not sure he's forgiven me for ruining things with Callie.

I place my groceries on the counter and bag the items after Hal rings me up. When I pay him, he hands me the receipt along with my change and one extra item I didn't pay for.

"This isn't mine." I hold up the coffee with a cozy around the mug.

"It looked like you could use it." His lip quirks ever-so-slightly. Finally I see it. This must be Hal's happy face. "We all have bad days. The problem is trying to go back to something that's not there. We just have to find a way to get through it."

It's this unlikely gesture from the person I least expected that gets me to break. I don't deserve kindness from anyone here.

"I'm a selfish person." I begin sobbing. "I ruined everything because I only cared about myself, and I hurt so many people. And now that the Blaire Fair isn't happening, the town will never make enough money to—"

Hal stops me. "The Blaire Fair is still happening."

I sniff, peering up at him. "What? How?"

Hal looks as confused as I am. "Don't know. It just is." He shrugs.

I recoil when I realize I made the mistake again of thinking I'm more important than I am. When am I going to get it through my thick head that the world does not revolve around Elena Ok?

"I haven't heard any updates about the Blaire Fair. Then again, I guess that makes sense. After the way I treated everyone, I'd be mad at me too." If I'm honest, I'm mad at myself.

"No one's mad at you."

I pause, unconvinced. "But I lied to everyone."

"When the news reporters started showing up, it began to make sense why you couldn't be completely honest with us. And it seemed unfair the way they were pawing after you, like you were sport. So we had to do something."

"We?" I ask.

"Officer Hartford drove the press out of Blaire by telling them their vehicles and equipment were interfering with the telescope. Then the mayor issued checkpoints on the two entry points to the town, making sure everyone who came through the town had a permit to enter."

"You don't need a permit to enter Blaire," I say. I would've remembered that detail.

"I know." Hal leans in. "But they don't know that," he says with a smirk, breaking the scowl on his face for the first time.

"Are you telling me that the police officer . . . lied?"

"If he's guilty, we all are," he says. "Jean fashioned archival badges they used to give out at the library and put them on utility vests to make them look like official law enforcement. They even got Callie to man the barricade with that other intern—you know, Dimples."

"Brennan?" I say.

"Yeah, that's the one. He smiles like it's his job."

I laugh. Who knew Hal had a sense of humor? "I can't believe everyone did that." A warm feeling begins to bloom in my chest, but it never fully rises. "I caused them so much extra work."

"They had to get all that stuff anyway. For the Blaire Fair," he explains. "They got the permit and everything, so everyone is planning on it. But now they're not sure people are going to show up with the way the press is saying how bad our town is."

As hard as it is to hear how my actions ruined the Blaire Fair, Hal is reminding me that there's something I can still do about it. Turning negative press into something positive is, after all, my specialty.

Later in the afternoon, we hear a commotion outside and gather around the windows to find a media van pulling up to our house.

"Why are they back? What did you do this time?" Gavin asks. Mom and Dad stand behind him, staring at me with the same judgmental glare that I can't say I don't deserve. But it's not what they think, not this time.

"I called them," I say. "I told them to make sure to come in a diesel-run van and with wired cameras that transmit recordings through video data."

They're taken aback by my admission, but instead of disappointment, curiosity fills their expressions.

"But why?" Mom asks.

"It was because of me that the town was being ridiculed. I was no better than the *Vogue* article. It's why I had to call the press back. Because that's what you do when you care about people. You show up for them when they need you, not when you need them." I look out at the camera crew. It's not the big horde I'm used to, and yet my fingers tremble when I go out to meet them.

The news reporter doesn't wait for me to get close before lobbing questions at me.

"Elena, we know your success in the media has been affected

by your family's business failure. Have you decided to give up your public image altogether? Is that why you're hiding in this town?"

I have a lot to say about that. I'm not hiding, and I don't care about my public image or the bankruptcy of my family's business. Not anymore, at least.

"Thank you for coming today. The purpose of this interview is to talk about something very important to me. I want to clear up some misconceptions about this town. Blaire is a remote town that is closed off from the rest of the world, but there's a good reason for it. The observatory here has a radio telescope that is advancing our understanding of space discovery. Due to the restrictions on radio wave interference, the town has to live in a National Radio Quiet Zone."

I explain what all of that means. How Wi-Fi and other radio wave signals can interfere with the work they're doing at the observatory. How the town has chosen to give up certain technologies for another technology that can serve the greater good of our population with its contributions. I end by explaining that the town's resources prioritize the observatory and that the Blaire Fair is a way to support the town's needs. I give all the details about when, where, and what goods will be sold. Still, the reporters try to press me for more about my personal life here, and I shut them down every time. After I say everything I want them to know, I thank them and leave.

"Do you think that worked?" Gavin asks as we watch the van drive away.

"I don't know. But I know I did what I felt was best in the situation. And I have no regrets."

"Elena." Gavin hesitates. "About before. I'm sorry about being so harsh. I know you have good intentions."

"I know. And I needed to hear it." I nod appreciatively. "I'm sorry too. For Callie."

His face falls as soon as I mention her name.

"I promise I'll make it up to you."

For the next two days leading up to the Blaire Fair, I lie low. Not intentionally, although I am nervous about meeting Callie, Brennan, and the rest of the town. I haven't been a good friend to any of them, and it showed. With all the different kinds of kimchi Mom makes with Gavin's help, we have our work cut out for us jarring all of it in time for the Blaire Fair. There's traditional cabbage, radish, and cucumber. There's even a "white" kimchi that is pickled in a clear liquid. In the evenings I work on a simple design for the labels, calling it Shik-gu Kimchi. Because our time together is what enhances the flavor, making it as tasty as it is unique. Mom loves it, and she agrees to seal each label with her signature.

"You are more capable than I gave you credit for." She gently pinches my chin, regarding me with admiration. "I would never have come up with a label this clever, let alone the Blaire Fair."

Being recognized for my efforts is all I've ever wanted from her. And as much as I'd like to take all the credit, I can't.

"Remember when you told me that the only person I can rely on is myself?" I ask Mom. She nods. "Well, I don't think that's entirely true. People need people. I've always believed that. We're not meant to live in solitude. And before you thought reliance on others was my biggest problem. But I think you were wrong. My biggest problem wasn't depending on people. It was the type of people I was depending on." I sit down next to her and explain how the Blaire Fair might have been my idea, but it wouldn't have happened if not for the help of good friends.

On Thursday morning we pack up all the jars of kimchi in boxes and load the tractor. Mom and Dad go ahead first, and Gavin and I walk behind them.

"Nervous?" Gavin asks, probably from the silence and definitely from the way I'm gnawing on my lower lip.

I nod.

"You did everything you could," he says reassuringly.

"Yeah, but you know how the media can be. They edit what they want. What if they leave out all the important details of the Blaire Fair and only zero in on me 'leaving Hollywood' or whatever?" I say, using scare quotes. "In trying to make the town look better, what if I only succeeded in making it seem worse?"

His silence only validates my fears. What happens if no one turns up? How else can I make it up to Callie and Brennan, the mayor, and the co-op? How can I prove to them that I care?

"No matter what the outcome, I know what your true intentions are." A beat later he adds in a quieter voice, "If that means anything."

"That does mean something." My voice cracks, and I'm unable to meet his eye. "It means a lot."

We walk the rest of the way in silence. Partly because the lump in my throat is literally preventing words from coming out. But also because I don't want to ruin the moment we shared. We've been through a lot this past month in Blaire, Gavin and me. Some of it was good, but mostly we were at odds with each other. It made me think we got along better when we lived separate lives. But now I realize the bickering isn't a sign we don't care—it's proof that we do.

As we approach the field sectioned off in front of the town hall, my eyes widen at the sight.

"This doesn't look like the same place."

"They must have finally mowed the grass for the booths," Gavin points out. "It looks great."

"Yeah, and so do all the displays." There's a clear pathway between the rows of booths, each one with its own specialty goods displayed. Callie is setting up her jars of honey with her mom on cute stands scattered around their table. Dr. Blaire brought an ice chest with her ice cream and yogurt. Jean has two booths, one for her eggs and the other for her flower arrangements. Even Hal has a booth set up with his cozies and naturally dyed clothes on display. I spot Mom in the corner, setting up her kimchi jars with Dad. I motion for Gavin to follow me to join them.

"Wow, Elena. It's better than I could've imagined," Gavin says, his eyes bouncing from one booth to another.

A grin instantly takes over my face. "I can't take all the credit, though. This is a collaborative effort. I only had the idea for the fair. Just hope people show up." As soon as I say this, we turn the corner, and I see them. About a dozen camera crews and reporters. When they notice me, they rush up to me, clamoring.

"Elena, tell us about your time here. What inspired you to create your own fair?"

"Elena, your resilience is an inspiration. Tell us how you coped with being isolated here."

"Elena, you're looking very svelte. What's your new fitness routine?"

"Elena, Elena, Elena . . ."

Stunned, we stand there in the middle of an aisle in the fair while the barrage of questions keeps coming. People around us stop setting up their booths to stare at us. Gavin and I exchange a glance. His expression asks if I'm okay. When I give him a look that says I am, he takes a step back.

With the attention on me, the reporters quiet down and shove their mics closer to my face.

"I'd be happy to tell you more about it, but now is not the time. I'm here to focus on the homegrown, handmade products Blaire has to offer," I tell the reporters. The less I say, the more relentless the press becomes.

"Have you done any treatments? Your skin looks amazing," a reporter shouts.

I decide to try something different. "This lavender milk bath is the reason my skin is so refreshed. And the calming effects of lavender help me sleep at night, so I'm always well rested."

"What's your love life been like here? Have you been dating?" another reporter asks.

"The only dates I've had are these date preserves." I hold up a jar so it gets as much coverage as my face.

Out of the corner of my eye, I see Jean, Dr. Blaire, and Annabel watching me with unreadable expressions on their faces. A media circus with me at the center of it. I have to explain to them that I'm not using this town to boost my self-image before they get the wrong idea, so I excuse myself and head over to them.

"I'm so sorry about this. It wasn't my intention to create a scene. I only wanted to spread the word about the fair to bring more customers to us." I look apologetically at Jean, Dr. Blaire, and Annabel.

"Honey, are you kidding? This is fantastic!" Jean claps her hands together.

That's when I look at the parking lot. It's full.

"People came?" I say, shocked.

Dr. Blaire nods enthusiastically. "We haven't seen this much interest since Daniel became the mayor of a town that shared its name with his wife"—she points to herself—"but even that was nothing compared to this."

"So you don't mind the media?" I peer up at them nervously.

"Mind?" Annabel says. "Why would we mind something that is doing so much good for our town?" She motions around us. We still have five minutes before the fair officially opens, and there are already people lining up at the stalls. "The sales from today's event alone will be more than the beautification fund has ever had, and if it continues, we'll be able to make all of the improvements," Annabel goes on. "Because of you, Blaire will finally get the attention it needs."

I want to continue our conversation, but the crowd keeps building, making it impossible. With a reassuring glance from each of the women, we part ways to divide and conquer. As I help Mom sell her kimchi, I feel the guilt wash away and turn into something else. Something warm and cozy, like one of Hal's creations. Without the attention from my family, I tried to fill the void by getting it elsewhere. From the media. From my fans. And from my association with this person or that. But no matter how much I tried to fill the void, I still felt empty. Doing something good for this town feels good, but what feels better is knowing I have relationships that aren't tethered to my popularity.

Mom hands me a phone, startling me. "It's for you," she says. In the busyness of the day, I forgot we could use our phones today and left mine at home.

"Who is it?" I ask.

"I don't know." She shrugs.

I take the phone from her. "Hello?"

"Elena, hon." A familiar voice at the other end takes me by surprise.

"Kiki?" I startle. I didn't expect to hear from her. "How'd you get this number?"

"I didn't get to be the best at what I do without having any connections. There isn't a number I can't find," she says. "I'm getting calls for you left and right. Let's start with the big ones first and see what you can manage. When are you back in town?" She stops herself. "What am I saying? We'll send you a car—we'll send a plane if we have to."

"Wow. All this for me?" I've never heard Kiki this excited. Not even when I got the highly coveted invite to the Met Gala.

"I know. I'm so proud of you. Not only did you take my advice to eat, pray, love your way through this crisis, but you also put the town of the forgotten back on the map. The people love you for your selfless efforts. I couldn't have planned it better myself."

But that's the thing. I didn't plan it. And like she said, she could have gotten in touch with me sooner if she'd wanted to. What happens when I lose my relevance again? Is she—and everyone else I surrounded myself with before—going to forget my number? I don't know if I can handle that type of fickleness.

"Kiki, I appreciate it, but I'm going to have to get back to you."

"When? We can't keep these people waiting. We have to strike while the iron's hot. Or else the public might forget about you again."

"Not if I forget them first."

NEWS UPDATE

Updated now

In response to the investigation and bankruptcy filing, It's Ok!'s CEO Dale Ok has stepped down from his position, handing control over to a board of directors consisting of a mix of existing and newly hired executives. Their first task as a board was to reassign the former CEO. The title of internal director was proposed to Ok, where he would have a large role providing valuable input in the day-to-day running of the company he built from the ground up. However grateful he was for the opportunity to stay connected with It's Ok!, Ok has ultimately decided to turn the position down. While he has expressed interest in retaining his shares, he does not intend to stay in the fashion business and is looking to move on to greener pastures.

ONE YEAR LATER

The Blaire Fair continued to generate foot traffic every month, and the profits from it made it possible to make significant improvements all around town. The grass is regularly cut in front of the town hall, the main road is now paved, and a sign welcoming people to Blaire has been erected. In fact, the success of the Blaire Fair helped fix many things around town, including Gavin and Callie's relationship. After seeing my continued efforts with the fair long after the media had moved on from it, Callie realized my dedication to the event, like my apology, was sincere. Gavin and Callie have made up and are taking things slow. She plans to attend Cal Poly in San Luis Obispo in the fall, pursuing a double major in agricultural science and engineering. Gavin now attends a culinary school in Santa Barbara and commutes from Blaire, which allows him to work part-time at the cafe on the weekends and help out on the farm, growing the things he feels inspired by in the garden Dad dedicated to him. And Brennan is back in NOVA, but we're all on a group chat that keeps us connected. He told us before his own parents when he got his acceptance to Caltech, and he can't wait to be back in California in the fall to get "the band back together again"—his words.

Mom's kimchi also got a lot of attention after the fair, and not just in Blaire. With interest from all sorts of investors, Dad tried to get involved and encouraged her to expand her business globally. But Mom has decided to keep the business small and local, and Dad has respected her wishes. Now they work together on the farm in Blaire and live a quiet but happy life. I've been living with them this past year, but I am also off to greener pastures.

While I continued to work with the town on improving the Blaire Fair, I finished my senior year online. By the time I got my diploma, I knew I had a knack for business, even more than I did before, which helped me to see that I had so much more to learn. Long story short, I ended up applying to colleges. More surprising still is that I got accepted to my top choice.

A full year after being shuttled off to Blaire in a run-down car, I am now back in LA, at the place I least expected: the University of Southern California. The dean's office of the business school at USC is the embodiment of academia. The hallways are decorated with plaques, cases of trophies, and so much oak furniture that it screams *academic institution*.

When I applied I wasn't sure if I wanted to be in LA, at the school Gavin was at before. But I had to think about my future and what was best for me. And if I want to pursue business, then USC—one of the finest in that department—is the place to be. I do, however, have one hang-up about it. So before I accept the offer, I want to make sure I clear the air.

"Ms. Ok, Dean Rutherford will see you now." A lady in a sleek bun calls me behind the partition and leads me to an office.

"Ms. Ok. It's a pleasure to meet you." Dean Rutherford holds out his hand to shake mine.

“Nice to meet you too,” I say, shaking his hand, then sitting in the chair across from him.

“I see that you’ve been accepted but you haven’t yet made up your mind. So what can I do to help change that?”

“It’s about the terms of my acceptance. I want to confirm that I’m not getting any preferential treatment. I want to know I got in based on my own merit.”

“Preferential treatment?” He frowns, then begins to scan his computer screen.

“My family connections,” I clarify.

“I’m sorry, I don’t see any indication about that here. We don’t have information that isn’t disclosed by the applicants.”

“You don’t know who I am?” I ask, not because I think everyone knows who I am. (Except, if I’m being honest, I kinda, sorta do.) It’s Ok! is a global company. Even if my dad’s not the owner of it anymore, it’s still a big deal.

“I’m afraid I don’t.” He seems as confused by my question as he is uncertain about who I am. “If I may,” he starts after a short pause, “I reviewed your application, and based on the admissions team’s recommendation, I agreed with their assessment. Creating an organized event to increase tourism and fundraising in a remote town as a way to compensate for the underfunded budget needed to improve the quality of life for the town’s inhabitants is no small feat. Your critical thinking skills are sharp, your ideas are innovative, and your philanthropic endeavors are commendable. The fact of the matter is, we think there’s a bright future for you here.”

Dean Rutherford isn’t telling me anything I didn’t already know about myself. But for so long, my signature catchphrase and lifestyle brand made it impossible for anyone to see the potential inside me. By choosing to be the version the public wanted, I kept my real self hidden. Hearing someone finally acknowledge the qualities I value in myself is making my tear ducts overreact.

"Thank you for your explanation, Dean Rutherford," I say, blinking rapidly. "That helped me a lot."

"I'm glad it did." He smiles proudly.

On my way out of his office, I pause and turn back to Dean Rutherford. "If you happen to google me after this," I say, "please don't."

After the meeting I hop into my diesel-run car and drive the familiar route back home with the windows rolled down. The air feels full of hope, like anything is possible. There's freedom in not being tied to the public for their approval. I no longer have to keep my guard up, portraying an image. I can be who I want to be. I can get my mail in my pj's, go to the store without makeup, and not worry that a tabloid is going to question whether I'm okay or not. But without the public support to carry my reputation, the pressure is now on me to find the success I'm seeking. I know I have my work cut out for me. And I know it's going to be harder than it is easier. But I'm more deeply rooted in relationships that will help keep me grounded to weather the challenges ahead.

After parking my car in the driveway, I open the door to our house.

"You're just in time," Gavin says, peering at me from the kitchen. He has oven mitts on and is pulling something out of the oven that is, no doubt, innovative and delectable.

I wash my hands and sit at the kitchen table. Gavin brings a dish and sets it on a potholder in the middle of the table. He sits down just as Mom and Dad join us.

"You're back," Dad says, wiping his brow with a handkerchief and stuffing it into the back of his jeans. After a year of living here, he's finally adapted to a more suitable choice of wardrobe.

"You've been gone all day. You must be hungry," Mom says, taking off her wide-brimmed hat and placing it on a hook.

"Yeah, I'm famished," I say.

"Music to my ears." Gavin's smile stretches wide. We wait for Mom and Dad to join us at the table before serving dinner.

"How was your meeting?" Mom asks just before we're about to dig in.

"It was good," I say.

"Does that mean you made a decision?" Dad peers curiously at me.

I smile, close-mouthed, not giving them an answer right away.

Immediately, the three of them ask me a barrage of questions, and I tell them all about it over dinner.

ACKNOWLEDGMENTS

To my brilliant editor, Zareen Jaffery, I don't know where this book would be without you. The initial pages of this draft read more like a tabloid than a story—as Gavin would say, it was "all vibes and no substance." But you helped me uncover the heart beneath the chaos, shaping it into the novel it is today. Bringing this charming town and its endearing characters to life with you was pure joy, and I am eternally grateful.

A huge thanks to my agent, Andrea Morrison, for believing in this story before I even believed I could write it. I've loved *Schitt's Creek* for years, but I never thought I could create something with that same mix of humor and heart. You were the one who saw the spark before I did, and that gave me the courage to run with it. I'm so grateful to have you in my corner, championing me on.

Thank you to the team at Kokila—Namrata Tripathi, Jasmin Rubero, Joanna Cárdenas, Tenisha Anderson-Kenkpen, Asiya Ahmed, Jenny Ly, and a special shout-out to Sydnee Monday for your thoughtful notes. To the production team—Rye White, Kaitlyn San Miguel, and Misha Kydd—thank you so much for combing through the manuscript. You've caught more inconsistencies and grammatical errors than I'd like to admit, and I'm eternally grateful for your careful reads. Thank you to Karter Powell in publicity, Christina Colangelo and Bri Lockhart in marketing, and Felicity Vallence and Shannon Spann in digital marketing.

A humongous thanks to Kristin Boyle for her vision with this cover and the talented Michelle Kwon for turning the concept into reality. I mean, it's stunning, right? It perfectly captures the fish-out-of-water setup and the hilariously-out-of-touchness of the Oks. I love, love, love it.

To the writers in my life—Jesse Sutanto, Margot Harrison, Marley Teter, Nicole Lesperance, and Kate Dylan. I'm grateful for our discussions and your friendships. I'm always in good company with you folks. To the Kimchingoos, Graci Kim, Jessica Kim, Sarah Suk, and Susan Lee. You're all such talented human beings who inspire me every day. And a special thanks to Nicole Bennett for reading an early version of this book when I was in a pinch. Your insight was much appreciated.

To my friends who give me moral support and daily encouragement, I could not do this without you. Sassy Six, (plus one, minus one), East Bay BBNG crew, and Webbies—you know who you are. To Jennifer Chang, thank you for always listening.

To Mom, Dad, Sue, and David—writing this book made me reflect a lot about our family dynamics. We may not always be on the same wavelength, but there's a connection there, deep below the surface. I love you always.

To Jin, thank you for your continued support. I know your Type A personality doesn't always pair well with the ups and downs of publishing, which is why I appreciate all that you do. Because of you, I'm able to pursue the career of my dreams. Tyler, Troy, Kate—of all the things I've accomplished, I'm most proud to be your mom.

I always thank my readers last because they are the most important part of this journey. They are the magic that makes my words become a book. So, to everyone turning these pages—thank you, thank you, thank you.